MARK
DAWSON

THE
HOUSE
IN
THE
WOODS

WELBECK

First published in 2023 by Welbeck Fiction Limited,
an imprint of Welbeck Publishing Group
Offices in: London – 20 Mortimer Street, London W1T 3JW &
Sydney – Level 17, 207 Kent St, Sydney NSW 2000 Australia
www.welbeckpublishing.com

First published in 2020
This edition published by Welbeck Fiction Limited, part of
Welbeck Publishing Group, in 2023

A CIP catalogue record for this book is available from the British Library

Paperback ISBN: 978-1-80279-583-7

Printed and bound by CPI Group (UK) Ltd., Croydon, CR0 4YY

10 9 8 7 6 5 4 3 2 1

To my family.

PART I

1

Detective Chief Inspector Mackenzie Jones was peeling potatoes and listening to Bing Crosby when her phone started to ring. She had been preparing tomorrow's dinner for the last two hours. Andy had offered to do the meal, just like he usually did, but she had told him that she wanted to do it. She wasn't as good a cook as he was and, not full of confidence that she would be able to pull it off, she had bought a meal box from Hello Fresh after seeing one of their ads on Facebook. She had a turkey, all the vegetables and sauces, and a booklet of instructions that even she could follow. She had selected her Christmas playlist on Spotify and had found, to her surprise, that she had enjoyed herself more than she had expected.

She wiped her hands on a tea towel and turned the phone around so that she could see who was calling.

It was Detective Sergeant Tristan Lennox.

She picked it up and put it to her ear. 'What's up?'

'Sorry for disturbing you, boss,' he said. 'Christmas and everything.'

'White Christmas' ended and The Waitresses' 'Christmas Wrapping' began. Mack turned the music down. 'It's not a problem. I was just doing the vegetables for tomorrow. What is it?'

'We've got a problem.'

'What?' She sighed. 'What is it?'

'Looks like we might have a murder.'

She stopped the music completely. '*What?*'

'That's what it looks like.'

'Where?'

'There's a farmhouse in Grovely Woods.'

'Casualties?'

'At least one dead.'

'You can confirm that?'

'I can't. But I've got a witness who says he saw a dead body.'

'*Shit.*'

'I know,' he said.

'Where are you? Are you there?'

'Yes. A civilian called 999.'

'Name?'

'Ralph Mallender. He said he went to the house and saw his father's body through the kitchen window. He doesn't have a key to get in, and the doors are all locked. I was closest when the call came in. I got here before uniform did.' He paused and Mack thought she heard the hoot of an owl in the background. 'I'm sorry, boss. I really think you need to get out here. The civilian says there were four people inside the house, and I'm fairly sure I saw movement in the window.'

She exhaled. *Christmas Eve.*

'Boss?'

4

'You called armed response?'

'On their way, but they're coming from Andover. I've got uniform covering front and back until they arrive.'

She laid the knife on the counter and propped the phone between her shoulder and cheek. 'Stay out of range. Nobody engages with anyone until the ARVs are there.'

'Understood.'

Lennox gave her directions. Mack noted them down and told him that she would call again from the car.

Andy was in the sitting room. He had the kids' presents set out on the coffee table and was struggling to wrap them.

'I'm no good at this,' he said, grinning at the mess of paper and sticky tape on the floor. He noticed Mack's drawn expression, and his own happiness fizzled out.

'I just had a call from Lennox.'

'Trouble?'

'He thinks there's been a murder.'

'It's Christmas Eve, Mack.'

'I know that.'

'And you have to go?'

'You know I do.'

He tried to hide his disappointment, but it was something that he had never been very good at doing. 'Fine,' he said, trying to smile. 'It's fine. It's not your fault. Not a problem.' He nodded to the kitchen. 'You want me to carry on with the prep?'

'Could you? I'm really sorry.'

He took a piece of tape that he had stuck to the edge of the table and used it to seal the final flap of paper on Daisy's present. He stood up and, seeing the concern on her face, stepped over the debris and drew her into an embrace. 'I'll take care of this. Just get home again as soon as you can.'

'Keep the bed warm,' she said.

* * *

Mack reversed off the drive and pulled away. It was late, and that, combined with the festive season and the cold drizzle that had been falling all day, meant that there was little traffic about. She left the ring road and turned onto Wilton Road, which led into the village and the entrance to Wilton House. Two large Christmas trees had been installed on either side of the gates to the house, and an adventurous local had clambered up the statue of the Earl of Pembroke and draped a length of tinsel around his neck. The houses on either side of the road glowed with lights in the windows. Drunks rolled home after late calls at the Greyhound and the Bear, and the congregation was just emerging from St Mary's and St Nicholas's, sheltering under umbrellas with collars turned up against the cold. It all looked festive and inviting. Mack drove under the railway bridge and then, glancing regretfully at the illuminations in the rear-view mirror, made her way into the enveloping gloom of the countryside.

She drove to Great Wishford and then followed the single-lane track to the north of the village. She passed between tilled fields towards the darker fringe ahead that signalled the start of Grovely Wood. It was dark, with no artificial light and all the illumination from the moon and stars blocked by the thatch of branches overhead. All she could see was what was directly ahead of her, the road and the underbrush illuminated by the light thrown forward by the high beams. She saw the shapes of the trees, the lines of beech planted on either side of the road.

She drove on and, eventually, saw blue light throbbing through the trees. The gate that marked the end of the track and the beginning of the farm's boundary was open. She drove up to it. A line of blue-and-white plastic police tape had been stretched between the gateposts, snapping in the light breeze. The blue light was from two patrol cars, and she recognised Lennox's Audi parked alongside them. She parked, opened the door and got out. The rain had stopped, and now the temperature had dropped so that the moisture, once it was on the skin, felt frigid. A hard frost had been promised. No snow, but not the kind of night you'd want to be outside.

She recognised the constable waiting by the cars. It was Sam Collison, one of the team who worked the countryside beat out of Wilton station.

'Boss,' Collison said. 'All right?'

'Freezing my tits off.'

'Where's Lennox?'

'With the civilian who called us. Son of the farmer who lives here. Says he saw a dead body through the window in the door.'

'Lennox told me he thinks there's someone still inside the house.'

'He thought he saw someone cross the upstairs window.'

Mack looked through the trees to the house. There was no sign of movement now.

'Did you see anything?'

He shook his head. 'The DS isn't sure, but he said we were to stay back. He's worried if there is someone still inside, they might take a potshot at us.'

7

2

'Evening, boss,' Tristan Lennox said.

Mack gestured to the house. 'Anything new?'

Lennox shook his head.

'You still think someone's in there?'

'Haven't been able to discount it.'

'We'll be careful. Are there guns inside?'

He nodded. 'Control ran the premises through the database. There are firearms registered to this address. Shotguns for the farm.'

'Bollocks.' She zipped up her coat. 'I need to take a closer look. Can I get close enough without putting myself in the firing line?'

'The barn over there,' he said. 'If we take it nice and slow, we'll be able to get a look at the house without giving ourselves away. Just keep your head down.'

Mack ducked under the police tape and, with Lennox, slowly approached along the track.

She looked over and noticed that the shoulder of Lennox's jacket had been ripped. She pointed to it. 'What happened there?'

'I was fixing the fence at home,' he said. 'Caught it on the post. Clumsy twat.'

'Didn't Sophie buy that for you?'

'Christmas last year,' he said.

'She's not going to be happy.'

He shook his head ruefully. 'Haven't told her yet.'

They reached the dark, looming shape of the barn and edged around the perimeter until they were able to squat behind a discarded pile of bricks that gave them a good view of the premises. The farmhouse was a large building, constructed in the Edwardian style and funded, no doubt, by the harvests of wheat that the fields within the woods had been producing for hundreds of years. There were lights on in one of the downstairs rooms and in two of the rooms above it.

'In which window did you see movement?'

'Top one, up there. Frosted glass.'

He pointed to a window on the first floor.

'Bathroom, maybe?' she said.

'Maybe.'

There was nothing there now. She took out her phone and shot a quick video, panning left and right so that the whole façade was included, and then signalled that they should return to the rally point. They retraced their steps. An ambulance had arrived while they had been away; Collison was at the door briefing the paramedics. It was standard practice: they didn't know what they would find once they went inside, and it was best to assume the worst.

'The two uniforms observing,' Mack said. 'Who are they?'

'Yaxley at the front and Edwards at the back.'

'Where's armed response?'

'Still twenty minutes out. Firearms controller has whistled for support from Avon and Somerset. They're sending extra units up.'

Mack noticed a lone figure sitting in the back of Lennox's car. It was a man, his head and shoulders occasionally illuminated by the flashing blues.

'Is that the civilian?'

Lennox nodded. 'His family lives here. Mum and dad. His brother and sister – Cameron and Cassandra – are back from university for Christmas. He thinks they're inside, too. Betts is with him.'

'Mallender?'

Lennox nodded. 'Ralph. Says he's worried about his brother. Told me he's unpredictable. Issues with his temper.'

'He thinks the brother did it?'

Lennox shrugged. 'He thinks he might've.'

'I'd better have a word.'

She crossed over to the car. She could see the occupants a little better now. PC Betts was in the passenger's seat and the civilian was in the back. They were talking.

She opened the rear door and climbed inside.

'Hello,' she said. 'Mr Mallender?'

'That's right. Please – call me Ralph.'

Mallender was in his late thirties, with thick black hair and striking, haughty features. He was pale, and his hands, laid in his lap, were trembling.

'I'm Detective Chief Inspector Jones.'

Mack extended a hand and Mallender took it. His flesh was icy cold and his grip loose.

'DS Lennox tells me that you saw a body in the kitchen.'

'Yes.' He swallowed. 'My father.'

'Are you sure?'

He nodded.

'Did you go inside?'

'Couldn't. Door's locked.'

'You don't have a key?'

'Not with me. Left it at home. And my father is very careful with security. They were burgled last year and he had heavy-duty locks put in afterwards. Once the doors are locked, that's that. And he wouldn't open them after dark unless there was a good reason.'

'So how did you see him?'

'I looked in through the kitchen window. That's when I . . .' He stopped.

'Go on.'

'That's when I saw him. He's lying on the floor. Wasn't moving. I saw blood.'

'And who else is inside?'

'My mother, my sister and my brother.'

'And what do you think might have happened?'

'I don't know,' he said.

'DS Lennox says you're worried about your brother.'

He nodded. 'He's had problems with his mental health.'

'What kind of problems?'

'His temper. There was a big argument this afternoon . . .'

'Involving him?'

'All of us. That's why I came back – I wanted to sort it out before tomorrow.'

Mack could see that there was a lot of detail that she would need to excavate and understand, but that would have to wait.

'We believe there may be firearms in the house – is that right?'

He nodded. 'Shotguns and a rifle. My father uses them to shoot rabbits.'

'Are they secure?'

'In the gun safe.'

'Anything else?'

'My father used to be a competitive shooter. Pistols. He kept the guns after the law changed. Shoots them in the woods.'

'And those are in the safe, too?'

He nodded.

'Would your brother have been able to get at the guns?'

He nodded again. 'He'd know where the key is.'

'Thank you, Ralph,' she said. 'I'm going to ask you to stay inside the car with Constable Betts while we get this sorted out. Okay?'

Mallender nodded. Mack climbed out of the car and kneaded her forehead.

Murder on Christmas Eve.

Peace on Earth and mercy mild?

Not tonight.

3

Mack fetched her phone from the car and found the number for Chief Superintendent Beckton. The call rang and, after a moment, it was answered. Beckton was annoyed at being disturbed, especially given the time of year, but she had no choice but to speak to him. The use of firearms would be controlled by the tactical firearms controller at the control room, but Beckton was the strategic controller, and Mack had been doing this long enough to know that it would be prudent to get him onside at the earliest opportunity. Beckton listened to Mack's summation of the scene and then gave her permission to deploy.

Mack ended the call. She turned to the track and saw someone approaching, a flashlight bouncing up and down. Mack guessed that the flashing blues had roused one of the neighbours.

She trotted over. It was a big man in jeans and a thick overcoat, Hunter boots splashing through the puddles, an Alsatian on a leash straining at his side. He held the dog's leash in his left hand and a shotgun in his right, the stock of the open weapon wedged beneath his shoulder.

'What's going on?' the man called out to Collison.

'Stay back, please, sir,' he said.

'What is it?'

Mack reached the gate at the same time as the man. 'Good evening, sir. Who are you?'

'My name's Robson.'

'First name, Mr Robson?'

'Jimmy.'

'Do you live here?'

He pointed. 'Just up the track.'

'And that shotgun – you got a licence for it?'

'I'm the gamekeeper,' he said. 'I work for the Wilton Estate. We had pikeys in here last week for hare coursing. Thought they might have been back. What's happening?'

'Have you heard or seen anything tonight? Anything unusual?'

He gave a shrug. 'Saw the lights of your cars,' he said. 'Dog started barking. Thought I'd better go and see what was what.'

'Have you seen anyone else?'

'No one save you lot. Why? What's happening?'

'I'm afraid I can't discuss it. Please give your details to the constable and then go home – there's nothing to see. Stay inside. It'll be Christmas in' – she checked her watch – 'five minutes.'

The man grunted something about the season and tried to look around the barn, but, at Collison's gentle urging, he turned away and provided his details. That done, he went back in the direction from which he had come. Mack told Collison to set up a cordon fifty feet from the gate and ensure that no one came in or out without her approval.

* * *

Mack saw the lights of two approaching police vans and jogged over to intercept them. They pulled up and the occupants disembarked. She recognised Sergeant Neil Blyford. He had seven men with him. They each went to the back of the vehicles and took out their weapons from the gun safe.

Blyford made his way up to Mack and shook her hand.

'Evening.'

'Boss,' he said.

'Sorry to drag you out tonight.'

Mack updated Blyford on the situation. He listened intently and then asked to speak to Mallender. The window was wound down, and Blyford crouched next to it and asked Ralph about his family and what they might expect to find when they went inside. He described the house, closing his eyes as he pictured it, explaining the layout: kitchen, boot room, drawing room and dining room on the ground floor; three separate staircases that led up to the first floor, with some of the upstairs rooms accessible only by one or another of the staircases. Mack watched him carefully, listening not so much to what he was saying but, rather, *how* he was saying it. There was nothing that suggested anything out of the ordinary. He was reacting just as she would have expected: distraught, frightened, shocked.

Blyford asked whether Mallender thought Cameron might be responsible.

Would he know where the shotguns were kept? Would he know how to use them?

Ralph answered yes each time.

Blyford reconvened with Mack and Lennox. She showed him the footage of the front of the house that she had taken on her phone.

'Thank you. Helpful.'

'Need anything else?'

'We're good,' he said.

Mack stood aside and let the officers go about their work. They were each armed with the same submachine guns and wore the same ballistic vests and helmets. One hefted a heavy ballistic shield, propping it up against the side of the car. The men clustered together and studied the video footage on Mack's phone.

Blyford walked over to Mack. 'I need all your officers to maintain their positions front and rear until we call in on the main channel that we're in position. Then I want them all the way back to the rendezvous point and not, under any circumstances, to advance without my express permission. We'll hand the scene back to you once it's secure, and call in the paramedics to deal with any casualties.'

'How are you going to do it?'

'Four men stay outside for containment. I'll take the other three, breach the kitchen door and call out to any occupants. If we get no response, we'll advance to the injured party. Then we'll go room by room to search for further casualties and will either arrest or neutralise any threats.'

The first team left to secure the perimeter.

Blyford turned to his men. 'On me. We'll give them two minutes to secure the perimeter, then we'll go in. Mack – listen in to the channel and be ready to advance with the paramedics.'

Mack nodded. The remaining four firearms officers all turned and made their way from the RVP towards the house. They left a tense silence in their wake.

Mack and Lennox stood in silence and then a loud crash was heard from the farmhouse.

'Armed police! Come out of the building with your hands up!'

Nothing.

The silence descended again before it was disturbed by a second, identical challenge.

Still nothing.

There came a series of shouts and crashes from the farmhouse as Blyford and his team stormed inside. Mack took a radio and risked a look around the side of the barn. She saw the glow of the team's flashlights spreading through the rooms on the first floor, and then, after a minute, they appeared on the second floor, too. Lights shone out of uncovered windows and suffused the curtains of those that were closed, and she heard more shouts and the splintering of wood as boots were put through doors.

Mack's stomach felt empty, her nerves buzzing.

Blyford's voice crackled over the radio. 'Backup, come forward.'

Mack pressed transmit. 'Status?'

'Bad,' he said.

'Signs of life?'

'Negative,' he said. 'Four bodies. They've all been shot.'

4

Mack sat down against a plough that had been left in the yard and pulled on a pair of forensic overshoes and a white forensic suit. The firearms team hefted all their kit as they made their way back to the vehicles, leaving just Blyford behind at the house. Mack hooked a mask over her mouth and nose, pulled the suit's hood up over her head, and pulled a pair of blue nitrile gloves onto her hands, snapping them into place over the cuffs of her suit. One of the paramedics stood by her, a weary-looking middle-aged man who carried nothing apart from a stethoscope. He also wore forensic overshoes and gloves.

'You're authorised to pronounce life extinct?' she asked him.

'Not my first time,' he said. 'Most times at Christmas it's suicides, though, not . . . whatever this is.'

'Follow behind and we'll go to each victim in turn. Understand?'

He nodded. Blyford stood next to her, his weapon aimed at the ground, also with forensic boots on his feet. Now was not the time to introduce anything new into the crime scene.

She checked that her gloves and boots were properly fastened.

'You ready?' Blyford said.

Mack nodded that she was.

Blyford led the way to the door, which was guarded now by Constable Britten. She felt a little sick with the anticipation of what she knew she was about to witness. It wasn't as if she had never seen dead bodies before; she had, and had learned to compartmentalise it as just another part of the job. But this felt different. The house had a brooding presence, a weight that she felt pressing down on her as she waited for Britten to step aside. The property was isolated and remote, yet, as she glanced into the trees that fringed the perimeter, she had an unsettling feeling that they were being watched.

The door opened into the scullery. Blyford led the way through the room and into the kitchen.

He stepped aside so that Mack could see the body.

It was a man, in his sixties or early seventies, lying spread-eagled across a chair that had fallen beneath him. His legs and left arm were in contact with the floor, and his head hung loosely, resting against the wall. He was wearing pyjamas and, if not for the blood that had stained his pyjama top and coagulated on the floor beneath his head, it might have been possible to mistake him for sleeping. Mack saw splatters of blood on the wall and across the glossy surface of the oven. The kitchen table had been shoved to the side and now sat at a diagonal across the room. A vase and a china bowl that must have been on the table had been dislodged, and now both lay in fragments across the tile.

The chairs had been disturbed, and one of them was lying on its back beneath the table.

The paramedic squatted next to the body and briefly touched his neck with two fingers. Mack had always found it odd that, whatever the state of a corpse, no police officer was allowed to assume that they were dead unless a medical professional certified it first.

The medic shook his head briefly and looked at his watch. 'Life pronounced extinct at three thirteen a.m.'

Blyford led the way down a corridor, up a step and then along a hallway to the front of the house. The front door was directly ahead of them, and there were doors to the left and right. Both were open: Mack looked through the door to the left and saw a dining-room table and eight chairs.

Blyford went to the door on the right. 'The others are in here,' he said.

She went inside. Blyford aimed his torch around the dim room. There were a table and chairs and three sofas arranged in front of a flat-screen TV that was fastened to the wall. The screen was switched on, frozen on the title screen for *Die Hard*. Mack took in the details, but her attention was focused on the slaughter that had taken place. A second body was sprawled out across a comfortable sofa. It was a woman, and she had been shot at least twice. There was a wound in her forehead and at least one more in her torso. Her face was obscured by a congealed mask of blood, and her shirt was crimson, with more blood pooled on the carpet around her.

The third victim was in an armchair. A blanket had been pulled up to just beneath the line of the head, and the body was angled away from the door. Mack stepped forward and around the chair and saw that the body belonged to a second woman.

She was younger than the first. Her blonde hair fanned across the back of the chair, and there was no sign of injury save the bloom of red that had gathered around the scorched holes in the blanket. She had been shot at least three times.

Blyford swivelled, sending the glow of the torch around the room until it found the fourth body. The victim was male, early twenties, and sitting with his back propped up against the wall. He was wearing a chunky cable-knit jumper, black jeans and a pair of fluffy slippers. His left leg was straight and his right leg was bent at the knee. His arms hung loosely to the sides and, just out of reach of his hand, a pistol rested on the floor. The man had a single gunshot wound to the left-hand side of his head, with a corresponding exit wound on the right.

Mack paused while the paramedic looked at each victim in turn. After the most cursory of torchlit glances, he shook his head once more. 'Life pronounced extinct for these three victims at three fifteen a.m.'

Mack saw cartridge cases scattered across the floor, glinting dully in the light from Blyford's torch.

'Jesus,' she said.

'It's a bad one,' Blyford agreed. He nodded down at the pistol. 'Looks like a Browning nine-millimetre. Illegal, obviously.'

'Everyone out,' she said gruffly. 'Let's secure the scene. No one else comes inside until the CSIs get here.'

Mack made her way back outside. The house felt even more oppressive now that it had divulged its bloody secret. The rooms were gloomy, with pools of thick blackness gathered in the corners, too dark to see into. She felt a sensation between her shoulder blades, a scratchiness, and the feeling that she was being observed grew stronger. The place had an atmosphere, an ominousness that had been underscored by what they had just discovered.

The house was secured, and no one would enter now until the CSIs arrived. The rooms would all be carefully photographed and filmed before any further examination took place. It would take days to finish the work. The dead, unlike the living, could wait; the preservation of the scene was everything if they were not to lose or contaminate evidence.

She thought about what might happen next. Four deaths would be a story in any event, but four deaths on Christmas Eve? It wasn't difficult to imagine how the press would react to it. There would be reporters here as soon as the news broke. It would be a big deal. She was damned if she was going to make a mistake in a case as big, and as scrutinised, as this one would most certainly be.

Lennox came over to where she was standing. 'What have we got?'

'Four dead bodies. Looks like three murders and a suicide.'

'Shit.'

'Yep.'

She looked at her watch. It was just before four in the morning.

'Happy Christmas, Lennox,' she said.

PART II

5

ONE YEAR LATER

Atticus Priest had been on a long walk around the city with Bandit. The dog had originally been loaned to him. The man from whom Atticus bought his pot – a malodorous and thoroughly undesirable man by the name of Finn – had neglected him, and Atticus, feeling lonely and sorry for the dog, had offered to take him off his hands for a week or two. That week or two had turned into three months, and there was no sign that Finn was even remotely interested in taking the hound back. Atticus didn't mind. Bandit was good company and an excellent reason to get a little daily exercise. Besides that, it wasn't as if Atticus was *busy*. He hadn't had a new case for a month, and, in truth, he had begun to entertain the dispiriting thought that he might have to look for something else to do with his life. The family business, even. He greeted that prospect with a shudder whenever he considered it, but he was running out of money, and there would come a point when he might have to admit to himself that it was necessary.

There would be a lot of humble pie to eat, but not yet.

Not *quite* yet.

Atticus's office was in the middle of the city on New Street, opposite the 1960s multistorey car park that looked so incongruous against the two-hundred-year-old properties on the other side of the road. He had found the place on Rightmove and had made an offer without seeing it. The property comprised two rooms on the first floor. The building was the middle one of what would once have been three houses, three storeys tall with brick walls and a slate-covered roof. The north-facing frontage of the three properties formed an approximately symmetrical four-bay façade in which the two middle bays of the first floor were occupied by a three-sided projecting window that stretched out over the pavement below. It was well situated, with an entrance gate that opened directly onto the pavement. The landlady, a pleasant enough if ruthless octogenarian who lived somewhere in Hampshire, owned the small complex of buildings that lay beyond the gate. The entrance passage led between a hair salon on the left and a bridal shop on the right and opened out into a garden that was only tended to when the tenants complained that it had become overgrown. There was a fitness studio, a jeweller's workshop and a dental practice.

The office would have been an excellent choice if there had been enough business for Atticus to justify the expense. Unfortunately, that hadn't been the case.

The door to the office was at the end of the passage, on the right-hand side. A woman was waiting for Atticus outside it. She was well dressed, wearing an oversized belted beige jacket over a skirt and top. She was good-looking, too, with lustrous hair that fell down past her shoulders. Her eyes were covered by a large pair of dark glasses. Atticus estimated that she was in her early thirties.

'Nice dog,' she said.

Atticus looked down at Bandit. 'He's a good boy.'

'He's gorgeous.' She knelt down and tickled the dog behind the ears. 'What's his name?'

'Bandit.'

'Hello, Bandit,' she said. 'You're a gorgeous boy, aren't you?'

Bandit wagged his tail happily. Atticus reached in his pocket for his keys. 'Are you looking for someone?'

She stood back up. 'I am,' she said. 'Mr Priest. I don't suppose you know him?'

Atticus's first instinct was that the woman had come to collect something. He owed lots of money to lots of different people and, indeed, was already two months in arrears for his rent. This woman didn't look like a debt collector, and she was too stylish to be a provincial solicitor, but he still felt uneasy.

He glanced at her warily. She spoke with a very soft accent that was difficult to place. 'Can I ask who you are?'

She tapped her finger against the bronze plaque that he had fixed to the wall. It read PRIEST & CO. – PRIVATE INVESTIGATORS. 'It's you? You're Mr Priest?'

'I am.'

She smiled warmly. 'Allegra.'

'I'm sorry—'

'Mallender. Allegra Mallender.'

Atticus paused. That name was familiar, although he couldn't recall where from. 'Do we have an appointment?'

'I *did* send you an email,' she said. 'You said I should come and talk to you. Four o'clock? Don't you remember?'

Atticus frowned. He didn't remember the woman, nor the email that she professed to have sent him, nor the appointment that he had apparently proposed. It wouldn't have been the first time that he had messed something up. Organisation was not his strong point, and there was no money in the budget for someone who might have been able to keep his diary for him.

'I need your help,' she said. 'Your professional help. I'm willing to pay for it, obviously.'

That was encouraging. Atticus knew that unless he found a paying customer quickly, the landlady would send someone to unscrew the plaque before evicting him.

'Of course, Ms Mallender. Sorry – is it Miss or Mrs?'

'Mrs.'

'I do remember, of course I do. I'm sorry – Bandit needed a walk, and I thought he was going to tear the place up unless we got out. Time got away from me.'

'Is it still convenient?'

'Of course it is. Absolutely.' He took his key out of his pocket and unlocked the door. 'Please. Come upstairs. I'll put the kettle on.'

6

Atticus unlocked the door, unclipped Bandit's lead and let the dog lead the way up the stairs. He looked down at the floor and saw the six months' worth of pizza leaflets that had been shoved inside, crumpled and dirtied as both he and Jacob – the upstairs tenant – had trodden on them, always meaning to clean them away but never quite getting around to it. The paint had been scuffed and chipped, and the carpet hadn't been vacuumed since he had moved in. The lackadaisical attitude extended to the rest of the common space; neither Atticus nor Jacob had taken responsibility for keeping it tidy.

He started up the stairs in the hope that if he moved fast, then Allegra might not notice. The staircase was narrow, with shallow treads and a sharp turn to the right before they reached the landing. If you turned back on yourself, you could reach the bathroom that came as part of Atticus's lease; he said a silent prayer of thanks that the door was shut. There was a smoked-glass door on the left that offered access to Jacob's flat on the second floor. Two doors opened into Atticus's two rooms, one to the office and one to the room he was using to sleep in: he unlocked the former, let Bandit inside and then invited Allegra to go through.

The rooms were in a mess, too. He stepped around Allegra and went to close the door to the bedroom before she could look inside; it was the more cluttered of the two, and he worried that it would look unprofessional if she realised that the rooms weren't exclusively used for business.

The office was furnished with a desk, upon which were perched his laptop and two monitors. There was a coffee table, with a spare keyboard for the laptop, a roll of one-dollar bills from his recent trip to the United States, and a pile of correspondence, most of which he had never opened. There was an antique chess set that was laid out to mirror one of the several games that he was currently playing online. Next to the table was a leather sofa that he had picked up while it was on special at World of Leather, and a small fridge sat in the corner.

'Please,' he said, indicating the sofa. 'Take a seat.'

The sofa was in the bay window that extended over the pavement below. Allegra sat down. Atticus had tossed a box of new business cards onto the sofa yesterday; the lid had come off and the cards were spilling out. Allegra picked up one of the cards.

'A. Priest and Co.,' she said.

'That's right.'

'Where's the "Co."?'

'It's just me, actually.'

She frowned, and he realised that that might make him look a little dishonest.

'Well, I say it's just me – I have people who work with me, of course. There's my secretary, for one. And other people I can call on for specialised help. Contractors.'

She turned the card around. 'And what does the A stand for?'

'Atticus.'

'*Atticus?*'

'I know,' he said. 'It's unusual.'

'I don't think I've met anyone called Atticus before.'

'My parents are a little eccentric.'

'From *To Kill a Mockingbird*? Atticus . . . Atticus . . .'

'Finch. That's right.'

'Atticus Finch. Of course.'

He had no interest in discussing the origin of his name or his parents' peculiarity, and, to his relief, Allegra moved off the subject. She opened her handbag, took out a set of keys, and then put them back in an inner pouch together with the business card.

'Can I get you a coffee?'

'Please,' she said.

He told her he would be right back and went out to the landing. There was a small cupboard beneath the stairs that led up to the flat above. His landlady, at some point in the past, had seen fit to install a tiny kitchen in the cupboard. She might have imagined that it would have meant that she could charge more – two rooms, bathroom, kitchen, central location in Salisbury – but to call this a kitchen was a disservice to the word. There was a counter, a sink, a lightbulb above, a switch for the light and, fitted into the smallest possible space, a hot water heater. Atticus flicked the switch and, while the water boiled, he went into the bathroom.

He had left his medication on the cistern. He picked up the bottles of Ritalin and Cipralex and put them in his pocket, then, when he decided that they were too bulky, he opened the cabinet over the sink and put them in there. He checked his reflection in the mirror. He looked tired. His dark hair was thick and unruly, reaching down to the top of his collar. At least he had shaved when he woke up that morning, and there was just the faintest sign of growth on his chin. His eyes were blue and clear, something of a miracle given the fact that he had been drinking all night, the evidence of that written in the dark pouches above his prominent cheekbones. He took off his coat and shirt and stared at his naked torso, at the sleeves of tattoos down both arms. He spritzed himself with deodorant. His last clean white shirt was on a hook behind the door, and he put it on, putting his suit jacket on over the top of it.

The water was ready. He opened the cupboard beneath the sink. He had several mugs, a box of teabags, and a jar of Nescafé. He took the jar, unscrewed the lid and looked inside. It was nearly all gone. He found a spoon, scooped enough for one mug, put a teabag in the other mug, and then filled both with hot water.

Allegra was standing next to the large whiteboard on the wall that bore his scrawled notes on Alfred Burns, the paedophile who had been acquitted before disappearing off the face of the earth.

'What's this?' she asked.

'A case I'm looking into.'

'Alfred Burns? I remember the name. The paedophile?'

'He was found not guilty,' Atticus said.

'And then disappeared,' she said. 'I remember.'

Atticus had investigated Burns for six months, bringing the case to prosecution and then watching, aghast, as he had walked free thanks to a procedural error on the part of the Crown Prosecution Service. He had continued to investigate the case to the point that Burns had complained to the Independent Police Complaints Commission that he was being harassed. Atticus had been reprimanded, and then, a week later, Burns had disappeared. His house was empty; he didn't go to work; none of his friends knew where he was. He had just vanished. Atticus knew what had happened. He was abroad, exporting his depravity to a vulnerable audience who had no idea who he was, misery trailing in his wake.

Atticus had been trying to find him ever since.

He stood the mugs on the table and took a bottle of milk from the fridge. He opened it and sniffed it surreptitiously; it was just about acceptable.

He carried both mugs back into the office area. Allegra took the coffee; thankfully, she drank hers black. Atticus sloshed milk into the other cup, found a sachet of sugar from the table next to his Bluetooth speaker, and tipped the contents into the brew. He swirled his finger in it and sat down in the reclining chair at his desk.

'So,' he said. 'How can I help you?'

7

Allegra looked at Atticus with an inquisitive, appraising eye.

'So you're a private investigator?'

'I am.'

'Are you a very good one?'

She was smiling, but Atticus could tell that it was an important question and that his answer would determine whether he was given any work.

'You're married,' he said. 'You run, but you've had a painful injury in the last two years. You took up running because you wanted to lose weight.'

Her mouth fell open a little.

'You've had some bad news today that has upset you. You lost a dog a little while ago, but you've replaced him with a puppy.'

'That's remarkable.'

'Not particularly.' He downplayed his demonstration with a smile. 'I have an eye for observation. I see the small details that other people miss, and then, when I see those details, I draw conclusions based on them.'

'But how did you guess all that about me?'

'They weren't guesses,' he corrected her. 'They were deductions. Your legs show excellent muscle definition, suggesting that you run, yet you walk with a very slight limp to the right. I would guess that it was a problem with your Achilles?'

'I tore it ten months ago,' she said. 'I've only been able to go out again the last month or so. Go on.'

He held up his left hand. 'The fact that you are married is simple enough.'

'My ring,' she said. 'Obviously. But losing weight?'

'There is a very slight indentation on your finger where the ring used to be a little higher. Your fingers have become more slender since you lost the weight, and the ring can now be worn lower down.'

She grinned as she realised how he had performed his parlour trick. 'And the bad news?'

'The fact you have come to enquire about hiring an investigator is suggestive, of course, but I can do better than that. You have black smears on the insides of your right index finger and your right middle finger. I suspect that is mascara – you've been crying, and your make-up has smudged.'

'And the dog?'

'When you took your keys from your bag, I noticed that you have a dog tag for a key ring. The fact that it is not attached to the dog's collar would seem to signify that the dog no longer has need of it. That, and the fact that you have it somewhere where you can see it, suggests that he or she might have died. Now, the puppy. You have stray hairs on the hem of your coat. Cats tend to climb – if the hairs had been on your upper body, I would have suggested you had chosen a cat, although I might have discounted that on the basis that I don't know anyone who would buy a cat after losing a dog. The hairs on your coat are lower, from where the dog has nuzzled your legs. They are below your knee, too, which is suggestive of a smaller dog. You don't strike me as the kind of woman who would choose a miniature breed, hence my suggestion that you have a puppy.'

'Jasper,' she said, then pointed at Bandit. 'He's a pointer. Like him.'

'Very good,' Atticus said.

She shook her head. 'I'm impressed.'

'All simple enough,' Atticus said with a self-deprecating wave of his hand. 'I was a police detective for several years, until quite recently. Ever since then, I've applied my talents, such as they are, to developing my private practice.' He sipped his tea and then wiped his hand over the damp circle that the cup had left on the table. 'Now – if that's enough to persuade you that I'm the right person for your particular problem, how can I help?'

'I mentioned it in my email . . .'

'Best to go through it again now, if you don't mind.'

She paused, as if fumbling for the right words to say what she wanted to say. 'I'm sorry. This is all a bit delicate. You were right about me being upset. I am. It's been hard the last few months.'

'You can speak freely. Everything you say in this office will be treated in confidence.'

'Have you been reading the newspapers?'

'Anything in particular?'

'The Christmas Eve Massacre.'

She wrinkled her lip in distaste as she spoke the words. The case was infamous and something of a cause célèbre, one of the higher-profile stories of the year and, seemingly, about to reach its conclusion. The appellation had been chosen by the seamier elements of the national press and it had stuck.

'Of course,' he said. 'Doesn't the trial start soon?'

'It's tomorrow.'

Atticus felt a quiver of anticipation as to the unexpected direction the conversation might end up taking. Atticus went to the coffee table and liberated the copy of *The Sun* that he had buried under a stack of other papers. The story was covered on the front page and two further pages inside. Atticus looked at the photograph of the man on the front page and then lowered the paper, looking at her in a different light.

'That's my husband,' she said.

8

Atticus stared at the photograph on the front page of the newspaper. There was something a little haughty about the way Ralph Mallender was looking into the camera.

'He didn't do it,' she said.

'Of course . . .'

'I know,' she said. 'I'm obviously going to say that. But he *didn't*. I know my husband. And there's just no way.'

Allegra said it with a passion and conviction that Atticus found persuasive. He stood, took the chair from behind his desk and wheeled it around so that he could sit closer to her.

'How do you think I might be able to help you?'

'I need someone to review the evidence. The police case is circumstantial. *At best*. There's no forensic evidence, for a start.'

'But he *was* there? I read what the papers said. He found the bodies.'

She exhaled. 'Ralph had gone back to try to mend an argument from earlier that afternoon. But they were all already dead when he got there. He saw his father in the kitchen and called the police.'

'Didn't they originally think his brother had done it? Cameron?'

'Yes,' she said. 'And we think he *did* do it, as hard as it is to say that. There's no other explanation. Cassandra was quiet – wouldn't say boo to a goose. His mother and father – well, they had their issues, God knows, but they wouldn't have been able to do this. Kill their kids? Impossible.' She stabbed her finger against the photograph of the farmhouse where the bodies had been found. 'No. The only explanation that makes any sense is that Cameron shot his parents and his sister and then shot himself. The police came to that conclusion themselves. It was only when the rest of the family got involved that they looked at it again, and now they say that they have evidence that Cameron *didn't* do it.'

'I remember.'

'Hugo's relatives – Hugo is Ralph's father – caused such a stink, the things they said . . . They persuaded the press and the TV that the case against Cameron was flimsy, and the press started accusing the police of botching it. And the police buckled. They just caved in. They decided Cameron didn't do it, but, once they did that, they needed to find someone *else* they could put it on. Ralph was in the wrong place at the wrong time. He was unlucky. That's all he's guilty of. Just bad luck.'

She swallowed and, for a moment, Atticus thought that she was going to cry. He picked up a roll of toilet paper from the desk and handed it to her.

'I don't know what else to do, Mr Priest.'

'Atticus,' he said. 'Call me Atticus.'

She looked up at him through wet eyes. 'Ralph's solicitors mean well, but they're completely *reactive*. I told Ralph that we should've gone to someone more experienced, someone from London, maybe – the case would never have got this far. There's no *spontaneity*, no drive to find the evidence that'd show that Ralph couldn't have done what they say he did, but we didn't.'

'Why not?'

'Neither of us thought that it would get to this. I mean, kill his family? Come *on* – he obviously didn't, not in a million years, and we just assumed that the police couldn't possibly think that he could've. I suppose there was an element of inertia in it. By the time we realised things were running away from us, it felt like it was too late to change.'

'And that's why you've come to me?'

She nodded. 'We need someone to look at everything, to interview witnesses, to find the evidence that shows that my husband is innocent. That's what we need you to do.'

Atticus looked at her. She was earnest, regarding him with hopeful eyes. He assessed her more closely: she was well dressed; her coat and shoes were expensive; the purse beside her on the sofa looked like it was Louis Vuitton. It looked like she had money.

'I'd be happy to help, if I can.'

'Is this the sort of thing you've done before?'

Atticus nodded, trying to look convincing. He had experience from the other side, investigating criminals in his short and inglorious career as a police detective, but he had no experience of the kind of work that Allegra needed him to do. The only cases that he had taken on since he had gone into business for himself had been investigations to provide evidence of cheating spouses and proof for insurance companies that customers who had claimed whiplash in road traffic accidents were, in fact, faking their injuries in order to take a payout. He had followed self-proclaimed victims to golf clubs where walking sticks were exchanged for pitching wedges, laid up in bushes and taken photographs of illicit trysts – the kind of grubby sleuthing that had given his own family so much to chuckle about – but he wasn't about to tell *her* that.

She looked at him and then nodded, encouraging him to provide her with examples of relevant experience.

Atticus thought quickly. 'Like I said, I used to work for the police,' he said, at least beginning from a position of truth. 'I was a detective in the CID.'

'Plainclothes?'

'That's right. I'm used to looking at this from their side, but the skills and experience are transferable.'

'Salisbury police?'

'Yes,' he said.

'Where?'

'Bourne Hill.'

'That's where they're running the case. Do you know the DCI there? Mackenzie Jones?'

'I do,' he said.

'She's the bitch in charge.'

'She used to be my boss.'

'You like her?'

Atticus shrugged, and she spoke again before he could answer.

'She's got it in for Ralph.'

He felt the need to defend her. 'She's probably just doing her job.'

It was a ridiculous impulse, given what had happened between them, and he realised as soon as he said it that it was foolish to take Mack's side over that of a potential client.

Allegra didn't seem to have heard him. 'Sorry,' she said. 'It's been an ordeal. The whole thing – total nightmare.'

'I'm sure it has.'

'Is there anything else that you need to know?'

'I don't think so.'

'So? Will you help?'

He started to weigh it up, whether he should get involved in something like this, already seeing how any work he did would butt up against the case that Mack had put together, and then chided himself. Who was he kidding? He was in no position to turn down the money, and Mack was a big girl. He didn't owe her anything and she'd cope.

'I charge my time at fifty pounds an hour, and I'll need paying up front for the retainer.'

'Of course.'

'Expenses, too. I can bill you for those separately.'

She reached into her bag and took out her purse. 'How much for the retainer?'

Atticus thought of the parlous state of his account. Four hundred would clear his overdraft.

'Five hundred, if that's all right?'

He watched with something akin to incredulity as Allegra took out a wad of notes and started to count them out.

'Here you are.' She handed them to him. 'You'll give me a receipt?'

He fumbled through the piles on his desk until he found a blank piece of headed notepaper. He wrote down that Allegra had paid £500 as a retainer, signed and dated it, and handed it to her.

'Thank you,' she said, folding the receipt and slipping it into her purse. 'What's next?'

'I'll need to talk to you again,' he said. 'A proper talk, about the case. Are you available tomorrow?'

'It's the first day of the trial. Maybe you could be there, too? You probably should.'

'What time?'

'Ten o'clock,' she said.

'Salisbury?'

'Yes.'

She stood, and Atticus took her offered hand. 'I'll be there.'

He showed her to the door.

'Thank you. You don't know how much of a *relief* this is. It feels like I've been doing this on my own for months.'

'Let's talk tomorrow.'

She thanked him again and made her way carefully down the staircase. Atticus closed the door and went to the bay window. She emerged from the passage below and took out her phone from her handbag as she waited for a gap in the traffic to cross the road. She looked first to the left and then to the right, the opposite of what might have been expected of a local. Atticus noticed it – it suggested that she was used to traffic approaching from the opposite direction – and then realised that her almost imperceptible accent was American. Boston, he thought, but certainly not working class. A well-educated New Englander who was either adept at hiding her accent or who had been here long enough for it to be softened away almost to nothing.

He watched as Allegra put the phone to her ear and crossed, turning right and then sharply left into the entrance of the multistorey car park. Bandit mooched over and Atticus scratched him behind the ears as he watched Allegra disappear.

'Happy days,' he said to the dog. 'Things are about to take a turn for the better.'

9

Atticus woke up early the next morning. He washed and dressed, put Bandit on his lead, left the office and locked the door behind him. He climbed down the stairs and let the dog drag him outside. The jeweller who had one of the workshops facing the garden was just opening up.

'Morning,' the man said.

Atticus nodded a greeting and made his way out onto the street. He walked to the junction with the High Street, turned left, then passed through the medieval gate and into the Cathedral Close beyond.

The cathedral's pale grey Chilmark stone glowed in the dawn light. He never tired of the view. The building was set amid immaculately kept grounds that accommodated a changing selection of sculptures and modern art. There were ancient trees between the grounds and the road that ringed them, and then a set of historic buildings that included a series of grand residences, some of which had been turned into museums. The cathedral, though, outshone them all. The spire reached high into the air, and, as he looked up, Atticus saw the pair of resident peregrines arcing around it in search of prey.

Atticus let Bandit stretch his legs and then made his way back to the office. He opened the door and climbed up to the landing. He took a can of dog food from the cupboard and rapped loudly on the glass panel of the door that led up to the flat above. He heard the sound of heavy footsteps and then saw the blur in the glass as Jacob came down.

He opened the door. 'Atticus,' he said, with a smile, 'you okay?'

'I'm good,' he said.

Jacob had been upstairs since before Atticus had rented the office. He made a decent living playing online poker and spent his spare time on *Fortnite*. He was in his late twenties, although he looked older. He had lost most of his hair and hid his baldness beneath beanies and ball caps. He wore a chain that linked his wallet to a belt loop, had fairly average tattoos on both forearms, and wore hoodies and baggy jeans to the exclusion of everything else.

'I know it's short notice,' Atticus said.

'You need me to look after him?'

Bandit wagged his tail.

'Do you mind?'

'Not at all. I like doing it. He's my lucky mascot. I made three hundred the last tournament he was with me. Got one starting in an hour.'

'That's great. He just told me he feels lucky today, too. Twenty quid?'

'Works for me.'

Atticus reached into his pocket and took out his wallet. He opened it and removed a £20 note. He folded it in half and handed it to Jacob.

'Give him a good walk,' he said. 'He likes the cricket pitch at Harnham. You can let him off the lead there. He likes going in the river, too.'

'I know,' Jacob said. 'Don't worry. I'll look after him.'

'Thanks. I'll be back late afternoon or early evening. Here's his food.'

He went back to the office, grabbed his notebook and slipped it, together with his phone, into his leather satchel. He locked the door, went down to the passageway and set off.

* * *

The courts were housed in a modern building that had been constructed at the turn of the century and shared the under-whelming architecture of the noughties. It had walls constructed from pale brick, a wide canopy that reached out over the frontage, and dark glass in the windows. Atticus went to the main door, next to stencilled letters that read SALISBURY LAW COURTS and a large royal crest, and checked his watch. It was nine fifty, meaning that proceedings would begin in ten minutes. There was a clutch of people circulating inside, and he pushed through the doors to join them. He looked up at the screen on the wall and saw that Crown v. Mallender was being heard in Court Number One.

He passed through the security gate, sending his phone, keys and loose change through the X-ray machine in a plastic tub. He took the stairs to Court Number One. The waiting area outside was as busy as it was downstairs. There was a collection of vinyl sofas set out on fresh grey carpets.

The area was full of members of the press and other onlookers who were waiting to go through into the public gallery. The trial was big news; the murders had excited the public ever since the first reports had broken, and the fate of the defendant was evidently and unsurprisingly an issue that held the Fourth Estate rapt.

Atticus looked around for Allegra, but couldn't see her. He made his way to the front of the queue, opened the door and went inside. The court was at the top of the building and was far brighter than many of the other courts that Atticus had been in before. It was a modern space, with skylights in the vaulted ceiling, white-painted walls and light-coloured wooden furniture. The judge's bench was on a platform raised above the rest of the room. Ahead of that was the desk for the court associate and then the benches for counsel for the prosecution and defence, with identical desks behind for instructing solicitors. To the right of the judge were two rows for the jury, with six chairs in each row. The dock was an enclosed space directly opposite the judge, with extensive glass windows allowing the accused to see everything that was happening. Next to the dock were the public and press galleries, and rounding out the space was the witness box. The court was equipped with thin LCD panels and a series of microphones.

Allegra was sitting at the end of a row at the front of the public gallery. The door squeaked as it closed, and she turned around and saw him. He raised his hand in acknowledgement and she stared back at him without responding; she was evidently worried about the start of her husband's trial.

That was reasonable.

He took one of the only empty seats behind Allegra at the back of the gallery. Most of the men and women sitting around him looked like reporters, conferring with one another in hushed, excited whispers. The remainder were harder to place; Atticus guessed that some would be relatives of the deceased, while others were students and interested members of the public. This was a big story, the culmination of a summer of lurid reports in the press as the details of the case were dripped out.

The barristers were already at their benches: two Queen's Counsel, one for the prosecution and one for the defence, both men with a junior to assist them. Atticus didn't recognise Ralph's brief, but the Crown prosecutor was familiar to him: it was Gordon Abernathy, a ferocious QC who had been bestowed with the nickname of 'the Bruiser' and a reputation for bullying witnesses, court staff and, it was said, even judges themselves. Atticus was aware of a story whereby Abernathy and the judge in a complex fraud case at the Royal Courts of Justice that had stretched on for months had been left with the necessity of arranging their evenings out at the Garrick on alternate nights so as not to be there at the same time. He was a fine choice for a trial of this nature and, were Atticus in Ralph's shoes, he would not have been encouraged.

The solicitor sitting behind Mallender's brief was a large and red-faced man. He looked back at Allegra and smiled at her. Atticus recognised him: Dafyd Cadogan, a lawyer from Salisbury with an office just around the corner from his. Ralph and Allegra must have chosen him to run the defence. It was not an inspiring choice. The partners of Cadogan and Crane

LLP had, variously, been investigated by the Law Society for embezzling client funds, been sued for negligence on at least two separate occasions in the last year, and were rumoured to be six months in arrears on the rent for their office.

Ralph Mallender was brought up from the cells by two burly security guards and ushered through a door opening directly into the closed-in dock. He was dressed in a smart dark blue suit with a crisp white shirt and a thin blue tie. His face was pale, and, as he looked over to the public gallery, he caught his wife's eye. Atticus glanced down and across at her in time to see her mouth, 'I love you,' and, as he looked back, he saw that Mallender had found a smile from somewhere.

Atticus saw the door at the front of the room open and watched as Detective Chief Inspector Mackenzie Jones made her way inside, followed by her sergeant, Tristan Lennox. She was wearing the same sober suit that he remembered from the last time he had watched her give evidence, matched with a white shirt. Her hair was down, immaculate as ever. She was carrying a folder that contained, Atticus guessed, some of the written evidence that would be examined at trial. She took her seat behind the prosecution brief. She didn't look back into the gallery and didn't appear to have noticed Atticus.

The associate came to the front of the room. 'All rise.'

Atticus stood and paid attention. The journalists took out their phones so that they could tweet developments as soon as they took place. The whispered conversations died out, to be replaced by the electric buzz of tension.

The Honourable Mr Justice Somerville came into the court. Atticus had googled him after seeing his name on the monitor outside: he was sixty-eight, assigned to the Queen's Bench Division and had previously had a successful practice as a Queen's Counsel specialising in criminal law. The rest of his biography was standard: educated at Charterhouse and Durham, with previous experience as a recorder. He had a reputation as something of a hanging judge. A sensational national newspaper columnist who had been given a stringent sentence for drunk driving had later described him as 'cold as a bag of frozen peas' and 'a bloodless dictator who sits in judgement on those unfortunate enough to pass through his domain'.

He was wearing scarlet robes, as was the custom in murder trials; the arbiters were 'red judges' when dispensing justice for the most serious crimes. He took his seat on the bench at the front of the room; the royal coat of arms was displayed on the wall behind him. It was slightly to the right of his chair; Atticus had heard that the reason for the placement was to suggest that the judge was sitting at the Queen's side.

The usher cleared his throat and, with a solemnity that befitted the archaic nature of the proceedings, said, 'Draw near all ye who have business in the trial of the Queen against Ralph Mallender.'

The associate stood and turned to the dock.

'Ralph Mallender, you are charged with murder, contrary to the common law. The particulars of the offence being that you, Ralph Mallender, murdered Hugo Mallender on 24 December 2018. How do you plead?'

'Emphatically *not* guilty,' he said. His voice was firm.

The associate repeated the process for the other three charges that had been laid against him, being that Ralph had murdered his mother, sister and brother. Ralph repeated his not guilty plea, his voice strong and clear every time.

'Please sit down, Mr Mallender,' the judge said. He turned to both sets of counsel. 'Is everything ready?'

Both barristers said that it was.

Somerville turned to the associate. 'Are the jury-in-waiting ready?'

'Yes, my Lord.'

'Bring them in.'

Atticus was familiar with the process and, even after seeing it so many times before, still found it deliciously anachronistic. There was an usher standing by the door to the rear of the courtroom. She went out through it and returned with a number of potential jurors; Atticus counted twenty of them. They were shown to seats next to the jury box.

Somerville turned to them. 'Good morning. You are members of a jury panel. Twelve of you will be selected as jurors to try the case in this court today. There are several guarantees of the fairness and independence of any jury. One of them is that no one on the jury should have any connection with the person being tried or anyone who is a witness in the case. This case involves an incident that happened at Grovely Farmhouse near Great Wishford in Wiltshire on Christmas Eve last year. Because a jury must decide the case only on the evidence given in court, it is *essential* that no one on the jury has any personal connection with, or personal knowledge of, the case or anyone associated with it. The defendant's name is Ralph Mallender, and he is the person standing in the dock. Mr Abernathy, who is prosecuting this case, will now read out the names of the people who may be called as witnesses or who are connected with the case. Please listen carefully to the names and think about whether you recognise any of them.'

Abernathy stood and read out a list of names. Atticus recognised several of them from his time in CID, including Mack and Lennox. Abernathy concluded the list and sat down. His opponent, identified by the judge as Mr Crow, took to his feet and read out a list of the witnesses that the defence would rely upon.

Somerville continued. 'If you think that you have any knowledge about any person connected with the case, including the defendant or any of the witnesses, please indicate that by raising your hand or writing a note explaining this and handing it to the usher.'

No one did.

The associate stood and picked up a number of paper slips. She shuffled them in her hands and then turned to the defendant.

'Ralph Mallender, you are about to hear the names of the jurors who are to try you. If you wish to challenge any of them, you must do this after the name has been called, but before they are sworn.' She turned to the two seated lines of men and women and said, 'Members of the jury-in-waiting, when you hear your name called, please answer "here" and proceed to the jury box.' Pausing for emphasis, she picked a slip and announced, 'Barry Gardner.'

One of the men stood, gave a strident, 'Here,' and allowed himself to be ushered across the courtroom and into the first row of the jury box.

'Abigail Winters.'

An elderly woman stood and made her way to the seat next to Gardner.

The associate continued, reading out another ten names.

The usher guided each new juror to the box.

Somerville nodded his satisfaction. 'Let the jury be sworn.'

One of the ushers went to the first person on the jury and asked on what oath the juror wished to be sworn. The juror said he was Christian, and was handed a Bible and told to recite an oath that he would faithfully try the defendant and give a true verdict according to the evidence. The usher thanked him, told him to sit down, and moved on to the next.

The process was repeated with the other eleven. They were an assorted bunch: eight men and four women, varying in ages, mostly white, mostly – at least to Atticus's eye – drawn from the middle class. They sat in their seats, some of them shuffling uncomfortably as the gallery assessed them. Atticus cast his eye over them, too. The man at the end of the row – Gardner – looked forward, his elbows resting on his knees and his fingertips pressed together. His posture suggested confidence, and Atticus made a bet with himself that he would be elected to be the foreman. Winters – the woman next to him – was smiling, but the smile was stronger on the right, suggesting that it was false. The woman to her left was stroking her hair, a classic gesture from pacifiers who were nervous and trying to maintain an air of calm. Atticus studied them, one after the other, and absorbed the details, building a picture of each. It was an automatic reaction, instilled by years of study and practical application. He would consider them a little more carefully as the trial began. Assumptions would form. He might be able to offer useful directions to the defence based upon what he observed.

The jury now duly sworn, attention turned back to the judge. 'Mr Abernathy,' Somerville said, 'shall we begin?'

10

Abernathy got to his feet and arranged his notes on the desk in front of him. He clasped his hands behind his back and thrust out his chest.

'My Lord, ladies and gentlemen of the jury, as you will no doubt have heard, this is a case of the utmost gravity. Mr Mallender stands accused of the murders, that being that he, as a person of sound mind, unlawfully killed four members of his own family with intent to kill or cause grievous bodily harm. My colleague, Miss Masters, and I will present witnesses to you, and they will provide the evidence in this case that, we will say, demonstrates beyond a reasonable doubt that Mr Mallender is guilty. I am addressing you now simply to give you an overview of the Crown's case and the theory of the Crown regarding the murders. I hope this overview will give you an indication of our evidence before we call our first witness.'

Atticus watched as Abernathy settled into the rhythm of his speech. He was dressed in a fine suit beneath his robes. His horsehair wig was old and grey, darker than the white of the wig worn by the junior counsel assisting him. It was a mark of his seniority; he had evidently owned it for some time, whereas the wig that Masters wore was fresh. Abernathy spoke with a confidence that strayed close to pomposity, but there was no question that he cut an impressive figure. Mallender's barrister would need to work hard to dispel the sense of gravitas that clung to him; his natural authority would be persuasive to a member of the jury not used to hearing someone like him present an argument.

'You will find that the police investigation of this case started in one direction and then took another turn altogether. The police who responded to the defendant's 999 call on Christmas Eve reached the conclusion that his brother, Cameron, had stolen a pistol from his father's gun safe and then used it to shoot their mother, father and sister before putting it to his head and shooting himself. The conclusion was reached because, amongst other reasons, the house was found to have been locked from the inside, and Cameron's body was found near to the weapon that was confirmed to have been used in the killings. It is a conclusion that you might well believe to be credible – the police certainly thought that it was. However, we will demonstrate that Cameron Mallender could *not* have killed his family and that, in fact, the murders were committed by the man you see standing before you in the dock today – the defendant, Ralph Mallender.'

Atticus watched Ralph, looking for any reaction to the accusations that were being made against him. He remained pale, his hands clasped in his lap, his thumbs pressed together. His eyes darted left and right, back and forth, a clear sign of insecurity. That was to be expected.

Abernathy jutted out his chin. 'The defence will try to persuade you that Cameron was responsible. The defendant has made that argument consistently ever since the murders took place. But the prosecution will demonstrate the flaws in that suggestion, not least that forensic evidence suggests that Cameron did not shoot himself, as might otherwise have appeared to have been the case, but that he was shot and that his body was arranged to give the impression that he had taken his own life.'

Atticus looked at Allegra. She was stiff-backed, her hands clasped in her lap and her face set hard, save for the bulge at her jaw where she was clenching and unclenching her teeth. Her legs were crossed at the ankles, and her arms were folded across her chest. She looked angry and uncomfortable.

Abernathy continued. 'We will bring additional evidence to show that Cameron Mallender had no experience with firearms, yet the defendant has suggested that he would have been capable of using a pistol – not just using it, mind, but using it with a degree of accuracy that meant that every one of the shots that were fired that evening found their mark. We will show you how there was no forensic evidence on the body of Cameron Mallender that would have gone towards the claim that he was responsible. There was no blood, even given the fact that the gunshots had produced a good deal of blood on the bodies of the victims and in their immediate vicinity. We will show you Cameron's clothing, and how it was free of any evidence that might suggest that he could have been involved in a struggle. We will show how swabs of Cameron's hands did not show the gunshot residue that would have been expected from someone who had loaded and fired a weapon. And we will show that the defendant was aware of a way to enter and exit the property without detection, thus allowing him to leave the exterior doors locked so that the assumption would be that the murderer remained inside.'

Atticus looked over to where Mack was sitting. She was listening intently, her eyes flicking between the jury to her right and the judge. She still hadn't noticed that Atticus was there.

'Finally, and most damning of all, we will hear evidence from a close friend of the defendant – a Mr Freddie Lamza – who will say that the defendant had confided in him that he hated his family and intended to kill them so that he could inherit their estate.'

Ralph shifted in his seat at the mention of Lamza's name. Atticus remembered reading about that in the papers: Lamza was a former lover, and the prospect of their relationship being aired in front of all these people must have been causing him tremendous embarrassment.

'The Crown will prove that the defendant had the means to commit the crimes. He knew how to leave the house secured so that it looked like the murderer must still be inside. We will show that he knew where his father kept his firearms and that he knew how to use them. And, when it comes to motive, we will show that there was a strong financial reason for the murders. The defendant stood to inherit a great deal of money. And, finally, we will show that he had the opportunity to kill them. The defendant was already at the farmhouse when Detective Sergeant Lennox arrived.'

Abernathy left a meaningful pause, glancing over at the jury with a sombre expression on his face. Those who were taking notes were busy with their pads.

'The facts of the case suggest that only Cameron Mallender or Ralph Mallender could have carried out these murders. We will show you how Cameron Mallender could *not* have been responsible. On that basis, there can only be one verdict. We will demonstrate, beyond all reasonable doubt, that the defendant had the motive, means and opportunity to murder his family on Christmas Eve last year.'

* * *

Abernathy went on to outline the Crown's case in more detail, telling the story of what they said had happened on that night. He took his time and still had not finished two hours later, as the hands on the wall-clock edged around to one.

'I have another half an hour,' Abernathy said to the judge. 'Perhaps now would be the time to adjourn for lunch?'

'I agree,' Somerville said. 'We'll continue at two o'clock.'

The usher stood. 'All rise.'

Atticus got to his feet with the others in the gallery, waiting for the judge to leave the court, and then anxiously watching as Allegra was one of the first to make it to the door.

'Excuse me,' he said as he bumped into his neighbour in an attempt to step around him. 'I'm in a bit of a rush.'

11

Allegra was waiting for Atticus in the reception space outside the courts. There was a clutch of reporters there and, as one of them recognised her, they all moved in her direction. Atticus shouldered his way through a gap and got to her first.

'We should go somewhere else,' he said. 'You're about to get hassled.'

'Where?'

He knew the locale well. 'There's a café down the road. We'll be okay there.'

She didn't argue and followed him as he led the way outside. It had started to rain during the proceedings, and Atticus regretted that he had left both his jacket and umbrella in the back of his car. Allegra had an umbrella and she raised it, sheltering beneath it as Atticus led the way down Wilton Road towards the city. The reporters followed for a moment, until only the two most determined remained in pursuit.

'Mrs Mallender,' one called out, 'how do you think it went this morning?'

They reached the building used by the Quakers for their meetings.

'Keep walking,' Atticus said.

'Did he do it? Allegra!'

'Keep going.'

'*Mrs Mallender!* Did Ralph do it?'

'Jesus,' Allegra said.

'It's down there on the right,' Atticus said, pointing down the street. 'By the roundabout. I'll see you in there.' Atticus turned round and blocked the pavement. They were being followed by a journalist and a photographer, most likely working together. The two men had no choice but to stop.

'Do yourselves a favour, lads,' he said. 'Piss off.'

'Who are you?'

'Mickey Mouse, and I asked you nicely. She doesn't want to talk.'

'Are you a friend?'

Atticus didn't reply.

'Does she still think Ralph's innocent?'

'Come on. She doesn't want to talk to you. Neither do I. I can't make it any clearer than that.'

The reporters didn't look as if they were going to pay attention to Atticus's suggestion. Instead of turning back, one of them tried to step around him. Atticus stood his ground and put up his hand, resting it on the man's shoulder. The reporter reached over and grabbed his wrist, moving his arm out of the way. Atticus stepped across to block the man's path again. The reporter's face clenched in anger, and Atticus readied himself for an escalation. The man squared up to him, but, before he could do anything other than bump shoulders, Atticus saw someone approaching them quickly from the direction of the court.

'Detective Chief Inspector,' Atticus said, deliberately loud.

The reporter frowned, backed away from him, and turned. Mackenzie Jones was behind them. 'What's going on?'

The reporter prodded his finger into Atticus's chest. 'He's trying to stop us going down the street.'

'And you are?'

'Steve Hawkins,' the man said.

She turned to the second man. 'And you?'

'Mark Lewis.'

'Which newspaper are you from?'

'Freelance,' Hawkins said.

Lewis added, 'I work with him.'

'They're bothering the wife of the defendant,' Atticus said. 'They want to ask her about her husband. She doesn't want to talk to them.'

'All right, then, lads,' Mack said. 'I'll tell you what I'll do. You go back to the court and I'll give you a quote and a picture, but best leave Mrs Mallender alone. This morning would've been difficult enough for her without you two making it worse. Her husband's on trial – not her. All right?'

It wasn't really a suggestion, and both men were sensible enough to realise that.

'Fine,' Hawkins said.

'Just give me a minute,' she said. 'I just want to have a word with Mr Priest.'

Hawkins and Lewis glared at Atticus, but did as they were told and made their way back to the court building.

Mack waited until the men were up the road before she turned to Atticus. 'Causing trouble again?'

'Hello to you, too, Mack.'

'I saw you in the gallery.'

'I was trying to keep a low profile.'

She looked at him with the concern that she seemed to reserve for their interactions. 'How are you doing?'

'Fine,' he said.

'I heard you got into trouble at the Wig and Quill.'

'Last week?' Atticus shrugged. 'Just a misunderstanding. I said the beer was off. Barry disagreed.'

'And called the police when you wouldn't pay?'

'What is this? Are you keeping tabs on me?'

'No, Atticus, I'm not. But you still have something of a reputation at the nick, and when you make a scene and an officer is called to take care of it, it's the kind of thing that gets shared during the morning briefing. There are people there who take pleasure in your mistakes, as you know.'

'Thank you for the concern. It's very touching, but there's nothing to worry about.'

'You're still doing the . . . you know, the detective thing?'

He sighed. 'Yes, Mack, I'm still a detective. It's going very well, thank you very much. In fact, I was just with my client.'

That brought Mack up short. '*What?*'

'Allegra Mallender wants me to look at your investigation.'

'And what does that mean?'

'She wants me to make sure that nothing was missed.'

'Good luck with that.'

'Why do you say that?'

'Because it's open-and-shut. And no, before you ask, I'm not going to tell you anything.'

'She says he didn't do it.'

'Of course she does. She's hardly impartial. She's his wife.'

'You must have spoken to her?'

Mack rolled her eyes. 'For hours and hours and hours.'

'And?'

'Weren't you listening? I can't talk to you about the case. Ask *her*.'

'But you think he did it?'

'We wouldn't be here if I didn't, would we? There's a ton of evidence. Were you listening this morning? He's got the motive; he had the opportunity; he doesn't have an alibi. Read the papers. That's all you'll need. It's all there.'

Atticus looked up at the rain clouds and shivered.

'Are you sure you're okay?' she asked.

'I'm fine. Really. Never better.' He paused, looked down, then looked back up again. 'How about a drink tonight? Just for a catch-up? We haven't seen each—'

'No,' she said, cutting him off. 'Not a good idea.'

The rain fell more heavily, drumming against the pavement, the tarmac and the passing cars.

Mack found a small umbrella in her bag and raised it. 'If you need anything on the case – anything I'm *able* to help you with – then come in and see me. Make an appointment. I'm sure the others would be pleased to see you, too.'

'Yeah.' He grinned. 'I'm sure they'd be *delighted*.'

She laid her hand on his arm. 'See you later.'

'Bye, Mack.'

'And, Atticus?'

'Yes?'

'Stay out of trouble.'

12

Atticus jogged along Wilton Road until he reached St Paul's Roundabout. The café was between a shop selling window blinds and an Indian takeaway. He opened the door and went inside. Allegra was sitting at a table in the back. She had two cups of coffee in front of her. He went over to join her.

'Honestly,' she said as he sat down. 'It's ridiculous.'

'The reporters?'

She nodded, her face set in a grimace of annoyance. 'They've been outside the house all week. It's a farce. An absolute farce.' She sipped her coffee, put the cup down and turned to look straight into his eyes. 'Ralph didn't do it. You have to help me to get him out.'

The change of subject and her earnestness took Atticus by surprise.

'I'll do my best.'

She reached across and laid her hand over his. 'It's just such a relief to have someone to help. I can't begin to tell you how much.'

He gently withdrew his hand. 'I can't offer any guarantees. I haven't seen any of the evidence yet. I'll approach it objectively and independently, and if I see anything that looks questionable – anything at all – I'll investigate it. All we need is to raise a reasonable doubt. That's it. They have to be sure that he did it. Not confident. Not satisfied. *Sure.* If they're not, they have to acquit. That's what I'll try to do – find the doubt that your husband needs.'

She stared out of the window at the handful of pedestrians hurrying along the sodden street. Cars swept around the round-about, throwing up parabolas of spray in their wakes. Allegra's enthusiasm seemed to melt away, replaced by an abstraction that Atticus couldn't quite place. He picked up the coffee, warming his hands against the polystyrene cup.

'What do you need from me?' she asked.

'I need to speak to Ralph's solicitor. It's Dafyd Cadogan, isn't it?'

'Yes. Do you know him?'

'I do,' he said, deciding not to impart his opinion of the lawyer and his firm. 'Tell him that I'm working for you and Ralph. I don't need long with him.'

'Before the trial starts again this afternoon?'

'Perfect.'

'Do you want me to be there, too?'

'It's up to you,' he said. 'It's not important – I just want to get a look at the files.'

She looked at her watch. 'We've got twenty minutes. Let's go and see him now.'

Atticus finished his coffee, stood, and dropped the empty cup into the bin. Allegra took her coffee with her. Atticus opened the door for her and joined her in the drizzle outside.

She put up her umbrella. 'Thank you,' she said. 'I'm so grateful. Ralph will be relieved, too.'

'You're welcome,' he said. 'I'll do my best, but you need to be realistic. Cases like this don't get to court unless the prosecution is confident.'

'But—'

'But there *will* be loose ends,' he said. 'There always are. I'll find them, pick at them, and we'll see what unravels.'

13

Allegra called Dafyd Cadogan as they walked back to the court, and the solicitor was waiting for them when they arrived in the waiting area.

'This is Atticus Priest,' she said.

'I know Mr Priest,' Cadogan said with a flat smile. 'Our paths crossed now and again when he was a police officer, didn't they?'

Atticus nodded with a forced smile. Cadogan was a large man in both stature and personality. He was wearing a baggy suit and a white shirt that was at least a size too small for him. His gut strained against the buttons, opening gaps through which Atticus could see his chest. He had represented several of the scoundrels that Atticus had investigated, and had always, without exception, been a right royal pain in the arse. He was pompous, full of the delusion that he had a modicum of talent, and seemingly blind to the fact that he was a two-bob provincial solicitor who earned his crust representing low-life criminal scumbags whose guilt was never really in question.

'I'll leave you two to it,' Allegra said.

She shook Atticus's hand and made her way back to the public gallery.

Cadogan glared at Atticus. 'What do you want? We start again in five minutes.'

'I need to see all of the documents in the case. Everything you've got and everything that the prosecution has disclosed.'

'There's a lot,' he said.

'I'm sure there is. I'd appreciate it if you could arrange for someone to copy them and bring them to my office. I'm just round the corner from you.'

'That's going to be expensive.'

He shrugged. 'I can't do my job without the evidence.'

'And what job is that?'

'I'm reviewing the case. Finding the errors in the evidence that you should have found.'

Cadogan curled his lip in annoyance. 'Is she paying for this?'

'She is. I'm sure you're already inflating your disbursements. You can add it to the bill.'

'I'm pleased to see you haven't lost your sense of humour, even after . . . you know, after all that unpleasantness.'

'I have a thick skin.'

Cadogan raised his chin and stuck it out, posturing defensively. 'She's deluded if she thinks this is going to be anything other than a waste of time. She's relentless. She calls me every morning to go through the case and to tell me all the wonderful new ideas that she's had to try to prove that her husband is innocent.'

'I'm sure you have the meter running.'

Cadogan didn't rise to the bait. Instead, he gestured towards Atticus and said, 'And now she's hiring the likes of you. Getting more and more desperate. She didn't think that they were going to arrest him, but they did. She didn't think they'd charge him, but they did. This morning in court won't have helped. I advised him to plead guilty, but he wouldn't.'

'So you think he did it?'

'I think the prosecution have a strong case.'

'That's not what I asked.'

'We're giving him the best defence possible. Do I think the jury will convict him?' He paused. 'Make up your own mind when you see the evidence. It's circumstantial, maybe, but there's a lot of it and it adds up. The jury will want something credible, and this is. *Someone* killed the Mallenders. In the absence of a more convincing explanation . . .' He shrugged.

'Your confidence in your client is inspiring,' Atticus said. He eyed the door, where the press was beginning to funnel back inside.

'I'm just being honest. And this' – Cadogan prodded a fat finger in Atticus's direction – 'is a waste of time and money.'

'We'll see. But at least I'll be able to tell her what a terrible job you've done. Get me the papers.'

14

Atticus retook his seat just as the associate called the court to order and the judge and jury came back inside. Abernathy resumed his spot and, with the same thoroughness he had displayed during the morning's session, continued his opening speech. He finished with another rhetorical flourish, his hands spread wide as he regaled the jury with his certainty that the Crown's case was strong. He finished with the suggestion – not far off an exhortation – that the evidence would leave them with no choice but to find Mallender guilty.

Abernathy thanked them and sat.

Somerville looked up from his notes. 'Thank you, Mr Abernathy. Are you ready to call your first witness?'

'Indeed, my Lord, we are. The Crown calls Jimmy Robson.'

*   *   *

The usher called out for Jimmy Robson, and the witness made his way into the court. He was a big man in his mid-twenties, shaven-headed and clearly unaccustomed to the suit that he was wearing for the occasion. Tattoos were visible above the line of his collar and down the back of his right hand. His eyes flashed around the room, but he didn't show the nervousness that might otherwise have been expected of someone here for the first time. Atticus wondered if he had prior experience of the criminal justice system.

'Mr Robson,' Abernathy said, 'please tell the court what you do for a living.'

'I'm a gamekeeper for the Wilton Estate. I look after the woods.'

'What does that entail?'

Robson shrugged. 'I keep an eye out for poachers, mostly. We've had gypsies coming in to try to shoot the deer. Had hare coursers in last week, setting their dogs loose in the fields. Had to chase them off.' He spoke slowly and deliberately.

'And you live near to Grovely Farmhouse, do you not?'

'I do,' he said. 'You get to their house and keep going down the track and you get to my place. Five minutes away. Owned by the Earl of Pembroke. Comes with the job. Nice little perk.'

'Thank you, Mr Robson. Please, would you tell the court how you know the Mallender family?'

'Used to work for Mr Mallender,' he said. 'Worked there since I got out of school until last year.'

'Do you know the family well?'

'Well as most, I reckon. I worked there the better part of ten years.'

'Would you say that the family had any enemies?'

'No, sir, I wouldn't. Mr Mallender had a bit of a temper on him, but no worse than others I know.'

'And the rest of the family?'

He shrugged. 'Wouldn't have said so. Everyone loved Mrs Mallender. Same for Cassandra. I didn't know Cameron very well, but he always seemed like a nice enough sort of bloke.'

'And the defendant?'

'I knew him a bit,' Robson said. 'Not all that well, like his brother.'

'Thank you, Mr Robson. Now – let's move to Christmas Eve. Please tell the jury about the last time that you saw Hugo Mallender.'

Robson cleared his throat. 'It was around half nine,' he said. 'Like I said, we've had poachers in the wood. I was going out to do a check. I went out by the house and saw Mr Mallender smoking a cigarette by the gate.'

'Did you speak to him?'

'No,' he said.

'But you're sure it was him?'

'Definitely.'

'And after that?'

'Well, I went home. I'm not into Christmas – I live on my own, and, well, you know, it can get lonely at that time of year – so I ended up having a drink and watching a film.'

'And what about later?'

'How do you mean?'

'Did you go out again?'

'I did,' he said. 'Saw the lights from the police cars. I walked Dave – Dave's my dog – up to the house and where the police had set up the cordon. I spoke to a couple of the police and they told me to go back home, so I did.'

*　*　*

The rest of his evidence was uncontroversial and had been included only to help establish the timeline that led up to the discovery of the bodies. It was coming up to three when Atticus decided that he had seen enough for the day. He got up and made his way along the row, mouthing apologies as he disturbed the others sitting between him and the aisle, stepping around them and over their feet. He reached the end of the row, noticed that Mack was watching him from her spot behind the barristers, and, after giving her a nod of acknowledgement, made his way to the door and went outside.

15

Atticus walked back to the office. He passed by the Playhouse and then down into the square with its ancient buildings, everything dominated by the tall finger of the cathedral's spire that was visible from almost everywhere in the city. He felt better and, buoyed by the confidence of his new work, he allowed himself to feel positive about his prospects for the first time in a long while. He found himself thinking about what his father had said about his change of career. Atticus imagined what he might say if he was able to influence the direction of a case as notorious as the Christmas Eve Massacre.

The old man would have no choice but to take him seriously then.

Atticus stopped at WHSmith and bought the things that he was going to need: fresh A4 pads, new markers for his whiteboards, a selection of stationery. He paid and walked back to the office.

A young man was waiting for him in the passageway. He had a porter's trolley and, balanced on it, three cardboard boxes.

'Atticus Priest?'

'That's right.'

'I'm from Cadogan's. Got these boxes for you.'

'Excellent. Good timing.'

Atticus opened the door and helped the young man to carry the boxes upstairs to the office. He cleared a space against the wall and stacked them there, then opened them up and started to arrange the contents across the floor. He saw that he had been given a copy of the core bundle. It included the indictments, witness statements and exhibits, with separate bundles for the disclosure material. The criminal justice system was supposed to run on a paperless footing these days, but Atticus had not been 'invited' into the digital case. It didn't matter; he preferred to have paper for a review.

He flicked through the crime-scene photographs and the report from the pathologist who had carried out the post-mortems on the family. There were reams and reams and reams of material.

'Need anything else?' the young man asked him.

'I'm good,' Atticus said. 'Thank you.'

The man disappeared down the stairs and shut the door to the passageway behind him.

Atticus knocked on Jacob's door and smiled as he heard the drumbeat of Bandit's paws thundering across the upstairs room and then down the stairs. He saw the dog through the smoked glass and heard the whacking of his tail against the wall.

'You're early,' Jacob said.

'Did what I needed to do. How was he?'

'Good as gold. We went for a long walk – he decided he wanted a swim in the river.'

'He loves it there,' Atticus said, rubbing behind the dog's ears. 'Thanks for looking after him.'

'Any time. I need the money.'

'You're my first port of call.'

Atticus led the way back to the office. Bandit slouched over and started to sniff the boxes.

'We're going to be busy,' Atticus said.

16

Atticus took Pink Floyd's *Dark Side of the Moon* from his collection, slid the vinyl from the sleeve and placed it carefully on the platter. He lowered the needle to the first song, adjusted the volume and waited for 'Breathe (In the Air)' to play. He whirled around the room for a moment, strumming in time with Dave Gilmour's guitar, and then, as the track finished and turned into 'On the Run', he went to sit down on the leather sofa in the bay window. He took two A4 pads and laid them out side by side on the coffee table.

On the right-hand pad he wrote DEFENCE.

On the left-hand pad he wrote PROSECUTION.

He started to take notes, beginning with the evidence that Ralph would give in his own defence. The account was based almost exclusively on his testimony, given first to the police at the farmhouse and then afterwards to the investigating officers and his own lawyers. The police interviews had been painstakingly transcribed into interview records that ran to several hundred sheets of A4 paper.

Ralph's account was that the Mallenders had gathered at the farmhouse for a pre-Christmas celebration on the day of the murders. Those present were Hugo and Juliet Mallender as hosts; the twins, Cameron and Cassandra Mallender, who had arrived from Bath University the previous day; and Brenda Grant, their cleaner, together with her husband, Keith. Ralph Mallender rounded out the attendees. Atticus wondered where Allegra had been, and, after skimming the papers, he found that she had reported feeling unwelcome at the farmhouse and had gone Christmas shopping in Southampton instead. Cellphone records confirmed that she had been in the city until the early evening.

Ralph said that he had had an argument with his mother and father. He said that he had brought up their treatment of Allegra and, specifically, that she didn't feel wanted at the house. He reported that the argument became heated and that he had left the house in anger at around eight. The police had interviewed a dog walker, who had testified that she had heard a car driving away from the farm at around the same time.

Atticus made himself a cup of coffee, flipped the album over onto the second side, and returned to the papers. Ralph said that he had gone to the Greyhound pub in Wilton after leaving the house. His presence there was confirmed by the landlord, who would later testify that Ralph had been in a black mood. Ralph ordered dinner and a pint and had been seen speaking to someone on the phone. Ralph said that was true, that he had called Allegra to tell her about the argument. The police had checked the calls that had been made and received on his phone and accepted that he had spoken to his wife. She had said that they had spoken, too.

Ralph testified that he had felt guilty at the direction the conversation with his parents had taken, and that he wasn't prepared to go home without at least trying to reconcile with them. It was Christmas Eve, he said, and he felt bad. He didn't want there to be an atmosphere over the dinner table when he and Allegra arrived the next day. He got back into his car and returned to the farmhouse. He said that he couldn't be sure precisely what time he arrived back at the property, guessing that it was somewhere around ten thirty. The publican at the Greyhound did not have CCTV and was only prepared to say that Ralph had left the Greyhound at some point before he called last orders.

Ralph said that he had tried the door to the farmhouse and found it locked. He did not have his key with him, but the kitchen light was on, and he had looked inside. He saw his father's body slumped on the floor with blood on his clothes and what he thought looked like gunshot wounds. He said that he froze, taking a moment to process what he had seen, and then he had been overcome with horror.

His 999 call was timed at 23.15 and a transcript was included in the file. Ralph – noted by the operator to have been in a panic – had reported that he thought his father was dead and that he needed the police to attend as quickly as possible.

Atticus flipped through to the police log. The attending officer was Detective Sergeant Tristan Lennox, who had been night duty CID cover that night. Lennox recorded that he had arrived at the property at 23.32 and found Ralph in the farmyard. Neither Lennox nor Ralph could say whether the rest of the house was empty, and given that Ralph had reported that his father had been shot to death, Lennox was not prepared to investigate without backup. He called for an armed response unit and then waited outside the property with Ralph Mallender for fifteen minutes before two uniformed constables – Ryan Yaxley and Vernon Edwards – arrived.

It was at this point that Atticus noted the first real point of interest. Lennox said that he thought he saw movement in one of the uncovered upstairs windows. Yaxley said that he remembered Lennox's statement, but, when questioned afterwards, said that he hadn't seen anything himself. He'd qualified that – most likely because he didn't want to drop his sergeant in it – by saying that he had been distracted. It was clearly going to be one of the pieces of evidence around which the case would turn: the defence would seize upon it, for, if someone was still alive in the house while Ralph was outside, it made it much less likely – and would certainly introduce reasonable doubt – that he could have been responsible.

The record came to an end and the stylus swung back to its cradle with a thunk. Atticus looked back at his notes and summed up what Ralph would say in his defence: he would admit that there had been an argument, and that he had decided that he would return to the house in an attempt to reconcile with his family. When he arrived, he found the door locked and, on looking through the kitchen window, he saw his father dead. He called the police. The explanation that he would suggest – the same one that the police themselves had originally posited – was that his brother, Cameron, had murdered his father, mother and sister sometime between Jimmy Robson's sighting of Hugo Mallender and Ralph's return to the house.

Bandit padded over.

'What do you think, boy? Did he do it?'

The dog cocked his head and nuzzled Atticus's hand.

'Exactly,' Atticus said. 'I agree. Doesn't look good for him.'

He put down his pen. He had taken six pages of notes, including a page noting the inconsistencies in the police case and the questions that he wanted to ask Ralph and his wife.

But it would have to wait. It was ten and he hadn't eaten yet.

17

Mack had gone back to the station after court to prepare for the second day of the trial. The first day had gone well. The opening statement was persuasive, and Robson had established the start of the timeline that they would be relying on. Abernathy had been satisfied and had departed with a cheery farewell, adding that he was looking forward to getting his teeth into the case properly in the morning.

Lennox was in the office with her. He was nervous about his own turn in the witness box tomorrow. His evidence – particularly the statement that he thought he had seen someone moving inside the house – was likely to be contentious. He still thought that he had seen someone and, given that Ralph was *outside* the property at the time, standing next to police witnesses, it was not helpful to the prosecution case that pegged Ralph as the murderer. But Lennox had reported it at the time and had noted it down. It was part of the case now, for better or worse.

Mack couldn't discuss his evidence with him – and she certainly couldn't coach him – but reassured him that he would be fine and that he had more than enough experience to handle anything that was thrown his way.

'Thanks,' Lennox said.

She leaned back and stretched. 'I mean it. You'll be fine.'

'It doesn't come as naturally to me as it does to you.'

'You think it comes naturally? I won't sleep a wink before mine. Nerves are fine. You *should* be nervous.'

'And I'm worried about . . . you know.'

'About what you think you saw?'

'It's their best evidence.'

'Probably.'

'And if I hadn't said anything, this would have been finished already.'

'Probably not. There's plenty of evidence against him. And there's no choice – you have to say what you think you saw.'

'Even if it means he gets off?'

'Just say what you think you saw, and the jury can decide. Abernathy is briefed. You know he has it all under control.'

'I know,' he said. He exhaled and looked at his watch. 'Fancy a pint?'

'Not tonight. I'm late as it is. Andy is going to kill me.'

Lennox nodded. He got up and stretched his arms. 'I might go and see if anyone's there for last orders.'

'Just one,' she admonished. 'And then get to bed. I want you fresh as a daisy in the morning.'

'Yes, ma'am,' he said with a grin.

18

Mackenzie and Andy Jones had a house in Bishopdown. It was a thirty-minute walk from the station, passing by the crematorium and Aldi and the small business park gathered around the roundabout that marked the start of the A30's north-westward exit from Salisbury towards Andover and the M3 to London. It was a peaceful district of newbuilds, with a nice community spirit, two new schools, quality housing stock and good access to the city. Being able to walk to work was a bonus, made easier since the station had moved from the old building on Wilton Road to its present location near the Greencroft. Mack didn't have time for scheduled exercise, so she often walked. It was good thinking time, too, an opportunity to consider work on her way in and how she might improve family life when she returned again. *Family life.* She had been thinking about that this evening as Lennox had driven them back to the nick.

Mack looked at her watch as she crossed over the pavement and walked up the drive: it was twenty past ten. She had promised Andy that she would be home an hour and a half ago. She braced herself. She wasn't worried about an argument –

they never argued, not like *that* – but that he would express his annoyance more subtly, with long silences and standoffishness; in some ways she would have preferred an up-and-down row. At least that way they would have had to work to find their common ground.

She opened the door and stepped into the hall. She could smell chicken cooking in the kitchen and could hear her husband's music playing. She took off her coat, left it on the bannister and went through into the kitchen. Andy was at the oven, his back to her. There was a chopping board on the work surface with diced chilli, onions and peppers.

'Hello,' she said.

Andy turned and smiled at her. 'Hello, stranger.'

'Sorry. I know I'm late.'

'It's all right,' he said. 'There's wine in the fridge.'

She saw that he had half a glass left on the counter next to the board. She took a glass from the cupboard, collected the wine, refilled his and then poured herself one.

'How were the kids?'

'Fine,' he said. 'Asleep. They missed you.'

'I missed them, too,' she said.

'How did it go?'

'Okay, I think.'

'Still confident?'

She took a gulp of wine, nodding as she swallowed. 'Early days.'

'It was on the news,' he said. 'They were outside the court.'

'The gallery is full of press.'

She sat down on one of the chairs next to the small dining-room table. Daisy's maths homework had been left there, her sums half finished. She had a test tomorrow, and Mack was about to ask why she hadn't finished them all when she realised that, under the circumstances, she was not in any position to criticise. Sebastian's toys were scattered over the floor, a Transformer locked in combat with a plastic T-Rex.

She took off her shoes and crossed her legs so that she could knead the arch of her right foot. 'How was your day?'

'Not bad.'

He gave her the potted version. Andy worked part-time for a web developer, three hours a day so that he could keep his hand in. He had taken a career break for eight years so that he could look after the children while Mack climbed the ladder at work. That, perversely, had led to difficult conversations between them. Mack loved her children dearly, but they had decided together that she had more to sacrifice and the most long-term potential. She was a DCI at thirty-eight, and the confidential nods and winks that she got from higher up the chain suggested that she had further still to climb. Andy had accepted that and had sacrificed his own career for hers. It was only now that the kids were both at school that he had the time to take decisions for himself.

He finished cooking and dished up. They took their plates into the sitting room and sat down; Andy found the recording of *EastEnders* from last week and queued it up. Neither of them particularly enjoyed it, but it was brainless and familiar, and that was often all they could manage at the end of the day.

'Did you remember we're going to see my mum and dad in London on Saturday?' he asked her.

'Shit,' she said.

'You forgot?'

'Yes,' she said. 'But it's fine. They shouldn't need me at the weekend.'

'"Shouldn't"?'

'Won't.'

'*Please* don't forget. It's her seventieth. It's been in the calendar for ages.'

'I'll remember,' she said, more sharply than she intended. She was curt because she knew that Andy was right – she *had* forgotten and she *did* need the reminder – and because that lack of focus was a failing that she had been working hard to fix.

Andy pressed play and the show started.

'You want to finish the bottle?' she asked him.

'Go on, then,' he said.

She put her plate on the arm of the sofa and went out of the room. She went upstairs first, checking that the children were both asleep. Daisy was curled up into a tight ball, her long limbs tucked up against her body; Sebastian was sprawled out, his plush dinosaurs spilling out from beneath the covers. She crept inside, arranged the covers over him and corralled the toys so that he wouldn't panic if he woke and couldn't find them. She leaned down to kiss him on the head. His hair was damp and smelled of citrus; Andy had washed and bathed them both, too. Mack sighed. She had missed bath time again, missed tucking them in, missed reading to them. She was missing a lot, and that needed to change.

She went downstairs and into the kitchen, collecting the bottle from the fridge and going back into the lounge. She emptied the contents of the bottle into their two glasses. She would try harder, she told herself. She had too much to lose.

19

Atticus went to McDonald's to get his dinner. He walked back through the city with the paper bag and felt alone. He watched the other people around him going about their business: the families and couples in the windows of the restaurants that faced the Market Square, the others emptying out of the Odeon at the end of whichever film it was that they had been to see. There was one elderly couple, still holding hands despite the years that he imagined that they had spent together, and he felt a pang of regret. He pictured the life that they must have had: a shared trove of memories to bind them close, a couple of children, perhaps grandchildren, too.

The prospect of a life like that seemed distant to him. Out of reach. There was no one that he would consider as a partner and, more to the point, he doubted that anyone would have him. He knew that this wistfulness had been provoked by his meeting with Mack earlier, but that didn't make it any easier to swallow.

He unlocked the outside door, went through the passage and opened the door to the office. Bandit was waiting for him upstairs, his tail wagging happily. Atticus sat down on the leather sofa and tore open the brown paper bag. The dog sat down immediately, his gaze switching between the food and Atticus's face. His tongue fell out between his lips, and his tail wagged against the floor.

'Don't worry,' he said. 'I got you one, too.'

He broke up one of the two cheeseburgers and dropped it into Bandit's bowl. The dog dipped his head to it and devoured it in five hungry gulps.

Atticus took his time over his, finishing it and then the carton of fries while he studied the moves that had been taken in the three games of chess that he was playing simultaneously on Chess.com. Atticus had started playing again to fill the time after he had been dismissed from the force. It gave him puzzles to solve and something to distract him from the boredom that he had found so difficult to alleviate.

The games were all on the correspondence basis, with each player making a move every day. Two of the games were humdrum, and Atticus had been toying with his opponents. The longest one was against a mouthy American with the username ChessCompressions16. Atticus had played an incisive Sicilian, and now saw that he could give up his rook for a bishop for a winning advantage. He made the move and waited for the inevitable abuse in the comments.

The second game, against a French player – SansLimite – had moved into an endgame where Atticus was a pawn down but had the advantage of the two bishops and his opponent's fragmented pawn structure. SansLimite had moved his knight to b5 and, after studying the board for a moment, Atticus took a calculated gamble by moving his king to h1. He suspected that he would be able to close out the position within the next three moves.

The last game was the most interesting. His opponent was Jack_of_Hearts, who Atticus had played against regularly for the last year. Atticus had no idea of the player's gender, but knew from the miniature Union Jack next to the username that they were also in the United Kingdom. He or she had proposed a game within a month of Atticus registering on the site, and had proven to be a worthy opponent. They had played fifty times, and Atticus was a whisker ahead with fifteen wins against twelve for Jack_of_Hearts and twenty-three draws.

This game had seen the two of them play out an aggressive Sicilian Sveshnikov, and it had progressed to a position with Jack_of_Hearts better on the board and ahead on the clock after fifteen moves. Atticus had reviewed a series of possible moves before assessing that he could castle when his opponent advanced pawns on the queenside. The trap had been closed, and Jack had gambled by moving his knight, realising, sometime after posting the move, that his position was hopeless. A wry note in the comments congratulated Atticus and predicted a resignation once the next move had been taken.

Atticus finished the last of the fries, chose the move to tighten the noose, and pressed send.

He picked up the notes that he had taken in his review of the documents. He had been thinking about the Mallender case and realised now that there was something about it that didn't sit right with him. There *was* a case against Ralph – Mack was an excellent investigator, and she wouldn't have moved this far with the prosecution unless she was confident in his guilt – but it still felt unfinished, as if there was a large piece of evidence that was missing and, without it, the puzzle couldn't be solved.

He just had to work out what it was.

He would start looking into it properly in the morning. He was tired now.

20

Atticus lowered the Venetian blinds and went to brush his teeth in the bathroom. He didn't have a shower here; he had been using the facilities at the gym near the Maltings, and resolved to visit tomorrow. He took off his shirt, washed and dried himself, and went back into the office. He locked the door, switched off the lights and went through into the second room. He could hear Jacob in the flat above as he padded from one side of his flat to the other, his weight jangling the light fittings overhead.

This room was smaller than the one that he used for his office, with enough space for a double mattress on the floor and a chair upon which he had stacked up a pile of clothes that needed to be washed. There was a low shelf that held some of his books: Blackstone's *Criminal Law*, manuals on forensic odontology and toxicology, a general text on criminal investigation that he was reviewing for an online forum that he contributed to. He had more than twenty crates of books and had put those in a storage facility in South Newton until he had somewhere larger to move to. There was a third door that led out of the room to a metal landing and the stairs that descended to the gardens in the quadrangle below. Atticus had bought a child's blackout blind from Mothercare and used the suckers to attach it to the glass so that the room was dark. He lowered himself onto the mattress and pulled his duvet over him. There was a plate on the floor next to the bed that he had been using as an ashtray; he remembered that he had a half-smoked joint there. He reached his hand down to it, fumbled through the ash until he found it, dug his matches out of his pocket and then lit it.

He lay back, put the joint to his lips and breathed in the sweet-smelling smoke, holding it in his lungs and waiting for the gentle buzz to prickle his brain. He exhaled, blowing the smoke into the darkness above his head.

He closed his eyes and let his thoughts drift to Mack.

Their affair had lasted for six months. It had been secret at the start, and they had worked hard to keep it that way. Mack was married and she was also Atticus's boss; there was no profit in anyone finding out about it until they were ready. They had been discovered by accident. Mack's husband was a perceptive man, and, like most cuckolds, he had seen the small hints and clues that could only reveal the truth when they were put together. Some might have chosen to be wilfully blind, but he had allowed his suspicion to consume him and had eventually found her password and accessed her personal email account. Mack and Atticus had been careful, but Andy found a receipt from the online drinks shop that Mack had used to buy Atticus a bottle of Chivas Regal for his birthday and, his suspicions freshly confirmed, had confronted her about it.

She had admitted the affair, and, displaying a decisiveness that Atticus would not have credited, Andy had thrown her out.

Atticus had been happy about that. He knew that Mack was miserable with her husband, and he had been telling her that she should leave him for weeks. She had resisted for the sake of the children. Atticus had seen what an unhappy marriage could do to a child – his own experience was instructive in that – and had argued that staying would not do them any favours in the long run, but she had resisted. In the end, the decision had been taken for her.

Mack had moved into the house that Atticus had been renting. It had seemed like a good idea at the time, but Mack was unable to put the children out of her mind. She had been loaded down with guilt, and their relationship had been unable to bear the weight. They argued and squabbled and, eventually, Mack had moved out and taken a room at the White Hart. Andy, knowing full well that Mack would not be able to abandon her children, had opted to be reasonable and played a waiting game. He had won. Mack had gone back to him and apologised, pleading for a second chance. He had given it to her on the condition that everything must end with Atticus. She had taken his offer.

Atticus knew that what had happened next was all his fault. He hadn't taken her decision well and had allowed his rancour to fester until it made working together impossible. He had been fired a month later, but that hadn't been the reason. An anonymous complaint had been made that Atticus had been seen smoking a joint on the job. The drug test had come without warning, and he had tested positive. Atticus had been suspended on the spot pending a professional standards hearing, but he knew that the writing was on the wall. His career was over, so he had resigned, preferring that to the indignity of a disciplinary panel.

He had bumped into Andy in the city the week after and had known, from the triumphant expression on his rival's face, that it had been he who had made the call. Andy must have found out from someone at the station and passed the tip along.

The marijuana might have been the precipitating event, but it was a symptom of Atticus's malaise if not the malaise itself. The true cause of his dismissal was the implosion of his relationship with Mack. Smoking on the job was a stupid risk, but he hadn't cared. He had known that he was sabotaging his career, and he had done it anyway. He realised now: he had *wanted* them to fire him. He had given them the ammunition and they had used it.

The rest of what happened after that was inevitable: he had allowed his compulsions to get the better of him and had spent his savings on chemical distractions that had helped him to forget. He had smoked and snorted his way through a small fortune, lining Finn's pockets at the expense of his financial solvency. He had cleaned himself up eventually, but the damage had been done. He was unable to afford the rent on his house without his police job and had been evicted.

All of that had brought him to this wretched point: sleeping on a mattress on the floor of a messy room, in the office of a failing business, with no one in his life save for the rescued dog who was curled up in the space behind his knees.

Atticus felt the emptiness in his gut and an ache in his heart. He drew down on the joint again, the red coal burning down to his fingertips, and then dropped it into the ashtray once more. He exhaled, closed his eyes, and tried to drift away to sleep.

21

Atticus woke to the sound of his alarm. He had deliberately left his phone in the office room so that he would have to get up to switch it off. He sat up and stretched out his aching limbs, his joints clicking and popping. Bandit had moved down to the bottom of the mattress in the night, and now he stirred too, getting up and shaking himself so that the tag on his collar jangled loudly. He padded up to Atticus and nuzzled him, his wet snout cold against Atticus's cheek. Atticus scratched the dog under the chin.

'Good morning, boy.'

Atticus felt better with the benefit of sleep, even if he could have done with a couple more hours. The pensive mood from last night was gone. He had a fresh puzzle to solve, and he would use that to distract himself from wallowing in self-pity.

The room was dark. He swung his legs around and stood up, stumbling through the abandoned clothes to the door. He opened it, the artificial light from the streetlamp outside the window drifting in through the dusty glass, and found his phone on the coffee table. He silenced the alarm and checked the time: it was just after five.

He took his pills with a glass of water, dressed, found Bandit's lead and attached it to his collar. He led the dog down the stairs and headed across the street to the car park. The dog hopped into the back of the Fiesta, and Atticus got into the front seat. He started the engine and drove out of the city to the west, heading towards Wilton. He passed the grand, stately pile of Wilton House, continued through the small town and then turned right onto Wishford Road. He passed beneath the railway bridge, passed the riding school and continued to the north until he reached the southern boundary of Great Wishford.

He stopped the car at the side of the road and got out. The first light of dawn lit the tops of the trees and silvered the wide-open fields behind him. It was quiet here and isolated. Arable land was laid out all around, and, to his left, he saw the dark green fringe of the forest. It was cold, too, with a northerly wind blowing over the open ground. Atticus looked at the forest and the road that passed deeper into it and imagined what it might have been like on the night of Christmas Eve. It was lonely here and would be even more so once he started into the wood. He remembered the area well. The Priest children had enjoyed exploring the countryside as youngsters, their parents often taking them on long Sunday-morning walks before finding a pub for lunch. It felt very different now, compared to his memories.

Bandit pawed the car's rear window, eager to be let out. 'Hold on, boy. You can run around in a minute.'

He got back into the car, turned to the left and continued on a narrow lane that was only just wide enough for one car to pass along it. He followed the track across the bleak, wide fields, the leaden skies stretching overhead as far as the eye could see. There were rows of trees planted to mark the boundaries of each field, and a fence on both sides of the road demarked those boundaries. After two or three minutes, Atticus arrived at a space that had been reserved for a car park. A single Land Rover, dusty and caked in mud, had been parked at the far end, and Atticus slid the Fiesta alongside it. He opened the door and stepped out, then opened the rear door for the dog. Bandit jumped out and shot off into the woods, his collar jangling.

Atticus went around to the boot and opened it. There was a lot of junk inside, including a pair of Hunter boots. He sat on the lip of the boot, removed his Converse trainers and pulled the boots on. He changed his leather jacket for a warmer overcoat, dug around in the junk until he found the leather pouch that contained his professional-grade lock-pick set, locked the car and started to walk. He whistled for Bandit and heard the dog change course, a blur of white and tan as he darted between the tree trunks to Atticus's left.

The start of the woods was marked by a blue sign that read GROVELY WOOD – PRIVATE WOODLAND. Vehicles were not allowed beyond that point, and, a few steps ahead, there was a second noticeboard that displayed a map of the area. Atticus checked it to refresh his memory. He remembered facts that had lodged in his mind as a child: the long straight avenues through the trees that were reputed to have been laid by the Romans; the arms dumps that had been hidden here during the war; the myths and fables that their mother had told them as they tramped along the damp and muddy trails. He recalled his favourite: legend had it that four Danish sisters who lived in Wilton had been suspected of witchcraft after an outbreak of smallpox had killed dozens of locals in the 1700s. The sisters were taken to the wood and murdered, their bodies buried a little way apart from one another so that they could not conspire in revenge against their murderers. Four ancient beech trees were said to have grown from the graves to remind the killers of what they had done. Atticus remembered visiting the trees and finding a hollow in the back of the largest one in which people still left pagan offerings.

The thought chilled him more than the weather. He zipped up his coat and set off down the track. The open fields were soon replaced by thick woodland on either side. Atticus followed the track as it bent around to the south, eventually reaching the junction with the First Broad Drive. The track continued on the other side of the avenue, and he hiked along it until he reached the Second Broad Drive. He paused there, standing still to watch and listen. It was eerily quiet. There was no one else in sight, and the only noise that he could hear was the call of a bird overhead and the rustle of a larger animal – most likely a deer – in the thick underbrush on his right-hand side. He put his fingers to his lips and whistled; Bandit crashed out of a bush, scaring a pigeon into the air.

The forest continued on the north of the Second Broad Drive, but it had been cleared to the south to open out onto a broad field that had been planted with wheat. Atticus took out his phone and looked at the Ordnance Survey map that he had downloaded. The farm was another five hundred feet to the south, following the continuation of the track that he had taken as it skirted the eastern boundary of the wheat field. There was a collection of buildings on the western side of that track; Atticus walked on, finding a gap in the overgrown hedges so that he could look at them.

Atticus saw a large farmhouse and a number of agricultural outbuildings.

Grovely Farmhouse, the scene of the Christmas Eve Massacre.

He continued along the track.

22

Grovely Farmhouse had been built on a corner of another large arable field. Atticus selected a satellite image on his phone and saw a large lawned area next to the house; the grass was a much darker olive green than the washed-out chartreuse of the fields, the latter marked by the patterns of the tractor tracks that swept across them in a left-to-right fashion.

The track ended at a gate. Atticus pushed it open and waited as Bandit bounded through. He followed, closing the gate after him. There was a garden to his left, its perimeter marked by a yew hedge. The buildings were directly ahead. There was a large barn first of all and then, behind that, the farmhouse itself. He walked up to the barn, opened the door and looked inside. There was nothing of note: unused mangers, neatly stacked bales of hay and bags of animal feed. An old Massey Ferguson tractor, missing both front wheels, was propped up on a stack of breeze blocks, ready to be attended to.

Atticus closed the barn door and continued to the house. It was empty. Atticus had seen the wills of Hugo and Juliet Mallender. They had left their estates to each other, with the stipulation that everything would be split equally between the children when they were both dead. Now that Ralph was the only one of the children still alive, he stood to inherit it all. But now the property was caught in limbo. Probate had been suspended until the trial's conclusion.

He walked all the way around the house, looking at the plan that he had photographed from the box of documents that Cadogan had provided and comparing it with what he could see. The front door faced him, with two large rooms on either side that were identified on the plan as the dining room and sitting room. Both rooms had wide windows that were obscured by the closed curtains inside. He continued around the house, following the wall of the sitting room until he reached the back door. He looked at the plan again. This door, as was so often the practice in the countryside, was the one that was used most often. It opened into the scullery, which, in turn, offered access to the kitchen and the downstairs den.

Atticus tried the handle: the door was locked. There were three locks securing it, all of them substantial. The house had reportedly been burgled in the months prior to the murders, and the experience had made Hugo fastidious about security. Atticus could understand why that might be: it was isolated here, far from anyone who might be able to help in the event that it was needed. The witness statements reported that Hugo locked the doors at dusk and was careful about opening them. That, of course, was a reason in favour of the defence's assertion that the killer must have been inside the property. It would have been difficult for someone outside to get in without the cooperation of someone inside.

The locks had been replaced after the police had smashed their way inside, so there was nothing to be gleaned from an examination of them now. Atticus crouched down next to the door and found the leather pouch that he had taken from the car. He unzipped and opened it. The lock picks came in a number of sizes, together with tension tools and a broken key extractor. He took out a torsion wrench and, using his left hand, slipped it into the bottom of the keyhole and applied just a little pressure. He slid the pick into the top of the lock with his right hand and pushed it all the way to the back. He scrubbed back and forth with the pick as he maintained the torque to the wrench. The pins became set, one by one, and the mechanism unlocked.

He repeated the trick with the second and third lock and then tried the handle.

It turned and the door pushed open.

He stepped inside.

23

Atticus had memorised the order of events that the prosecution had constructed and had no need to refer back to his notes. He paused again, soaking in the atmosphere and trying to imagine what the night of the murders might have been like. He wanted to transport himself back there – to will himself to be an observer – as a way to test the competing explanations that would be made by the prosecution and the defence. Some of the facts were not in dispute – the locations of the bodies, for example – but it was how they came to end up where they were found that needed to be ascertained.

Bandit came inside, but, rather than go into the kitchen, he stayed close to Atticus. The dog's tail was clamped between his legs, almost as if he knew what had happened here.

'It's all right, boy,' Atticus said, scrubbing the back of the dog's head.

Atticus closed his eyes, listening. He couldn't hear anything. He opened his eyes and looked around: the door to the kitchen was open, but the room was dark, the curtains drawn across the window. He went over and opened them. The room was rustic, with horse brasses fixed to wooden beams. There was a large Aga, a butler-style white ceramic sink and a painted wooden dresser that bore a selection of crockery. A rug sat on the bare floor next to the range.

Atticus took out his phone and found the photos that he had taken of the crime-scene evidence. He had recorded all of the crime-scene photographs that had been disclosed, and now he scrolled through them until he found the ones that had been taken here. Hugo Mallender had been found next to the range. The oven was next to a door that gave access to the service stairs leading up to the first floor. The chair was still in the same place as it had been in the pictures. Atticus knelt down next to it, looking at the photograph of Hugo's body. Hugo had fallen across the toppled chair, his body jack-knifed over it. The chair supported the weight of his body, with his head coming to rest atop a coal scuttle. There had been blood smeared across the beige paint of the range, a puddle that had congealed on the floor beneath his body, and spatters that had fallen across the wooden legs of the chair.

The prosecution's explanation made sense. Hugo was paranoid about security and would only have opened the door to someone that he knew. He would certainly have opened it to Ralph, his son, who had then murdered Hugo and his wife and other children. The police contended that Ralph had shot his father once and then struck him on the side of the head with a blunt object, but that the older man had still been able to put up a fight. The struggle had been violent, and the heavy oak kitchen table had been knocked all the way back to the worktop. The bowl of fruit that had rested atop the table had been overturned and was found smashed on the tiled floor.

Atticus considered the alternative. The defence's suggestion was that Cameron Mallender had attacked his father. Both scenarios were possible, with their own strengths and weaknesses. Atticus would continue to test them until one was left standing.

He stood. Everything had been tidied now, the debris cleared away and the blood scoured from the surfaces. Atticus was a practical man who preferred science to superstition; he did not believe in psychic echoes, yet it was undeniable that the room had an unusual atmosphere that was, given the context and what he knew had happened here, unsettling. Bandit was feeling it, too; the dog remained close, his muzzle brushing up against Atticus's leg.

'Let's keep looking.'

Atticus continued through the kitchen and into the hallway. The front door was ahead of him now, with the doors to the sitting room and dining room to the left and right. He would deal with those last of all. The main stairs were to his left, and he climbed them to the first floor. There was a box room at the front of the house, and to his left a door led to the master bedroom. The bed was made, and everything was neat and tidy, as if the occupants had gone away for a few days but would shortly be returning to take up residence once more.

He went to the guest bedroom on the opposite side of the landing, where Cassandra Mallender had been staying. Atticus scrolled through his phone until he found the pictures that had been taken here: there were two single beds, a dresser and a table that had been littered with a collection of make-up products, a hair dryer and straighteners. The table had been cleared and was empty now.

Atticus returned to the landing and took the short stair up to the hallway that ran down the middle of the floor.

There were three more bedrooms, together with a WC and the family bathroom. Cameron Mallender had been staying in his old bedroom, on the right-hand side of the hallway. Atticus pushed the door open and stepped inside. It was the smallest of the three bedrooms that he had visited, with a single bed in the corner and a fitted cupboard next to the door. Atticus stepped inside and went over to a bookshelf. Books from Cameron's childhood were still arranged there: Choose Your Own Adventure and Fighting Fantasy game-books, a complete set of *The Lord of the Rings*, books by Stephen Donaldson and David Eddings. Atticus ran his finger across the spines, all of them bearing creases that suggested that they had been well-loved. He had read the same books as a child.

He closed the door behind him and went back downstairs. He put his head around the dining-room door, saw nothing of interest, and crossed the hall to the drawing room. Bandit padded after him but, as he opened the door, the dog stayed where he was. Atticus left him there and went inside.

This was where the remaining three members of the family had been found.

It was a large space. Atticus swiped to the pictures that had been taken here. There had been a Christmas tree in the bay window, but that had long since been taken away. The main pieces of furniture had been a three-seater sofa and then two smaller sofas arranged in front of the flat-screen TV on the wall. The larger sofa and one of the smaller ones were still in place; the second smaller sofa had been removed, and a rectangle of carpet that had been underneath had been cut out to reveal the floorboards. Atticus could guess why: the sofa and carpet had been soaked with Juliet Mallender's blood. She had been found sprawled out across the seat. Cassandra Mallender had been found on the three-seater and, as Atticus crossed the room to get a better view of it, he saw that two of the cushions had been removed. They, too, must have been soaked in blood.

He turned and looked back to the wall. Cameron had been found slumped up against it. The Browning nine-millimetre had been found on the floor a reasonable distance from the young man's body. It was close enough to have fostered the suggestion that he had used it last, yet far enough away to lend credence to the counterargument that it could not have been fired by Cameron and still find its way to its final resting place.

Atticus went over to the wall and lowered himself so that he was sitting in roughly the same position that Cameron had been when he was found. He put his index finger and middle finger together and held them against the side of his head. He imagined what it must have been like to pull the trigger, and then allowed his hand to flop down. The gun would surely have landed in his lap or, perhaps, might have fallen onto the floor nearby. That wasn't where it had been found, though; it had been more than a metre away. Even if he allowed for the possibility that Cameron's arm had jerked spasmodically just after he had pulled the trigger, it was still a stretch to suggest that the pistol could have travelled the distance across the room to the location where it had been recovered. It was impossible to be sure, but, on the balance of probabilities, Atticus found the suggestion difficult to credit. That was unhelpful to Ralph's version of events.

Bandit started to whine in the corridor outside. Atticus zipped his overcoat to his neck. It was cold in the house and, after his walk, he felt colder. He went out of the room and ruffled the dog's fur.

He went to the study. There was a desk and two free-standing shelves that had held ring binders of documents that were relevant to the running of the farm. Those had been removed now, and the leather-topped desk swept clear. The gun safe sat in the corner behind the door. It was just over a metre tall, thirty centimetres wide and thirty centimetres deep. The door was open. It looked as if it would be large enough to store four or five long guns, but it was the handgun that had been inside that was relevant now. Atticus had read in Ralph's statement that his father had been a competitive shooter, and that he had refused to hand in his pistols when the government had outlawed them following the Dunblane massacre. He had kept two – a Browning nine-millimetre and a Smith & Wesson M19 .357 – together with ammunition. Both weapons had gone missing before the murders, with only the Browning subsequently being found. The Smith & Wesson had never been recovered. The defence version of events was that Cameron must have opened the safe and taken both. The prosecution said it was Ralph.

Atticus took out his magnifying glass and studied the lock. There were the usual small scrapes and scratches in the immediate vicinity of the keyhole, but nothing that suggested that the lock had been forced or even that it had been picked. If it had been opened, it looked as if it had been opened with the key.

Bandit whined.

'Nearly,' Atticus said. 'One more thing to look at.'

24

Atticus went back to the hallway and found the door to the cellar. A flight of steps descended into total darkness; he felt against the wall for a light switch, found one, and flicked it on. A single bulb had been hung at the top of the stairs, with another down below. Bandit stayed where he was, his tail still clamped between his legs. He clearly had no interest whatsoever in following Atticus down the stairs.

'Woof if you hear anything. I'm going to take a look down here.'

There was enough light now for him to be able to make his way down. The boards were narrow, old and weak, creaking every time he put his weight on them. He reached the bottom and found himself in a large cellar that seemed as if it ran the length of the house. The walls were composed of bare brick, patches of lichen growing against the damp surface. There was an empty rack of shelving that might, at one time, have been used to store wine. There was a stack of large boxes, the cardboard similarly damp and fragile to the touch. The light from the bulb illuminated only the area nearest to the bottom of the stair, so Atticus had to light the rest of the room with his phone's flashlight. He shone it left and right and confirmed that the rest of the space was empty, save for bait boxes that had been left there to take care of rodents.

The coal hole was at the front of the cellar. He made his way there, noting how the storage area was, in effect, a small antechamber that bulged out of the far wall. It was also constructed from naked brick and was narrow enough that he could touch the walls to the left and right with his arms still bent at the elbow. He shuffled forward, casting the light from his phone around. The space was empty. He knelt down and touched his fingertips to the floor, turning his hand over and aiming the light over it; his skin was darkened by a residue of fine soot, probably years old. There were prints in the soot; the police would have been over every inch of it looking for evidence. Atticus recalled the photographs from before that had happened. There had been several prints, too many overlapping one another to make very much out.

He stood and looked up. A thin line of the morning's early light framed a square in the ceiling, probably the coal-plate that offered access to the cellar from the outside. In the old days it would have been opened by the coalman, who would then empty his sacks straight into the cellar, pouring the coal in to be stored until it was needed. Atticus reached up, placing his palm against the cold metal of the plate, and pushed. It gave a little and then stopped; he pushed again, harder, and heard a metallic rattle. The plate had been secured with a padlock sometime after the murders. That made sense.

This, according to the prosecution case, was how Ralph had exited the farmhouse while making it appear that it was locked from the inside. Atticus would check for himself when he was outside, but the pictures that had been taken by the police suggested that the coal-plate had been left untended for years and had been obscured by vegetation that had been allowed to grow over it. The plate was difficult to see and might only have been noticed by those who had lived in the house for long enough to know that it was there. It had always been left unsecured; it would have been a simple thing for Ralph to make his way through the cellar, open the coal-plate and then get outside.

Atticus took a quarter-turn and felt a sharp scratch against his shoulder. He swayed away from it and brought the flashlight up to examine what he had touched; a nail had worked free from a wooden board that had itself been fixed to the wall. Atticus had no idea what purpose the board served, but it was coming loose and the nail had popped partially out.

He shone his torch on it and then turned the light down onto the floor. He knelt down, running his fingertips through the light coating of dust. He found fragments of debris that had worked loose from the wall over time – little rough pieces of brick and mortar – and then saw the light catch against something that looked out of place. He lowered himself further, holding his phone steady and reaching down with his left hand. It was a small square – maybe a centimetre by half a centimetre – of a thin, papery material. He brought it closer to his eye, then gently rubbed it between thumb and forefinger. It looked like the dense polyethylene that was used in Tyvek, the material in the disposable oversuits that were worn by crime-scene examiners. Atticus had a small plastic baggie in his pocket; he took it out, opened it, dropped the remnant inside, and sealed it up.

He backed out carefully and made his way back to the stair. Bandit was at the top, looking down at him. His tail thwacked against the wall as Atticus climbed back up to him.

'Come on then, boy,' he said. 'Let's get out of here.'

25

Atticus opened the door and Bandit bounded out, racing around the farmyard as if relieved that he could be away from the oppressive atmosphere of the house. Atticus locked the door and walked around the perimeter of the property until he reached the front, then looked down at the weed-choked path until he found the coal-plate. It was similar to a manhole cover, just a little smaller. Atticus guessed that it was around twenty-five inches across. The plate was set into an outer metal ring that was then cemented into the path. It was decorated in an attractive geometric pattern and marked with a foundry mark: Hayward Brothers of London. Atticus crouched down and ran his fingers over it. He dropped onto his belly so that he could look more closely at it. The weeds that had obscured the cover had been pulled up, most likely by the police when they were examining it.

Atticus wondered how easy it would be to slide through the hatch. It would have been simple enough for someone slender to enter the house this way, but more difficult to climb out. It would have been necessary to have something to stand on – a chair or a box – before reaching up and boosting oneself out.

Atticus got back to his feet. Ralph was reasonably slim. He wondered if he was slim enough to fit through the narrow opening. He didn't recall seeing any analysis by the defence to investigate the possibility that he *wouldn't* fit, and made a mental note to raise that with Cadogan when he was back at the office.

Atticus was just brushing the dirt from his clothes when he heard the sound of a car approaching along the track. Bandit sprinted away to investigate. Atticus walked back around the barn and made his way to the gate.

A squad car had pulled up and Bob Carver was stepping out of it, grumbling to himself as he put his feet into a muddy puddle. Bandit was waiting by the gate, barking loudly as Carver spoke into his radio.

'Morning,' Atticus called out.

Carver looked over and then scowled in recognition. 'Bloody hell,' he said. 'What are you doing here?'

'Just having a look around.'

'Trespassing.'

'No, Bob, not trespassing. I'm working for Ralph and Allegra Mallender. I wanted to see the house.'

'But—'

'Technically,' Atticus continued, cutting him off, 'Ralph owns the house. It was left to him in his father's will.'

'That'll all change when he gets convicted.'

'*If* he gets convicted,' Atticus corrected him.

Carver snorted. 'Like he's not going to.'

'What are you doing here, Bob?'

'We got a call that someone was nosing around.'

'That would be me. No need to worry, as I said – it's all above board.'

Carver shook his head. 'I still want you to leave.'

'I'm not finished, Bob. And, actually, it's you who's trespassing.'

'Piss off.'

'Do you have a search warrant?'

'Of course I don't.'

'Do you think someone is about to be killed or injured?'

'No.'

'The property's about to be damaged?'

'I don't know—'

'Or there's a breach of the peace?'

'No, but—'

'So you don't have permission to be here, and the law doesn't allow it. *You're* trespassing.'

Carver stepped forward, his boots squelching through the mud. 'You always were a smarmy arsehole.'

Atticus closed the gate and turned his back on Carver as he went to secure it with the padlock. He felt hands on his shoulders, shoving him forward. Carver leaned against him, the weight of his body pinning him against the wooden gatepost. Bandit started to growl. Carver grabbed Atticus's wrist and dragged his arm behind his body, his fingers digging into Atticus's flesh as he yanked up.

'I don't like you, you prick. Never did, not from the first moment I saw you.'

Bandit started to bark. Atticus ground his teeth together. Carver's mouth was next to his ear, and it would have been a simple matter to have jerked his head in that direction, butting him in the face. He didn't, though; he knew that was what Carver wanted – any excuse to arrest him. Carver wasn't the sharpest tool in the drawer, but he had a certain base cunning, and Atticus knew that he would have no problem fitting him up if he gave him any reason. The story would be easy to concoct: Carver responded to a call about a trespasser at the farm; there was an argument between the two of them; Atticus assaulted him. A bloody nose would be all the proof that Carver would need; Atticus's reputation would do the rest. The last thing he needed was a conviction for assault.

'You hear me, you smarmy bastard?'

'Loud and clear.'

Carver let go of Atticus's wrist and stepped back. Atticus turned around just in time to see Carver's knee as he brought it up, burying it in his groin. It was a peculiar pain: a momentary pause and then, suddenly, a deep ache that morphed into something much more unpleasant. Atticus gasped and dropped to his knees, splashing down into the middle of the quagmire.

'Take that as a warning.'

Carver left Atticus in the puddle and turned, starting to negotiate the quagmire so that he could make it back to his car. He probed for firmer ground and, distracted, didn't notice as Bandit sprang at him. The dog was heavy and he had plenty of momentum as he planted his front paws right between Carver's shoulder blades. He toppled over, slamming into the mud with a heavy splash.

Atticus reached back for the gate and used the bars to help him get back to his feet. He stepped onto the verge where the footing was more secure and made his way around the puddle where Carver was still floundering in an attempt to get up.

'Oh dear,' Atticus said.

The pain subsided, turning back into a throbbing ache. Atticus checked that he still had his phone and his keys and his picks and, finding them in his pocket where they were supposed to be, he followed the fresh tyre tracks and started back to his own car, Carver regaling him and Bandit with colourful imprecations as they left him behind.

26

There was a tap at the back of the office that the gardener used to irrigate the garden. Atticus tied Bandit to a drainpipe, cranked the tap and washed him off in the jet of cold water. The dog was unimpressed, clamping his tail down and bowing his head.

'Sorry, boy,' Atticus said.

He hurried upstairs for a towel, came back down and dried the dog, then let him bound inside. Atticus took off his own muddy clothes and pulled on a pair of jeans and a shirt he found on the floor. He reminded himself that he couldn't put off his visit to the launderette any longer. He would go tonight, for sure, with no more postponements. He grabbed a large IKEA bag and stuffed it to the brim with his dirty washing. He spritzed himself with deodorant, grabbed the bag of clothes and pulled on his coat.

Bandit trotted up to him and Atticus knelt down to scrub behind his ears.

'All forgiven?'

The dog licked him.

'Good boy. Now – let's see if Jacob can look after you.'
Bandit wagged his tail happily.

* * *

Atticus called Allegra and arranged to meet her in the café that
they had visited yesterday. He drove to court, leaving his car in
the car park next to the medical centre nearby, and then made
his way back down the road. Allegra was waiting next to the
counter when Atticus pushed his way through the door.

'Good morning,' he said.

'What can I get you?' she asked, gesturing to the menu
above the counter.

'I'll get them,' he said, taking out his wallet.

'Thank you,' she said. 'A cup of tea, please. Shall I go and
get a table?'

Atticus took his place in the queue and watched as Allegra
went over to one of the empty tables. She was dressed smartly
again, in a sober black jacket with a matching skirt and low heels.
He was reminded, again, that she was an attractive woman.

'Attic . . . Attica . . .' The barista was struggling with his name.

'*Atticus*,' he said.

'Sorry?'

'Att*icus*. That's my name. *Atticus.*'

'Weird name.'

'It's from a book . . . oh, never mind.'

He smiled with exaggerated forbearance, thanked the barista,
and took the drinks to the table Allegra had chosen near the
window. He sat down and handed her the tea.

'Thank you,' she said, sipping it gingerly.

'Get any sleep?'

'Not much,' she admitted.

'How did you find it yesterday?'

She looked down into her drink and, when she looked up again, her eyes were filmy with unshed tears. 'Awful. *Awful*. Just to hear what they think of Ralph – what they say he did. It was horrible.'

'I can imagine.'

'I watched the jury and all I could think was that our future is in the hands of twelve people whom we've never met before. I don't know the first thing about any of them.'

'You could have ended up with a worse jury,' he said.

'How do you mean?'

'The woman on the far left – the one who was wearing the twinset? She raised her eyebrows when your husband was brought into the dock.'

'So?'

'It often indicates positive feelings. Lowering the eyebrows would be the opposite. That was a positive first impression. And you might not have noticed, but she had her arms folded when Abernathy was speaking. It's become a bit of a cliché, but it's still a classic sign of disapproval.'

'But that's just one out of twelve.'

Atticus sipped his drink, then replaced the cup on the table. 'Generally speaking, when people are presented with someone or something they find distasteful, they'll turn their bodies a little to the side. It's very subtle, but you can see it if you know what to look for. I only saw two of the jurors angle themselves away. Two of them – the elderly man in the suit and the young mother – actively leaned forwards. That's a strong sign of a positive first impression.'

She frowned. 'I didn't see a mother there.'

'Second row, two from the right. There was a discoloration on the left-hand shoulder of her jacket. I suspect she was winding a baby and it was sick. There hadn't been time to change into something else, and, although she'd done her best to clean it, the stain was still visible, even across the room.'

'Come on,' she said. 'You're reaching.'

'Perhaps a little,' he said with a smile. He had studied body language for years and was confident in the accuracy of his cold reads. But he didn't want to belabour the point now.

'And if they believe what they're being told . . .' She didn't finish.

'There's a long way to go yet,' Atticus said. 'We've only had the first day.'

'I know that,' she said. 'But there's so much uncertainty. The police have their case; they're going to hammer Ralph with it again and again and again. It's just so upsetting.'

'How long does Cadogan think the trial will last?'

'Two weeks.'

Atticus had assumed it would be something along those lines; it didn't give him very long to find anything helpful. He would have to work quickly.

She sipped her drink and then replaced the cup in the saucer. 'What have you been doing so far?' she asked him.

'I've started my review of the evidence.'

'And?'

'There are a few things that could do with a little examination. DS Lennox's suggestion that there was someone inside the house when he got there, for one. I know they'll say that he could have been mistaken, but I'd like to speak to the other officers who were there.'

'You can do that?'

'There's no property in a witness,' he said. 'It's perfectly legal to talk to them, ask questions.'

'But they've closed ranks,' she said. 'You won't get anywhere.'

'Maybe. But it's worth a try.'

Atticus tried to sound optimistic for her benefit, but he suspected that she was right. The police would be very reluctant to talk to someone from the defence. He knew, from experience, that they tended to divide people into two classes: members of the public and villains. Once the decision had been made that someone was a villain, they could be very awkward indeed.

'Anything else?'

'I'd like to see whether Ralph could even have fitted through the coal hole at the house. Did you know about it before all this happened?'

She nodded. 'Ralph told me ages ago.'

'It's pretty small,' he said.

'You've been to the house?'

'This morning, before I came here. I should probably have asked.'

'It's fine – but it's locked.' She looked at him questioningly.

Atticus shrugged. 'I picked the lock,' he said. 'I didn't think you'd mind.'

She shook her head. 'Of course not.'

'Did Cadogan look at whether Ralph would fit?'

'Sort of. Ralph said he thinks he can probably still get through it, but that it's tight.'

'Did he actually try?'

'He's been remanded in custody the whole time. He hasn't had a chance.'

'That might be worth doing. I think it'd be difficult for him to get out.'

'I'll speak to Cadogan.'

'What about the shoes that Ralph was wearing?'

'I think the police have them – why?'

'There's a thin layer of soot on the floor of the coal hole. If he went out that way, I'd expect to see traces of it in the soles. I'd also like to check to see whether the police were able to match prints from the shoes he was wearing to the ground around the coal hole. The ground was damp and muddy that night. I didn't see anything in the file to suggest that they paid much attention to that, but if Ralph *did* come out that way, then I'd expect to see prints in the coal dust and in the dirt around the hatch.'

'And they could tell it was him?'

'You look for matching patterns or brand or logo marks. You can analyse wear patterns so that you have an idea about the angle of footfall and weight distribution. You'd be surprised how much you can tell – it can prove to be as specific as a fingerprint. I've studied it extensively.'

She finished her coffee. 'Do I need to do anything?'

'No,' he said. 'I'll look through the evidence again. I'm interested in Cameron. The police thought it was him. They fixated on him for the first few days.'

'Yes.'

'And you and Ralph think he did it.'

She sucked her lip. 'I think it's possible.'

'Why?'

'It's all in the papers,' she said. 'Haven't you—'

'I haven't read them *all* yet,' Atticus said, cutting across her. 'I'll finish tonight. But it would be helpful to hear it from you – why you think he might have done it.'

She paused a moment, evidently thinking about the best way to start. 'Cameron had serious issues,' she said. 'Their father – Hugo – he had this reputation in Wilton for being the nicest man. He was generous, friendly, the kind of person who would do anything for you. He fooled me, originally. I thought the same as everybody else. It was only later that I found out what he was really like.' She took a sip of her tea and looked away; when she returned her gaze to him, Atticus saw that her eyes were flinty with anger. 'He used to beat them when they were children. Not just slap them – I mean *really* beat them. His fists. Belts. Anything that was to hand. Ralph told me about it eventually. And there was always such a bad atmosphere in the house. There were arguments and fights; most of the time I just couldn't wait to get away again. There was this one time, last summer, when there was a big fight at the family barbecue they held in the garden every year. Cameron was *so* angry. I've never seen anyone as angry as that before. Hugo said something and Cameron just went for him.'

'"Went for him"?'

'Tried to hit him. Ralph tried to hold him back, and Cameron elbowed him in the face; he said that it was accidental.

Ralph's nose was broken – we had to go to Accident and Emergency. Ralph told me everything while we were waiting to see the nurse.'

A member of staff came to collect their empty cups.

Allegra paused until they were alone again.

'It seemed to get worse,' she said. 'We found out that Cameron was having trouble at university. Ralph would get phone calls from him late at night. I don't exactly know what he said, but the gist of it was that Cameron was having nightmares. And he had this terrible temper. *Terrible.* Ralph said it had always been there, but that recently it had seemed to get completely out of control. He was arrested for brawling in the street last year. Something happened in a bar that he was in, and he ended up headbutting a student in the face. The police got involved – Ralph drove to Bath at one in the morning to get him out of the police station. There was rumour that he was going to be asked to leave the university, but they managed to talk them around.' She shook her head. 'There were other times, too. We went out for a drink on Cameron's birthday, and he ended up having a big go at Ralph. Hugo came up in the conversation and he just lost it. There were many arguments in the house. It had got to the point where I used to dread going there for anything.'

Atticus drew a line under his notes.

'Anything else?' she asked him.

'Cassandra?' Atticus said.

She nodded. 'What do you want to know?'

'The police didn't find anything out about her.'

'There wasn't much to find.'

Atticus looked back at his notes. 'She was at Bath, like Cameron. Some suggestion that she had trouble settling in, but then she got on top of it. She was religious.'

'That was a recent thing.'

'How recent?'

'The last year.'

'She was a hard worker.'

Allegra nodded.

'No boyfriend,' Atticus added. 'No reason to think that she had any cause to hurt her family.'

Allegra nodded again. 'I don't think it was her. She wasn't . . . like that. Not like Cameron.'

'All right,' Atticus said. 'A couple of other things. The first is awkward.'

'You want to ask me about Freddie Lamza?'

'I'm sorry,' he said. 'But I do.'

27

Atticus would have preferred *not* to bring Lamza up, but there was nothing else for it. His testimony was crucial. The prosecution's case rested upon what he would say. In the absence of strong forensic evidence that could be used to convict Ralph, the Crown had fallen back upon establishing a case based upon circumstantial evidence, all of it underpinned by Lamza's testimony that Ralph had evinced a desire to see his family killed. It was the fulcrum upon which everything else turned.

'Freddie Lamza,' Allegra said, sighing. 'What a mess *that* is.'

'I'm sorry,' Atticus said. 'But we can't really ignore him.'

She sighed. 'I know we can't,' she said. She folded her hands on the table in front of her and took a moment to compose herself.

'Is he gay?' Atticus said. 'Ralph, I mean.'

'No. I know what Lamza says, that he is, but it isn't true. I've spoken to him about it, of course.' She laughed, humourlessly, once more. 'Jesus, we've spoken about it for *hours*. Ralph says that he's wondered for years about whether he might be bisexual. He was in London on business a year ago, and he said he saw one of those cards in a phone box. You know . . .' She trailed off.

'The ones left by prostitutes,' Atticus finished.

'Yes. Those. He saw one that Lamza had left there and called him. He says he doesn't know why he did it. We'd been going through a rough patch – caused by his family, of course, and the way they treated me – and he says something just clicked in him. He called the number, Lamza gave him an address and explained what would happen, and then Ralph went and visited him.'

'Lamza says that they started to have an affair.'

'He can say what he wants,' Allegra snapped, 'but it wasn't like that. Ralph *isn't* gay. I'm sure about that.'

'Ralph's sexuality doesn't make any difference either way. Not to anything. It wouldn't matter if Lamza was a woman. It's what he will say that Ralph said to him. That he hated his family and was going to kill them. That's what's important.'

'I know,' she said. 'Ralph says he didn't say it.'

'So why did Lamza say that he did?'

She snorted. 'Isn't it *obvious*? He's a jilted lover. Ralph said he wouldn't see him again, and Lamza's feelings were hurt. That's it. He saw Ralph on the news and he saw a chance to put the boot in. That's all it is – as simple as that. Revenge. The whole thing is a pack of lies.' She looked away. 'I'm sorry for snapping at you. This is unbelievably stressful.'

'It's fine,' Atticus said with a smile. 'I understand.'

'What can you do about him?'

'I'll see what I can find.'

She looked at her watch. 'I need to be getting on – there's a conference with Crow at nine thirty. Is there anything else?'

'One more thing,' Atticus said. 'I need to talk to Ralph. I've read most of his evidence, but that's no substitute for speaking to him. There might be something that he says that gives me another angle to investigate.'

'He's not in a good way,' she warned. 'This whole thing – he's not handling it well.'

'I'd be concerned if he was. You don't need to worry about that. I've interviewed people in the same situation before.'

'I'll need to be there, too,' she said.

Atticus bit down on his lip, wondering about the good sense of that. He would have preferred to speak to Ralph on his own. Allegra had a powerful personality, and, from the brief recollection that Atticus had of her husband in court, he suspected that she would be the dominant party in their relationship. On the other hand, Atticus needed Ralph to open up to him. Perhaps a compromise would be a first meeting with the two of them, and then a second meeting could take place with Ralph alone. Atticus put that to one side for now; the details could be worked out later.

'Of course,' he said. 'Could you ask Cadogan to take care of that? I'd like to see him as soon as possible. After court today would be ideal.'

28

The kitchen was a scene of barely controlled chaos. 'Get your clothes on!' Mack said as she flew around trying to prepare her bag for the day ahead.

'Sebastian put his tongue out at me!' Daisy complained.

'No, I didn't!' Sebastian protested.

'Yes, you did!'

Mack turned her back as she took a ballpoint pen out of the drawer and was only dimly aware of the shape of her son as he barrelled across the room towards her daughter.

'He hit me!' Daisy exclaimed. 'Oh my God, Mum! Sebastian hit me!'

'Sebastian, get your uniform on. You need to leave for school in' – she checked her watch – 'shit, two minutes.'

'You *swore*, Mummy,' Daisy said. 'You said "shit".'

'Shut up, Daisy. Brush your teeth and brush your hair and get your shoes on *now*.'

Mack tried to put the folder of evidence into her bag, found that it didn't fit, took it out and tried to make space for it. She was exhausted. Sebastian had suffered from a nightmare that night, and she had stayed with him for an hour until he had stopped crying and settled back to sleep. She had hugged him against her own body, inhaling the smell of him, her mind drifting back to the first few months of his life when he had slept so badly. She remembered it as a surreal time, an almost hallucinatory blending of night into day, marked by a bone-deep fatigue and eyes that scratched and itched from lack of sleep. She had breastfed him for three months before she had returned to work, afraid that a longer absence would be held against her. Andy had taken over, feeding their son from a bottle and sacrificing his own sleep so that she was able to function.

'Mum!' Daisy wailed. 'I can't find my shoes.'

She wanted to swear, but bit her lip.

'I've got them,' Andy said, sweeping into the kitchen with Sebastian's PE kit, Daisy's spellings and the shoes for both children. He had polished both pairs, and, after depositing the duffel bag and folder on the counter, he knelt down between the two children and helped them to put them on.

'Thanks,' Mack said.

'I'll take them,' he said.

'It's my turn,' she said, grateful and guilty at the same time.

'You've got to get to court. I know it's important – just go. I'll take care of them and we can see you tonight. Okay?'

'You're a lifesaver,' she said, bending down to kiss him on the top of the head. 'What would I do without you?'

'Let's not find out,' he said, looking up with a smile.

Mack kissed the children, told them to behave, gathered up her bag and the folder, and made her way out to the car on the drive. She opened the boot, dumped her stuff inside, and got in.

It was late. Lennox was due to give his evidence first thing once proceedings resumed; she needed a clear run if she was going to get there in time.

She reversed out just as Andy shepherded the kids to his car. He held up his hand as she shoved the car into first and pulled away.

*　　*　　*

Mack parked the car in the Waitrose car park and then struggled to the court, balancing the trial bundle in her arms while her bag swung from her shoulder. She arrived in front of the building at the same time as Allegra Mallender was braving the phalanx of reporters waiting outside. She reached the door first, nodding her thanks to the member of staff who held it open for her and then stopping it with her foot as Allegra finally cleared the scrum and came inside.

'Thank you,' Allegra said, but then she recognised Mack, and her expression changed to one of sour dislike. She bustled by her and joined the queue for security without saying another word.

Mack took her foot from the door and turned away so that she could follow Allegra inside.

'Charming!'

She turned back. Atticus was making his way inside and the door had closed on him.

'Sorry. In a rush.'

They joined the queue for security together.

'You okay?' Atticus asked her.

'I'm fine,' she said.

'Still confident?'

'Come on. I'm not going to talk to you about the case.'

She dumped her things on the belt and stepped through the arch. Atticus followed her. She hoped that it might bleep so that he could be detained for a moment to allow her a chance to get away, but it did not. He intercepted her as she scooped up the trial bundle, and snagged the strap of her handbag for her.

'Thanks,' she said, shrugging it onto her shoulder.

'I've been to the house.'

That brought her to a halt. 'What?'

'The Mallenders' place. I visited it this morning. I wanted to see it for myself,' he said.

'And? Find anything to make my life difficult?'

'I don't know. Have you looked at whether Ralph would fit through the coal hole?'

The details came to her easily. 'It has a diameter of twenty-five inches. Ralph's slim. He can get through it.'

'Might be a tight squeeze.'

The glossy folders slipped against each other; she clamped her hand down to secure them. 'So tell the defence to raise it. We can take him out there and drop him through it, see what happens.'

She set off again.

Atticus followed. 'What about his shoes?'

'What about them?'

'Did they have coal dust on them?'

'They had all kinds of shit on them.'

'Because there would have had to be coal dust. The floor down there was covered in it. Still is.'

Mack remembered the shoes. They had been sent for analysis, and the report had found trace evidence from a number of different sources: there was skin, body hair, fibres from the carpets used in the house, and soil particles from a number of distinct locations. There were also traces of coal dust that had been matched with the samples found in the cellar.

'Read the forensic report,' she said. 'He's been down there.' She reached the door to the prosecution's conference room and stopped. 'I don't have time to talk now.'

'Maybe later, then?'

She smiled thinly at him, but didn't reply. He turned and continued down the corridor to the room that the defence was using. Mack watched him go, realising that her confidence in a case that had appeared solid was just a little less certain now. Atticus hadn't found anything yet, but the very thought of his involvement had her questioning herself. She knew why: he was brilliant, incisive, not bound by convention or rules or anything else, and, if there was anything amiss with the investigation – if she had erred in any way – then he would find it.

She took a breath. There was no need to panic. There was nothing wrong with the investigation, and nothing for him to find. They had done a good, thorough job.

She pushed the door and went inside.

29

The others were already sitting around the conference table when Mack came inside.

Abernathy stood. 'Good morning, Detective Chief Inspector.'

'Morning,' Mack replied.

Abernathy was dressed in a suit and tie. His wig and robes would be in the robing room, waiting for him to put them on prior to the start of the morning's proceedings. His junior, Suzanne Masters, was seated at the table. Harry Probert – the solicitor from the Crown Prosecution Service – was alongside her, flicking through two open ring binders that were set out on the table before him. Tristan Lennox was on the other side of the table and, judging by his demeanour, Mack could tell that he was nervous.

She looked at her sergeant. 'Tristan?'

'A few butterflies, boss.'

Lennox had given evidence before, but none of those cases had the profile that this one did. That was reasonable enough; none of the cases that Mack had worked before had enjoyed the same profile, either. Lennox was a steady, solid policeman. He was reliable and diligent, the kind of officer who would not let you down. If there was a weakness, it was that he was not – at least in Mack's opinion – blessed with the sharpest of minds. Her meeting with Atticus in the corridor came back to her. Atticus and Lennox had clashed while they had both worked the Burns case, and Mack knew that Lennox's resentment towards Atticus was entirely because Lennox found it impossible not to compare the two of them. Inevitably, Lennox knew that he would always come up short. Mack had wondered whether the revelation of her affair with Atticus had bothered Lennox, too; he had always thrived on her approval, and now here was evidence that she preferred his rival in every way. She remembered his gleeful reaction to the news of Atticus's dismissal and had wondered whether he had been the one who had tipped off Andy. They had never spoken about it.

He was looking at her now as if for a blessing. 'You'll be fine,' she said, trying to find a reassuring smile. 'Just answer the questions.'

'Just what I said,' Abernathy said.

'But Crow is sharp. What if he trips me up?'

'Stick to the facts,' she said. 'No one is going to ask you to speculate.'

'And the movement in the window?'

'We can't talk about the evidence now,' Abernathy said. 'You just have to deal with it.'

'But if the jury agrees with me . . .'

Abernathy spread his hands. 'We put our case against Mallender to the best of our ability. If they can introduce a reasonable doubt to say that he didn't do it, then we have to take that on the chin and accept it.'

'You'll be fine,' Mack said again.

Abernathy looked at his watch and stood up. 'I agree. For what it's worth, I don't think they can do too much damage. We've got Lamza's testimony, the arguments at the house, the fact that Mallender would get a fortune in the event of the deaths of his family members. We've got enough. You'll be fine, Sergeant, like Mack says. And so will we, even if today is a little bumpy. We'll all be fine.' Abernathy took off his glasses and slipped them into his pocket. 'I'll see you inside.'

They all stood as Abernathy left for the robing room.

Mack went to Lennox and patted him on the arm. She noticed that he was wearing a new suit and that the caps of his shoes had been buffed to a high sheen. 'I'm not worried at all,' she said. 'You've got this.'

'Thanks, boss,' he said.

'You ready?'

He nodded. 'Let's get it over with.'

30

Atticus took his seat and looked around the courtroom. The second day was just as busy as the first, with the small public gallery once again full to capacity. Journalists were pressed together shoulder to shoulder as they discussed proceedings in hushed and excited terms. Allegra was sitting in the same seat as yesterday. He scanned the court for Mack and saw her in the same seat as before, her arms crossed as she waited for the proceedings to begin.

The associate called for the court to rise and everyone did, the shuffle of feet accompanying the judge as he came inside and sat down.

'Are you ready, Mr Abernathy?'

'Yes, my Lord. The prosecution calls Detective Sergeant Tristan Lennox.'

The usher opened the door and called Lennox inside. Atticus watched as the detective made his way to the witness box to be sworn in. He looked apprehensive, with a sheen of sweat on his forehead that caught the harsh glare of the overhead lights. Atticus wasn't fond of Lennox, and he knew that the antipathy was mutual. Lennox had found him smoking a joint in the toilets at Bourne Hill, and his fateful drug test had been just a day or two later; the suspicion that Lennox was responsible for it was easy to credit.

'Can you confirm your name, please?' Abernathy said.

Lennox leaned forward, a little too close to the microphone; a buzz of feedback burst out of the speakers.

'Sorry,' he said, causing it to feed back again.

'No need to be quite so close,' Abernathy said gently. 'Your name and rank, please.'

'Detective Sergeant Tristan Lennox. I work at the major crimes unit, Wiltshire Constabulary.'

'Thank you, Detective Sergeant. I would like to begin with your summary of the events of Christmas Eve last year.'

'Of course,' Lennox said. 'I was duty CID that night. I was passing through Wilton when I heard the call from the control room. A civilian reported that he had observed a body in a property in Grovely Woods, near Wilton, and that he suspected that foul play was involved. I immediately drove to the property.'

'This is Grovely Farmhouse?'

'Yes, sir. I arrived there soon after the 999 call.'

'And you were first on the scene?'

'I was.'

Abernathy led Lennox through the narrative of his testimony: his arrival at the farmhouse, his early interactions with Mallender – what he said, his behaviour and what Lennox made of him – and then the arrival of reinforcements. Atticus watched. He could see that Lennox was nervous at the start, but at Abernathy's patient prompting he found his confidence and settled into a more relaxed delivery.

'Could you speak a little about the house itself?'

Lennox took a sip of water and nodded. 'The external doors were found to be locked from the inside. All of the windows were latched. The rear door had been secured with a mortice lock, and the key had been left inside. The window to one of the upstairs spare rooms was open, although access through it was discounted as extremely unlikely given that scaling the wall at that part of the house would have been almost impossible.'

'And your initial view – taken at that early stage – was that it would not have been possible to get into the house?'

'Yes.'

'But that changed?'

'It did. Hugo Mallender's brother subsequently demon-strated to us that access was possible through an old coal hole at the front of the house. The misapprehension that the house was secured from the inside had lent weight to our initial theory that it must have been a murder-suicide, with the killer taking his own life.'

'Because it wouldn't have been possible for someone else to have committed the crime and then lock the doors from the outside?'

'Exactly.'

'And until you were told about the coal hole, you believed that Cameron Mallender was responsible?'

'We did.'

'Please explain what you found inside the house, Detective Sergeant.'

Lennox described the crime scene in precise and unemotive language. 'Hugo Mallender was found in the kitchen. His wife,

Juliet, and his daughter, Cassandra, were found shot to death in the sitting room where Cameron Mallender's body was also found. The pistol at Cameron's side was later confirmed as the weapon that was responsible for all four deaths.'

'That fact is not in dispute,' Abernathy noted to the jury.

Lennox went on. 'The crime-scene technicians spent several hours going about their work. They took more than three hundred photographs, including shots of the victims, their positioning in the rooms in which they were found, the disturbed furniture in the kitchen, the firearm, the spent ammunition, and anything else that might have been of subsequent interest. The bodies were then removed from the property after the technicians had released it to us, and were taken to Holly Tree Lodge Mortuary in Dorset.'

'And what happened next?'

'The defendant was taken to Bourne Hill CID in Salisbury for interview. Detective Chief Inspector Jones and myself were responsible for that. Mr Mallender admitted that there had been a row with his mother and father earlier in the evening, and that, after stopping for a drink in the Greyhound pub in Wilton, he had decided to return so that he might smooth things over.'

'How did you find the defendant?'

'Much as you would expect, under the circumstances.'

'Did you find him credible?'

'At that stage, yes, I did. The other officers who interacted with him, too – we all did.'

'We'll hear from them all in due course,' Abernathy said, nudging Lennox away from giving hearsay evidence. 'What happened next?'

'We worked through the whole of the next day.'

'This was Christmas Day?'

'It was,' Lennox said.

'My sympathy,' Abernathy said, turning to the jury with a knowing look. 'I doubt that went down well with your family.'

'I'm single,' he said. 'But it didn't go down well for my boss.'

There was a titter of laughter, and Atticus couldn't prevent a wry smile. He knew that Andy, Mack's husband, would have kicked up a stink. He had never really understood his wife's dedication to her job and had often complained that she pursued her career to the detriment of her family. And this was Christmas Day. Atticus could imagine how he would have reacted to her phone call telling him that she wouldn't be home.

Abernathy pointed back to the dock. 'And was the defendant still not seen as a suspect?'

'No,' Lennox said. 'Not at that stage.'

'When did that change?'

'The post-mortems took place on Boxing Day. The first time we realised something wasn't quite as it appeared was when the pathologist reported that it was his opinion that the weapon had been fired into Cameron Mallender's head in such a way that made it unlikely that he had fired it himself.'

'Meaning?'

'It was *possible* that Cameron had fired it, but it was more likely that it was fired by someone else. That, obviously, made us question our working assumption that this was a murder-suicide.'

Abernathy turned to the jury. 'We'll hear from the pathologist in due course,' he said. He returned to Lennox. 'What else made you change your mind?'

'We were approached by several people – relations of the Mallenders, mostly – who said that the defendant's relation-ships with his family were not what he had suggested to us. They told us that there was no love lost between them. There was also reported to have been an argument earlier on Christmas Eve between the defendant and his family.'

'Go on, Detective.'

'I interviewed the cleaner – Mrs Grant. She was there that afternoon, and she said that the argument between Ralph and the rest of the family was much worse than he had told us.'

'Again, we will hear from Mrs Grant.' Abernathy flipped the pages in his folder of notes.

'We learned about the coal hole, too,' Lennox said. 'We realised that there was a way in and out of the house even when it was locked. That opened up the pool of potential suspects beyond the victims inside the property.'

Abernathy flipped pages. 'You were also contacted by Mr Freddie Lamza.'

'Yes, sir.'

'Once more, members of the jury, we will hear from Mr Lamza in due course, but he will say that the defendant expressed hatred for his family and said that he wanted to kill them.'

'That's what he said,' Lennox said.

'And did that change your opinion?'

'It made me question the conclusion that we had drawn. All of it did.'

'So, you no longer thought the killer was Cameron?'

'No,' Lennox said.

'And your new conclusion?'

'We started to look very closely at the defendant.'

'Indeed,' Abernathy said. 'Now, then – we need to address something that you note in your witness statement. You said that you believe you saw movement in the upstairs window of the house soon after you arrived. Is that correct?'

Atticus leaned forward, his attention focused on Lennox. Lennox took another sip from his glass. 'It is, sir.'

'Would you mind telling us what you thought you saw?'

'I've given it a lot of thought since then,' Lennox said. 'And the honest answer is that I don't know. It was dark. There was no light in that particular window. I thought I saw something moving.'

'What do you think you saw?'

'A person.'

'I see. And how confident are you that you saw someone?'

'Can I swear to it? No, I can't. But do I think it is possible that I saw what I thought I saw? Yes, I do. It's possible. I'm sorry I can't be more certain.'

'That's fine. Thank you, Detective Sergeant. Please stay there – Mr Crow will probably have some questions for you.'

31

Abernathy sat down. Atticus watched Lennox as he looked over at Mack. She smiled back at him, and Atticus could see that she was trying to impart a little confidence. They would both have known that his evidence-in-chief would be the easy part, and that the cross-examination would be where things might become more difficult.

Christopher Crow stood up and folded his arms behind his back so that his elbows protruded. 'I do indeed have some questions,' he said. 'Detective Sergeant Lennox – I think I only need detain you to clarify one point of your evidence. It's the matter of the person you saw in the window of the farmhouse.'

'The person I *thought* I saw.'

'Indeed. And this is a crucial question, is it not?'

'Yes, sir.'

'Because, Detective Sergeant, if there was someone in the house who was still alive when you arrived, then it means the case against the defendant could not possibly be made.'

'I suppose so, sir.'

'You suppose so? I think we can be more categorical than that. If someone was alive inside the house while Mr Mallender was outside it, then surely the suggestion that he was responsible for what happened can finally be described for what it really is: patent nonsense.'

'Those are your words.'

'Then perhaps you could give us some of *yours*, Detective. If the defendant was outside the house with you when someone else was still inside, what impact would that have on the question of the defendant's guilt or otherwise?'

'It would make it less likely,' Lennox said.

'"It would make it less likely,"' Crow repeated with a stagey, knowing look at the jury. 'I should think it would. Do you still believe that you saw someone moving in the house?'

Atticus leaned forward, watching carefully; Lennox was known for having a bit of a temper, and he knew him well enough to know that he would find Crow's attitude both pompous and aggressive. He had seen him lose his rag to lesser provocations.

'All I can say is what I said before. I thought I saw something that night. I've thought about it a lot since, and I still can't say for sure.'

'But it is possible?'

'Yes. It's possible.'

Crow smiled. 'Thank you, Detective Sergeant. I have no further questions.'

Abernathy was quickly back on his feet for his re-examination. 'I think we ought to just reiterate the evidence that you gave, Detective Sergeant. It was dark and there was a lot going on in the farmyard – that's correct, isn't it?'

'It is.'

'And when I asked you earlier, you couldn't say for sure that you saw someone – is that still your evidence?'

'It is.'

'It could have been something as simple as a reflection? The moon, perhaps? Or a torch?'

'Yes, sir. It could.'

'Thank you, Detective Sergeant. That is all. You may stand down.'

The judge looked to Abernathy. 'I see that it is nearly one o'clock. Perhaps this might be an opportunity to break for lunch?'

'Of course, my Lord.'

'Good. We'll adjourn and continue with the prosecution's next witness this afternoon.'

The judge stood.

'All rise,' the associate called out.

32

Atticus followed the rest of the gallery out into the lobby and saw that Allegra was waiting for him with Dafyd Cadogan. The solicitor saw him approaching and instinctively reached down to button his jacket. It was defensive, closed body language that Atticus recognised; it often signified that a person was uncomfortable. Cadogan was full of bluster, but Atticus could see beneath it easily enough and didn't mind at all that he had that effect on him.

'I asked Dafyd about you going to see Ralph,' Allegra said.

'I'm not sure what it'll achieve,' Cadogan said, barely attempting to conceal his disdain.

'I like to be thorough,' Atticus said. 'Is it possible?'

'He can see you this evening.'

'What time?'

'Court should finish between four and five. Ralph should be back in prison by six. We have some things to do first – you should aim to arrive around seven. I'll arrange for a Visiting Order to be left for you.'

'Where's he being held?'

'HMP Winchester. Main building. You'll need to bring ID.'

Atticus was tempted to tell him that he had visited people in prison before and knew the procedure, but held his tongue. 'Thank you.'

Allegra thanked Cadogan and waited as he made his way to the exit. She took Atticus aside.

'What did you think? About this morning?'

'Lennox?' he said.

'You say you're good at reading people.'

'He was clearly very uncomfortable. I doubt he wanted to be there, but that's not surprising. No one enjoys giving evidence, not even the police – it's stressful. Stress and discomfort actually make it more difficult to read a person. When someone is comfortable, the nonverbal signs that might suggest deceit are easier to see. The trouble with an environment like a courtroom is that we can't find a baseline.'

'But you thought he was telling the truth?'

'I don't know why he would lie about something like that. I thought it was helpful to Ralph's case. He could've said that he had thought about what he thought he had seen and had decided that he was mistaken, but he didn't. It's an element of doubt.'

She smiled. 'That's what I said to Dafyd. We only have to introduce reasonable doubt.'

'That's right,' he said, 'but you're not there yet. They still have a lot of evidence. It was a good morning, but you'll need a few more like that before you allow yourself to be confident.'

She laid a hand on his arm. 'That's why we have you.'

* * *

The afternoon in court was taken up with the evidence of the firearms officers who had attended the scene that night. Atticus would have liked to have watched all of the evidence, but time was not on his side; he needed to find weaknesses in the case before the trial came to a conclusion, and the pieces of evidence he needed to attack were the big ones, not the minutiae of how the crime scene was administered in the early stages of the investigation. That was a job for Cadogan, not him.

He decided to skip it. He left the court and made his way back to his car. He drove to the Washing Well launderette on Chipper Lane, took the bag of dirty clothes that he had packed earlier, and found an empty machine. He loaded it up, poured in powder and conditioner, and thumbed four pound coins into the slot. The programme would take a couple of hours to complete. He walked to the gym, went inside and showed his card to the receptionist – hoping that she didn't check the date, since his membership had expired six weeks ago – and then made his way through into the changing rooms. He stripped off and showered, standing under the tepid water for fifteen minutes and using soap from the dispenser until he was clean.

* * *

Atticus opened the door to the office and let Bandit go in first. He followed, kneeling down to cuddle the dog, then got up and opened a tin of food for him. The sight of the dog clearing his bowl reminded him that *he* hadn't eaten today, so he went down to the coffee shop on the High Street, ordered a flat white and a sandwich to go, and took both back to the office.

Bandit had settled on the leather sofa. Atticus went to the desk and fired up his laptop. He navigated to Chess.com to check whether his opponents had played a move in the three games that he was engaged in and saw that they had. Chess-Compressions16 had accepted that his position was hopeless and had given up, departing the game with a flurry of insults. SansLimite had tried to defend against Atticus's attack by sacrificing a pawn; Atticus ignored his clumsy trap and set up checkmate in the next move.

Jack_of_Hearts had resigned his position, as Atticus had predicted, and had created a new game, opening by pushing out his pawn to e4. Atticus considered the options and decided to try the Alekhine Defence, where black allowed white to chase his knight all over the board. White would be allowed to gain control of the centre of the board, and black would counter by undermining white's overextended pawns. Atticus had been studying the defence and had been looking forward to experimenting with it. Jack was a good enough player to test him properly. He moved his knight to f6 and logged off.

He started to work. He had decided to begin with Cassandra Mallender. Cameron's life had been dissected and splayed out in the defence's case, yet Cassandra had seemingly been ignored, at least by comparison. Mack's investigation appeared to have been thorough, but he had found nothing in her background that had given him pause.

That made Atticus suspicious.

Everyone had secrets.

He started to read the documents that had been disclosed by the prosecution, cross-referencing them with information supplied by Ralph. Just like Cameron, Cassandra had been studying at Bath University. They were both in their second year: she was studying law while he studied business management. The police had interviewed her tutors, and they had all reported that she was an excellent student: hard-working, intelligent, diligent. She had applied for a training contract and had secured a place at one of the most impressive firms in the City. They would pay for her to study at the College of Law and then take her to London to begin her career.

Atticus read through the witness statements and ended up with an almost clean page of A4 where his notes should have been. There really was nothing of interest. No loose edges to pull at, nothing to prod or poke. She was bland. Boring, even. There was an interest in religion; she liked to run; she was an avid reader. But that was that.

He didn't buy it for a moment and, undeterred, moved on to her friends.

Once again, the police had been thorough. Cassandra had a small collection of acquaintances, most of whom were drawn from Bath City Church. He read a statement from one of the church elders that said she had only recently become religious, with her conversion coming between the end of her first year and the start of her second. She had never shown any interest in religion before, they said, but she had embraced the church with enthusiasm and vigour. She had volunteered to work at the soup kitchen attached to the ministry and had been an active participant in the weekend services. Atticus looked back through the statements for anything that might suggest why she had turned to God, but found nothing. That, too, struck him as odd:

there must have been a reason, some precipitating event that persuaded her that she needed religion in her life. The fact that she had been abused by her father, perhaps? He noted that he should speak to Ralph about it, and moved on.

He opened up his laptop again and started with Google, searching Cassandra's name in the hope that she might have posted something that would give him a better insight into her character. There were pages and pages on the court case that had shrouded her in posthumous infamy, but little else; Atticus found it grim that the sum of the young woman's life had been distilled to her grisly end, but it was something that he had seen before.

He moved over to Facebook. He had often found success there, often because its users posted things without thinking, and those things were never really gone, especially if you knew how to look for them. Atticus had taught himself how to inter-rogate the platform in a forensic fashion, using a number of software tools that allowed him to build a detailed picture of the person he was studying.

He found Cassandra's profile – it had been memorialised under Facebook's recent policy for deceased users – and started to scroll back through the public posts that had been left on her timeline. The tributes started to appear on Christmas Day, the day after the murders. Friends told of their shock and of how much they would miss her. There was much talk of God, and how He moved in mysterious ways, and how He would take her to Heaven to be with Him. Atticus read them, taking down the names of the posters and noting relevant information beneath them, and then scrolled further back.

Cassandra's own posts were not unusual: an article from the *Independent* on 'How to Tell a Good Lawyer from Bad'; a post to a video that had dubbed Donald Trump quotes over a clip from *Star Wars*; links to music mixes on Soundcloud. He scrolled further back still and found more personal updates: photographs taken at church, at the soup kitchen, at a football match.

He went further back and saw a marked change. The posts during the last year of her life were frequent, but then there was a period of time – six months – when Cassandra seemed to have neglected her account. There were no posts, no photos, no updates at all.

Atticus scrolled back until the posts began again. He straightened up in his chair. The updates that preceded the period of silence were different from the ones that followed it.

The earlier posts showed the kind of student life that was absent from the latter ones. Atticus saw nothing unusual in them, save they were so different to what came after. Cassandra appeared to be a typical student, doing typical student things. She was pretty; she smiled a lot; she had a lot of friends. There were pictures in bars and pubs. She looked drunk in some of them. There was a series of pictures taken in Ibiza with Cassandra looking *very* much the worse for wear. There were references to drugs, and Atticus found one picture with her smoking what looked like a joint.

He noted down some of the names that had been tagged to these pictures and compared them to the names of the witnesses who had spoken to the police. There was no crossover at all: the police had concentrated on her current friends and did not appear to have spent significant time with those whom she had known in her first year, before she had found religion. He started to feel the first buds of optimism, the possibility that he had a fresh line of enquiry.

He opened his notes application and composed a quick message, explaining who he was and how he was working on the investigation into Cassandra's death. He was intentionally vague beyond that, leaving it to the natural curiosity of the recipients to respond. He pasted the text into Messenger and sent it to the half-dozen people who appeared most often in the timeline.

He crossed his fingers and waited for a reply.

33

Atticus looked at his watch: it was six thirty. Time had run away from him. He cursed: he needed to make his way to Winchester for his appointment with Ralph. He took Bandit to the launderette to collect his washing, and then made sure that he had enough food and drink for the evening. He took the things that he would need for his visit: his notepad and pen, a digital recorder and the summary of the prosecution evidence that he had prepared.

'I'll be back later,' he said to Bandit. 'Be a good boy.'

The dog wagged his tail, hopped onto the sofa and curled up.

Atticus locked the office door and got back into his car. He set off, heading east for the second time that day. He plugged his phone into the stereo, selected Genesis's *The Lamb Lies Down on Broadway*, and set it to play. He thought about the notes that he had taken during his review of the disclosure in the case, distilling them into the most salient points and then considering the questions that he wanted to ask Ralph. The trial was already well underway. He didn't have very much time. In the event that he was able to find evidence that might cast doubt on Ralph's guilt, it would be better for everyone if that evidence could be presented before a verdict was reached. It would be easier to dismiss the charges against Ralph now rather than seek to introduce them later at an appeal. Allegra should have hired him earlier, but there was no point in dwelling on that now. It was what it was.

He would just have to ensure that he made the most out of this visit; there might not be time for another.

* * *

Winchester Prison was on Romsey Road. It was a category B establishment, housing both adult prisoners and young offenders. He had been here several times before, but only in his capacity as a detective. This was the first time that he had visited as a civilian. He knew that there was no parking on site, so he left his car in the city's park-and-ride and took the bus.

He got off outside the hospital and walked the short distance to the prison. It was a bleak building, with four large wings that met in a central hub. It was not a particularly well-regarded facility. The inspectorate's most recent report had noted that it was 'teetering on the edge of a major incident' and had placed it in special measures. The cells were small and unpleasant, and violent altercations among the inmates were regular. Mallender was middle class and out of his depth; Atticus suspected that he would be eaten alive by the more experienced lags.

He walked up to the guardhouse and waited for the man inside the booth to notice him and toggle on his microphone.

'Sorry,' he said. 'Visiting time's finished.'

'I'm here professionally,' Atticus said.

'Still got to make an appointment.'

'You have a prisoner here who's on trial at the Crown Court. Ralph Mallender. I'm working for him. You should have a Visiting Order for me.'

The man grumbled something under his breath. 'Wait.'

The guard clicked off the microphone and referred to a clipboard that he picked up from the desk. He took a telephone receiver and held it to his ear as he conferred with another member of staff and, seemingly satisfied, he replaced the receiver and toggled the microphone again.

'Go on,' the man said. 'They'll sort you out in reception.'

The guard opened the gate and Atticus walked through, following the signs to the visitors' centre. He gave his name and waited as the woman behind the counter checked his identification against the Visiting Order that had been arranged for him. She told him to take a seat while she sorted out his credentials. To his surprise, Atticus found that he was nervous. He had met murderers before, but their crimes were usually spontaneous. Ralph Mallender was different. He had been accused of a premeditated plot to murder four members of his family and, from Atticus's review of the evidence and his faith in Mack's investigation, he believed that there was a good chance that he was guilty as charged. The prospect of the meeting had him on edge.

'Atticus.'

He looked; Allegra Mallender had just come inside.

'Hello,' he said.

She looked tired. Her eyes were red-rimmed and her cheeks were pale; it didn't look as if she was getting enough sleep.

'I know,' she said, anticipating him. 'I'm done in.'

'How was the afternoon?'

She shook her head. 'Not as good as the morning. They're making it look as bad for him as they can.'

That's their job, he thought, but he kept it to himself.

'Who was it? Anyone other than the armed response officers?'

'No – just one of them after the other. It was ruthless.'

'Did Crow get anything out of them in cross-examination?'

'Not really,' she said glumly. 'I spoke to Ralph afterwards – with the lawyers. He's desperate. We need to offer him some hope. I don't know if he'll be able to get through this unless he thinks there's a chance.'

She looked beaten already.

'It's never easy to hear the prosecution case,' Atticus said. 'They're going to make Ralph look as bad as possible. That's the whole point of it. The defence will balance it out.'

It was as if she didn't hear him. 'Do you have anything for us to go on?'

'Not yet,' he said.

'But you reviewed the files.'

'Yes.'

'And visited the house.'

'I did,' he said patiently. 'I've got some angles I'd like to explore.'

She looked expectantly at him.

'Lamza's testimony is the most damaging. He's my focus. I'm looking at Cassandra and Cameron, too. But a lot of it will depend on what Ralph tells me now.'

'I don't mean to be rude,' she said, 'but you need to move faster. They think the case will be finished this time next week. If we haven't been able to introduce something new, and if they find him guilty . . .' The sentence drifted away.

'I'm working as quickly as I can. You have my exclusive attention – this is all I'm doing. The only case. If there's anything to find, I'll find it.'

She nodded, at least putatively satisfied, and then exhaled, her shoulders slumping as she looked down at her feet. Atticus felt sympathetic. He had never been in her position, but he had watched the families of defendants that he had brought to trial, and he could imagine the sense of helplessness that they must all have felt. The criminal justice system was like a machine. Their loved ones were passed through it, chewed up and spat out, and there was nothing that they could do to influence the result that was eventually dispensed.

'Hello?'

Atticus looked up; the woman behind the counter beckoned them both over. She gave them laminated badges with their names on them.

'You can go through to the visitors' hall,' she said. 'Mr Mallender will be brought through in a moment.'

34

The visiting room was separate from the space where visits usually took place. It was much smaller, with just a pair of tables and chairs rather than the several rows that were in the main area. It shared the same air of drabness, with the same shade of magnolia on the walls, the same cheap tiled floor, and the same grime and dirt that had accreted over the course of years without proper cleaning. Atticus held out one of the chairs so that Allegra could sit down, and then took the one next to her. He ran his fingertips over the pitted surface of the table; the vinyl had been scratched, with graffiti scored into it.

He turned to Allegra; she looked nervous, her face pinched, as she bit her lower lip. He was about to offer something to reassure her when the door opened and her husband was ushered inside.

She stood, bumping clumsily against the chair as she made her way around the table so that she could get to him. He was a little taller than she was, and she had to reach her arms around his neck to draw him down so that she could kiss him.

'How are you, darling?' she asked as soon as she had disengaged.

'How do you think?' he said sourly. 'Bloody dreadful.'

'I know,' she said, immediately sympathetic. 'I'm the same.'

'How can you *possibly* be the same?' he snapped. 'You're not the one about to go to prison for the rest of your life.'

'You're not going to prison,' she said.

'Really? Not what it looks like from where I'm standing.'

Atticus had already guessed at the state of their relationship from the things that Allegra had told him and what he had observed in court, but the diagnosis was all the more obvious now. Ralph was curt and impatient, with Allegra quick to intervene in order to deflect his temper. Atticus had investigated cases of domestic abuse before, and he saw plenty of symptoms that were grimly familiar.

'This is Atticus,' Allegra said, taking a quarter-turn so that Ralph could look down at him.

Atticus stood and extended a hand. 'Hello.'

Ralph left his hand there for a moment before he took it and squeezed it more tightly than necessary. Atticus had expected this kind of show of strength, and, as Ralph looked into his face, he showed no discomfort or any other reaction. Ralph squeezed a little harder, Atticus held his gaze and, with a flicker of annoyance, Ralph released his hand.

'Come on, Ralph,' Allegra said. 'He's on our side.'

'Really?'

Allegra turned to her husband and put her hand over his. 'Please, darling. You need to trust him. I'm doing everything I can to show them you didn't do it. Atticus can help us to do that.'

Ralph glared at Atticus, a muscle in his cheek pulsing as his jaw clenched. There was anger there and a quick temper. He was not a pleasant man. The defence was planning to call Ralph as a witness; Atticus wasn't sure that that would be wise.

Ralph took a deep breath and exhaled. 'I'm sorry.'

'It's fine.'

'This is all very stressful.'

'Of course.'

'And my wife is desperate. It would be easy to take advantage of that.'

Allegra groaned. 'Ralph—'

'It's fine,' Atticus said. 'It *would* be easy. But that's not what I'm doing. Between us, I think you should have had someone looking at the evidence earlier.'

'The lawyers are shit,' Ralph said sourly.

'They're doing their best,' Allegra said, although there was no conviction in her voice.

'I told you Cadogan was a bad choice,' he said, bitter once again. 'I told you, didn't I? I *said*.'

'Maybe I can find something that will help,' Atticus intervened, trying to reassure them. 'I'm going to do everything I can. I'm not working for anyone else at the moment. I've cleared all my other cases.'

Other cases. Ralph looked at him, and Atticus wondered whether he was perceptive enough to see through his lie. They locked eyes for a moment before, finally, Ralph breathed in deeply and then exhaled.

'Fine,' he said. 'Let's carry on. What do you want to talk about?'

'A few things, if you don't mind.'

Ralph gestured around the room with a sweep of his arm. 'I'm not going anywhere.' He pulled out the chair on the other side of the table and dropped down into it, his legs out straight and crossed at the ankles.

Atticus sat down, too; Allegra did not.

'Go on, then,' Ralph said.

'Shall we start with your brother?'

'What do you want to know?'

'I've read through all the papers,' Atticus said.

'And?'

'His anger.'

'What about it?'

'Do you have any idea why he had such a problem with it?'

He shook his head. 'I don't know.'

'Nothing in his history? When you were children?'

'It wasn't a happy childhood,' he said.

'How do you mean?'

He paused for a moment, perhaps picking out the right words. 'My father was a difficult man.'

'How so?'

'He was in the army before he took over the farm. Discipline was important to him. He was old-fashioned about bringing up children.'

'Better seen and not heard?' Atticus offered.

'That's one way to put it.'

'He beat you.'

Ralph glared at his wife. 'You told him?'

'Of course,' she said. 'It might be important.'

Atticus glanced down and saw that Ralph had turned his feet towards the door. It was a classic sign of discomfort, an unconscious indication that he was considering the exit, and how he might forestall the rest of the conversation.

'You and Cameron?'

'Yes,' Ralph said.

'What about your sister?'

Ralph chuckled bitterly. 'Cassie was the apple of his eye. It wasn't the same for her. It was me and Cameron. We both got it bad.'

'And you think that explains Cameron's problems?'

'I don't know. I'm not a psychiatrist. I've no idea why he ended up the way he did.'

'Angry,' Allegra added. 'Angry and bitter.'

'And violent?'

Ralph nodded. 'He could be.'

'Do you think he was angry enough to do what's been suggested?'

He looked troubled. 'Maybe,' he said. 'I wouldn't have said so, but who else was there? I know it wasn't me. There's no way my mother or father would ever have done something like that. And Cassandra?' He shook his head. 'No way. Unless someone else was in the house that night, and no one's suggesting that. It could *only* have been Cameron.'

Atticus let that sit for a moment, wondering whether he should press further. Ralph had put both hands onto his knees, another clear sign that he was uncomfortable and ready to end the meeting. Atticus suspected that Ralph hadn't told him absolutely everything, but he wasn't sure whether what might have been left to say was worth the cost of digging it out. He had other questions to ask and, with time already moving on, decided to change tack.

'Can we go back to Christmas Eve?' he said.

'Must we?'

'I've read the statements.'

'So what do you want to know?'

'The argument with your family – what was it about?'

'The way they treated Allegra,' he said, glancing over at his wife. 'They never accepted her. My mother and my father. Never.'

'Why?'

He exhaled wearily.

'They think I'm a gold digger,' Allegra said. 'It was his mother more than his father – wasn't it, Ralph?'

'Yes,' he said.

'Why?'

'I'm too young, apparently. And we got married too quickly.'

'How did you meet?'

'Online,' she answered.

'How quickly did you get married?'

'Six months after we met,' she said.

'That *is* fast.'

'Why wait?' she said, laying her hand on her husband's. 'We both knew we wanted to be together.'

'And to say that she's a gold digger is hilarious,' Ralph said. 'There's no gold to dig. It's not like I have all that much.'

'But you *could* have.'

'I'm not interested in his inheritance,' Allegra said.

Atticus smiled. 'Tell me more about how they reacted.'

Ralph snorted. 'To Allegra? It was just the attitude. They didn't make her welcome at the house. They wouldn't speak to her. We tried to ignore it. We thought, eventually, they'd realise that they were wasting their time, that they'd realise that we love each other and that nothing was going to change, but it was getting worse and not better. I told them that unless they made Allegra feel welcome on Christmas Day, then that would be the end of it.'

'What do you mean?'

'That I'd consider us to be estranged.'

'And then?'

'And then I went to the pub.' He paused. 'This is all in the statement.'

'I know. But it's helpful to hear it in your own words.'

'I went to the pub and had a drink. I had second thoughts. It felt like I ought to give them a second chance. I'd been angry, and I wanted to explain to them – calmly and rationally – why what they were doing was so upsetting. I wanted them to under-stand. I drove back over there and . . .'

He stopped.

'And they were dead,' Allegra finished for him.

35

Ralph went over what he had found when he arrived back at the farm that evening. His recounting tallied exactly with the testimony that he had given in his witness statement: the locked door, the kitchen light on, a glimpse through the window to see his father's body on the floor. He related his call to the police and the wait for them to arrive. Atticus probed with a handful of questions of his own, but found nothing new that might be helpful: no, Ralph couldn't say that he saw any sign that there was someone else in the house, as DS Lennox had suggested; no, there was nothing outside that suggested someone had visited the house in the time he had been in the pub; no, he couldn't think of anyone else who might have had a reason to do the family harm.

'What about the coal hole?' Atticus said.

'What about it?'

'Can you fit through it?'

'I used to be able to,' he said.

'When's the last time you tried?'

'I don't know. The time I locked myself out of the house.'

'When?'

'Five years ago? I got inside through the cellar then.'

'And now?'

'I think I probably still could.'

'I don't know, Ralph,' Allegra said. 'You've put on a little weight since then.'

'Thank you, darling.'

'I don't mean it like *that*,' she said. 'I'm just saying. It's in our best interests that you *can't*. If they can't find a way for you to get out of the house while leaving it locked from the inside, the case collapses.'

'I know,' he said wearily. He shook his head. 'I haven't tried, but I think I *would* fit. And I'm not going to agree to the charade of going out there and trying to show that I wouldn't.' He chuckled bitterly. 'Is this what we're left with? O. J. Simpson? "If it doesn't fit, you must acquit"?'

'It *did* work that time,' Atticus said.

Ralph stretched out, straightening the kinks in his back. 'But not this time. You need to do better than that.'

Atticus nodded. There was no obvious weakness in the prosecution case, and he had done as well as he could with the tiny inconsistencies that he had been able to uncover. He agreed with Ralph: he thought he probably would have been able to squeeze through the coal hole, and now was not the time to push the suggestion that he couldn't. It was too late to test the hypothesis now unless they were sure that it had value. The danger of taking the judge and jury to the house and then finding that he could get through would be significant; it would make them look desperate. The defence should have investigated that earlier.

'Are we done?' Ralph said.

'I'm afraid not.' Atticus held Ralph's eye.

He slumped back in his seat. 'Let me guess. Freddie?'

'We need to talk about him.'

Allegra stiffened, and Ralph sighed. Atticus felt bad about forcing Allegra to listen to her husband speak of his infidelity more than once. But it wouldn't be the only time that was required, nor even the worst: listening to the testimony in a packed courtroom was going to be bad enough.

He decided to abbreviate his questions to the most essential. 'He's key to the prosecution case. If we can discredit him . . . well, I'm not going to make any promises, but it would be helpful.'

'What do you want to know?'

'You met him a year ago.'

'Something like that.'

'I don't need all the details,' Atticus said, casting an eye at Allegra. 'I've read what you've said, and I've read what he says. You're saying that he's not telling the truth about you telling him that you wanted to kill your parents.'

'It's a pack of lies.'

'So why would he say that? Why would he put himself in a position where he's going to have to stand up in court and give that evidence in front of everyone and perjure himself?'

'Because he bears a grudge.'

'That's a serious grudge.'

'He hates me.'

Atticus looked at Allegra.

'It's fine,' she said. 'I know what happened. We've spoken about it. It doesn't matter.'

Ralph laced his fingers and put his hands on the table. 'Allegra and I were having trouble with our relationship. I was working too hard, not coming home. We weren't talking . . .'

'It was both our faults,' Allegra said, laying her hand atop her husband's.

Ralph smiled at his wife, then looked back to Atticus. 'I was in London, I was lonely, and . . . well, you know what happened.'

'Please – go on. In your own words.'

'It was a moment of madness. I saw a card in a phone box. I saw him. I thought . . .' He stopped. 'I don't know what I thought.'

'But you called him?'

'I did. He told me where he was, and I went to see him. We . . . well, you know what happened next.'

'And then?'

'And then I saw him whenever I was in London. Four or five times over the course of six months. He said he had feelings for me. I know it was stupid, but I was flattered.'

'And then?' Atticus prompted.

'He got it into his head that we had a future together. He's nuts – you'll see when he gives evidence. He's loopy. But he started talking about how he would stop working, about me leaving Allegra and moving to London so that we could be together. I'd realised by then how stupid I was, that I love my wife very much and that I didn't want to throw away my marriage, so I told him that it wasn't going to happen. I said we couldn't see each other any more and he just lost it. *Lost* it. He said I was joking, and then, when he realised that I wasn't, he was all about how he was going to tell Allegra, how he was going to ruin my life.'

'A lover spurned,' Atticus suggested.

'Exactly. You've read his witness statement. He saw the news about my family over Christmas and called the police to say that he had something that he thought would be relevant. But it's bullshit. The whole thing – none of what he says is true. I never said what he says. Not a word of it.'

'Thank you,' Atticus said.

'Anything else?'

Atticus stood up, the legs of the chair scraping against the linoleum floor. 'No,' he said. 'I have enough to be getting on with.'

'So, what now?'

'I'm going to concentrate on Freddie. That's the most important testimony they have, but I think it might be the flimsiest. We'll see.'

'Are you going to speak to him?'

'Probably.'

'But isn't that – you know – tampering?'

'Depends how it's done,' Atticus said. 'There's no property in a witness.'

'What does that mean?'

'It means that, as long as I don't try to make him change his evidence, there's nothing to worry about. You can relax. I'm very discreet.'

Allegra got to her feet now, and Ralph followed suit.

'Thank you,' Ralph said. 'Sorry for snapping at you. Like I said – this is a nightmare.'

Atticus nodded. The apology felt hollow, almost as if delivered by rote, and he could see no sincerity there. More likely Ralph had seen the possibility of a crease in the prosecution's case and, realising that – and that he had very few friends – he was trying to present a slightly better impression in the hope that Atticus might, after all, be able to widen that crease. It didn't matter. Ralph was still Atticus's client, and he would be professional. He would do the best job that he could, regardless of how he felt about the man. That was what he was being paid to do.

'I'll be in touch,' Atticus said.

Ralph put out his hand and Atticus took it, locking eyes with Ralph in the event that he tried to squeeze hard again. He didn't, releasing his grip and turning quickly to his wife. Atticus turned away as they embraced, and knocked on the door and waited for the guard to unlock it. He went outside into the waiting area and sat down. Allegra followed him a minute or two later.

'Was that okay?' she said.

'It was.'

He looked at his watch. It was nine. He could be back in Salisbury by ten.

'What are you going to do now?'

'There's someone I want to talk to,' he said.

36

Mack had arrived back at the station at six and had been at her desk ever since. It was ten now, and she was beginning to flag. The work that was necessary to ensure that a trial proceeded smoothly was significant. She knew that there would be a series of late nights until proceedings came to a conclusion with the jury's verdict, but, even though she had warned Andy that that would be the case, she still felt bad. She couldn't keep pulling these late shifts. Time to go.

She locked her PC, pushed herself away from her desk and got up.

'Done for the night, boss?' Lennox said from the other side of the room.

'I've been looking at the same page for the past twenty minutes,' she said.

'Another half an hour for me.'

'Don't work too hard,' she told him. 'I'd rather you came back early tomorrow than stay later tonight.'

'Understood,' he said. 'I won't be long.'

She grabbed her jacket and bag and, with a final wave, left the CID room and took the stairs down to the ground floor.

*   *   *

The Bourne Hill area of Salisbury was close to the city centre, yet might just as easily have been miles away. It was set around a large park, with an abundance of trees, shrubs, flowers and wildlife. There was a tended lawn area and neatly arranged flowerbeds, but, apart from that, the rest of the grass was left to have a wild feel. The medieval ramparts of the city had run right through the gardens and, although most of them had long since been removed, there still remained a small monument on one of the footpaths that wound its way between the trees. The council had chosen the area for its administrative buildings and, following the closure of the old nick on Wilton Road, the police had been moved here too. Mack liked it better. It was more peaceful, and she liked to be able to walk into the city for a change of scene during her lunch break.

The police station had been rehoused in one of the council's newer buildings. It was a surprisingly modern design for a city like Salisbury and had been built at the back of the old council office, its modernity shielded by the eighteenth-century façade. The main body was composed of a concrete shell that was, seemingly, suspended beneath a long rank of concrete arches. A smaller glass construction emerged from those arches, its sleek, dark shine providing a contrast to the dullness of the rest of the building.

Mack came out of the main entrance, turned left and followed the path down to Bedwin Street.

She was at the junction when she saw Atticus.

She stopped. 'What are you doing here?'

'I thought you'd be working late.'

'And?'

'I came to say hello.'

'No, you didn't,' she said. 'What is it? What do you want?'

'I meant what I said earlier,' he said. 'I haven't seen you for ages. Can't we have a drink to catch up?'

'And *I* meant what *I* said,' Mack replied. 'No. Absolutely not. Bad idea.'

Mack saw Atticus's expression change as he looked over her shoulder, back towards the building. She turned to see Lennox making his way towards the road. He slowed his pace as he recognised Atticus, his eyebrow kinking up in surprise.

'All right, boss?' Lennox said to Mack.

Mack sighed, exasperated; the last thing she wanted was to be seen with Atticus. 'I'm fine.'

Lennox stayed where he was, eyeballing Atticus.

'Get off home, Tristan,' she said.

Lennox leered at Atticus. 'Still doing the weed?'

'Just at the weekends.'

'Go home,' Mack said to Lennox. 'I'm fine.'

Lennox said goodnight to her and continued on his way. Mack turned back to Atticus. 'All you do is cause trouble. What do you want?'

'I just want to talk.'

'About?'

'Ralph Mallender.'

'So make an appointment.'

'You *really* want me to come into the nick?'

'I can't stop you.'

'Can't we just have a private chat?'

'No.'

'You know how stubborn I'll be about it. I can be annoying when I put my mind to it.'

'That's probably the most truthful thing you've said all day.'

'Come on. One drink. Just business – I promise.'

There was no point in fighting with him. She knew very well that he meant what he said: he would be back here again tomorrow, and he would return until she gave in. He could be relentless.

'Fine,' she said. 'One drink.'

37

The Royal George was a whitewashed building that had its name painted in large blue text on both the front and side elevations. It was close enough to the station to serve as the local for the officers who worked there. It was well known for live music, and it had thriving pool and darts teams. Atticus opened the door and held it for Mack as she went inside.

There was a low-ceilinged bar area covered with traditional horse brasses and laid out with tables and chairs. There was a dartboard on the wall, and two TVs were tuned to the replay of the Manchester United match on Sky. There was a restaurant area at the rear of the bar with a dozen tables, together with a separate pool room at the back of the pub. The bar was quiet, save for four regulars, who were watching the football.

Mack was relieved to see that there was no one in from the station tonight. She had wondered whether it might have been more sensible to go somewhere a little further afield; the last thing she wanted to do was to have to face knowing looks from the others when she reported to work tomorrow. The more talk there was, the better the chance that Andy would find out who it was that she had been seeing.

'The usual?'

She nodded and watched as Atticus went to order the drinks. There was no denying that he was an attractive man. She noticed that he had changed his hair since the last time she had seen him. He had previously worn it in a wavy crewcut but had opted, instead, to grow it out so that it was down past his collar. His face was long and aquiline, his blue eyes sparkled with intelligence, and his cheekbones were fashionably gaunt. He was tall, an inch or two over six feet, and he had a certain sartorial style that was all his own. Today, for example, he was wearing the black leather bomber jacket with a shearling collar that he had bought from the vintage shop on Fisherton Street, matching it with a pair of skinny black jeans, biker boots and a faded Guns N' Roses T-shirt.

There was no point in pretending that she didn't find him attractive, because she did. Physically and, especially, mentally. She reminded herself that there was no point in pursuing that line of thinking to its ultimate destination. She had tried that before, and it hadn't ended well.

He brought the drinks to the table, placed them down and took the other seat. He took off his jacket – revealing the sleeve of tattoos that ran down his both arms from shoulder to wrist – and held up his glass. 'Cheers.'

She touched her glass to his.

'Good to see you, Mack.'

'Hmm,' she replied.

'We haven't spoken for ages, have we? I mean, not really.'

'That was what we agreed.'

'Come on,' he protested. 'You're not still worried about that?'

'I don't think things have changed, Atticus.'

'But you're still here,' he said with a smile.

'Because you wanted to talk about Mallender. And because you're stubborn enough to bother me if I didn't.'

She didn't mean to sound hostile, and leavened the suggestion with her first smile. She regretted it at once: Atticus saw it, took it as an invitation, and immediately moved the conversation onto more personal territory.

'How's Andy?'

She shook her head. 'No,' she said. 'No, no, no. We're not talking about him.'

'Domestic bliss?' he said.

'I said no,' she said firmly.

'The kids?'

'Atticus,' she said sternly, 'I'll talk to you about the case. I won't talk to you about my personal life. If that's going to be too difficult for you, I can go right now.'

He looked chastened. 'Sorry,' he said. 'You're right – just business, nothing personal. Understood.'

He had never been good with emotions, either his own or those of others. Mack knew that it was not his fault, that it was a symptom of the very mild Asperger's that he usually kept under control with medication. As far as she knew, he had only ever confided his diagnosis to her; none of the others at the station knew anything about it and attributed his diffidence and lack of social skills to rudeness. He could probably have made his professional life a little easier by confiding in the others, but he had insisted to her that the disorder was mild and that he would much rather keep it to himself. She would never have dreamed of abusing his trust and had not breathed a word of it to anyone, not even to her husband.

She sipped her drink and watched him over the rim of the glass. 'So?'

'I spent the day looking through the files for the Mallender case.'

'You're serious about that?' she said. 'You've really taken that on?'

'I told Mrs Mallender that it was probably going to be a waste of time, but she insisted. And if she's determined to pay me, why should I say no?'

'Because her husband is guilty?'

'Maybe,' Atticus said. 'But I don't blame her for wanting to kick the tyres a bit. I've got a list of questions that need to be answered.'

She exhaled wearily. 'This is going to be *so* much fun.'

He grinned at her, lifted up his half-empty glass and downed the rest of it. 'Another?'

'I said just one,' she said.

'Understood,' he said, taking his glass back to the bar.

She took out her phone, expecting to see a message from Andy asking when she would be home. There was none; he knew that she would be late, and was being reasonable about it all. That made her feel even worse about being here. She was taking advantage of his good nature.

Atticus returned to the table with two drinks. He set hers down without a word, but a smile twitched the corner of his mouth. She exhaled and then barely managed to stifle a laugh. He was impossible.

He held up his pint and, knowing that she was indulging him, she accepted the drink and touched it against his. She sipped the lager. 'So, what is it you really want?'

He put the glass down on the table and wiped the back of his hand across his lips. 'I have some questions for you.'

'I can't say anything. You know I can't. The trial has started. Jesus, if Beckton knew that you were working for the other side and that I was here having a drink with you, he'd string me up.'

'I won't tell him if you won't,' Atticus said. 'Look, I know you won't be indiscreet, and I'm not asking you to be. I just wanted to get a sense of what you thought of the case. I've been through the papers, like I said. There are inconsistencies that I'm going to have to tease out. I'm just interested in what you made of him.'

'Who?' she said. 'Ralph?'

'Yes.'

'Have you spoken to him?'

'Tonight, actually. I've come from the prison.'

'And?'

'And he's not the most sympathetic character I've ever met.'

'We can agree on that, at least.'

'I wanted to know what you thought about him. You were at the farmhouse that night.'

She nodded. 'You've read my evidence.'

'Yes. You didn't think he had done it, did you? Not at first.'

She rubbed her forehead, wondering whether this was a line of conversation that she ought to be encouraging. 'You know I didn't.'

'I trust your judgement, Mack. I can read people, but you have intuition that I don't.'

She knew that he was flattering her, but, as usual, she rather enjoyed it. Atticus was sparing in his praise, and when he blessed someone with a compliment, it was something to be savoured.

'No,' she said after a moment's thought. 'I didn't think it was him. He was in pieces when I got there. Exactly like you'd expect him to be.'

'And the others thought the same thing?'

'We all did. Ralph told us that Cameron was struggling at university, and that he had problems with his temper. And that was all true. You take that about Cameron, add the way Ralph reacted with us, and then add the way the crime scene looked that night . . . It was difficult to come to any other conclusion.'

'I'm not criticising,' he said.

'That's encouraging,' she said, knowing that that was precisely what he was about to do.

'But it just seems that the investigation switched to Ralph too easily, and then, once it had, it focused on him so much that every other possibility was ignored.'

'We looked at everything objectively.'

'Why did you flip from Cameron to Ralph? The family?'

She nodded. 'They were smart about it. Getting the press on their side early, getting into the papers and then onto the TV. Beckton was getting it in the neck, and you know what that means – shit runs downhill as far as he's concerned. He made me go over it again. And when we did, I started to see it in a different light. The gun was too far away from Cameron's body for him to have shot himself, for a start. There was a way to get out of the house while it was locked. And the more we looked at Ralph, the more we saw that he had the motive to kill them all, the opportunity to do it and the means. Read the file, Atticus. Look at what the cleaner said. Look at the arguments that the family had been having for months about Allegra and everything else. Ralph discovered the bodies. He had the best opportunity to kill them all. He knew about the coal hole. You know the statistics as well as I do. The suspect with the most obvious motive is almost always the one who ends up being found guilty. And, in this case, it's him. He did it.'

'Maybe,' Atticus said. He finished the rest of the second pint and put the glass back down on the table. 'And maybe not.'

'You're not an independent judge,' she said. 'You can milk the Mallenders out of a lot of money if you give her hope.'

'Come on,' he protested. 'That's unfair.'

She leaned back in her chair and nodded. 'I'm sorry. Low blow. It's been a long day, and, honestly, I'm not looking forward to having to tussle with you over this.'

'It won't come to that,' Atticus said. 'I'm not saying you're wrong. All I promised her was that I'd look into it. There are some inconsistencies that I need to check out, but, between you and me, I think you're probably right. He does look guilty.' He stood and collected their glasses. 'One for the road?'

She stood, too. 'I can't. I shouldn't really have even had one, and definitely not two. Andy is expecting me. I'm already late.'

To her surprise, Atticus conceded defeat. 'Thanks.'

'For what?'

'For being frank with me.'

She shrugged herself into her jacket and picked up her bag. 'It's good to see you again.'

He smiled, as if surprised that she would say that. 'Likewise. Fancy doing it again?'

She sighed. Atticus was fearsomely intelligent, but *so* naïve with it. He could deduce things about people from the slightest piece of evidence, but he was a wide-eyed innocent when it came to personal relationships. That artlessness was one of the things that she liked most about him.

'I don't think so,' she said.

He nodded, put his hand on her shoulder and leaned in to kiss her on the cheek. She let him, reminding herself of the musky scent of his skin.

'See you in court,' she said.

38

Bandit woke Atticus up the next morning. He had wriggled up the bed and had pressed his wet muzzle into the space between Atticus's chin and shoulder. Atticus reached for his watch and held it in front of his face, waiting for his eyes to adjust.

'It's six o'clock,' he groaned.

Bandit licked Atticus's face.

'All right, all right. You want a walk. Fine – come on, then.'

He rolled off the mattress, dressed in clean clothes and pulled on his boots. Bandit trotted into the other room and returned with his lead in his mouth. Atticus clipped it to the dog's collar. He swallowed his pills and led the way down the stairs.

It was fresh and cold outside, the dawn just breaking around the vaulting spire of the cathedral. He followed his usual route, through the Close, crossing the river by the Harnham Bridge and then back along the Town Path. Bandit trotted happily alongside him, darting ahead and then waiting for him to catch up.

Atticus took the opportunity to consider the case and what he was going to do today. Hugo and Juliet Mallender's surviving family members were due to go into the box. The prosecution was coming to the end of its evidence, building towards the testimony of Freddie Lamza on Friday or early next week. Atticus knew that would be the defining moment of the trial. If Lamza was credible, Ralph was in trouble. If he wasn't credible, or if Atticus could find something with which they could discredit him, perhaps there was a chance. Atticus was walking back through Queen Elizabeth Gardens when he felt his phone buzz. He whistled for Bandit to stop while he reached into his pocket and unlocked the phone. He saw that he had a Facebook message. A man named George had responded to one of the messages that Atticus had sent following his trawl of Cassandra Mallender's social media posts the previous afternoon.

He sat down on a bench and read it. George said that he had been following the case and that his memory of Cassandra was very different than the picture that had been painted in the newspapers. He said that he would be happy to talk about it. Atticus messaged him back and asked when would be a good time. George replied, proposing a café in the centre of Bath and saying that he would be there after he finished work at three that afternoon.

Atticus said that he would see him then.

*   *   *

Atticus took Bandit back to the office and arranged for Jacob to look after him again. He slid his laptop and a notebook into his rucksack and set off on the walk to court.

39

Mack had a meeting with Gordon Abernathy first thing and had to ask Andy to get the kids ready and off to school again. There was an atmosphere in the house. Last night hadn't gone well. Andy had been annoyed that she had been late again, and she had felt guilty about seeing Atticus and it made her feel defensive. He had told her that he had kept her dinner warm; she had told him he was behaving like a martyr; he had retorted that she was behaving as if she didn't want to spend time with her family and had gone upstairs to bed.

She blamed herself this morning. She had been taking advantage of him, and she really ought to do something to remind him of how grateful she was for the flexibility that he allowed her. She didn't tell him that she was thankful nearly enough, and, as she drove away from the house and set off for court, she promised herself that she would make more of an effort. They hadn't been out on a date night for months. She would arrange for a babysitter and take him out for something to eat and then a film at the Odeon. He had mentioned that there was a new Terrence Malick film that he would like to see.

It would do them good to have some time alone together, away from the kids and the pressure of her work. She couldn't do it yet – the trial made a social life impossible – but she would sort it out as soon as it was done and Mallender had been put away.

* * *

Mack took her usual place behind Abernathy and glanced around the court. Atticus wasn't there. She started to wonder where he was – or, more to the point, what mischief he might be causing – when the doors opened and he came inside. He made his way into the gallery, said something to Allegra, and continued up to the back where, with copious apologies, he edged along the line towards the only two empty spaces. He sat down, exhaled, and, as he noticed she was looking in his direction, smiled and raised his hand in greeting.

Mack returned the smile and then quickly turned her face away. She shouldn't have gone out with him last night. She had promised Andy that she would have nothing to do with him, and going back on her word – and not telling him about it – felt like a betrayal, even though nothing had happened.

No more, she told herself.

That was the last time.

No more mistakes.

The usher cleared his throat. 'All rise.'

* * *

Mack jotted down her thoughts as Abernathy presented a series of police witnesses. She watched as Yaxley and Edwards, the first officers to reach the farmhouse after Lennox, gave their evidence. The testimony was not particularly controversial, dealing, for the most part, with both men going through the details that they had entered into their notebooks. By the end of their evidence-in-chief, Abernathy had confirmed the summary that Lennox had provided yesterday. Abernathy also worked to mitigate the damage that had been caused by Lennox's testimony, with both officers confirming that they had not seen or heard anything inside the house that might have suggested that someone was still alive while Mallender was outside with them.

The defence accepted most of their evidence, with Crow concentrating his cross-examinations on the suggestion that it would have taken only a moment for someone to be inside, and that it was possible that they might have missed what Lennox said he had seen. The officers admitted that it was possible, but reiterated what they had said before: they had not seen anything themselves. Crow did not press the issue and the officers were dismissed.

* * *

The civilian telephone operator who had taken Ralph Mallender's panicked 999 call came next. The call had been recorded, and the courtroom was rapt for thirty seconds as it was replayed. Mack had heard the call many times before, but hearing it here – with everyone leaning forwards, tension fizzing through the air like electricity – lent it an urgency that had her holding her breath just like everyone else.

'Emergency services. Which service do you require?'

Mallender's voice came over the speakers. 'I need help. My father has been shot.'

'Slow down, sir. What's your name?'

'Ralph Mallender.'

'And where are you?'

'Grovely Farmhouse. In Grovely Woods. Near Great Wishford.'

'Where is your father now?'

'Inside the kitchen. The door's locked – I can't get in. I think he's been shot.'

Mack looked up at Mallender; he was staring straight ahead, his face expressionless save for a tic that twitched in his cheek.

'Is anyone still inside the house?'

'I don't know. I told you, the door's locked.'

'I understand, sir. There's a car on its way. They'll be there as soon as they can.'

'How long?'

'No longer than ten minutes.'

'Please tell them to hurry!'

The call ended.

Abernathy said that he had no questions, and Mallender's brief indicated that there would be no cross-examination from the defence. The operator was dismissed.

Abernathy stood. 'Now might be a good time to adjourn for lunch, my Lord.'

'Very well,' Somerville said. 'We'll adjourn.'

40

There was half a mile between the court and the station, and Atticus covered the distance at a brisk walk. There was a train at nineteen minutes past the hour, and he was keen to be on it so that he could get to Bath in plenty of time for his meeting with Cassandra's friend. He was sweaty by the time he arrived. He bought a ticket from the machine, fumbled it into the ticket barrier, and hurried across to the correct platform. The doors were just closing as he reached the train; he pushed them apart and squeezed on board. It was busy, and the only space was next to a prim matron, who glanced up at him with disdain as he sat down next to her.

The journey would take an hour. There was time to do a little extra research. He took out his laptop, tethered it to his phone and opened a fresh Word document. He typed FREDERICK LAMZA across the top, copied it and then pasted it into Google. It was an unusually distinctive name and, thanks to that, Atticus was rewarded with a series of useful hits.

The first was a report from the *Camden New Journal* from the summer. He copied and pasted it into a fresh document.

FREDERICK LAMZA, aged 28, of Sapperton Court, Islington, was found guilty of soliciting. The incident took place on 27 June at Camden High Road. He has been fined £220 and has been ordered to pay a surcharge of £30 to fund victim services, and to pay costs of £135.

There was a picture of Lamza looking straight into the lens of a police camera. He glared angrily out of the shot, his lip curled up at one side with unhidden contempt. He looked scruffy, and his hair was long and unkempt.

A second hit led to a YouTube video. It was a BBC documentary on the sex industry in London, with a focus on male prostitution. Freddie Lamza was noted in the description as one of the interviewees, and Atticus scrubbed through the film until he found him. The interview had been recorded eighteen months ago.

'I started off with one or two people a night,' he said, 'and then more and more.'

The video was shot from behind Lamza so as not to show his face, but Atticus could see from a comparison with the newspaper photograph that it was the same man, and that he wasn't being portrayed by an actor. His hair was the same, and he had the same build: slim, with a slender neck that made his head look a little outsized.

Atticus took notes and allowed an impression of Lamza to form. He was feminine and spoke with a sibilance that Atticus suspected was manufactured; he gesticulated to punctuate his sentences, a theatricality that verged on flouncing. The shot from behind changed to a close-up of Lamza on the phone, speaking with a client.

'One hundred and fifty pounds is a full service,' he said, 'and we can negotiate extras separately.'

The woman sitting next to Atticus was surreptitiously watching over his shoulder, but she blew her cover with an audible tut as the camera showed a neon sign that promised BONDAGE, SPANKING, HETERO & GAY. Atticus looked over at her and smiled, turning the laptop a quarter in her direction so she had a better look. She shook her head with exaggerated disgust and made a show of reading her magazine.

Atticus let the video play and continued with his notes.

41

Mack took her seat as the afternoon's testimony began. The first witness was Brenda Grant, the cleaner who, together with her husband, had been present at the gathering on Christmas Eve. Abernathy encouraged her to talk about the atmosphere inside the house and the argument between Ralph Mallender and his father.

'Mr Mallender – Ralph – complained that his wife didn't feel welcomed by the rest of the family. The whole thing just escalated into a shouting match. Hugo said he would write Ralph out of his will unless he agreed to leave her. Ralph picked up a glass bowl that Juliet liked and threw it against the wall before storming out of the house and driving away. I had to clean up the mess.'

As Mack had expected, she made an excellent witness: she was persuasive and unemotional, sticking to the facts and avoiding the kind of speculation that might have appeared prurient.

Abernathy thanked her and sat down.

'Mrs Grant,' Crow said, 'had you ever seen this kind of incident before?'

'No, sir.'

'Had anyone told you that there was a problem in the family?'

'No.'

'Thank you,' Crow said as he looked knowingly over at the jury. 'I have no further questions for you.'

She was dismissed.

☐ ☐ ☐

Hugo Mallender's surviving family members came next: his brother, Colin, together with his son and daughter, Ralph's cousins.

Colin gave evidence that he had received a telephone call from his brother in the early evening of Christmas Eve, and that he had been fine. There was no suggestion of a problem at home, although Hugo had made reference to the argument that had taken place that afternoon with Ralph. Colin went on to say that, in his opinion, Ralph had always seemed to be aloof from the rest of the family. He said he was a 'cold fish' with whom he had never felt very close, and noted that Hugo had told him on more than one occasion that he felt that Ralph was drifting. Colin said that Hugo had told him that Ralph seemed to have no purpose in life and little in the way of prospects.

Crow stood up for the cross-examination. He suggested that Colin and the rest of his family had an interest in Ralph being found guilty of the murders, since Colin would be the next in line to inherit the estate if Ralph forfeited it by reason of his guilt.

'That's ridiculous,' Colin said.

'Is it? Who would stand to inherit your brother's estate if Mr Mallender is found guilty?'

'That's not relevant,' he blustered.

'Please – answer the question.'

'Well, I suppose I would,' he said.

'Thank you.'

Crow was about to sit when Colin spoke again. 'Are you saying that I'd lie about this so that I could benefit?'

'No, sir. I'm just pointing out that you stand to become a very wealthy man if Mr Mallender is convicted.'

'I don't care about the property or the money. I'd give it all up to have my brother back again.' He glowered across the court at Crow. 'And I have to say, I find your insinuation absolutely disgusting.'

Mack gritted her teeth. They had known that Colin had the potential to react badly – he had been the same during the witness preparation – but they had hoped that he would be able to keep his temper. She glanced across the court and saw disapproving expressions on the faces of several of the jurors.

'Thank you, Mr Mallender,' Crow said. 'I have no further questions.'

Abernathy rose for the re-examination and attempted to make up for the damage that Colin's haughtiness had caused. He focused on the loss of his brother and the stress of attending the trial and, after five minutes of gentle cajoling, he decided he had remedied things as much as he could and sat down.

Colin Mallender was dismissed.

42

The train was delayed en route, but, to Atticus's relief, George had messaged to suggest they meet at four. The train pulled into Bath Spa at half three. Atticus hopped down to the platform and made his way through the station, beating the crowd of commuters and setting off for the coffee shop that George had suggested. The place was called Colonna & Small's and was on Chapel Row, a half-mile to the north of the station. Atticus had half an hour, so he ambled along, looking around at the city as he passed along its grand streets. He liked Bath. The buildings were impressive, crafted from the honey-coloured limestone that was so common here. It was an affluent city and the streets were busy with locals and tourists who had come to visit.

The coffee shop was between an estate agency and a wine shop. It was small, with a stencilled sign in the window that made much of the fact that it used only sustainable beans. It was busy inside, catering to a mixed crowd of hipsters, students and middle-class yummy mummies with expensive pushchairs parked against the wall. Atticus went inside. He had refreshed his memory of the pictures that he had grabbed from George's

Facebook profile and, after standing awkwardly in the door for ten seconds, he saw him sitting at a table at the back of the room.

He went over to him. 'Hello.'

George looked up. 'Mr Priest?'

'That's right. And you must be George.'

'I am.'

'Can I get you a drink?'

'Thank you,' he said. 'A flat white, please.'

Atticus went to the counter and ordered two coffees. He paid and waited while the barista set to work, looking back across the room to where George was sitting. He was smartly dressed, wearing a woollen cardigan, jeans and a pair of Chelsea boots. He guessed that he was in his early twenties, around the same age as Cassandra had been when she had died.

'Two coffees for . . .'

'*Atticus*,' he said, shaking his head as the barista struggled to read the name that had been scrawled on the sides of the cups.

'Atticus,' the barista repeated. 'Like in the book?'

'Just like in the book. Thank you.'

He took the coffees back to the table, set them down, and pulled out a chair opposite George. He sat down.

'Thank you,' George said, putting the cup to his lips.

'Thank *you*. I appreciate you finding the time to see me.'

'How can I help?'

'I'm working on the investigation into Cassandra's death,' Atticus said.

'You said. But for who? The police?'

There was no point in lying. 'I've been hired by Ralph Mallender.'

'Her brother?'

'That's right.'

'But they said he did it.'

'He's been charged,' Atticus said. 'The trial is taking place now.'

'So what does it have to do with you?'

'I'm a private investigator.' He took out a business card and slid it across the table.

George took it, examined it, and then slipped it into his pocket. 'I see,' he said. 'I wondered whether you were police when you messaged me. But then I thought police probably don't use Facebook to get in touch with people.'

'You'd be surprised,' he said. 'But no – I'm not police. They finished their investigation a long time ago. I'm looking at the evidence that they've put together against Mr Mallender to make sure that it all stacks up.'

'And does it?'

'I'm not sure.'

George sipped the coffee and then put the mug back down onto the table. 'I couldn't understand why they didn't speak to me before.'

'The police didn't get in touch?'

'No. Not a word. I know they were here, but . . . nothing. It was the same with all the old crowd.'

'Who did they speak to? Do you know?'

'People at Cassandra's church. The university, too, and her new flatmates. But not me or any of the others.'

Atticus took out his phone and opened the voice recorder. 'Do you mind if I record this?'

He shrugged.

'So – let's start at the start. You were friends with Cassandra?'

'Yes.'

'Close?'

He nodded.

'I saw you used to be on her timeline all the time.'

'The good old days,' he said with a wistful smile.

'And then you're not on it at all.'

'Things change,' he said. 'People change.'

'This was about a year ago?'

George nodded. 'At the start of our second year.'

'What do you mean by "people change"? What happened?'

'She ghosted me,' he said. 'And not just me. She was like that with everyone.'

'What do you mean?'

George leaned forward, both elbows on the table. 'There was a crowd of us. Six of us had rented a house. It was really good – we all got on, we went out together, hung out all the time. We went home at the end of the year, and then when we all came back' – he snapped his fingers – 'she stopped seeing *everyone*. It was the strangest thing. One day she was part of the crowd, best friends with everyone, popular, going out all the time, all that, and then the next day . . . nothing.'

'Why?'

'I blame the church. You know about that? The church?'

'I know she was religious,' Atticus said.

'Didn't used to be. The complete opposite. It was that summer, after the first year – when she came back in September, she was really into it. Services two or three times a week, volunteering for their charity stuff.'

'She hadn't been into it before?'

'The opposite. She was into Marx – thought the whole thing was a scam, opium of the masses and all that. She was an atheist.'

'Did you speak to her? Ask her what happened?'

'Just once. She'd changed her phone, so I had to go and find her. She said she was sorry, but she was unhappy with her old life and she wanted to make a new start. I said that was fine, I was okay with that, but it didn't make any difference. She said she was going to concentrate on the church and her studies and that she would rather we didn't see each other any more.'

It was obvious that there was something that George was unhappy about discussing, and Atticus decided that he would need to approach it with tact if he was to persuade him to go into detail.

'Let me backtrack,' Atticus said. 'You said you and Cassandra were friends?'

'That's right.'

There was a hesitation before he answered, and Atticus could see there was more to their relationship than that.

'George? I'm sorry – I need to ask. Were the two of you seeing each other?'

'For a bit,' he admitted. 'We met in Freshers' Week. It wasn't serious.'

'And then?'

'And then she dumped me for the guy from home.'

There was a clipped dismissiveness to the way he said that. Atticus could see at once that his motivation for speaking to him might not be entirely altruistic. George had been spurned, and now Atticus knew that there was a chance that his snubbing might colour anything that he said. He resolved to bear that in mind.

'I didn't know that she was seeing anyone at home,' Atticus said.

George shrugged.

'Do you know his name?'

He furrowed his brow. 'Can't remember.'

'Can you try? It could be helpful.'

George closed his eyes. 'No. I don't know.'

'Do you have a picture of him?'

'Why would I have a picture of him? He was awful. No one liked him.'

'Why?'

'He was older, for a start.'

'How old?'

'Mid-twenties?'

'And Cassandra was seeing him romantically?'

George shrugged. 'He came up four or five weekends in a row and stayed in her room – so, yeah, they were seeing each other. That was when she started to go off the rails. I mean, we all do, now and again. Right?'

'You're students. That's part of the job description.'

'Exactly. Getting drunk at the weekends, all that. But Cassandra started to get into drugs, too. We were all smoking weed, but she'd started to do coke. I'd never even *seen* coke before. She'd disappear with him into the bathroom at house parties and they'd come out rubbing their gums and talking, non-stop talking. It was starting to get embarrassing.'

'Where did she get it from?'

'From him,' he said. 'He was into it in a big way.'

'That's helpful,' Atticus said. 'I've read what the police said about her. I wouldn't have thought that she was the type to be into that.'

'She *wasn't*, not before – that's just it. Before he showed up, she was just like us. Booze and weed, that's it. And then, when she came back after the holidays, she didn't even touch alcohol. She went from being normal, to this crazy coked-up party girl, to completely straight-edge. Like I said – it was totally weird.'

Atticus could see that George had crept up to the thing that he was reluctant to talk about, and prompted him gently. 'Why do you think she changed?'

He bit his lip. 'Do you remember Stacey Dickinson?'

'The name's familiar,' he said.

'She was part of our group,' George said. 'She was probably Cassandra's best friend.' He paused. 'Look – what happened got reported in the papers and on the TV, so that's probably the reason you've heard about her. There was a house party one night. There were six of us in our house-share, like I said: me, Cassandra, Stacey, Eddie, Connor and Raif. We all went to this party, including the bloke from home. It was the usual night out – everyone was smashed, people were passing weed around, the same old shit. And then someone found this bag of tabs on the table and offered them out. I'd never done E before and I said I wasn't interested, thank God. Stacey took one and then, really quick, she started to get this bad reaction. She got hot – really hot – and she couldn't stop drinking. Pints and pints of water. Then she couldn't stand – she collapsed, lost conscious-ness. We called an ambulance and they took her into hospital, but it didn't make any difference. She was in a coma when they admitted her, and she never woke up. She died early the next morning. Water intoxication, the inquest said. Who knew you could die from drinking too much water?'

'Hyponatremia,' Atticus said. 'Not enough sodium in the blood.'

'That's what they said. The police got involved, obviously, but no one could ever prove who brought those pills.'

'And you think it was the man Cassandra was seeing?'

'He said the week before that he was going to bring some with him the next time he came, so, yeah, I think it was him.'

'You told the police that?'

'Of course. I think they questioned him about it, but they couldn't prove it. I never saw him again after that.'

'She stopped seeing him?'

'I guess so. She came back for the second year and ignored all of us, like I said. What happened that night was when it started.' He exhaled, his story concluded, and sat back. He spread his arms in a gesture of helplessness. 'It was a mess. It messed all of us up. I was on track for a first, but I'm scraping a two-two now, and that's if I'm lucky. If I had my life again, I would never have got involved with her. I'm sad about what's happened now, but it looks like she had a way of attracting trouble.'

Atticus switched off the recorder. 'Thank you, George.'

'Do you need anything else?'

'No. I think that's all for now – you've been great. Very helpful.' Atticus stood up. 'Is it okay if I get in touch with you if I have any other questions?'

George shrugged. 'Of course.'

'And if you happened to find a picture, or if you could remember his name, you'll let me know?'

He nodded. 'Sure.'

Atticus put out his hand and George took it.

'What do you think happened to her?' George asked. 'Was it her brother, like they say?'

'I don't know,' Atticus said. 'Maybe. Maybe not. I'm going to try to find out.'

43

It was five when Mack awoke. She lay there for a moment, her mind immediately buzzing with the trial. She knew that there was no way she would be able to get back to sleep, so, sliding out of bed carefully so as not to wake Andy, she went downstairs to the kitchen and boiled the kettle.

She made a cup of coffee and took it to the table. Her thoughts snapped back to the trial. It had reached the fourth day, and this one promised to be the most consequential yet. Freddie Lamza was the prosecution's most important witness. They had evidence that suggested that Ralph Mallender could have been responsible for the murders of his family, but it was Lamza who would tie it all together. He would testify that Ralph had told him that he hated his family and wanted them dead. If he could persuade the jury that what he said was credible, they would have taken a big step towards getting a conviction. But Lamza was a flamboyant and divisive man, and if the jury didn't take to him – if they didn't believe him – then the opposite would happen.

The prospect of that made her very nervous.

* * *

Mack showered and woke the children. They had the rare treat of sitting around the kitchen table together, the two children eating boiled eggs with toast soldiers and Andy and Mack enjoying bacon sandwiches. Andy took them to school, and Mack grabbed her things and drove to court.

Abernathy was waiting for her in the corridor outside the courtroom.

'Everything okay?' she asked him.

'I just wanted to make sure you had a word with Lamza before he gives evidence. We don't want him to be overwhelmed.'

'You think he might be?'

'We live and breathe all this,' he said, gesturing to the corridor and the monitor with Crown v. Mallender displayed on it. 'I doubt he's ever set foot inside a court before. I've seen witnesses fall apart – you must have, too.'

'Plenty.'

'Well, we can't have that today. We'll have trouble if he doesn't perform. Can you find him and tell him to read his bloody statement before he gives his evidence?'

'Of course.'

'How do you think it's going?' he asked her.

'Seems to be going well. What do you think?'

'The jury are on our side,' he said. 'I've been watching Mallender during the evidence. He's not doing himself any favours. There's something about him.'

'The arrogance,' Mack said.

'Exactly,' he agreed. 'Looks like he thinks he's too good to be here.'

'He was the same when we were interviewing him. It was like he was tolerating us.'

'That's exactly what it is. There's that way he almost sneers when someone says something that he doesn't like. The jury sees it. One thing you can say about him is that he draws the eye.'

'I noticed,' Mack said. 'Some of them can barely take their eyes off him.'

'They're seeing it all, and it's not doing him any favours. And, out of all of them, I'll lay odds he reacts worst to what Lamza has to say.'

'I'll speak to him,' Mack said.

44

Mack went to the prosecution witness room and peered through the window in the door.

Freddie Lamza was the only person inside. He was pacing from one wall to the other, his hands clasped in front of him. He was dressed in a suit that was perhaps a touch too blue, with a hint of coral, and had matched that with a crisp white shirt. He was wearing a tie that was fastened with a fat Windsor knot, and a silver tie bar worn between the third and fourth buttons of the shirt secured both the front and back of the tie to the placket.

Mack opened the door. 'Freddie.'

He stopped, unfolded his hands and turned to face her. 'Hello, Detective Chief Inspector.'

'Are you okay?'

He smiled wanly. 'A bit nervous.'

'That's fine. I've done this a lot and I still get that way.'

'Really?'

'It's normal. Have you spoken to the witness care officer?'

'When I arrived,' he said. 'She wasn't much use.'

'You'll be fine – I promise.'

'It's the cross-examination I'm worried about.'

'I know. It might feel rough, but you just need to remember that it isn't personal. It's the brief's job to make sure that you haven't made a mistake with your evidence.'

'I haven't.'

'I know that,' she said reassuringly. 'And just remember that it's Ralph, and not you, who's on trial. His brief isn't going to try to make people think that you're stupid, or call you a liar. Nothing like that. And Mr Abernathy will intervene if the questions are too aggressive.'

Lamza nodded that he understood. 'I know,' he said. 'It's fine – just butterflies. I'm ready to do what needs to be done.'

It was ludicrous – given the way that he made his money – but Lamza had always made a show of his moral values. Lamza had told her, at the first interview, that he was very keen to 'do the right thing', no matter the personal cost. It was virtue signalling – conspicuously obvious, too – and Mack found the charade vaguely nauseating.

He went to the window and looked out. 'How long will I have to wait?'

'You're first, so not long. The best thing you can do while you're in here is to reread your statement. Do you have it?'

He held up the brown envelope that he had placed on the chair next to him.

'Look through it again,' she said. 'Mr Abernathy is very keen that it's fresh.'

The door opened and the pathologist who was presenting the Crown's forensic evidence came inside.

'DCI Jones,' the woman said, putting out a hand.

'Judith,' Mack said, 'you okay?'

'I'm good. They told me to get here early.'

'You might have a wait,' Mack said apologetically. 'Mr Lamza is on first.'

'It's fine. I've got my book.'

Mack didn't want to be seen with Lamza for fear that it might look improper, so she decided to make her way back to the court. 'Just answer the questions, Freddie. Nice and easy; don't elaborate. You'll be fine.'

'I've got it,' he said, taking out the statement and sitting down to read it.

Mack said goodbye to them both, opened the door and took the corridor back to Court One.

*   *   *

The court was slowly filling up, with a queue of spectators waiting to get inside. It had been full each day, and today – the most important of the trial so far – looked to be no different.

There was a commotion at the door to the public gallery. Mack looked back and saw Atticus bustling through the crowd. He had two large cups of coffee balanced precariously on a ring binder and, as he slid between Hugo Mallender's brother and his wife, he was jostled and almost lost them onto the floor. The wife said something, her face stern, and Atticus offered something back; Mack couldn't hear but, judging by the blush of red that infused the older woman's cheeks, it was delivered with Atticus's trademark derision.

Atticus made his way towards her, almost spilling the coffee again. Mack rolled her eyes. Food and drink weren't allowed in the courtroom, and the usher would blow a gasket if he noticed.

She turned away and pretended that she hadn't seen him.

'Mack!'

She sighed.

'*Mack!*'

She sighed again. She wasn't going to be able to ignore him. She turned as he arrived alongside.

'Here,' Atticus said, offering her one of the coffees.

'You're not supposed—'

'Skinny hazelnut latte.'

He had remembered her favourite. 'Not in the court,' she said.

'They're too busy to worry about things like that. I got it from the café downstairs. It's probably awful, but it's the best I could do.'

She took it, intending to dispose of it as soon as she could. 'Thank you.'

He leaned against the wall. 'How's it going?'

'Going well.'

'Today's a big day.'

'It is.'

'What about Cassandra Mallender?'

The non sequitur caught her out. 'What?'

'Cassandra?' he repeated.

'I know who she is. What about her?'

'You didn't go back very far with her.'

'Meaning?'

'Meaning she's not all sweetness and light. Not like the picture that was painted of her.'

'I don't have time for games, Atticus. If you've found something relevant, just share it.'

'I'm not sure if I have found anything. I spoke to one of her friends, from before – before the friends that you spoke to. She wasn't always religious. She was a typical student – drink, drugs, exactly what you'd expect. She's been dismissed as a suspect, or as a reason for what happened. I think that might have been hasty.'

The queue moved forward.

'This is completely unhelpful,' she said.

Atticus smiled, as if he hadn't heard her rebuke. 'Good luck.'

He reached out and touched her on the shoulder before going through the door and making his way to the gallery. She found herself off balance and left with the sensation that Atticus knew more than he was letting on, and it wasn't for the first time. She tried to put him to the back of her mind as she followed him inside. He went to the gallery and she took her usual spot behind Abernathy.

'All rise.'

The judge came into the court, seated himself, and indicated that everyone else should sit, too. He looked down at the papers on his desk, adjusting his spectacles.

'Good morning,' Somerville said. 'Let's get started, shall we?'

45

The court was silent save for the associate tapping out something on his computer and the rustle of a paper bag as one of the jurors offered sweets to her peers.

'Do you have a witness for us, Mr Abernathy?' the judge asked.

Mack involuntarily caught her breath as Abernathy stood to address the court. 'I do indeed, my Lord. The prosecution now calls Mr Frederick Lamza.'

The usher opened the door. 'Mr Frederick Lamza,' he called out.

Everyone turned as the door that led to the witness room was opened and Freddie Lamza was admitted. He paused there, looking left and right, and then continued to the witness box. Mack found herself wondering about the impression that he would convey to the jury. His dress recalled the formality of the forties and fifties, but his personality – shrill and dramatic – made for a discordant mix. There was nothing to be done about either now; all they could do was to cross their fingers and wait.

Lamza was sworn in, his gaze flicking from the associate to the jury, to the judge and then, finally, to Abernathy.

'Hello, Mr Lamza,' Abernathy said.

'Good morning,' Lamza replied.

Mack watched Lamza as Abernathy guided him gently through the first of his questions. She had always found him slightly irritating: he was effeminate almost to the point of parody, and she had wondered how much of it was an act and how much of it was real. He spoke quietly to begin with, but, at Abernathy's polite insistence, he raised his voice and spoke more clearly. Abernathy asked him to briefly give a little of his background, shepherding him on to another topic once it became clear that he would be happy to speak about himself all day.

Abernathy moved him briskly along to the night in London when he had met Ralph Mallender, and then invited him to speak about the relationship that had developed between the two of them. Lamza became more confident as he settled into his evidence, with Abernathy skilfully encouraging him to fill out the relevant details. There was brief talk of the relationship that had grown between the two men, Lamza recounting the details without even a shred of embarrassment; indeed, he spoke with pride, his chin pushed out.

Mack turned back to the dock; Ralph's cheeks were red and his jaw was clenched. His composure looked to have been disturbed as his affair was exposed to the court. Mack looked from him to his wife. Allegra was looking down at her feet, unable to look at Lamza as he took obvious relish in describing the relationship that he had enjoyed with her husband.

Abernathy kept the witness on a tight leash, intervening on several occasions when it looked as if Lamza was about to regale the court with intimate details of the affair, but, even so, Mack could see how embarrassing the experience must be for her. She had no fondness for the woman, but it was difficult not to feel pity.

She found her gaze drifting across to Atticus. He was watching the jury, his eyes wide and concentration etched across his face.

She went back to what he had said to her. What had he meant about Cassandra? That was worrying. What had they missed? The prospect of someone like Atticus poking into her evidence had always been an unwelcome one, but now she was concerned that he had found something.

Would he give her more of a warning?

Probably not.

Not now.

It would have been different last year, when she was his boss. When they were on the same team. He would have been unable to resist a demonstration of his ability. She remembered the way he had explained the deductions that he had made that had broken open cases that had otherwise seemed insoluble: the deductive reasoning that had elicited the password to the hard drive full of child pornography belonging to Alfred Burns; the confession that he had extracted from Leigh Manning, the squaddie who had killed a woman in a hit-and-run outside the army camp at Bulford. Atticus's loyalty was to his clients now, not to her, and the question of disclosure or not would be one for Allegra and Ralph to make.

She couldn't get the thought out of her head: what had he been referring to earlier?

Was *that* his warning, the furthest that he'd felt able to go?

She stared at him, Lamza's voice fading into an abstract buzz, until Atticus realised what she was doing and angled his head a degree or two so that he was looking at her. He smiled and she turned away, her face reddening, irritated with herself.

46

The morning session was spent on Lamza's background, his present circumstances, a description of his meeting with Ralph Mallender and the relationship that had subsequently developed between them. Abernathy's examination was only halfway through by the time the court rose for lunch.

Mack met Lamza on the way to the witness room.

'How was I?' he said.

'I can't talk to you in the middle of your evidence, Freddie.'

'Did you see how he was looking at me?'

'I can't—'

'Ralph,' he said, not even hearing her. 'He *hates* me.'

It was heavy on the melodrama, and, despite the wetness in his eyes, Mack could tell that he was over-egging it for effect.

'If it's upsetting you,' Mack said, 'then look at Mr Abernathy. Or look at the jury. Don't look at Ralph.'

Lamza said that it was difficult – Mack knew that he was fishing for attention – but that he would try. Mack smiled, told him to get a sandwich and eat it in the witness room, and made her way outside.

☐ ☐ ☐

There was a sandwich shop near to the court, and Mack made her way to it, enjoying the fresh air and a moment of peace. She bought herself a ham and cheese baguette and a Diet Coke and, seeking somewhere quiet, she took the subway under the round-about and found an empty wooden bench on one of the paths that led to the other subways. Traffic rushed around the road above the little hollowed-out depression, but at least it was secluded.

She found herself thinking about Andy. It was Friday today; there was a good chance that Somerville would rise early and, if he did, she might be able to get home at a reasonable hour. She wondered whether Anne, their babysitter, would be available on short notice. It would be good to go out, to do something that normal couples did, to get away from Ralph and the trial and everything else that went along with it.

She took out her phone and was about to call Andy to see if he fancied it when she felt someone at her side.

'This seat taken?'

She looked up. It was Atticus.

'Can I?'

She gestured to the half-dozen empty benches all around. 'You have a wide choice.'

Atticus ignored her and sat down. 'Interesting morning.'

She found that she was curious as to his opinion. 'What did you make of it?'

He started to unwrap his own sandwich. 'I thought he was a melodramatic queen.'

'Anything in particular?'

'He's clearly a narcissist. Lack of empathy. Very touchy. And the humblebragging . . .'

'That can be annoying,' she admitted.

'I also got the very strong impression that he assumed that everyone that he liked and respected must share his opinions, and those whom he did not like would not. And, of course, I doubt you missed the way he looked at his reflection in the glass panel of the door as he came into the court.'

Mack hadn't noticed that, but found – as usual – that she felt the urge to burst his bubble. 'You don't have to be particularly observant to see that Freddie Lamza loves himself. Got anything better?'

'He's moved on from his previous "employment".' He spoke the final word with a disdainful little kink of his eyebrow.

'From the prostitution?'

'Yes. I don't think he does that any more. Can't say for sure, but I'd lay odds that he has very recently started a business as a hairdresser.'

Her mouth fell open in surprise, and she was immediately annoyed with herself. She shouldn't have found Atticus's parlour tricks impressive, but she couldn't help it.

'How could you possibly know that?'

'Am I right?'

'Yes. But it wasn't mentioned in evidence.'

He smiled and turned his finger in the air to indicate that she should continue. 'Go on . . .'

'At the risk of inflating your already ridiculous ego? Whatever. Freddie trained as a hairdresser at college. He started renting a seat in a salon two weeks ago. I'll let you show off – how did you know that?'

'His dominant hand is his right, yes? He has cuts on the middle finger of his left. That's often the case for hairdressers, particularly those who lack experience. The dexterity with a pair of scissors takes a little while to develop.' Atticus took a bite of his sandwich. 'I suspect that he also has some experience in amateur dramatics. He breathes from his diaphragm and often has his hands behind his back – actors do that to improve projection.'

'He likes musicals,' she said.

'Of course he does.'

'Do you think he's acting now?'

'No. Not when it comes to the broad strokes, in any event. I don't think anyone is going to doubt that the two of them had an interlude together.'

'An "*interlude*"?'

He grinned. 'The *looks* Freddie was giving Ralph.'

She couldn't help but smile. 'The pouts?'

Atticus pursed his lips and flashed a look at her from beneath lowered lashes. 'A lover spurned,' he said vampishly.

'You didn't have to interview him for two days.'

'One of the benefits of being told my services were no longer required.'

She looked up at him and wondered whether he was making a point.

'Relax,' he said. 'I'm just joking. I'm not bitter.'

'We never really spoke about it, did we?'

He held up his hands. 'What is there to say? I made a mistake; your husband grassed me up; they sacked me. There's nothing to speak about.'

She found that she had the need to explain to him. 'It wasn't my decision. What happened – between you and me . . . It wouldn't have made a difference to me being able to work with you.'

'It would have made a difference to me,' he said and, for a moment, the playful edge to his words was gone, replaced by an honesty and a wistfulness that was immediately disarming. He looked as if he was going to say something else, but then changed his mind. 'Look,' he said, 'it's all water under the bridge. You get to interview a hysterical queen, and I get to work for someone who might very well have murdered his entire family. All's well that ends well.'

His smile had returned, but Mack knew him well enough to know that he was forcing it.

'So you think he did do it?' she asked him.

'I think you have a circumstantial case with a lot of questions to answer, but if you're asking if he had the opportunity to do it, I think he did. He had the means, too.'

'And the motive?'

'The money, obviously. He stands to be a very wealthy man.'

'But . . .?'

He paused.

She almost didn't want him to answer, but couldn't resist it. 'Atticus?'

'The defence has raised some interesting issues. I think Cameron's problem with anger could be relevant. He makes a reasonably persuasive suspect. I can see why you might have been drawn to him. It would certainly have been convenient.'

'Convenient?'

'A murder-suicide would have been a lot easier to clear up than a case as controversial as this one.'

'But Cameron *didn't* do it.'

Atticus shrugged. 'So you say.'

'And if it wasn't Cameron,' she went on, 'it has to be Ralph.'

'Not a third party?'

'There's no evidence of that at all.'

'I'm not sure. I read through all of the police notes. It didn't look like anything was taken, apart from the two handguns from the gun safe – we know where one of those is, but not the other – and Cassandra's crucifix. The relatives said that she never took that off, yet it wasn't around her neck when she was found.'

'True. The pistols can be explained – we know where one of them ended up, and the other is probably where Ralph—'

'Or Cameron.'

'—stashed it.'

'The crucifix?'

'We don't know. But it's small and would be easy enough to lose. The cleaner couldn't say for sure whether Cassandra was wearing it that afternoon. Maybe she'd lost it.'

'I don't like maybes,' Atticus said. He clicked his tongue against his teeth. 'What about the figure at the window?'

'Lennox was wrong.'

'What if he wasn't? It couldn't have been Hugo or Juliet – they would have raised the alarm rather than pacing around the bathroom. How about Cassandra?'

'The pistol was nowhere near her,' she said. 'And what did you mean when you mentioned her this morning?'

'I can't say now. But I promise to give you warning if it turns into anything.'

'But if it's not a third party, or Cassandra, or Ralph, or the parents ...' She paused. 'If it's not them, then we're left with Cameron.'

'As Ralph would like you to believe.'

'Go on, then. You tell me. What happened?'

'Here's one possibility,' he said, leaning back. 'Cameron takes his father's pistols from the safe and shoots him in the kitchen.'

'The others don't hear anything?'

'They were watching *Die Hard*. If the TV was loud, they might not have realised what was happening.'

She nodded. 'Go on.'

'He goes to the sitting room and shoots his mother and sister. They're both killed outright. His father is not fatally wounded and tries to call for help. Cameron finds him, but the pistol misfires when he tries to finish him off. The two men struggle – there would've been no opportunity for Hugo to fight if the gun had been working correctly. In desperation, Cameron uses the pistol to bludgeon his father to death. At some time shortly thereafter, he hears Ralph at the door and hurries upstairs.'

'Why? Why not just shoot himself there and then?'

'Because the pistol is jammed. He's confused – perhaps the gravity of what he has just done has overcome him. He goes upstairs in a panic to try to unjam it. I've seen the ballistics report – there are scratch marks inside the action. I would say it is arguable that he went to find something that he could use to remove a round that had become stuck in the chamber. If it had been my investigation—'

'Which it wasn't.'

'—then I would've looked for tweezers that might have matched the scratch marks.'

'We didn't find anything like that,' she said.

Atticus shrugged that off. She didn't press, because she knew what he would say: just because you didn't find them doesn't mean that they weren't there.

'Ralph sees his father. He can't get inside and calls 999. Cameron is still upstairs when Lennox arrives. The window where Lennox thought he saw movement is the bathroom window – perhaps that's where he found the tweezers. He knows that he needs to finish what he started, so he goes back downstairs to his mother and sister, sits down, and uses his freshly unjammed pistol to shoot himself.'

She shook her head. 'No one heard a shot. Lennox and the uniform were there. Ralph, too.'

'I agree,' he said. 'That's the main problem with the defence. But shots can be muffled. They can be missed. It's not impossible.'

'I don't buy it,' she said.

'All right,' Atticus said. 'Fine. You say it was Ralph – what about the lack of forensic evidence on his clothes?'

'He wore something to prevent contamination.'

'No gunshot residue on his hands.'

She took a bite of her sandwich and gestured with the half that remained. 'Gloves.'

'So he disposed of everything between killing them and calling 999? The timeline is already tight.'

'You've spoken to him. He's cunning. That wouldn't have been beyond him.'

'Where?'

'I don't know. He buried it all in the forest.'

'Find anything like that?'

'You know we didn't,' she said.

'It has to be somewhere.'

'It doesn't matter. There was no residue on Cameron's hands, either. And there were no marks or injuries on his body that would have indicated a fight with his father.'

'That's easy enough,' Atticus retorted. 'Hugo had already been shot. He was on his last legs. Couple of bangs on the head and it's all over.'

'A couple of bangs on the head? You saw the blood in that room.'

He shrugged and took another bite of his sandwich.

Mack found that she was enjoying the banter even as Atticus picked at her evidence. 'Got anything else?' she said.

He swallowed. 'I could do this for days. How did Ralph get into and out of a locked house?'

'The coal hole.'

Atticus raised his hands and held them a short distance apart. 'It's narrow. Would he fit?'

'He hasn't *said* that he wouldn't.'

'A mistake,' Atticus suggested. 'I think it would be a tight squeeze. He might not.'

'You'll have to account for the pistol if you're going to prove that it was Cameron,' she said. 'We found it too far away from his body.'

'How careful were the CSIs with the evidence?'

'Come on,' she protested. 'You're not seriously suggesting that they moved it? You're reaching.'

'Yes, but I'd still raise the possibility in evidence. You remember the Baxter murder? The CSI who knocked over the table with the knife on it?'

'Only too well.'

'So it *does* happen.'

'Only this time it didn't.'

'Go on, then,' he replied with a smile. 'Your turn. What happened?'

She nodded and, looking him right in the eye, laid out the prosecution's case with a little extemporising for added colour.

'Ralph goes back to the house after the argument. His father lets him in. He pulls the gun and shoots him, then goes through to the sitting room and shoots his brother, sister and mother. Hugo is still alive. The gun jams when Ralph tries to shoot him. Ralph uses the gun to bludgeon him to death. He puts the gun on the floor near to Cameron and locks the door from the inside.'

'He doesn't put the gun in Cameron's hand? Or in his lap?'

'He makes a mistake.'

'Now *you're* grasping.'

She ignored that. 'He takes off whatever it was that he was wearing to reduce the chance that he picks up any forensic evidence. Maybe he has a shower to make sure he's clean – the shower tray was damp when we got there. He goes into the cellar to the coal hole, pushes the cover off and climbs out. He hides the gloves and the clothes somewhere and calls the police.'

'It's all circumstantial,' Atticus said. 'Lots of evidence that suggests it could be him, nothing determinative.'

'We've got Lamza,' she said.

'You do. And we'll see how he holds up this afternoon. I suspect the case will be decided by the time we are adjourned for the weekend. Anyway – thanks.'

'For what?'

'For the conversation. It's good to have at least one friendly face in CID. Everyone else hates me.'

She was about to respond when she saw that he was joking. The flippant mask was back, put aside for just a moment before he put it on again. Mack knew that Atticus didn't like to show weakness, and that he covered up his vulnerability with self-deprecation and sarcasm. It had taken weeks for him to put that aside for her, even when she told him that she could see through the façade. She had told him that he didn't have to pretend to be someone else for her, and that she preferred the authentic Atticus to the face that he showed to the world. She had wondered if she would ever see that vulnerable side again and, now that she had, she was reminded how attractive she found it.

A bus rumbled to a stop at the red light above them. The signage on the side of the vehicle was visible from where they were sitting: it was an advertisement for the film that Andy wanted to see. Mack felt a flash of guilt that she had spent lunch with Atticus, and decided it was time to bring it to an end.

'We'd better go back separately,' she said. 'Wouldn't want people talking.'

She took another bite of her sandwich and dropped the rest into the bin.

'That was fun,' he said. 'Hashing out a case together. Just like old times.'

He gave her a wink, wished her good luck for the afternoon's session, and set off for the subway. Mack watched him go, gave him a minute to start up the road, and then followed.

47

Atticus watched Freddie Lamza carefully as he made his way back to the witness box. He had been surprised by his appearance when he gave his evidence in the morning session. He looked nothing like his mugshot from the solicitation conviction or his appearance in the BBC documentary that he had watched on YouTube. His clothes were obviously not cheap: the suit looked new, and, given the way it fitted, was likely bespoke; the white shirt looked new, too. His hair had been styled and his skin was fresh and clear. He had been dressed cheaply before; his hair had looked dirty and unkempt, and his skin had looked greasy and unhealthy, scattered with acne.

Abernathy guided Lamza through the rest of his evidence, eventually settling on the subject of the things that Lamza claimed Ralph had told him about his family. Lamza testified that Ralph had made regular comments about how rich the family was, about how much land the farm had and how profitable it had been for such a long time. The farmhouse, he reported, was worth in excess of a million pounds, and there was a large estate both around it and in the fields nearby. Ralph had said that he would inherit it one day and that he couldn't wait for that day to come.

Abernathy gently guided the evidence along, moving Lamza to the central thrust of the case against Ralph.

'Mr Lamza,' he said, 'I would like to take you back to the conversation that you had with the defendant in your flat in London in October of last year. Would you tell the court what you say the defendant said to you?'

'He said that he wanted them all dead.'

The nature of the allegation was well known from the newspaper reporting of the case, but, even so, the suggestion provoked a flutter of excitement and consternation in the public gallery. The reporters leaned forward a little, their pens poised over their notepads. Lamza noticed that he had a rapt audience and played up to it, preening a little and putting his chin out.

'He told you that, Mr Lamza?'

'He did.'

'Can you remember exactly what he said?'

'That he hated them all and that he couldn't wait until they were dead. I told him that was a horrible thing to say – I think I told him it was callous – and he just laughed. He said that he had been thinking about it for months and that he was tempted to take matters into his own hands.'

'Really?'

Lamza nodded.

'What else did he say?'

'He said he'd be doing them all a favour. "Putting them out of their misery." He said his mother had been miserable all her life, his father was a bully and deserved everything he got, his brother was an idiot, and his sister was a slut.'

'*Liar!*'

Atticus turned to the dock. Ralph was on his feet. The urbane, arrogant sheen was gone, and in its place was seething, livid anger.

'Mr Mallender,' the judge said sternly, 'please sit down.'

'He's a bloody *liar!*'

'I won't tolerate outbursts in my courtroom. Mr Crow – I suggest you explain to your client why it is in his best interests to regain his seat.'

Crow waved for Ralph to take his seat again. Atticus turned back to Lamza just in time to notice something that immediately snagged his attention: Lamza was looking at someone in the public gallery with an expression on his face that Atticus could only describe as jubilant. The journalists there were scribbling notes frantically, aware that the defendant's outburst had added an element of sensationalism to the copy they would file as soon as the day was done. The person at whom Lamza was looking was to Atticus's right, and, from that angle, it was impossible to identify him or her.

Ralph had slumped back into his seat in the dock, the security guard who was with him now standing a little closer.

'Please,' Somerville said. 'Mr Abernathy – please, continue.'

Lamza went through the rest of his evidence without further interruption from Ralph. Abernathy anticipated the questions that would be asked during cross-examination, specifically why Lamza hadn't reported the threats to the police at the time that they were made. Lamza said that he hadn't taken them seriously, and it was only when he had seen the news on Christmas Day that he had remembered what had been said and what, with hindsight, it might mean. Lamza was melodramatic, occasionally choking up and wiping away the tears that gathered in his eyes.

Atticus watched him carefully, looking for body language that might betray a lie. He was good, but there were subtle signs that indicated, at the very least, that he was exaggerating. Abernathy's direct suggestion that he was lying was met by Lamza leaning away from him, a signal of discomfort that was difficult to mask. Other questions were accompanied by little touches to the neck and mouth, pacifying gestures that suggested that the enquiries had upset his equilibrium. There was nothing that suggested an obvious lie, but enough that Atticus was sure that Lamza wasn't being completely honest.

Lamza concluded by saying that he knew that Ralph would characterise his evidence as the revenge of a lover spurned; Atticus had to stop himself from rolling his eyes as Lamza said that he expected that, that he would never do such a thing, how he blamed himself for not speaking out sooner and that all he wanted to do now was to 'get justice for that poor family'.

Abernathy concluded his examination and sat down.

'We'll adjourn for today,' Somerville said. 'Mr Lamza's cross-examination will start first thing on Monday morning. Mr Lamza, please do not discuss the case with anyone in the meantime.'

'I won't, sir.'

The judge turned his iron gaze onto Ralph. 'I hope we can use the weekend to consider how we should conduct ourselves and then continue without any of the interruptions that we've seen this afternoon.'

Somerville rose and made his way to his chambers.

Atticus got up and, without waiting for the other people on the row to stand, he stepped over their legs and hurried to the exit.

48

Atticus was one of the first to leave the building. He waited outside as the court emptied. There was a private door that was reserved for court officials and witnesses who did not want to run into the families of those men and women against whom they had just testified. Atticus knew that Lamza was most likely to use that exit, and, with that in mind, he made his way to a bench where he could see both ways out.

He sat down and waited.

Allegra left through the main entrance, heading towards the car park at Waitrose. She looked tense, as well she might; today had been a bad day for her husband's prospects. Cadogan followed soon after, and then Abernathy and the CPS solicitor. Atticus looked at his watch, worrying that he had been too slow, but then, as he was wondering whether he had missed his chance, he saw Lamza come out of the exit. He was impossible to miss: medium-sized, slender, his bouffant hair bouncing as he walked.

Atticus gave him a short head start and then, making sure that he wasn't observed, he followed. Lamza turned onto Wilton Road and then Fisherton Street. Atticus had already guessed where he was going: the CPS typically used the Red Lion on Milford Street to accommodate witnesses who were required to give evidence for more than a single day. It was a pleasant hotel with a bar and restaurant on the ground floor and then two further floors that were given over to bedrooms. Lamza looked down at a piece of paper that he held in his hand – Atticus assumed that he was checking that he had found the right place – and then crossed the street and went into the sheltered courtyard that offered access to the main part of the half-timbered building.

The bar and restaurant were next to the desk, and Atticus took a table close enough to hear the conversation between Lamza and the receptionist. The woman asked him for his name and address, confirmed that a room had been reserved for him, and printed a key card. She said that he was in room 203 – on the second floor, next to the stairs – and hoped that he had a pleasant stay.

Lamza thanked her and made his way to the stairs.

Atticus waited.

* * *

The restaurant was quiet save for the conversation between the receptionist and another member of staff who, Atticus quickly gathered, was replacing her as the shifts changed. Atticus went up to the bar to order a pint. He took it back to the table and sat down at a chair that allowed him to watch the restaurant and the flight of stairs that led up to the bedrooms.

He didn't have long to wait.

Lamza came down the stairs just after five. Atticus was ready to follow him into the city, but Lamza didn't head out; instead, he took one of the other empty tables and went to the bar to order a drink. Atticus watched him. He had changed his clothes and, judging by hair that looked a little damp, he had taken a shower.

Lamza took a gin and tonic back to the table. He sat down and tapped out a message on his phone. Atticus finished his pint and went to order another and a plate of fish and chips from the bar. He went back to the table and sat down so that he was facing away from Lamza. He could still see his table by looking into the mirror that was hung above the room's large inglenook fireplace.

Atticus's food had just been delivered when a man came into the bar. He waited in the doorway for a moment, said something to the new receptionist and then, looking into the restaurant, saw Lamza and made his way over to him. Lamza stood and shook the newcomer's hand; the two men shared pleasantries and the newcomer offered to buy Lamza another gin. Lamza thanked him and the man went to the bar.

Atticus glanced up at the mirror. The second man's face was visible, and Atticus had seen him before.

The man returned with the drinks and sat down.

'So?' Lamza said.

'So what?'

'So how was I?'

'You were great,' he said. 'Really great, Freddie.'

'That reaction from Ralph . . .'

The man chuckled. 'I know. He didn't do himself any favours.'

'And for you?'

'What do you mean?'

'The story – him losing his shit like that. It must've helped?'

Atticus watched in the mirror as the second man winced. He looked up and, for a moment, he stared into the mirror and at Atticus. The man turned his attention back to Lamza and said something in a quiet voice that Atticus couldn't hear. Lamza started to protest, the man said something again – Atticus detected a note of reproach – and then both of them stood up. Atticus pretended to concentrate on his food, but he saw Lamza put on his jacket and heard the sound of footsteps as the two of them crossed the room to the door. Atticus saw them pass before the window, and then they were gone.

Atticus realised where he had seen the man before.

It was Steve Hawkins, one of the reporters who had followed Allegra on the first day of the trial.

49

Atticus finished his meal, sank the rest of his pint and went to the desk. The receptionist was in the room behind the desk. Her back was turned. Atticus looked down at the desk and saw a plastic tray, about the size of an A4 sheet of paper. The tray was evidently used to store the forms filled out by guests when they checked into the hotel. Atticus took his phone, switched to the camera, and, with a quick lean across the desk, snapped a three-shot burst of the form at the top of the tray.

He put his phone away and cleared his throat.

The receptionist turned. 'I'm sorry, sir. Can I help you?'

'I can't find my room key,' he said. 'I went out and it must have slipped out of my pocket. Would it be possible to have a replacement?'

'Of course, sir. What room are you in?'

'It's 203,' he said.

'Room 2-0-3,' the woman recited, tapping on the keyboard. 'And the name, sir?'

'Lamza. Freddie Lamza.'

* * *

Atticus took the stairs to the second floor and found room 203. The hotel was quiet, and, as he waited and listened, he couldn't hear anything that made him worry that he might be noticed. He took the replacement key card from his pocket and held it over the reader. The lock buzzed and the door opened. He pushed it with his fingertips and, after satisfying himself for a second time that there was no one inside, he stepped into the room.

Freddie had dumped his suitcase on the bed and left it splayed open. There was a damp towel on the floor, and a pile of clothes, still neatly folded, had been placed on the bed next to the case. Atticus went over to it and looked through it. There was nothing of interest. He had wondered whether Freddie might have brought a laptop or a tablet that might have proven useful, but he had not. The case contained a wash bag, fresh underwear and a pair of shoes. Atticus checked the clothes, but there was nothing in any of the pockets.

He wasn't disappointed. He knew that this was a long shot, and that it was always likely that he would have to work a little harder to excavate anything that might be helpful in discrediting Freddie.

He wasn't ready to give up yet.

He left everything exactly as he had found it and made his way back to the door. He opened it a crack, listened until he was sure that there was no one outside, and then left the room.

*　*　*

Atticus went back down to the bar and ordered another pint. He took it to the snug and sat down next to the fireplace.

There was an armchair there and, after he turned it a little, he was able to see everyone who came in through the hotel entrance.

He took out his phone and looked at the pictures that he had taken. Freddie Lamza was booked in for four nights: Friday, Saturday, Sunday and Monday. His address, telephone number and email were all recorded, too. Atticus was pleased. The details would all be helpful.

He sipped his pint and waited.

*　*　*

Freddie Lamza was on his own when he returned to the hotel. Atticus got up quickly and intercepted him before he could continue up to his room.

'Hello,' he said.

Lamza paused and smiled uncertainly. 'Hello?'

'Freddie?'

'That's right.'

'I'm sorry for disturbing you – but you were *excellent* today.'

'I'm sorry – do we know each other?'

'We don't,' Atticus said. 'My name's John Nicholls.'

Atticus knew that what he was doing was dangerous. He was an agent of the defence and he was prepared to lie to a witness in an attempt to get inside information. Should the judge find out, then he might very well decide to discharge the jury mid-trial and lock Atticus up for his temerity.

But the trial was pressing on, Ralph was looking at life behind bars, and Atticus had to do *something*. You had to break an egg or two, he noted to himself grimly, if you wanted to make an omelette.

Lamza kept his eyes on Atticus and, after a moment, a smile cracked the corner of his mouth. 'You were sitting in the gallery.'

'That's right. All four days.'

'I saw you. I remember.'

'Well, like I said, you were excellent. Very convincing.'

'Convincing? You think so?'

'Well, *I* believed you.'

'Good,' he said. 'That's because it's true.'

Atticus detected just the faintest trace of indignation. 'I don't doubt it for a minute.' He pointed over to the bar. 'Buy you a drink?'

Atticus noticed the flick of his glance as Lamza looked from his eyes to his lips and back again. 'I suppose one wouldn't hurt,' he said. 'Thank you.'

Atticus went to the bar and ordered two pints. He turned back as he waited for the barman to pour them. Lamza was looking at his phone, his finger sliding up and down the screen. He was slouched in his chair, and Atticus wondered if he might already be a little drunk. He imagined that he might have gone out for dinner with Hawkins, and that, perhaps, there had been alcohol involved. That would make the conversation he was planning much easier.

He took the drinks back to the table and set them down.

'Cheers,' Atticus said, holding up one of the pints.

Lamza took the other and touched glasses. 'Cheers.'

Atticus noticed his fingers. They were long and slender, and the nails bore the unmistakable signs of having been recently manicured. He remembered the close-up shot of a phone pressed to Freddie's ear in the BBC documentary; his fingernails then had been cracked and dirty, very different to how they were now. The cuts on the middle finger of his left hand were healing, but still noticeable.

The clothes, the clear skin, the manicure.

All the evidence pointed towards it: Freddie had recently come into a sum of money. Could his new career have been that lucrative? It seemed very unlikely.

'You're staying here tonight?'

'All weekend, actually. The CPS are paying. I'm being cross-examined on Monday.'

'You're not going home for the weekend?'

'I've got friends in the New Forest. I'm going to see them. Are you here tonight, too?'

Atticus shook his head. 'I'm on the last train back to London.'

Lamza sipped his pint. 'What do you do?'

'I'm a journalist. I'm writing about the trial.'

'Who for?'

'Freelance.'

Lamza shuffled a little uncomfortably. 'I'm not supposed to talk to reporters,' he said. 'The judge . . . you heard what he said.'

Atticus winked. 'I won't tell if you don't.'

Lamza drank off half of the pint and stood the glass back down on the table.

'Looks like you need that,' Atticus offered.

'I do. *Long* day.'

'Nervous?'

Lamza exhaled. 'A bit. They said it'll be harder. I only got here today – what's the defence brief like? I haven't seen him yet. What's his name?'

'Christopher Crow. He's not as aggressive as Abernathy, but he's no pushover, either. He'll say you're lying. That Mallender didn't say the things you're saying.'

'I know *that*,' he said. 'He can say what he wants. I know what happened. It's my word against Ralph's.'

'His reaction today won't have helped him.'

'I *know*,' Lamza said, grinning. 'I couldn't believe that. The way the judge shut him down.' He laughed. 'Oh my God. That was *hilarious*.'

Atticus saw movement behind Lamza and noticed Hugo Mallender's brother and his wife making their way over to the reception. It looked as if they were staying here, too.

Lamza was too self-absorbed to notice. 'Be honest,' he said. 'You were watching – I was all right?'

'You were good,' Atticus said.

'Really?'

'I was watching the jury.'

'And? You think they believed me?'

'Definitely.'

Atticus watched him carefully as he spoke. Why was Lamza so keen for praise? In his experience, most witnesses didn't concern themselves with that. They took the stand, told their story, and were done with it; it was an ordeal that they were glad to have behind them. But Lamza seemed anxious about how he had been received. It might have been because he was an egoist – that much was obvious – but it might have been something else; Atticus started to wonder whether Lamza was looking for confirmation that he was credible because he knew that his story was false.

Atticus took a sip of his own pint. 'Have you given evidence before?'

'No,' Lamza said.

'Did you go to the police?'

'I did. And I had to work hard to persuade them that I was telling the truth.'

'Who did you speak to?'

'DCI Jones,' he said. 'I don't think she likes me very much.'

'If you help her win the case, you'll be her best friend for life.'

'Honestly? I just want it to be over. I've been asking myself why I'd put myself through this.'

Atticus didn't buy that for a moment. He could see that Lamza was fishing for sympathy.

'Why did you, then?' he said. 'Put yourself through it?'

'Because it's the right thing to do. Ralph's a dangerous man. What he did? To his family? It's *evil*. I wouldn't have been able to live with myself if I'd kept what he said to myself.'

'I agree,' Atticus said. He chose his words carefully. 'Look, Freddie, I was wondering – my story's already good, but it would be even better if I could get you on the record.'

Lamza shook his head, but there was a smile playing on his lips. 'Is that what this is about?' He pointed at the almost-empty glass on the table. 'Trying to get me drunk?'

'Not at all. But if you did happen to be interested in earning some money, I'm pretty sure I could pre-sell your story to a national. They'd pay well to get an interview with you. Probably very well.'

'I can't.'

'Don't dismiss it out of hand. For something like this, you'd be looking at a minimum of fifty thousand.'

'*Really.* I can't.'

'Why?'

Lamza paused, biting his lip, obviously wondering if he should say anything else.

His reaction was all the confirmation that Atticus needed. 'You've already sold it.'

'I can't talk about it,' he said, but his body language said plainly that Atticus was right.

'I understand,' Atticus said, showing Lamza the palms of his hands. 'No judgement here. I don't blame you at all. I'm just annoyed someone else got to you first.'

Lamza finished the pint and looked at his watch. 'Actually, I think that'll do it for me. I'm going to call it a night. My friends have got a dog – we're going to walk in the forest tomorrow. Don't want to do that with a hangover.'

Atticus stood. 'Nice to meet you, Freddie,' he said. 'Good luck on Monday.'

'You going to come and watch?'

Atticus put out his hand and Freddie shook it.

'Wouldn't miss it for the world,' he said.

50

Atticus allowed himself the luxury of a lie-in the next day and eventually got out of bed at nine in the morning. Bandit was in the other room, standing on the sofa with his paws on the back so that he could look out of the wide bay windows and into the street outside. Atticus took his pills, changed into fresh clothes, pulled on his boots and clipped the dog's lead to his collar. Jacob had exercised Bandit during the week, but Atticus had not been able to spend as much time with him as usual. He missed that – he always had his best thoughts when he was walking – and determined to put it right this morning.

'Ready for a walk, boy?' he said.

Bandit bounded around him excitedly.

'Me too.'

*   *   *

They set off for Old Sarum, a two-mile walk to the north. They reached the site of the old settlement fifty minutes later and, once they were safely away from the road, Atticus unhooked the lead and let Bandit run free. The dog rushed away, bounding through the fields in pursuit of two other dogs who were chasing each other up and down the slope.

Atticus gave thought to the events of the past week. He found himself considering his thoughts about Ralph and decided that he was still uncertain about the question of his guilt or innocence. His client was not a particularly pleasant man, but that was irrelevant. Atticus was only interested in the facts and the inferences that could be drawn from them. Mack had overseen a reasonable case, and there was enough evidence for it to be brought to trial. The defence had still to present its case, but, as it stood at near the halfway point of the trial, it didn't look good. He had been watching the members of the jury during the presentation of the prosecution evidence and, if he had been forced to guess, he would have said that the odds of a conviction were much higher than an acquittal. He wondered how high and settled on eighty-twenty in favour of a guilty verdict, maybe worse.

On the other hand, the Crown's evidence was circumstantial, and Atticus knew that he only had to find a couple of weaknesses to improve Ralph's chances. If he could do that – if he could introduce enough doubt – then Ralph would be acquitted.

He tried not to dwell on how Mack would react to that.

His phone rang.

'Hello?'

'It's Allegra Mallender.' She didn't sound pleased.

'Hello, Allegra.'

'I was looking for you last night after court.'

'I had a couple of things I needed to do.'

'About the trial?'

'Of course.'

'Well? What were they?'

'I'm looking into Freddie Lamza.'

Her voice tightened. 'He really had fun yesterday, didn't he?'

'He did seem to enjoy the attention.'

'Poisonous little *queen*. What are you doing about him?'

Atticus had a plan, but it was not one that he was prepared to share with her for a number of reasons. 'I'm going to look into his character. If we can show that he's unreliable, maybe we can discredit him.'

'He's a *prostitute*, Atticus. He's the definition of discreditable.'

'*Used* to be a prostitute,' he said. 'He's a hairdresser now.'

'What? *Please*.'

'I know,' he said, pacifying her. 'His history is useful. There's scope to make him look unreliable. I'll let you know if I get anything useful.'

The line was silent.

Atticus wondered if she had been cut off. 'Allegra? You still there?'

'I need you to do better,' she said. 'You've been on this all week and you haven't found anything useful yet.'

Her tone was harsh. It was the first time that Atticus had heard recrimination from her. It was to be expected, he supposed: the week would have been an ordeal; her husband's future looked bleak; she was desperate.

'I'm working hard, Allegra. I've got several lines of enquiry.'

'You keep saying that,' she said, 'but I don't see any results. I haven't seen *anything*.'

'You came to me the day before the trial,' he said. 'You didn't give me very long.'

'Come *on*,' she snapped. 'Don't use that as an excuse. You were happy enough to take my money. I want something in return for that. Something that will help Ralph. Cadogan told me this was a stupid idea. He said you wouldn't be able to help. Maybe he was right.'

Atticus stopped walking and took a breath. 'I'm happy to stop if that's what you want,' he said. 'I can bill you for the time I've spent and close the file. It's up to you.'

Bandit trotted over with a tennis ball in his mouth.

There was another pause, this time punctuated by a long sigh.

'No,' she said wearily. 'No. I'm sorry. I shouldn't take it out on you. I'm just ... it's just that it feels like I'm in a tunnel and there's no light at the end of it. Nothing. I've tried everything – you're our last chance.'

'I can't begin to understand what this might feel like for you. For Ralph, too.'

Atticus wasn't good with empathy. His instinctive response would have been to tell her that he couldn't pretend to understand what the ordeal must feel like, that he couldn't pretend to care, but that it wouldn't make a difference in what he did for her and Ralph, but he had learned enough about what was expected of people in situations like this to offer something else instead.

Bandit dropped the ball and looked up at Atticus with hopeful eyes. There was another pause before Allegra spoke again.

'You've heard most of the evidence. And you've read the file.'

He held his breath; he knew what was coming next.

'Be honest – do you think he did it?'

Atticus took a beat. 'No,' he said, putting as much confidence into his voice as he could. 'I don't.'

'It's so good to hear that,' she said.

'The case has not been proven. The evidence is flimsy. But I don't know if the jury will feel the same way. I'm trying to find something that will make them share my opinion. I'm going to be doing that this weekend and all of next week. Okay?'

'Thank you, Atticus,' she said. 'Call me if you find anything.'

'I will.'

He ended the call and put his phone away.

Bandit lowered his snout and pushed the ball against Atticus's foot.

'Where did you find that, you little thief?'

Atticus stooped down to collect the ball. Bandit enthusiastically wagged his tail.

Atticus launched the ball as far as he could and watched as the dog hared after it. There was no rush to get going. He was going to be busy, but not until much later tonight. He could put off what he was proposing to do until then.

51

Atticus spent the rest of the day working on the files, but found nothing of use. He took a break at lunchtime to see whether Jack_of_Hearts had played his or her next move in their current game. He or she had pushed his pawn out to e5 and had left a comment.

> *The Alekhine Defence, unless I am very much mistaken.*
> *I look forward to testing it.*

Atticus fetched his chess books and turned to the pages that were dedicated to an analysis of Bobby Fischer's games against Boris Spassky in '72. Fischer had famously abandoned the Sicilian Defence for the Alekhine, deploying it twice against Spassky in what had evidently been an unpleasant surprise for the Russian. Spassky had not analysed the variations for white because Fischer had always played the Sicilian, and, caught unawares, he made mistakes. Atticus spent twenty minutes reviewing those games. Fischer's gambit had led to him seizing the initiative and snatching a pawn. Spassky had been wary of the position that he would be forced to take if he sought to retake the pawn and had abandoned it, choosing to make a kingside attack instead.

Atticus reset the board on the table and adjusted it to show the three moves that had been played so far: white's opening move of pawn to e4, black's knight to f6 and white's pawn to e5. He looked down at the board. White was playing the four-pawn attack, trying to control the centre while chasing black's knight. Atticus picked up the knight and patted it against his hand as he decided what to play. He moved the knight to d5, aiming to persuade white to overextend his centre. He was happy with the move, replicated it on the computer, hit the button to confirm it, and typed out a reply.

> *Fischer overcomplicated the end game against Spassky.*
> *I won't make that mistake.*

He posted the comment and logged out.

□ □ □

Atticus ate an early dinner at McDonald's and then visited the DIY section of Poundstretcher in the High Street to pick up the things that he was going to need for the evening: a pair of thin fabric gloves, a roofing hammer, a crowbar, a centre hole punch and electrical tape. He paid for the things, bagged them up and then went to the tailor's shop on New Street and bought a plain black hoodie and a ball cap with NYC on the front. He went back to finish his preparation. He dressed in black – black jeans, black boots, the black hoodie and a black jacket – and made sure that Bandit was fed and watered.

He collected the additional things that he thought he might need. He took out his lock picks and a Maglite and put them into a small rucksack with the items that he had purchased earlier. He added the book on forensic toxicology that he had started to read the night before and zipped the bag closed.

He scrubbed Bandit behind the ears. 'Wish me luck,' he said. 'See you in the morning.'

Atticus made his way down the stairs and into the passage-way. It was cold, with a mist of light rain hanging in the air. He pulled the cap onto his head, pulled up the hood of the hoodie and started the walk to the station.

The last train from Salisbury to London was the 22.26. Atticus bought a ticket from the machine and boarded. It was almost empty, and he was sharing the carriage with just one other person. He sat down, put the rucksack on the seat next to him and took out his book.

52

It was a slow train, stopping at all the stations along the way, and it was twenty past midnight on Sunday morning by the time it finally pulled into Waterloo. The station was quiet, with small clutches of travellers looking for their last trains back to the suburbs after a night out in the city.

Atticus was hungry and joined the end of the queue in the station's branch of Burger King, taking his meal up to the second-floor seating area. He took out his phone and checked the details on the hotel booking form. Freddie Lamza had listed his address as Sapperton Court in Gee Street, Clerkenwell. Atticus wasn't in any hurry and, indeed, preferred to wait a little before making his way there. He took out his phone and logged into his account at Chess.com. Jack_of_Hearts had made a third move, responding to black's knight to d5 by pushing a pawn to d4.

There was another comment.

> *Spassky was taken by surprise. I'm wise to you.*

Atticus opened the greaseproof wrapper and started on his burger while he analysed the board. He pushed up his pawn to d6 and played the move. He left his own comment.

> *Let me guess? Kingside attack? I'll be waiting.*

He finished the last of the fries, drained his drink and disposed of the rubbish in the bin. He checked the time on his phone. It was one in the morning. He had waited long enough. Time to go.

He went down into the underground, followed the directions to the Northern Line and waited for a train.

*   *   *

Atticus took the Northern Line to Old Street, disembarked and made his way up to the surface. Gee Street was a fifteen-minute walk and he arrived there as the clock was coming around to half past one.

Sapperton Court was ex-Local Authority housing stock. It was twelve storeys high, with external passageways that accessed the front doors of the flats on each floor. It had clearly been renovated prior to the flats being sold, and was still in good condition, although the final letter of the art deco-styled COURT had come loose and fallen off. The communal space outside the entrance was neat and tidy, too. The buildings that faced the block were newer, a mixture of newbuilds and extensively remodelled warehouses that were characteristic of the area. There were offices on the ground floor, and the cars that were parked outside them were expensive. It was a typical London street: the rich and poor living cheek by jowl.

Atticus waited outside the building for ten minutes, sheltering from the rain beneath the overhanging ledge of the office at number 47. The street was close to the main road, and, despite the hour, there was still a decent amount of traffic passing along it. He looked up at the building, noting that some of the windows were still lit. He took out his phone and shuffled through to the photograph of the check-in form. Lamza had given his address as flat twelve; that looked as if it would be on the fourth floor. There was no light in any of the flats on the fourth floor.

The main entrance looked as if it led into a lobby, and Atticus guessed he would find the stairs and lifts there. He saw a man staggering towards the building along the other side of the road. The man was wearing a suit with his tie loosely fastened around his neck. It was obvious that he had spent his Saturday evening out drinking and was now rather the worse for wear. Atticus put his phone back into his pocket and looked left and right: there was no one else on the street. He crossed the road and walked casually to the building.

The man stopped, tapping a code on the keypad and grumbling when the door did not unlock. Atticus dawdled behind him, but the man was too drunk to notice. He finally managed to key in the code. The door opened and the man pushed it back and went inside.

Atticus moved quickly. He jammed his cap down so that the brim covered as much of his face as possible, and draped the hood of his hoodie over the top of it. He jogged ahead and intercepted the door before it closed and locked again. The drunk was halfway up the first flight of stairs and hadn't seen him come inside. Atticus waited on the ground floor, pretending to do up a shoelace in the event that someone else might come in. He heard the sound of the man struggling with another lock on the first floor and waited for him to open the door and then go through into his flat. Atticus heard the door close.

There was a security camera above him. Making sure that he kept his head down, shielding his face with the hood and the cap, he went up the stairs himself. There were numbers on each landing indicating the flats that were on each floor; his guess had been correct, with flat twelve on the fourth floor. He reached the landing, paused to listen carefully once again, and then pushed open the fire door that opened out onto the corridor.

He took the rucksack from his shoulder and took out the fabric gloves. He put them on and then took out the leather pouch with his lock-picking set. He took a moment to listen for movement, heard none, and knelt down to address the door. It was secured by a simple pin tumbler lock. Atticus slid the tension wrench into the bottom of the keyhole and pulled down, applying very slight pressure to the teeth inside. He inserted the rake in the top of the lock and, while maintaining the torque on the wrench, he scrubbed the pick backwards and forwards inside the keyhole. He arranged the pins in the correct position and turned the lock.

The door opened, the hinges squeaking a little.

Atticus went inside and shut the door behind him. The flat was quiet, save for the ticking of a clock in the kitchen and the creaking of a pipe somewhere below. He waited in the hallway, acclimatising himself to the sounds and atmosphere of the place:

he heard the sound of a siren passing by on the high street and footsteps in the flat above, a heavy tread that rattled a loose bathroom fitting.

He took out his Maglite, switched it on and started to investigate the flat. It was split over two levels and wasn't particularly generous: the first level offered access to two bedrooms and the bathroom; there was then a short flight of stairs up to a half-landing that, in turn, opened out onto the kitchen-diner. Atticus started here. Lamza had IKEA furniture: he recognised the same sofa and dining table that he had bought with Mack. There was a bookcase filled with books, and a flat-screen television had been fitted to the wall. He looked at the books; there were titles on meditation, on career change, and, next to that, an introduction to hairstyles through the ages. He dropped down to the next shelf and found a framed Diploma in Hairdressing from the College of North West London dated eight years previously.

He went to the breakfast bar and shone the light over a pile of documents. There was a stack of bank statements showing an account that was three thousand pounds overdrawn. Atticus shuffled through the pile and found a statement from Lamza's American Express card. Again, he had run up a lot of debt: more than six thousand pounds. He was obviously in financial difficulties.

Atticus arranged the statements on the bar and, with the Maglite held in his teeth and shining down, he took photographs of them one by one.

He went to the low coffee table in the centre of the room and saw a pile of holiday brochures. The holidays were high-end and expensive: the Maldives, Tenerife, St Lucia. Atticus flipped through the pages of glossy images of glamorous models in luxurious surroundings.

He took the stairs down to the hall and went into the first bedroom on the left-hand side. There was a neatly made bed with bedside tables on either side of it and a desk with two lights and a laptop. The desk also held a jam jar full of coloured pens, another with coloured pencils and a tidy with paper clips and erasers and a mug of cold coffee. Atticus automatically made a number of deductions: he assumed from the two desk lamps that Lamza was accustomed to working through the night, and confirmed what he already knew – that he was right-handed – by the fact that the mug of cold coffee was to the right of the laptop, with its handle pointing to the right.

Atticus tapped the keyboard to wake the screen; the computer was locked.

He went to the bedside table: he saw loose change, a packet of Marlboros and a lighter, a glass with an inch of water in it, and a copy of the latest Lee Child thriller. He pulled out a drawer and found a leather-bound notebook. He opened it: two yellow Post-it notes had been stuck to the first page. One of them looked interesting. Someone had written out a long combination of letters, numbers and symbols that looked similar to automatically generated passwords.

Atticus took the notebook to the desk, woke the screen on the laptop and, when he was prompted for the password, tapped out the string of characters.

He pressed enter and the screen unlocked.

Easy.

There was a chair behind the desk. Atticus sat down and took out the DataTraveler flash drive that he always carried in his bag. He fitted the drive with a USB-C adaptor and slid it into one of the MacBook's empty ports. He opened the email client that Lamza used, selected all the emails, and dragged them over to the drive to copy. He did the same for the files stored in the Documents folder and on the desktop. The computer reported that it would take twenty minutes to complete the operation.

Atticus was about to start to read the documents when he heard the sound of a muffled voice coming from the corridor outside the flat. He froze, listening, his stomach falling as he heard a key being pushed into the lock and the squeak of the hinge as the door opened.

53

Atticus looked at the laptop screen. The transfer of the files to the USB stick was not complete, with the bar showing a final third still to fill. He got up from the chair as quietly as he could, sliding it back into the position that he had found it in, and listened as Lamza walked into the kitchen. He was on the phone, speaking more than loudly enough for Atticus to be able to hear his side of the conversation.

'That's what I said. Salisbury. I *know*. Pretty, but so boring. I don't want to go back, but there's nothing I can do about it. I've got to finish giving the evidence.'

Atticus looked back to the screen and saw that the bar was edging to the right, still not quite all the way there.

Come on.

He turned away from the screen so that he could look around the bedroom more carefully. There was a free-standing cupboard, but it didn't look sturdy enough to bear his weight should he try to hide inside it. The bed was raised off the floor a little, just enough for him to slide underneath. That looked like it might be the best that he could do. Freddie was in the kitchen and would see him the moment he stepped outside the bedroom.

Atticus checked: not *quite* finished.

Come on.

Lamza was pacing, his feet noisy across the wooden floor.

'I was supposed to be staying with Matt and Helen this weekend. I *know*. We were going to go for a walk in the forest, country pub for Sunday dinner and all that shit, but she's ended up sick or something and they bailed. I came back this morning. I thought I might as well go into the salon and do a couple of hours' work.' He laughed at something the other person must have said. 'I know. It's not like I *need* the money, but it's better to keep appearances up. I don't want to make it too obvious. I'll probably end up investing some of it in the salon anyway, at least once I've had a little bit of fun. Did I tell you what I decided? Two weeks in the Maldives. Next month.'

The computer bleeped as the transfer completed; Freddie stopped talking. Atticus swiped the drive out of the port, closed the lid of the laptop, and hurried across the room to the bed. He dropped down to his belly and slid beneath it. It was a tight fit, with the wooden rails that supported the mattress pressing against his shoulder blades.

He heard footsteps.

'It's nothing,' Lamza said. 'I thought I heard something.'

Atticus slid further beneath the bed and turned his head so that he could look out from beneath it to the doorway. The angle was shallow, and all he could see were the bottom of Lamza's legs up to his knee. His legs were clad in black fishnet stockings and he was wearing a pair of red high-heeled shoes. It was incongruous, and it took Atticus a moment to process it.

'They had the drag karaoke,' Lamza said, answering a question that Atticus couldn't hear. 'Yeah – at the Two Brewers. Clapham. Danny was there. I *know* – Sum Ting Wong. It was hilarious. I mean, he looks like he put his make-up on while he was wearing a *blindfold*, but he can sing. Was a good night. I know – I'm pissed, and I'm supposed to be going back to Salisbury today so that I'm there for tomorrow. It's such a *drag*.' He tittered. 'Pardon the pun.'

Atticus realised he had left his phone on Lamza's desk, next to the computer. He couldn't see it from where he was hiding, but, as he patted his pocket, he knew he didn't have it.

Shit.

He held his breath. He watched Lamza approach the bed. He turned around and then lowered himself down, the mattress pressing on Atticus's shoulders a little harder as Lamza reached down with his hand to take off his left shoe and then his right. He dropped the shoes on the floor, and Atticus saw the red soles that said they were Louboutins. They looked new, too, with only mild scuffing to the underside. Atticus knew that Louboutins were expensive. Lamza wasn't shy about showing off his newly found affluence.

'I'd better go to bed now,' Lamza said. 'I need to sleep and I know I'm going to have a pig of a hangover. I'll speak to you when I get back. Love you. Kiss, kiss.'

Atticus heard the beep as the call was ended and closed his eyes in exasperation as Lamza flopped back on the bed, his feet kicking up into the air as he straightened out. He didn't know what he would do if Lamza saw the phone on the desk; the evidence that he had found would be admissible despite the fact that it had been obtained illegally, but the value of his discovery would not protect him from burglary charges. He was wondering whether he might be able to strike a bargain with Lamza when he got up, yawned volubly, and padded across to the bathroom.

Atticus waited until he could hear the sound of Lamza urinating, and slid out from beneath the bed. He crept to the desk, swiped his phone and made his way as quietly as he could out of the bedroom and through the flat to the front door. He turned the lock, winced as the hinges creaked, and stepped outside. The door creaked again as he closed it, but he didn't wait around to see if Lamza had heard it. He descended the stairs hastily, pushed open the door to the outside, and headed straight for the road.

*　*　*

Atticus walked back to Waterloo Station, arriving as the first light of dawn stained the sky between the high-rise buildings on the South Bank. The first train back to Salisbury left in an hour, and he had something that he needed to do first. He googled nearby internet cafés and found one – Caffe Deniro – on Webber Street. It opened early, and light from inside cast a welcome glow onto the pavement as Atticus approached. He paid for an hour and sat down at an empty desk. He took out the flash drive and, after plugging it into the computer's USB port, he selected the most interesting emails and documents and moved them into a folder, one by one. He opened the browser, navigated to Gmail and created a new account. He opened a second window and found Dafyd Cadogan's email address, copied it and pasted it into a new email. He dragged the folder to the email so that its contents would be added as attachments, and pressed send. There was no need for an accompanying message. The documents would speak for themselves.

Atticus closed down the browser window, retrieved the flash drive, emptied the terminal's cache and left the café. He looked at his watch: it was twenty past five. He had a few minutes to get to the station if he wanted to catch the first train.

54

Wilton Shopping Village had been running a Christmas ice rink for the last few years, and it had become something of a Jones family tradition to visit it in the week before the big day. The rink was built on the lawn within the inner courtyard that had once been used to stretch out the carpets that were woven here, with wooden sheds erected around the perimeter where local traders could sell their festive goods. There was a mulled wine stall and Mack had already enjoyed a glass. It had been a little stronger than she had expected, and had gone to her head a bit. That was the cause – and not any innate lack of balance or ability – of her unsteadiness. That was what she told herself, in any event.

They had enjoyed a pleasant weekend so far. They had gone to Andy's parents' for his mother's birthday yesterday, putting on a brave face for the benefit of the assembled relatives. The kids raced around the house, always on the verge of knocking something over, but they had been happy and hadn't bickered and, eventually, Mack had been able to relax. Andy had offered to drive home, and she had enjoyed a couple of glasses of wine, the alcohol relaxing her enough that she was able to rest a hand on her husband's knee as they drove back.

Today had been fun, too. She shuffled around the edge of the rink, gripping onto the rail with her left hand and extending her right for additional balance. She watched as her kids slid across the ice. Both Sebastian and Daisy were able to stay on their feet, which was more than could be said for her. Her parents had never taken her to anything remotely similar when she was growing up, and her first time on skates had been two years ago. She had been awful then and she was only marginally less awful now, mulled wine notwithstanding.

She had reached the end of the rink and was about to try to negotiate the stretch without a rail when she felt her phone buzzing in her pocket. She anchored herself with her left hand and fished out the phone with her right.

She sighed. It was the station. She was tempted to ignore it, but knew that she couldn't. They wouldn't call on her day off unless it was important.

'Hello?'

'Hello, boss. It's Francine.'

DC Francine Patterson was a newly qualified detective. She was young, smart and eager to make progress in her career. Mack liked her and, as a woman who had blazed the trail before her, had decided that she would do everything that she could to ease Patterson's transition into plainclothes.

'What is it?' she said.

'I'm sorry to disturb you on a Sunday.'

'It's fine. What is it?'

'We've had a walk-in.'

'And?'

'It's the Mallender case.'

Mack straightened up a little. 'Go on.'

'It's a woman – she says she has information for us.'

'Did she say what kind of information?'

'Says she's a doctor, was treating Cameron Mallender before he died.'

'Treating him for what?'

'She wouldn't say anything more than that – she'll only talk to you.'

Mack sighed. There was no way she was going to be able to get out of this. 'All right,' she said. 'Where is she?'

'I've got her in an interview room.'

'Tell her I'll be there in half an hour.'

She put the phone back in her pocket, her foot sliding out from underneath her as she struggled to fasten the zip. She caught herself on the rail before she could fall, but it was far from a graceful recovery.

Andy slid over to her. 'Careful.'

'I'll never get the hang of this,' she muttered.

'Probably help if you weren't on your phone?'

'I have a problem,' she said.

'Please don't say that was work.'

'I'm sorry – I have to go in.'

'On a *Sunday*?'

'I know.'

'*Jesus*, Mack,' he hissed. 'It's nearly Christmas. We come here every year. You can't go to work now.'

'You know how it is – I don't get to choose.'

'Bullshit,' he said. 'You're a DCI. Send someone else. Call Lennox – he can bloody well do it. Call Best or Boyd. Get one of them to go in for you.'

'You think I *want* to go in?'

'I don't know,' he said, suddenly sullen. 'Do you?'

'No, I don't. But it's the Mallender case. I don't have a choice.'

'You'd better make sure he goes down,' he said, 'because this isn't feeling like it's worth it at the moment.'

He pushed off.

'Andy!'

He spun around so that he was facing her and sliding gently backwards. 'Go. I'll tell our children why Mummy can't be here for the rest of the afternoon.'

He spun around and skated away before Mack could say anything else. She was aware of a sharp pain in her lip and realised that she had bitten down on it, hard. She wanted to go after him, to rail at him that it was unfair to make her feel guilty, that it wasn't her choice that she was going, but he was already too far away and, if she was honest, she knew that he was probably right. She knew plenty of coppers who ended up with other coppers; it made sense. Sometimes only someone who worked the same job and suffered the same unsociable hours and demands could understand what police work was like. Her thoughts jerked to Atticus, and how he would have understood what it meant, before she banished the thought of him from her mind.

The affair had been a mistake.

A dreadful, weak, dangerous mistake, and one that she was never – *ever* – going to repeat.

A mother on the rail between Mack and the changing area where she could remove her skates looked at her and stumbled as she slid out of the way. She had a look of alarm on her face, and it was only when Mack was past her that she realised why: she was wearing a ferocious scowl.

55

Mack called for a car to pick her up and take her to the station. She went up to the CID room. Francine Patterson was waiting.

'Where is she?'

'In the interview room.'

'Anything that I need to know before I talk to her?'

'Not really. She wanted to wait for you. I don't know anything more than I've already told you.'

'Okay. Come in with me and take a note.'

She led the way to the interview room, knocked on the door and went inside. The interview rooms at Bourne Hill were reasonably new, and in much better condition than the ones that they had replaced before the constabulary had moved here. They were used by officers for interviewing suspects and witnesses, and by solicitors who needed privacy when consulting with their clients. The room was painted in two tones of grey, with a small table against the wall and three chairs. One of the chairs was occupied by a middle-aged woman. Mack estimated that she was in her late forties. She had a thick head of naturally curled dark hair, a slender and almost elfin face, and was dressed in clothes that were obviously on the more expensive end of the scale.

'Hello,' Mack said, offering her hand. 'I'm Detective Chief Inspector Jones.'

The woman stood up. 'Audrey Sandeau.'

'Thanks for coming to see me,' Mack said.

The woman nodded a little nervously. 'I'm not completely sure I'm doing the right thing.'

'I'm sure we can work that out.' Mack gestured to the chair. 'Please – sit down. Have you been offered a drink?'

'I'd love a coffee.'

Mack turned to Patterson. 'Could you get a couple of coffees, please?'

'Right away.'

Patterson went outside and closed the door behind her. Mack decided to get started. 'You said you had information about Cameron Mallender?'

Sandeau looked down at the digital recorder on the table. 'That's not recording, is it?'

'Not now,' Mack said.

Sandeau turned and gestured up at the camera fixed at the junction of the wall and ceiling. 'And that?'

'That's off, too, but if you think you have something that might be relevant to the trial, we'd have to go on the record and switch them on.'

'Can I talk to you about it first? You could tell me if it's important.'

'We can do that,' Mack said.

There was a knock on the door and Mack got up and opened it. Patterson was waiting outside with two cups of coffee in her hands. She came inside, closing the door with her foot, and set the mugs down on the table.

Sandeau thanked her.

Patterson took a pad of paper and a pen from the table. 'DC Patterson is going to take a note,' Mack said.

'That's fine. How do we start?'

'Just tell me whatever it is that you want me to know,' she said.

Sandeau nodded. 'I'm a psychiatrist,' she said. 'Until quite recently I had a practice in Bath. One of my patients was Cameron Mallender.'

Mack felt a quiver of anticipation. 'Go on.'

Sandeau took the coffee and sipped at it. 'He came to me at the start of last year. He was in a bit of a mess.'

'There was never any suggestion that Cameron was seeing anyone.'

'Why would there be? He wasn't referred to me. It was his decision. He was a private client – I'm not sure he would've told anyone else. He never said that he had.'

'Why did he come?'

'He had a problem with his emotions. Anger, especially. It was a long-standing condition, but it had been getting worse. We had a series of sessions over the course of last year. The last one was in November. I didn't see him again. And then . . .' She let the sentence trail off before finishing it. 'And then he was murdered.'

'Why was he angry?'

'He had a very difficult childhood. He was abused by his father.'

'What kind of abuse?'

'Sexual,' she said. 'Did you know?'

Mack shook her head. 'We didn't.'

'He said it started around the age of six and continued until he was ten. His father would come into his room at night and touch him. He told me he'd been suffering with memories of what had happened for years – he couldn't sleep, got flashbacks. Abuse like that can cause PTSD, and he showed classic symptoms. Hypervigilance. Intense physical reactions when he recalled what had happened. Hyperacusis – reduced tolerance to loud noise. Irritability and anger.'

'How long did you see him for?'

'Seven months. We had two sessions a week at the start; then we dropped down to once a week. He certainly made progress, but that kind of experience isn't one that you can ever forget about. I tried to teach him some techniques that would help him to deal with it. And, of course, just talking about it is therapeutic.'

'So, are you here now because you think he might have done it?'

'What? Murder his family? No. Definitely not. It couldn't have been him.'

'But if you're saying his father abused him—'

'Oh, he hated him,' she cut in. 'He really did – but his anger didn't express itself that way. He directed it inwards. Towards himself – he had expressed suicidal ideation and had tried to kill himself twice prior to coming to see me. The second time was the trigger to find help. He didn't want to die. Cameron was in a pattern of self-destructive behaviour, but he wasn't dangerous to anyone else.'

'How can you be sure?'

'Because I've seen a lot of patients with his kind of issues, and I know how to identify someone who might be a threat to others. And, added to that, if he was still on the same medication as he was when he saw me, it would have made that kind of violent act very difficult indeed.'

'Can I ask what he was on?'

'Of course. Haloperidol decanoate. It's an antidepressant – he was on two-hundred-milligram doses. Trifluoperazine, too. That's an antipsychotic. He would have been docile. Low energy. It helped him keep his emotions at a level that he could easily control.'

Patterson noted that down, drew a line under it and then turned to a fresh page.

'Thank you, Doctor,' Mack said. 'That's helpful. Go on.'

'I read what Ralph Mallender is saying about Cameron – that he was responsible, killed the family and then himself – and I didn't feel I could stay silent. The poor boy is dead – he can't defend himself. But I can report what he told me, and I can give my professional opinion. Even if we allowed the possibility that he might have acted with violence towards his father – which I don't believe is likely – I don't believe that there is *any* possibility that he could have harmed his mother and sister. He was devoted to them both.'

Patterson kept writing. Mack instinctively knew that this was valuable. The defence was going to focus on the suggestion that Cameron had killed his family and then himself; this was strong, unbiased, *professional* evidence that would refute that suggestion.

'I have to ask,' Mack said carefully. 'It's very late in the day to come to us with this. The trial has started.'

'So why didn't I come to you earlier? I'm afraid it's been one of those things. I haven't been in the country for many months. I'm French. My husband stays in Paris while I work here. *Stayed* in Paris, I mean. He was diagnosed with cancer just after last Christmas. I took a leave of absence to nurse him. Unfortunately, it was a particularly aggressive cancer and he died last month.'

'I'm very sorry to hear that,' Mack said.

'Thank you,' she said. 'I've only just returned to the country – yesterday, actually. I read everything I could find about the case and then called you. It's awful. Absolutely *awful*.'

'And you'd be prepared to give evidence?'

'What would that entail?'

'We'd take a statement and then ask you to answer questions at the trial.'

'And it would be helpful? For Cameron?'

'Very.'

She nodded. 'I still have responsibility towards him as a former patient, but, in the circumstances, I also have a duty to help you in any way that I can. If you think it would be helpful, I'd be happy to do whatever is necessary.'

* * *

Mack asked Sandeau if she wouldn't mind waiting and went outside with Patterson.

'What do you want me to do, boss?' Patterson asked.

'We're going to need to take a statement. Call Lennox. Get him to come in – the two of you can do it together. I need to speak to Abernathy. This is important.'

Patterson said that she would do that, and hurried away to make the arrangements.

Mack went to the vending machine outside the CID room and paid for another cup of cheap coffee. It was midday now, and they would need to get the statement ready for disclosure to the defence tomorrow morning. They were going to be busy for the next few hours. It wasn't ideal, especially at the weekend, but there was nothing that could be done about it.

She would make it up to Andy and the kids, but, until the trial came to an end, she had to put work first.

56

Atticus took the tennis ball that Bandit had delivered to him, wound his arm back and threw it as far as he could. The dog rushed away, his paws pounding a drumbeat over the ice-hard playing field. It was a cold day, and they had it to themselves. The Avon wound its slow course ahead of them with the water meadows beyond it, both providing a bucolic foreground to the majesty of the cathedral. Atticus often wondered how much the view had changed in the eight hundred years that the cathedral had stood. This particular aspect contained only a few buildings, and it wasn't difficult to erase them and imagine what the cathedral must have represented to local inhabitants who would have shared this view in years gone by. Some of them, living in medieval squalor, would surely have been dumbstruck by its majesty. Constable had been similarly taken and had painted some of his most impressive landscapes from vantage points along the route of their walk. Atticus had one of them – *Salisbury Cathedral from the Meadows* – as the screensaver on his laptop.

Bandit trotted back, his tail swooshing left and right, and dropped the ball.

Atticus reached down to collect it when his phone started to buzz in his pocket. He took it out and glanced at the screen. It was a landline that he didn't recognise.

'Hello?'

'It's Allegra Mallender.'

'Afternoon,' he said.

'I need to see you,' she said. Her tone was undercut with excitement. 'Actually, we all do.'

'I'm out with the dog at the moment,' he said, playing it out.

'It's urgent.'

'Why? Is everything okay?'

'There's been a development in the case. I'll explain when you get here.'

'Where are you?'

'Cadogan's office. Can you come?'

Atticus had been expecting the call, although he couldn't say that. He knelt down to grab Bandit's collar.

'I'll be there in twenty minutes.'

*   *   *

Atticus hooked up Bandit's lead and led him through the North Gate to Cadogan's office on the High Street. He knocked on the door and, rather than the receptionist, it was opened by Cadogan himself. He glanced down at the dog and looked as if he was about to protest; Atticus walked inside before he could say anything.

'What's going on?' he said.

'I'll tell you inside,' Cadogan said. 'We're in the conference room.'

He led the way along the corridor and turned into the first room on the left. There was a table with ten chairs around it. Allegra Mallender and Christopher Crow were there already, engaged in conversation. There was a pile of stapled documents on the table.

'Good afternoon,' Atticus said.

Allegra turned around. Her eyes shone with excitement. Atticus unhooked Bandit's lead, and the dog trotted over to her and nuzzled her hand until she scratched his ears.

'Take a seat, Mr Priest,' Crow said. He was wearing jeans and a baggy jumper and looked very different without his robes and wig.

'What's happened?'

Cadogan sat down, reached for the documents at the top of the pile, and slid them across the table. Atticus made a show of looking through them.

'What is it?' he asked guilelessly.

'Emails between Freddie Lamza and Steve Hawkins.'

'Steve Hawkins?'

'He's a journalist. Please – read them.'

Atticus looked through the emails, feigning ignorance as to their contents, and then turned to the contract that had been attached to one of them.

'What? Lamza has already done a deal with the press?'

'Indeed he has,' Crow said. 'He's already received the first payment, too. That, in itself, would be damaging for his credibility. But that's not the worst of it. Look at the email at the top of the pile – the one sent last week.'

Atticus knew which message he meant, since he had read it in the café near Waterloo just a few hours earlier. Nevertheless, he had to play along with the charade, so he picked out the correct page and read it.

"'It's in your interests to make your evidence as compelling as possible. It goes without saying that you need to be truthful, but the more interesting your story, the better the chance that we would be able to secure additional interviews for you once the case has come to an end. And, of course, there will be little interest in what you might have to say in the event that Ralph is acquitted.'"

'Can you believe it?' Allegra said.

Atticus put the paper on the table. 'So Lamza has a financial motive for sensationalising his evidence?'

Crow nodded solemnly. 'I think there's the beginnings of a strong case for perjury against him.'

'And perverting the course of justice against Hawkins,' Cadogan added.

'Even if we can't get far enough to show that,' Crow said, 'all of Lamza's credibility as a witness is gone. His evidence is prejudiced. It's worthless.'

'Isn't it the *best* news?' Allegra gushed.

'It's great,' Atticus said. 'But how did we get this?'

Cadogan leaned back in his chair and looked at him from hooded eyes. 'It was emailed to me this morning.'

'By?'

'We don't know,' Cadogan said. 'It was sent anonymously.'

'So how did whoever sent them get hold of them? These look like private emails.'

'That's impossible to say,' Crow said.

'The obvious explanation is that either Lamza or Hawkins has been hacked,' Cadogan said.

Atticus laid a finger on the topmost sheet. 'But can we use them?'

Crow nodded. 'We can,' he said. 'Mr Justice Compton's *dictum* has always been relevant: "It matters not how you get it; if you steal it, even, it would be admissible in evidence." There was a case two years ago that made it very clear that there is no prohibition of the use of illegal or covertly obtained evidence. The courts will allow it to be presented if it is relevant to the case. And this – plainly – is relevant. It goes towards the character of the main prosecution witness. The real issue is one for Mr Cadogan.'

Cadogan drummed his fingers on the table. 'I could be struck off if I was involved in breaking the law to get the evidence.'

'But you weren't involved,' Atticus said, 'were you?'

'Of *course* I wasn't.'

'I'm sorry, then – I don't understand the concern.'

Cadogan and Crow both stared at Atticus from the other side of the table.

'Let's just be absolutely clear,' Cadogan said. 'Did *you* get these?'

'No,' Atticus replied. 'This is the first time I've seen them.'

'You're absolutely sure?'

'I'm sure. I'm not usually shy when it comes to taking credit, but this time I'm afraid I can't.'

Crow and Cadogan exchanged glances.

'All right,' Crow said.

'Well?' Allegra said. 'What do we do next?'

Crow got up. 'We have work to do.'

57

Mack arrived at court with five minutes to spare and in a bad mood. It had been a struggle to get the kids out of bed, and they had been in a dreadful mood. It had been an exercise in diplomacy to get them to eat anything for breakfast and even more difficult to get them washed and dressed. Andy had slept badly, too, and was less patient than he normally was. He had barely spoken to her the previous evening, making it plain how annoyed he was that she had abandoned the family tradition to work in the afternoon. Mack had volunteered to drop the children at school, but the whole process had taken about twenty minutes longer than it should have. She was in a foul temper by the time she arrived at court.

Sunday had been busy. Lennox and Patterson had taken a witness statement from Dr Sandeau, and it had been emailed across to the CPS solicitor and to Abernathy. Both lawyers had then requested a conference, and Mack had ended up on the phone with them for ninety minutes. They all agreed that Sandeau should be called as a witness and, while not impossible, there were procedural requirements that needed to be negotiated with the defence before that could happen. Introducing evidence at this late stage in the trial was unusual, but this was relevant and potentially important. It went to the heart of Mallender's defence: they were arguing that Cameron murdered the family before killing himself, but here was evidence that said that he wasn't violent and would likely have been rendered docile by his medication. Cameron wasn't able to defend himself, so that job fell to the prosecution. Abernathy said that he would see the judge and Christopher Crow in the judge's chambers before the morning's proceedings began so that they could hash out the best way to proceed.

Mack looked at her watch: 9.55. Abernathy would already have raised the question of adducing the new evidence. She wondered whether he had been successful.

☐ ☐ ☐

The courtroom was busy; the cross-examination of Freddie Lamza was scheduled for the morning and, given the explosive outburst from Ralph Mallender that had punctuated Friday's evidence, it was obvious that the reporters were hoping for an encore.

Mack scanned the rest of the court: Christopher Crow wasn't here yet and neither was Dafyd Cadogan. Allegra Mallender was usually in the gallery by this time, but, as Mack turned to look for her, she saw that she wasn't there, either. That was strange. Atticus was in the front row and, as he saw Mack glance across, he raised his hand in greeting. Mack nodded back at him in response, but he was distracted.

Something wasn't right.

Abernathy emerged from the entrance to the judge's chambers and made his way to his desk. He turned to address Mack and the CPS solicitor.

'I spoke to Somerville,' he said in a low voice. 'He's fine with us admitting the evidence from Sandeau. I've disclosed it to the defence, and I don't think they'll have an issue with it.'

'When will she give evidence?'

'Probably tomorrow morning,' he said. 'I'll make sure she's here.'

Abernathy looked concerned, as if something was bothering him.

'Is everything else okay?' she asked.

'I don't know,' he said. 'Crow was nonplussed when I told him about Sandeau. He ought to have complained about it, but he didn't – nothing beyond the perfunctory grumble, anyway. I've known him for years. He's got something up his sleeve.'

'What?'

'He says they're going to call Mallender's solicitor.'

'Cadogan?' Mack said. 'Why?'

'He said, "We shall have to wait and see." He wouldn't give me anything else.'

Mack turned back to the gallery and saw Allegra picking her way along the crammed seats to one that Atticus had saved for her. She looked different; there was something in her face that Mack hadn't seen before. She was smiling, and, as she sat down next to Atticus, she turned to whisper something into his ear.

Abernathy had seen it, too. 'She's happy about something.'

'But what?' Mack said. 'What can Cadogan add?'

'I don't know. But Christopher can be devious when he wants to be. I have a bad feeling.'

Crow came through the door with Cadogan following close behind. Mack looked at their faces for any sign that might explain why they were late; Crow was concentrated, which was not unusual, but Cadogan looked exultant.

Mack was still looking over at Atticus when he turned and held her gaze. As he did, he mouthed a single word that was impossible to mistake.

Sorry.

Mack frowned in confusion, but Allegra was talking to Atticus and he had to look away. Mack was about to press Abernathy for an explanation, but was forestalled by the arrival of the associate.

'All rise, please. All rise.'

58

Atticus felt uncomfortable with the course of action that had been chosen. Crow had decided not to give advance disclosure of the evidence of Lamza's perfidy, and, essentially, to ambush him and the prosecution with it. Crow had studied the procedural rules around defence disclosure and had concluded that he was within his rights to introduce the evidence as he saw fit, eventually deciding that he would call Cadogan – who had received the correspondence – as the witness who would give evidence about it.

The emails between Lamza and Hawkins concerned a flaw in the prosecution's main witness that, Crow argued, the prosecution should have already been aware of, and, in addition, the defence had only become aware of the evidence the day prior to the cross-examination. Time had been spent considering the probity of the emails and how best to deploy them, and that, he had argued, was more important than ensuring the prosecution's comfort. His job was to use all lawful means to further his client's interests, and the course of action that he had chosen fell squarely within that duty.

It had been settled.

Atticus knew that Mack would be blindsided just as badly as anyone else, and had argued – for her sake, although he didn't admit that – that an application for an adjournment so that the evidence could be properly adduced would be the more equitable way to proceed. Allegra had looked at him as if he had sprouted two heads, and had brusquely asked him how equitable the prosecution had been in its relentless hounding of an innocent man. Atticus had ceded the point. There was no sense in an argument, and, after all, his loyalty was to his client and not to the Crown, the police or Mack.

He still felt bad about it.

The usher stood. 'Mr Frederick Lamza.'

The courtroom settled down, a buzz of anticipation hanging in the air. Lamza came inside. He was wearing a different suit, this one a little more sober than the electric blue outfit that he had sported on Friday and a *lot* more respectable than the outfit that he had been wearing the last time that Atticus had seen him. He was noticeably more hesitant as he took the stand. He knew that he would be tested this morning; he didn't know just how much.

He was reminded of his oath and, at the judge's invitation, he took his seat.

Christopher Crow stood up. 'Good morning, Mr Lamza,' he began.

'Good morning.'

'How are you?'

'I'm fine.'

'Thank you for your evidence on Friday afternoon. It was very interesting. I have a few questions that I'd like to put to you.'

'Of course. I'm happy to help.'

'That's very kind, Mr Lamza. Very kind.'

Crow opened the slim document folder that he had brought into the courtroom with him and took out a sheaf of papers. Atticus looked over at Mack; she was leaning forward, the tension obvious in the way she was fretting with the hem of her skirt.

Atticus felt the buzz of anticipation in his gut. He knew what was about to happen: a bomb was about to be dropped right into the middle of the prosecution's case.

'Mr Lamza,' Crow said, 'could you tell the court whether there is anything that influenced your evidence?'

'What do you mean?'

'Let me put the question a different way. *Why* did you give your evidence on Friday?'

Lamza looked puzzled. 'Because it was the right thing to do.'

'It was your civic duty?'

Lamza nodded. 'Exactly.'

'And there was no other reason?'

Lamza turned to the judge for guidance.

Somerville frowned. 'Where are you going with this, Mr Crow?'

'My Lord, I'd like to hand up a selection of documents that have been brought to the attention of the defence. I have copies for the prosecution and members of the jury, too.'

The usher came forward, collected the stapled sets of papers from Crow and handed one up to the associate, who passed it to the judge. The usher took the rest to the jury, where they were passed along the line so that each juror had a copy. Crow collected three additional sets from his desk: he handed one to

Abernathy, one to the CPS solicitor behind him and one to the returning usher to deliver to Lamza.

Abernathy stood. 'What is this?'

'New evidence,' Crow said. 'I'm afraid we only became aware of it yesterday.'

'My Lord?'

Somerville was looking through the papers, flipping pages.

'My Lord,' Abernathy pressed, 'the prosecution has been made aware of additional evidence from Mr Cadogan. I presume that this is it, but this is the first that we've seen of it. I would respectfully suggest that if it is important, then we should adjourn so that it can be considered.'

'I disagree,' Crow said. 'I think the witness should be asked to comment on the evidence now. It raises some troubling questions as to his motive in appearing for the prosecution. Speaking bluntly, it questions Mr Lamza's honesty. I'd like to question him before he has the opportunity to fabricate a story by which he might try to explain it away.'

The judge thumbed through the papers. 'I'll permit it,' he said. 'We can discuss the timing of the disclosure later.'

'Thank you, my Lord,' Crow said. 'Now, Mr Lamza – can you tell me what you see?'

Lamza looked down at the papers. His expression had passed from confusion to fear. His mouth opened and closed, but he didn't answer.

'Mr Lamza?'

'They're emails,' he said quietly.

'Louder. The jury need to hear you.'

'They're emails.'

'That's right – they are. *Emails*. Who are they between?'

'Between me and . . .'

He looked away.

Atticus turned his attention to Mack. She was trying to get a look at the copies that had been given to the CPS.

'Mr Lamza, would it be fair to say that these emails are between you and a member of the press? Would that be accurate?'

Lamza swallowed.

'Mr Lamza?'

'Yes,' he said quietly.

'Is the person with whom you were corresponding in court today?'

No answer.

'Mr Lamza,' Somerville said, 'answer the questions, please.'

'Yes,' Lamza said. 'He is.'

'Would you point him out to us?'

Freddie looked over at the press gallery, raised his hand, and pointed to the front row.

'Who is that, Mr Lamza?'

'His name is Hawkins. Steve Hawkins.'

'That's right,' Crow said. 'You were corresponding with Mr Hawkins.' He turned to the jury. 'Mr Hawkins is a freelance journalist who has written for most of the tabloid newspapers.'

The jury turned as one to look at the man in the front row of the press gallery. Atticus turned to look at him, too. Hawkins's cheeks were red and he was nervously scratching at his chin.

'Mr Lamza,' Crow said, 'would you read the passage in the first email that I've highlighted? This is from an email that you sent to Mr Hawkins a week ago. Please.'

Lamza looked up at Somerville, but, if he was looking for an instruction that he did not have to do as he had been asked, then none was forthcoming. Abernathy was no help, either; he was hunched over his desk, his face hidden, as he read through the papers he had just been given. Atticus glanced down at Mack; she looked as white as a sheet.

'Mr Lamza,' Crow pressed firmly, 'read the passage, please.'

Lamza cleared his throat and, when he spoke, it was in a hushed and tremulous voice. '"Thanks for going the extra mile for me. You've been very generous. I promise I won't let you down."'

'Mr Lamza,' Crow said, 'please tell the court *how* Mr Hawkins has been generous.'

Lamza was barely audible. 'He arranged the contract between me and the newspaper.'

'Louder, please.'

'He arranged the contract between me and the newspaper,' he said, his voice still quiet, but – in a courtroom that was as quiet as a tomb – perfectly audible.

'And he's been very generous indeed, hasn't he? I believe the newspaper he's sold his story to has agreed to pay you a considerable amount of money for an exclusive.'

'Yes.'

'But there's a stipulation in that contract, is there not?'

Abernathy got to his feet. 'This is ridiculous. I've only just seen these—'

'Just a moment, Mr Abernathy,' the judge said. 'Answer the question, Mr Lamza.'

Lamza swallowed. 'The newspaper has paid me half. They'll only pay the other half if Mr Mallender is found guilty.'

There was an audible gasp from the gallery. Atticus turned to the jury and saw the same reaction. Those who were taking notes were scribbling furiously; the elderly woman at the end of the line was shaking her head, her disapproval obvious.

'And I understand you've been promised additional payment for subsequent stories if the defendant is convicted, have you not? Beyond the money you've already agreed.'

'I have.'

Crow held up the sheet of paper with the email. 'What did you mean when you said that "I won't let you down"?'

'I don't know.'

'I think I do.' He took a second page from his desk and adjusted his spectacles so that he could read it. 'This is an email that Mr Hawkins sent to you the day before the email you just read out. He says, and I quote, "It's important that you tell the court everything that you told me. Don't spare anything. It's going to be important to your story that all the salacious detail is included. You asked me whether I thought you should exaggerate anything – of course, I can't possibly condone that, but I will say that adding a few judicious bits of colour won't go amiss."'

Atticus watched Mack as Crow read the passage. She had her eyes closed. He knew how she must be feeling: the pieces of her carefully constructed case against Ralph Mallender were detaching and tumbling to the floor. He felt bad about that, but Crow had been adamant: this had to be an ambush to get the most from the disclosure. Crow could not do anything else, and Abernathy would have known that. There was the possibility that he might be ostracised by colleagues and that Somerville might be censorious, but he was still prepared to press ahead, because, Atticus presumed, the benefits to his career of success in a trial as big as this one would outweigh any temporary opprobrium from his colleagues. Money tended to salve all wounds, and Crow was banking – with good reason, Atticus thought – on a win bringing in a flood of new work.

Abernathy was on his feet again. 'I'm sorry, my Lord, but this is simply *intolerable*. We haven't had sight of these documents until just now. We don't know where they came from. We don't know how they were obtained, but we have to consider the possibility that it was by criminal means.'

'They were emailed to my instructing solicitor yesterday morning.'

'From whom?'

Crow shook his head. 'From an anonymous source. You'll have the chance to cross-examine Mr Cadogan when the defence calls him.'

'And where did this source find Mr Lamza's personal emails?'

'I don't know,' Crow said, 'but, given how important his evidence is for the prosecution's case, it would be highly prejudicial for them not to be considered.'

Abernathy was flustered. 'My Lord, I really do think a conference is necessary.'

'I disagree,' Somerville said. 'This evidence is clearly important. And you confirm that Mr Cadogan will be called?'

'He'll be called, my Lord.'

The judge nodded. 'Then I think we are fine to proceed. Carry on, Mr Crow.'

Atticus turned to the dock. Ralph Mallender was smiling at his wife. Atticus looked back to Mack. She noticed him, and their eyes met for a second; she stared at him, her lips pursed and white and her eyes cold. Would she guess that he had found the emails? Perhaps. She knew him well, better than most, and he had always been prepared to push the boundaries of what was acceptable when he had been working for her. Getting his hands on something explosive like this, regardless of how he came by it?

She would see his fingerprints all over it.

59

The prosecution gathered for a meeting during the lunchtime adjournment. A CPS paralegal had gone out to buy sandwiches and coffees from Pret, but they remained on the table, untouched; they had all lost their appetites.

Mack was slumped in her seat. It felt as if months of grinding, hard graft had just been flushed away. She had been confident that Ralph was guilty, and what they had just learned from the pitiless demolition of Freddie Lamza had cast all of that in doubt. That, in itself, would have been bad enough, but, as she waited for Abernathy to arrive, Mack found her thoughts settling on Hugo, Juliet, Cameron and Cassandra Mallender. She wanted to deliver justice for them, and now she didn't know if she could.

Abernathy came into the room and took the spare seat near the door. He had a face like thunder. 'What the hell just happened?'

Harry Probert, the CPS solicitor responsible for the case, just shrugged. 'I have no idea.'

'The emails? They just *appeared*?'

'Who knows?'

'"Who knows", Harry? We'll have to do rather better than "who knows".'

'Perhaps Lamza forwarded them to someone and they – I don't know – they sent them to Cadogan.'

'Lamza says he didn't.'

'So perhaps Hawkins did.'

'Why would he do that?'

'I don't know,' Probert said, slumping back.

'It would have been immeasurably helpful if you could have found out that Lamza was not to be trusted *before* I called him as our key bloody witness!'

'There was no way we could have known,' Probert protested. He turned to Mack, ready to pass the blame. 'Detective Chief Inspector?'

Mack bit down on her lip until it hurt.

'Mack?'

Now Probert and Abernathy were both looking at her.

'I'll speak to Lamza,' she said. 'The obvious answer is that he's been hacked. But it won't hurt to be thorough. I'll look into it.'

'What now?' Probert said.

Abernathy leaned back in his chair and sighed loudly. 'Crow is going to finish his cross. It'll be unpleasant for Lamza, I'm afraid – *very* unpleasant – and it might get worse. I wouldn't be surprised if he ends up being investigated for perjury. And Hawkins is probably looking at a charge of perverting the course of justice. But what happens to them isn't of any concern to us.'

'And the case?' Probert asked.

Abernathy looked at Mack. 'Do you have any other witnesses who will say that Mallender said he was going to kill his family?'

'If we did, we would have told you.'

Abernathy exhaled. 'Then I'm afraid we're going to be struggling. We have Sandeau next. We should be able to show that Cameron wasn't the murdering type, but, since they've blown holes in our case that Ralph *is*, we just get to stalemate.'

'And then it's me,' Mack said.

They had decided to leave her evidence until the end of the prosecution case. It would give them the chance to use her to pick up any incongruities that had developed during the evidence. Abernathy had said that it would be all over bar the shouting by the time that she was called, but it didn't look that way now.

'Yes, Detective Chief Inspector,' Abernathy said, picking up on Mack's obvious trepidation. 'This afternoon is going to be unpleasant for Freddie. But tomorrow is going to be unpleasant for you, too. I suspect Crow is going to lay all of the failings of our case at your door. Everything. He's going to rake you over the coals.'

60

The cross-examination of Freddie Lamza continued for another hour. Mack watched, aghast, just as if she were observing the aftermath of a particularly nasty car wreck. It was purgatory for her and, for Lamza, something more unpleasant entirely. Crow took him through his emails in detail, having him read them out loud line by line. The exercise must be excruciatingly embarrassing; every answer made it more obvious that he had been prepared to lie in order to secure his payday and his moment in the sun. He seemed to shrivel in on himself, and the fine clothes that he was wearing suddenly looked like badges of shame, purchased with the proceeds of his corruption.

Crow ratcheted up the stakes even more as he drew towards the end of the cross-examination, suggesting that Lamza had perjured himself, that it was a serious offence, and asking sternly whether he knew the consequences should he subsequently be prosecuted and found guilty.

Lamza said that he did not.

Crow told him that he might expect to be sent to prison for two years.

Abernathy interceded at that point, and Somerville warned Crow that the proceedings were about Mallender and not the witness, and, addressing Lamza, said that he didn't have to answer if he felt he might incriminate himself. Of course, it was too late for that by then; Lamza was up to his neck in ordure. He was as pale as a sheet and looked as if he was about to be sick.

The jury's view of him – and everything that he had said – had been comprehensively, utterly, irretrievably poisoned. Crow concluded his cross-examination and Abernathy passed up the opportunity to re-examine; the damage was done, and there was nothing that he would have been able to do to fix it.

'It's two o'clock,' the judge said. 'I had anticipated that Mr Lamza's evidence would need all of today to be heard, but things have evidently changed. Mr Abernathy – you have an additional witness before you conclude the Crown's evidence with Detective Chief Inspector Jones.'

'That's correct, my Lord. Dr Sandeau. I think it might be possible to get through her evidence this afternoon.'

'Very well. Let's get on with it. Call the witness.'

▢ ▢ ▢

Dr Sandeau's evidence would have been important had it not just been preceded by the implosion of the prosecution case. She was an excellent witness, sober and respectful – diametrically opposed to Lamza – and, by the time that she had answered all of Abernathy's questions, much of the defence's anticipated negativity as it pertained to Cameron Mallender had been rebutted. It was impossible to remove the possibility that he might have been responsible for the murders, but Mack was sure that the jury would have a harder time believing it than had been the case before.

She didn't know how important that was any longer. She doubted that they would suspect Ralph, either.

Abernathy concluded the evidence-in-chief. Crow asked a few perfunctory questions, then sat down.

Somerville looked down from his desk. 'I think this might be a good point to adjourn for the day.'

'Yes, my Lord,' Abernathy said.

Crow nodded his agreement.

'We'll reconvene in the morning for the Detective Chief Inspector.'

Abernathy nodded. 'Very good, my Lord.'

'Then we are adjourned.'

61

The atmosphere in the defence conference room was jubilant. Allegra Mallender was sitting with a wide grin on her face that looked as if it might be permanent. Atticus leaned against the wall, watching. Ralph was still on remand and had been taken downstairs to the cells to await his transfer back to prison. Only the lawyers were able to see him at court, and Allegra was anxiously waiting for them to return with news of his reaction.

She didn't have to wait long. Crow and Cadogan opened the door and came inside. Both of them were beaming.

'Well?'

'He's happy,' Crow said.

'Mr Crow has a gift for understatement,' Cadogan corrected him. 'He's *ecstatic.*'

'As he should be,' Crow said. 'That was a very good day.'

'A very, very good day.'

Both men sat down, still smiling.

'We just bumped into Abernathy, too,' Crow said.

'It would be fair to say that he didn't enjoy proceedings as much as we did,' Cadogan added.

'He thinks I should've given notice before I introduced the evidence,' Crow said. 'I disagreed. My duty is to do everything lawful in my power to help Ralph. Abernathy can call it an ambush if he likes – I just used the ammunition that I was given in the most effective manner I could. He would have done the same. I'm not bothered that I've caused him an inconvenience. It's just spilt milk. He's a big boy – he'll get over it.'

Cadogan steepled his fingers on the table. 'He said that the evidence must have been obtained by criminal means, and shouldn't have been admissible.'

'Which is utter nonsense,' Crow said. 'The judge has discretion to allow or exclude evidence and, when the evidence speaks to the motivation of a witness to testify – and possibly even to perjure himself – it would be manifestly unfair to exclude it.'

'So what does it mean?' Allegra asked.

Crow smiled at her. 'How does it affect the case?'

'Yes. The practical effect.'

'It means that Lamza's evidence is worthless. I can't see any possibility that the jury believes what he said about Ralph's conversations with him now.'

'And without that?'

'Without that, they're going to have a very difficult time proving that Ralph did what they say he did. There's more, too. Lamza was at least fifty per cent of their case. We've shown that he is, at the very best, untrustworthy, and at worst, mendacious. That stain will pollute everything else. The jurors will have in the back of their minds that the Crown was prepared to rely on someone like Lamza. If him, who else?'

Allegra had a hopeful expression on her face. 'So how do you see our chances?'

Crow pursed his lips and tapped his fingers together. 'Well,' he said, 'before this, I would've said it was seventy-thirty against, as you know. But now? The opposite, in our favour, and even that might be pessimistic. It might be better.'

'Is there even a case to answer?' Atticus asked.

'I'll make an application when they finish that there isn't,' Crow said. 'It's hard to know what Somerville will say. It would be good to dismiss the case now, but I don't think it'll make much practical difference. I think we can agree that we've had the best day of the trial.'

'The best day I've had in months,' Allegra added.

Cadogan slapped his hands on the table in agreement.

'So where did the emails come from?' she said.

'We don't know,' Cadogan replied.

'And I'm not sure we really *want* to know,' Crow said. 'It would appear that your husband has a friend who was not prepared for him to go to prison based on the evidence of a perjurer.'

Allegra leaned back. 'Well,' she said, 'whoever it was, I'm grateful.'

Atticus said nothing.

'Will they still put DCI Jones up?' Allegra asked.

'They have to,' Crow said. 'She's going to have to work to try to fix the problems we've caused.'

'But you'll be able to go after her? You know – you'll put the boot in?'

'I certainly will,' Crow said. 'I'm afraid she's going to have a very awkward morning indeed.'

62

There was a buzz of electricity in the lobby. Reporters spoke to their editors, knowing that their stories would find their way to the front pages of tomorrow's editions. The proceedings today had been dynamite, and they all knew that they would be given all the space that they needed.

Atticus was tired. He hadn't slept on Saturday night, and last night had been disturbed by the prospect of today's evidence. Fatigue was beginning to get the better of him. His eyes felt scratchy and raw and his eyelids were heavy; he wanted to get home and go to bed.

He looked around, concerned that he might see Mack. He knew that she would be angry, and that there was a good chance that she might try to take it out on him. He could do without that today.

'Atticus!'

He stopped and turned. It was Allegra.

'Could we . . .' She paused, glancing around at the others waiting in the lobby. 'Could we have a chat?'

'Of course.'

'Can I give you a lift home?'

☐ ☐ ☐

Allegra drove a brand-new Mercedes. They got in and she picked her way through the rush-hour traffic that choked Salisbury's medieval streets. Allegra said nothing for five minutes. The *Play for Today* was on Radio 4 and they listened to it together in silence; Atticus knew that something was on her mind, but he decided to wait for her to bring it up.

She reached over and turned down the volume.

'Can I ask you a question, Atticus?'

'Of course.'

She turned her head to look at him. 'Did you find those emails?'

Atticus concentrated on maintaining a straight face. 'No.'

'Are you sure?'

'No,' he repeated. 'I didn't.'

'Because they made all the difference.'

'Whoever found them broke the law. I work hard for my clients, but there are lines I won't cross.'

She drove on for a moment, her attention on the road ahead, flicking the car into the outside lane to pass a parked bus and then sliding back again.

'I don't believe you,' she said.

'I can't do much about that.'

'Those emails didn't just appear.'

'No,' he said. 'They didn't. Someone's certainly on your side.'

'A guardian angel,' she suggested with a brief hint of sarcasm.

'That's one way to describe it.'

'Well, whoever it was, they've made a huge difference. You heard what they said – Crow is actually confident now. Jesus. That's a first. He's been doom and gloom until now.'

'He should be confident.'

'You think so?'

'Discrediting Lamza helps. There's no question about that. I agree with what was said. The prosecution case is thin now.'

She looked across the cabin at him. 'I want you to know that we appreciate all the work that you're doing. Ralph and I – really, we do. I know that I was a bit sharp with you over the weekend, but I was desperate. We were getting nowhere and the case was coming to an end. I know you've been working hard.'

'It's all right,' he said. 'It's a very stressful experience.'

'Understatement,' she said, chuckling bitterly. 'But then this, today. I don't know . . . I feel able to relax for the first time in months.'

Atticus wanted to tell her that there was still a long way to go. Yes, it was true that the defence had enjoyed a strong day in court. But nothing was guaranteed. Things could go wrong. The judge might decide that there was still a case to answer. Ralph was planning to take the stand, and that offered all sorts of traps and pitfalls. But, as he looked back at her, he didn't have the heart to suggest that she shouldn't raise her hopes. He had no experience of the position in which she had found herself, but it was obviously disquieting.

She deserved an evening where, for the first time in weeks, she might allow herself just a modicum of hope. He was happy to have been able to give her that.

63

Allegra dropped Atticus outside Wagamama on Bridge Street. He picked up two takeouts and two bottles of Asahi and strolled down the road, the smell of the food wafting up from the paper bag. He went up to the office and knocked on Jacob's door.

Bandit clattered down the stairs and pawed at the glass. Jacob came after him and opened the door.

'Hi,' Atticus said. He held up the bag. 'What do you like? Chilli prawn and kimchee ramen or teriyaki beef donburi?'

'You didn't have to do that.'

'You've been a big, big help. Go on – pick.'

Jacob picked the donburi. Atticus took one of the beers and handed it and the food to Jacob, together with a twenty-pound note.

'Same again tomorrow?'

'Is that okay?' Atticus said. 'I don't want to take advantage.'

'You're not. Bring him up whenever you want.'

'I should be back to normal by the end of the week. The job I'm on is nearly done.'

'It's not a problem.'

'Thank you.'

Atticus opened the door to the office and let Bandit lead the way inside. He took off his shoes and put Supertramp's *Crime of the Century* on the player, carefully sliding the needle onto the vinyl. The wistful harmonica introduction to 'School' started to play. He logged onto the game of chess that he was in the middle of and saw that Jack_of_Hearts had not made their next move, but that a message had been left in the comments.

> *I'm sorry that I haven't been as attentive to our game as normal. I've been a little busy. I'll make my move shortly.*

Atticus typed out that that was fine, sent the message and closed the lid of the laptop. He dropped down onto the sofa and stretched out his legs, resting his feet on the coffee table. He tore the lid off the carton, split the chopsticks and started to eat. It had been a long day, and the weekend had been testing, too. He decided that he would go to the cinema – there was a brainless Marvel movie that would do an admirable job of taking his mind off the case – and then turn in for an early night. There was nothing for him to do on the Mallender case and, even as he looked over at the boxes of documents from the Alfred Burns case that had haunted him for so long, he found that he didn't have the energy or the enthusiasm. Better to eat, distract himself for an hour or two, get ready for bed and then read a chapter or two of Dvoretsky's *School of Chess Excellence* that he had been meaning to read for weeks.

64

Atticus woke to the sound of a determined knocking at the door below. He lay back on the mattress for a moment, hoping that the knocking would stop. But it didn't stop. It continued, more determined than before, a constant banging that he could only ignore by putting his pillow over his head.

Finally, the person at the door gave up.

Atticus took the pillow away and exhaled. He reached for his watch and looked at the time: midnight. He had only been asleep for half an hour.

He closed his eyes to try to get back to sleep.

'Atticus!'

The voice was at the foot of the flight of outdoor stairs that led from his bedroom to the garden.

Atticus groaned. He recognised the voice.

'*Atticus!*'

He heard the sound of footsteps rattling up the steel treads. There came a *rat-tat-tat* against the glass panel in the door.

'*Atticus!* I know you're in there. Open the door.'

'For pity's sake, Mack,' he groaned. 'It's midnight.'

'I don't care. Open the door now, Atticus.'

'What is it?'

'Open the door.'

Atticus sat up and swung his legs around so that he could stand. He looked in vain for his dressing gown and, instead, pulled on a pair of jeans and a T-shirt that he found amid the welter on the floor. He looked at the bedroom: it was a shocking mess, with clothes strewn around, together with empty Amazon packaging and the discarded Wagamama bag and carton from his meal. He grabbed the rubbish and stuffed it into the already overflowing bin in the corner of the room.

'*Atticus!*'

'Hold on, hold on.'

He found the key for the door on his bookshelf and peeled the blackout blind away from the glass. Mack was standing outside on the exterior landing. Her arms were crossed and the security light shone down onto her, revealing the stern expression on her face.

Atticus unlocked the door and opened it.

She came inside and looked around. '*Jesus.*'

'I know. I need to give it a bit of a clean.'

'A *bit* of a clean?' she said. 'It needs to be fumigated.'

'That's an overreaction.'

'Is this where you work? In this?'

Atticus realised that she had never visited him here before.

'The office is next door,' he said.

Bandit padded in from the office, his tail wagging. She hadn't met the dog, either.

'This is Bandit,' he said. 'Bandit, this is Mack. She's the reason we live in a two-room flat rather than a nice place like normal people.'

Bandit wagged his tail even more vigorously and negotiated the mattress so that he could get closer to Mack. He nudged her leg until she reached down to rub his head. She looked as if she was going to say something about the dog, but – perhaps because it would be pleasant and might deflect her from the haranguing that Atticus knew she had come here to deliver – she straightened up, stepped over the clothes, picked a path around the mattress and went through into the office.

Atticus followed her.

'What are you doing here?' he asked.

'You need me to tell you?' she said, clearing a pile of papers from the sofa but then changing her mind about sitting down.

'Yes, please,' he said.

'What the hell are you doing?'

'Still not following.'

'I mean, really. *Really*. What are you *doing*?'

'Still nothing.'

'Piss off, Atticus. Just piss off. The evidence about Freddie Lamza. The emails.'

'Oh,' he said. 'Those.'

'Where did they come from?'

He shrugged. 'Can't help you. Do you want a drink?'

'No, I don't want a *pissing* drink, you dick. I want you to be honest with me, for once, just once, and tell me what you know.'

'I know the prosecution was relying on the evidence of a witness who was apparently prepared to send a man to prison in return for a big payday. There's a word for that. Begins with *P*.'

She waved that aside. 'Where did they come from?'

'I know as much as you do – Cadogan got an email on Sunday morning. Anonymous. He doesn't know who it was from.'

'As simple as that?' Mack said, not even trying to keep the sarcasm out of her voice.

'As simple as that.'

'Convenient.'

'It was certainly good timing.'

'Very.'

'I don't know what you want me to say.'

'Fine,' she said. 'Let's try this another way. Where were you on Saturday night and Sunday morning?'

'Here.'

'Really?'

'Really. Ask Bandit – he was with me.'

The dog cocked his ear at the sound of his voice.

'That's your alibi?'

'Afraid so.'

'A dog?'

'What can I say?'

'You're going to lie to a police officer?'

'Are you investigating me, Mack?'

'I don't know. *Should* I be investigating you?'

'I was here with Bandit,' he said patiently. 'I had an early night. I can't prove it, but you can't prove that I didn't.'

She sighed. 'Let me tell you what I think. I think you've done something really, really stupid. *Really* stupid. The kind of thing I won't be able to help you with if you get found out.'

Finally, she did sit down on the sofa. She reached into her pocket and took out her phone. She handed it to Atticus. There was a still image from a security camera on the screen. Atticus looked down at the screen: there was a figure in the shot.

'Who's this?'

'Come on. Don't insult my intelligence. That's you.'

Atticus made as if he was looking more carefully at the image. It *was* him; of course it was. He had noticed the security camera in the lobby of Freddie's building and had made sure that his face was covered by the hood when he went inside. He looked at the image again and confirmed that there was nothing there that could identify him.

She took the phone from him. 'You were wearing gloves, I suppose?'

'Mack – it wasn't me.'

She shook her head and stood up, straightening out her coat. 'Fine,' she said, sliding the phone into her pocket. 'I didn't expect you to admit it. But you've *got* to stop. Breaking into the flat of the prosecution's main witness? Come *on*. You couldn't do that when you were in the police. You *definitely* can't do it now.'

'I'm doing what I've been asked to do.'

'Break the law?'

'No. Investigate the evidence.'

She made her way towards the door as if she was about to leave, then turned back to him. 'How easy do you think it would be for me to find evidence that puts you in London on Saturday night? How did you get there? Should I check the CCTV at the station? How did you pay for your ticket? You wouldn't have been stupid enough to pay with a card, would you?'

'Of course not. I'd pay cash.'

'So you *did* go to London?'

'No,' he said. 'That was a hypothetical.'

'You're *impossible*.'

'Come on, Mack. I've told you it wasn't me. If you think it was, we'd better continue this at the nick in front of a lawyer. I'll call Cadogan.'

She shook her head and sighed. 'You know what you'd get for this kind of burglary?'

'A year. I know. I'm familiar with the law.'

'The CPS would throw the book at you. An ex-police officer with an axe to grind. Breaking into the property of a prosecution witness to find evidence to disrupt an ongoing case being overseen by the DCI with whom he had an affair.'

'This is nuts,' he said. 'You—'

'A year might be on the optimistic side,' she said, talking over him. 'You'd get seven years for aggravated burglary.'

He almost corrected her – there would need to be damage to the property for aggravated burglary – but there was no way he could have known what had or had not happened at the flat. He stopped himself just in time.

'Even if it was me,' he said instead, 'which, before you say anything, it wasn't, I don't see the issue. Those emails corrected a very likely miscarriage of justice. Freddie Lamza was being paid to lie, Mack. He was going to give evidence about something *that did not happen*. And, if he hadn't been found out, Ralph would probably have been convicted. Did I find that evidence? No, I did not. But if I *had* found it, you would be better to *thank* me than to come in here and *threaten* me.'

She shook her head. She looked tired, wrung out. 'I'm not threatening you. I'm warning you. For some reason – Lord knows why – I still think fondly of you. And you're going to get into trouble. The kind of trouble that will make a mess of the rest of your life. And, next time, I'm not going to be there to get you out of it.'

She turned back to the main door, but, before she reached it, she noticed the whiteboard that was covered with Atticus's scrawled theories about Alfred Burns.

She pointed at it. '*Still?*'

'He's out there,' he said. 'He'll do it again – you know he will – and I don't want that on my conscience.'

'Have you been taking your pills?'

'This has nothing to do with that,' he protested.

'Really?' she said. 'Obsessive behaviour?'

'Yes,' he said, 'I *am* obsessed, because he's still out there and he's still dangerous.'

'But you're taking your medication?'

He went over to the table and picked up the two bottles.

He shook them and the pills rattled inside. 'Happy?'

Mack looked as if she might reply, but changed her mind and turned the key in the lock. She opened the door and made her way onto the landing. Atticus started after her, but he heard her footsteps on the stair and then the door opening and closing. He went to the bay window and looked out as she passed along the pavement beneath him, crossing the road and disappearing out of sight. She didn't look back.

He stayed in the window, staring, his thoughts running away from him. Had he thought about how Mack would react if he started to dismantle her case? It had crossed his mind, but he had pushed it down. He reminded himself: he was being paid to do a job of work. He didn't owe the police anything. They had dismissed him without a second's thought.

Why would he care about making them look bad in court?

He told himself that he didn't owe Mack anything, either, but that one was a harder sell. It was her case; losing it would reflect badly on her, and losing it because the investigation had been sloppily handled would be a black mark against her record. And she was due to give the evidence that would close the prosecution case tomorrow.

She was going to get destroyed.

He locked the main door and went back into the bedroom. He closed the door to the stairs and lowered himself down onto the mattress again. Bandit padded over and lay down beside him. Atticus closed his eyes, tried to put the sadness and regret out of his mind, and waited for sleep to come.

65

Mack went home in a foul mood. She knew that Atticus was responsible for the emails, but knew – despite her threats – that she wouldn't be able to prove it. She realised, as she walked through the quiet streets back to Bishopdown, that it wasn't so much what he had done that had annoyed her, but that *she* had been found wanting. Her first impression of Lamza had been negative, and she had never really trusted him; that being said, his claim to have been in a relationship with Ralph had not been disputed, and there was no obvious reason that he would have put himself through the ordeal of a trial just so that he could perjure himself. Greed was a powerful motivator, and he had been susceptible to it.

She had missed it.

She had seen the weight and heft that his evidence would lend to the prosecution case, and had allowed it to blind her to his obvious shortcomings.

She let out a long, tired sigh. She wondered how Atticus had come to the conclusion that Lamza was bent. She had worked with him for long enough, and she knew that his frequent flashes of insight were less magic and more the aggregation and assessment of small pieces of evidence that, once viewed as a whole, could reveal interesting truths. He had been a valuable asset in her team. He had made breakthroughs that were beyond anyone else; beyond her, too. She doubted that Lamza would have been able to fool them all if Atticus had been there to assess him.

No sense in dwelling on that now. He was gone. Long gone. Water under the bridge.

It was one in the morning by the time she opened the front door to their house. She crept inside, listening at the foot of the stairs until she heard the deep in and out of Andy's breathing. She poured herself a glass of water and took it upstairs. She checked the children – both were sound asleep – and then went into their room. Andy was sleeping deeply. They still hadn't had the chance to discuss the argument from the skating on Sunday. She considered going to the spare room, but decided that would escalate things when all the two of them needed to do was talk. She undressed and slid between the cold sheets. Andy mumbled something, but did not wake.

Mack decided to leave him be. There was no point in trying to untangle their emotions now. It could wait until the morning.

66

Mack found it difficult to sleep, and, when she awoke and checked the clock, she found that she had forgotten to set the alarm and had overslept.

It was eight fifteen.

Shit.

She was due to give her evidence this morning. She had wanted to be there in plenty of time to run over her witness statement again and to prepare herself for the ordeal she knew that she was going to have to endure.

Today, of all days, was not the one to be late.

Why hadn't Andy woken her?

She swung herself out of bed and stumbled to the head of the stairs. She listened for sounds of activity from the kitchen, but heard nothing. Andy and the kids must have already headed out. She went to the window and looked down onto the drive. Andy was getting the kids into the car, tossing their school bags into the boot and then making sure that they were strapped in. She knocked on the window, but Andy didn't hear her – or ignored her – and got into the front of the car. He reversed out and drove away.

She sighed.

They couldn't go on like this. They really needed to talk.

She stumbled into the shower, put her hair inside a cap to keep it dry, and quickly washed. She dried herself and dressed. She couldn't find the kitten heels that she wanted, so had to make do with a pair of black patent brogues that she had picked up on a whim from Next.

She checked her watch – eight thirty – and decided that she would have to get breakfast at the court's café, and hurried outside.

She tried to start the car.

Nothing happened.

Shit.

She tried again.

The engine spluttered once, twice, and then died.

She slapped her hands on the wheel.

Shit, shit, shit, shit, shit!

She took out her phone and stared at it helplessly. Lennox wouldn't be near enough to come and pick her up, and she couldn't really call the nick and have them send her a car. She found her thoughts drifting to Atticus, but dismissed them immediately. He was the last person in the world whom she could call.

No.

The *absolute* last.

She called Triple 7 and sat back in her beached car, waiting for the taxi to arrive.

67

Atticus took his usual seat as the preliminaries for the day's evidence were dispensed with. Abernathy rose and cleared his throat.

'The prosecution calls Detective Chief Inspector Mackenzie Jones.'

Mack came into the court and crossed to the witness box. She was wearing a slim-cut navy suit with a white shirt and brogues. Her jewellery was limited to a simple watch and earrings. She stared across the court until she found Atticus and locked eyes with him. She laid her hand on the Bible, cleared her throat and – still looking at him – spoke into the microphone.

'I swear by Almighty God that the evidence I shall give shall be the truth, the whole truth and nothing but the truth.'

'Thank you,' Abernathy said. 'Could you introduce yourself, please.'

'Detective Chief Inspector Mackenzie Jones, senior investigating officer at Wiltshire Police.'

'Thank you. Could we begin by giving the jury a flavour of your role in this case?'

'Of course. As senior investigating officer, my role is to capture and examine all of the evidence as a whole, to decide on investigative strategies and to manage a team of detectives charged with carrying out the investigative actions that I set.'

'Thank you, DCI Jones,' Abernathy said. 'I'd like you to go over your own experience on Christmas Eve last year.'

Mack spoke succinctly and authoritatively, furnishing the facts and leaving out her opinion until she was asked for it. She was an experienced and persuasive witness. She proceeded to describe the events of Christmas Eve from her perspective, including her interactions with Ralph Mallender; she defused Lennox's concern that there was still someone inside the property; she spoke of the arrival of the armed response vehicles and the storming of the house. She went over the time that she'd spent inside the property, reinforcing the evidence that had been given by the other officers who had attended that night.

Atticus knew from his own experience that the exercise was designed to highlight the strongest points of the prosecution case: the family argument on the afternoon of Christmas Eve; the ability to exit the house through the coal hole, so that the killer might still have been inside; the new evidence from Dr Sandeau demonstrating that Cameron Mallender was an unlikely suspect. Abernathy stayed away from any reference to Freddie Lamza's discredited evidence, and, while he had no choice in that, its absence was obvious and underlined the fact that the Crown's case was significantly weaker now, and perhaps even crippled.

Abernathy continued to a review of Mack's interviews with Ralph, allowing her to set out how her suspicions as to his involvement had developed over time.

'We were operating on the basis of the evidence before us,' she said. 'The first few days suggested that Cameron was the most likely suspect. The house appeared to be locked from the inside, and the murder weapon was close at hand.'

'But not close enough,' Abernathy said.

'That's right. We initially believed it was possible that the pistol might have ended up there after Cameron discharged it, but subsequent expert analysis has rendered that less likely.'

'And what do you think happened now?'

'I think that a third party shot the family and wanted to make it look as if Cameron was responsible. They wanted us to think that it was a murder-suicide.'

'And that third party?'

Mack looked to the dock. 'I believe it was the defendant.'

'I don't want to preclude the defence's cross-examination of you, DCI Jones, but their statements suggest that they will say that you were unduly influenced by the family of the victims, and that it is in their best interests that the defendant is convicted since, if that happens, it will be they – and not he – who stand to inherit the estate. What do you say to that?'

'The investigation was not influenced by external pressure in any way.'

'But you spoke to the family?'

'Of course. They made their concerns known, but it didn't influence us at all. We simply followed the evidence as we found it. At first, the evidence pointed to Cameron Mallender. As we investigated further, it pointed more clearly to the defendant.'

Abernathy moved on to ask how Ralph had appeared to Mack when she first spoke to him, and then about the content of the interviews that had been conducted both prior to and after his subsequent arrest. Atticus listened. She maintained her composed delivery, but her answers started to sound defensive, unsurprising given the fresh context that had been delivered by the evidence heard yesterday. Mack had already been given a tough time in the papers following the abrupt about-turn from Cameron to Ralph as the main suspect; some less charitable legal commentators had suggested that the investigation had been botched, and there had been calls for an inquiry to establish what had gone wrong. Atticus had always found those calls hysterical, but he knew that they would be made again now that it looked as if the investigation had taken another wrong turn.

Atticus had sympathy. A case like this was a living, breathing thing, and it was normal for it to take divergent courses when new material was presented. His confidence in his own abilities lent him the belief that he would not have made those errors, but he was not about to damn Mack because she had.

Abernathy finished the evidence-in-chief after an hour. 'Thank you, Detective Chief Inspector,' he said. 'Please remain there – I'm sure that my learned friend will have some questions for you.'

Abernathy sat down and Crow took to his feet.

'I most certainly do,' he said.

Atticus felt nauseous.

68

Crow smiled and laced his fingers behind his back.

'Detective Chief Inspector,' he said, 'I'd be surprised if this trial has gone the way that you thought it would. Would that be right?'

'I don't know that I'd say that.'

'But you can't *seriously* still think that the defendant is guilty?'

'That's for the jury to decide.'

'We can agree on that, at least,' Crow said, looking over at them with a meaningful arch of his eyebrow. 'Do you think that the defendant is guilty beyond all reasonable doubt?'

'Again, Mr Crow – that's for the jury.'

Crow left a short pause as he flipped through his trial bundle.

'You have said that your initial suspicion was that Cameron Mallender was responsible for the murders.'

Mack nodded. 'That's right.'

'What changed to make you suspect the defendant?'

'The evidence made it clear to me that Cameron could not have been responsible and that there was a strong case against the defendant.'

'You allowed yourself to be pushed away from Cameron and onto Ralph?'

'"Pushed"?'

'Influenced.'

She shook her head. 'The direction of the case changed, but we were not influenced by anyone.'

'Not the family?'

'No, sir. Not at all.'

He flipped pages again, leaving a weighty pause. It was a clichéd move, but that didn't make it any less effective. Mack was doing a good job of maintaining her composure in the face of the avalanche of criticism and derision that she must have known was about to fall upon her, but Atticus was astute enough to see the signs of her discomfort: she reached up with her left hand to touch her neck, then laid both hands on her legs and gently rubbed them down to her knee. Pacifying gestures. It was difficult to notice what the hands were doing when the brain was focused on something else.

Crow settled on a page. 'How did you feel when Freddie Lamza made contact with you?'

'What do you mean?'

'I imagine it must have felt like a significant moment?'

'It did.'

'And you must have thought his evidence was very important?'

'Yes,' she said. 'We did.'

'I imagine that you and your team must have been thrilled.'

'I wouldn't say that.'

'Really? Mr Lamza was prepared to give evidence that Mr Mallender hated his family and wanted them dead. That was the missing piece in the prosecution's case. Here was his motive. Surely you must have been elated?'

She shook her head. 'We weren't thrilled or elated. It was an important piece of evidence. We investigated it, just as we would investigate any other piece of evidence.'

'But that investigation was a travesty. The Criminal Procedures Investigative Act demands that you investigate all reasonable leads, whether they point towards or away from a defendant's guilt. Would you agree that you failed in that regard, Detective Chief Inspector?'

Mack smiled, thin and curt, and shook her head. 'No, I do not.'

'But it has been demonstrated that Mr Lamza perjured himself. That he was prepared to *lie* in order to gain a measure of revenge on the defendant while also being paid handsomely for doing so. Isn't that right?'

'I have been disappointed by what I have learned about Mr Lamza over the course of the trial.'

The line came smoothly. Atticus knew that Mack would have prepared it in advance.

Crow pointed behind himself to the dock. 'Not *nearly* as disappointed as Ralph Mallender. He is disappointed that you did not see Mr Lamza for what he is – a duplicitous perjurer – until the defence did your work for you.'

Mack's eyes flashed with anger, but she held her tongue.

'He is disappointed that you have turned his life upside down. He is disappointed that the manifest and repeated failures of the investigation that you were responsible for have meant that who-ever murdered his family has not been brought to justice.'

'It remains my position that the defendant is responsible for what happened that night.'

'What *nonsense*.' Crow turned to look at the jury. 'The pros-ecution case is a sham, isn't it? A failure from start to finish. It was Cameron; then it wasn't. It was Ralph, but now it isn't. Isn't it the case that your personal conviction of the defendant's guilt led you to ignore all of the investigative avenues available to you?'

'No, sir. It did not.'

'Who really killed the Mallenders?'

'There is still evidence against the defendant,' Mack said icily. 'Mr Mallender had the means, motive and opportunity to murder them. All I can do is to speak to the evidence that the investigation assembled. There is a lot of evidence that he was responsible for what happened.'

'A lot of unsubstantiated, circumstantial evidence.'

'You can say that, sir, but I don't agree. And, with respect, it doesn't matter what we think. The jury will decide whether he is guilty or not.'

'Indeed,' Crow said with another look across the court at the eight men and four women, who were all rapt as they watched the exchange. 'Thank you, Detective Chief Inspector. I have no further questions for you.'

69

The atmosphere in the court fizzed as Mack went back to her seat behind Abernathy. She felt a curious mixture of emotions: humiliation at the shortcomings of the investigation being pinned solely on her; anger that she had been shamed so publicly; and relief that the ordeal was over.

Mack looked over at the gallery. Allegra Mallender was there, in the same seat as before. She had glimpsed her while she had been in the box, and had seen how she had leaned forward, staring at her, a thin smile often playing across her face. Mack couldn't really blame her. She knew that Allegra held her responsible for what had happened to her husband, and it wasn't unreasonable that she should find pleasure in Mack's discomfort.

Atticus was there, too. She was surprised that he had come. He could deny being involved in the character assassination of Freddie Lamza as much as he wanted, but Mack knew that it was his work. Not *literally*, perhaps – Atticus was too careful to do something as foolish as that – but she knew that it had been him.

There wasn't much else for him to do now. His work was over.

A job well done.

Christopher Crow got to his feet and cleared his throat. 'My Lord, now that the prosecution has concluded its case, I feel it is incumbent upon me to submit that there is no case to answer. The prosecution's case relied upon the testimony of Mr Lamza, and he has now been thoroughly discredited as a perjurer motivated by money. There is no forensic evidence against Mr Mallender. No motive has been proven. All we are left with is the fact that he was – arguably – in the wrong place at the wrong time. Accordingly, I must suggest that the charges against my client be dismissed.'

Mack found that she was clenching her fists. The anxious anticipation of her own evidence had distracted her, and she had forgotten that the case could end as soon as this morning; right now, in fact.

'Thank you, Mr Crow,' the judge said. 'I had anticipated that you might make this application, and I gave it some thought overnight. I would have been happy to grant the application if there was no case to answer against the defendant, but, on balance, there is some evidence that a jury, properly directed, could possibly convict upon it. My ruling is that the case should proceed, and any evidence that you might wish to put forward should now be heard.'

Mack exhaled in relief.

Crow bowed his head in acceptance of the decision. 'Are you ready to begin the defence?' Somerville asked. 'I am, my Lord. I call Mr Ralph Mallender.'

70

The fireworks from Lamza's evidence yesterday were still fresh in Mack's memory and, although they had seriously undercut the case against Ralph Mallender, now that the trial was confirmed to carry on to a verdict, everyone knew that what came next was important. It had the potential to be dramatic, too. Mallender had sat in the dock throughout the proceedings and, save his outburst against Lamza – now seemingly justified after the demolition of the prosecution's star witness – he had been calm and still throughout.

His cross-examination would test that sangfroid.

Ralph took his place in the witness box. Mack had been unsure whether he would still give evidence, given that the case against him had been weakened so significantly. The prosecution's case was precarious now, and she had wondered whether there was more for Mallender to lose than gain by going into the box.

Crow got to his feet and began the evidence-in-chief. The questions were straightforward and the answers all carefully rehearsed: what happened on Christmas Eve; what did he see when he returned to the farmhouse; how did he feel; what did he think might have happened? Mallender answered them eloquently and with just the right measure of emotion. He took out a handkerchief when he was asked to describe how he felt about what had happened to his family so that he could dab his eye. Crow asked him what he had thought when he had seen his father's body, and his eyes filled again with tears.

It was an accomplished performance, but Mack found it all a little bit *too* perfect. But, she concluded, it probably didn't matter. Mallender didn't make any major errors, and, given what had happened with Lamza, just getting through without a gaffe was all that he needed to do.

'One final question, Mr Mallender,' Crow said. 'Did you shoot your family?'

'Absolutely not, sir,' he said. 'I did not.'

'Thank you,' Crow said. 'Please wait there. I'm sure Mr Abernathy will have some questions for you.'

Abernathy stood and pushed his shoulders back. 'I do.'

71

The atmosphere in the court changed, as if a ratchet had been very subtly tightened. Abernathy made Mallender wait while he arranged his notes on the desk, running his finger down a page, drawing it out, letting the defendant know who was in charge, letting him *sweat*. Mallender drummed his fingers on the rail of the witness box; Mack could see that he was nervous.

She started to wonder whether Abernathy might be able to draw something out of him after all.

'Mr Mallender,' Abernathy began, 'I expect you think this is going rather well.'

Mallender took a sip of water. 'Is that a question, sir?'

'*Do* you think your defence is going well?'

'That's not how I would describe it. This has been the worst ordeal of my life.'

'Worse than finding that your family had been killed?'

'Of course not,' he said. 'I mean the *whole* thing – what happened at the house, being investigated, charged with it . . . then this. Do you know what it feels like?'

'I do not.'

'I wouldn't wish it on my worst enemy.'

'I'm sure you wouldn't.'

Mallender took another sip and then put the glass down. Mack could see that his hand was shaking. Abernathy took the sheet of paper, adjusting his spectacles as he looked down at it.

Somerville cleared his throat. 'Do you have a question for the defendant, Mr Abernathy?'

'Yes, my Lord. I do. I'm not going to start with what happened that night – we'll get to that in time. I'd like to start with your relationship with your family.'

'What do you want to know?'

Abernathy started in a discursive manner, taking Mallender through a review of his childhood, his teens and then his early adult years. He asked gentle questions, simple enquiries that Mallender didn't have to work too hard to answer. Mack could see that Mallender was on edge – a mixture of anxiety and suspicion at the affable nature of the questioning – but, as the first half-hour passed into the second, he visibly relaxed.

Abernathy put the paper down on the desk and hooked his thumbs into his gown. 'As you know, the prosecution has a witness – a psychiatrist, Dr Sandeau – who gave evidence that your brother, Cameron, was in therapy in order to deal with his problems with anger. You are aware of that?'

'I became aware of it yesterday when she gave her evidence.'

'You didn't know before?'

'I did not.'

'You heard her testify that Cameron told her that your father, Hugo, abused him when he was younger.'

341

Ralph's voice dipped a little. 'Yes.'

Abernathy took off his glasses and stared at Mallender. 'Did your father abuse you, too, Mr Mallender?'

Mack observed Mallender carefully; he was gripping the rail and, as she watched, he gripped so tightly that his knuckles showed white. He bit down on his bottom lip.

'Mr Mallender,' the judge said, 'please – answer the question.'

'I'd rather not.'

'Please, Mr Mallender,' Abernathy said. 'Your father – did he abuse you as a child?'

Ralph looked to Somerville. 'Is this really relevant?'

'It might be. Please – answer the question.'

Ralph kneaded his hands together.

'You're hesitating, Mr Mallender. Is that because he did?'

Mallender spoke quietly. 'Yes.'

'Louder, please.'

'Yes. He did.'

Abernathy leaned forward. 'Could you tell us about that?'

'What do you want to know?'

'What happened?'

'Why is that relevant?'

'Please answer the question.'

Ralph turned to the judge. 'I don't see how this is relevant.'

Somerville looked down at Abernathy. 'Mr Abernathy?'

'My Lord, I'm exploring a line of questioning that will, I hope, assist in exploring the motivation that the prosecution seeks to ventilate.'

'Please make sure it remains relevant,' the judge said. 'Of course, my Lord.'

'Please, Mr Mallender. Carry on.'

Ralph glared at Abernathy. 'He . . . touched me.'

'And?'

'He made *me* touch *him*.'

'Sexual touching?'

'What other kind is there?'

'I'd just like to be clear.'

'I *said* he abused me.'

'When did this happen?'

'When I was a boy.'

'When did it stop?'

'When I was ten or eleven. I don't know. I tried to forget it.'

'*Why* did he stop?'

'I don't know.'

'No idea at all?'

'Maybe I was getting older. I don't know.'

'And he switched his attention to your brother?'

'Yes.'

'Speak up, Mr Mallender.'

'Yes. I suppose he did.'

'Did Cameron talk to you about that?'

'Yes,' Ralph said. 'He did.'

'So when you say, "I suppose he did," what you meant to say was, "Yes, he did."'

'Yes,' Ralph said, his eyes flashing. 'He did.'

'Thank you, Mr Mallender. I'm just trying to set out exactly what you knew.'

'Fine.'

Abernathy looked over his spectacles at Ralph. 'How did that make you feel?'

Mallender frowned. 'What do you mean?'

'The fact that he abandoned you for Cameron – did that make you feel less loved?'

'*What?*'

'It's perfectly straightforward, Mr Mallender. Did you feel less loved?'

'Don't be so preposterous.'

'I've prosecuted cases where victims have testified to that.'

Mallender turned to Somerville. 'Do I have to answer that, too?'

'Please.'

Mallender shook his head derisively. 'This is ridiculous. Of course not. Of course I didn't feel less loved. That's a ridiculous suggestion. Ludicrous.'

Crow stood up. 'I'm not sure why this is relevant. It feels very much like my friend is baiting Mr Mallender.'

'I'm paying close attention,' the judge said.

Abernathy bowed his head. 'I am obliged, my Lord.' He turned back to Ralph. 'How did you feel when Cameron told you what your father had done to him?'

'Awful. Dreadful. The main thing I remember is wondering if there was anything that I could have done to protect him.'

'But you were young, Mr Mallender. What could you possibly have done?'

Ralph didn't answer.

Abernathy pushed his glasses back up his nose and looked down at his notes. 'Let's move on to your feelings towards your father.'

'What do you want me to say?'

'I want you to answer truthfully.'

'I am answering truthfully.'

'Did you forgive him for what he did to you?' Mallender swallowed.

The pressure was building. Abernathy was skilfully probing and poking, finding sore spots and digging into them.

'Mr Mallender – did you forgive him for what he did to you?'

'No,' Mallender snapped. 'What he did is not the sort of thing that you can forgive.'

'So it would be fair to say that you were angry with him?'

'Would you have been angry if your father had ...' He swallowed. 'If he had *interfered* with you?'

'Yes,' Abernathy said. 'I most certainly would. But this isn't about me, is it? It's about you.'

'Of course I was angry.'

'How angry?'

Mallender started to speak, but caught himself.

'How angry?'

Allegra Mallender leaned forward.

Ralph stammered. 'I ... I ... I ...'

Abernathy rested his hands on his desk and leaned forward. 'You *hated* him, didn't you?'

Mallender's face blanched and his larynx bobbed up and down as he fought a dry mouth. Mack looked at Crow and the solicitors behind him; they suddenly looked concerned. The confidence that they had shown after what had happened to Freddie Lamza looked like a memory now. She felt a prickle of excitement pass up and down her spine. Abernathy was goading him, and Mallender was close to losing his temper.

Allegra could see it, too. Mack could see that she wanted to tell him to stop, but that was impossible. He was on his own.

'Mr Mallender?'

Ralph was struggling to master himself, trying not to react.

'You *hated* your father, didn't you?'

'I don't . . .' he stumbled. 'I didn't . . .'

'Mr Mallender,' Abernathy repeated, raising his voice, 'answer the question.'

'Yes,' Ralph barked out. 'I hated him. He was a sick old bastard and I fucking hated him.'

There were gasps. Abernathy ignored them; he smelled blood.

'What about your mother? Did she know what your father had done to you?'

'Oh yes,' Mallender said angrily, lost amid the sudden welter of his fury. 'She knew. She knew from the start.'

'And did you hate her, too?'

'I hated them both. He ruined my life and she let him do it.'

'You killed them on Christmas Eve, didn't you?'

Ralph started to speak, then stopped. Realisation broke across his face. His mouth opened and closed as the enormity of what he had just said finally dawned on him.

'No. No – I didn't.'

'Yes, you did.'

'Mr Abernathy,' Somerville intervened sternly.

Abernathy ignored the scolding, pushing his luck harder. 'You had an argument with them that afternoon, didn't you? What was said?'

Ralph was sweating. 'It was about my wife.'

'Just one more thing to add to the long list of things you hated your parents for. Your father abused you. Your mother ignored it. And now, after all of that, after all those years of *misery*, here they were trying to prevent you from finding happiness with your wife. A litany of things that you hated them for. I can't imagine how that would have made you feel.'

'I don't . . .' Ralph looked to the judge, then to the jury, then into the public gallery. 'No. I didn't . . .'

Abernathy spoke over him. 'You waited until you knew you could find them at home, you went back to the house, and you shot them. You knew that you stood to inherit everything if you were the sole survivor, so you shot your brother and your sister, too. That's what happened on Christmas Eve. Isn't that true?'

'No, it is not—'

Abernathy spoke over him again, anger vibrating through his voice. 'I don't believe you, Mr Mallender. You shot them and then, if that wasn't enough, you defiled the memory of your brother by making it look like *he* killed them. Isn't that true?'

'*No*. I did not.'

'We've heard evidence from Cameron's psychiatrist that he wasn't violent, at least beyond his self-harm. You used his mental illness as a diversion. A diversion designed to take attention away from what *you* did.'

'No, it's not like that.'

'No? Really? So what *was* it like, Mr Mallender? Did you panic? You lost your temper for a moment and then, when you realised what you'd done, you panicked. You made it look like Cameron had killed them. You wiped the pistol down and put it down near to his body, although not near enough. You locked the doors so that it looked like the killer must have been inside the house. You went out through the coal hole, and then you called the police. Isn't that what happened?'

'*No.*'

Mack had seen Ralph like this before, during the interviews that she had conducted with him before he had been charged. She had chipped away at him, asking the same questions over and over again, each repetition another drop of poison added to the mix. He was brimful of anger and superciliousness and disdain, and, if handled *just* so, it was possible to lead him all the way to a place where he couldn't stop that mixture from detonating. He was close to that place now. He had exploded once; another larger explosion was coming.

Abernathy sensed it, too. He prodded and probed some more, provoking him, daring him to react, encouraging him to lose control. The barrister was ramrod straight, his eyes burning, staring at Ralph, almost taunting him.

'You've told a pack of lies today, haven't you?'

'No.'

'Everything you've told us about what happened on Christmas Eve is a lie.'

'No, it's not. It's true. I didn't do what they said I did.'

'Lies, lies, lies.'

'No, sir.'

'Your father abused you for years.'

'No . . .' Ralph paused, confused.

'No?'

'I mean yes. I'm not lying.'

'He abused you for years.'

'Yes.'

'He stole your childhood from you.'

'Yes.'

'Your mother was complicit.'

'Yes.'

'A mother should protect her child, shouldn't she?'

Ralph was lost now, swept away. 'Yes.'

'But she didn't. She made it all possible.'

'Yes.'

'You hated your mother and your father and you wanted them dead.'

'*Yes, I fucking did.*'

He shouted, a sudden eruption that echoed around the court. There were gasps from the public gallery. Mack leaned forward, avid, knowing full well that this was the fulcrum upon which the case would be decided. Lamza was suddenly no more than an inconvenience.

The investigation, the trial . . . it all came down to this.

Abernathy leaned in, too, a hawk ready to swoop. 'You killed them.'

'He was a bastard. The only thing that made him happy was making my life a living hell. They were both evil.'

Abernathy let the moment hang and then, taking off his spectacles and slipping them into a pocket beneath his robes – letting the moment stretch out a little longer – he closed his folder and stood back.

'I have no further questions.'

72

The atmosphere in the defence conference room was *horrific*. Atticus was in his usual position, leaning against the wall and, from there, he was able to look at the others ranged around the table: Crow looked stunned, trying to start a summing-up of the car crash that he had just witnessed but unable to find the diplomacy to do it; Cadogan looked bemused, jotting pointless notes on a legal pad so that he wouldn't have to offer an opinion; Allegra was shocked, her mouth open, her right hand obsessively kneading her left. Ralph had been taken back down to the cells until the end of the lunchtime adjournment. Crow and Cadogan had been to see him and had reported that he was in a bad way. That, Atticus thought, was not surprising. He had allowed his temper to run away with him, and the potential cost of that momentary slip could be his liberty.

'Right then,' Crow said, trying to sound cheery. 'That didn't go well, but it's not the end of the world.'

'Don't sugar-coat it,' Allegra muttered. 'That's it, isn't it? He's done. We're cooked.'

'He didn't do himself any favours. But . . .' Crow looked down at his notes. 'Like I said, it's not the end of the world. We can recover.'

'Abernathy took advantage of him,' Allegra said. 'He goaded him.'

'That's his job,' Crow said.

Allegra looked up from her lap, her eyes flashing. 'So Ralph should've taken a deep breath. We told him, didn't we? We said, "You can't lose your temper." *Jesus*. Toddlers react like he did. He knew what Abernathy wanted him to say, and then he said it anyway.'

'Let's not panic,' Crow said, his hands raised. 'What's done is done. It didn't go well, but it's just a setback. We can recover from it.'

Allegra looked as if she was going to say something more, but decided against it and went back to an examination of her hands.

'We'll put it to one side,' Crow said. 'I'll work on a way to minimise it. I get to re-examine Ralph after lunch. I'll try to repair as much of the damage as I can. And then we've got Cameron. We'll put the focus back on him. His anger. When he got in trouble with the police and Ralph had to go and bail him out. The violence. We'll focus on that, just like before, just like we said.'

'They've already undermined all that,' Allegra said. 'Sandeau said Cameron *wasn't* violent.'

'I know she did,' Crow said. 'And we have plenty of witnesses who will say otherwise. He was arrested for beating someone up – that's not speculation, it's not professional opinion, it's recorded fact. The jury will decide which story is the most credible. I think we'll win this one.'

'I don't know.'

'We can add in the abuse now, too,' Cadogan said. He turned to Crow. 'Right?'

'We can,' Crow said with a nod. 'It cuts both ways – what Hugo did is a motive for both brothers. Ralph *and* Cameron.'

Atticus felt his phone buzz in his pocket. He took it out and saw that he had a Facebook message. He opened the app and navigated to Messenger.

It was from George, Cassandra's ex-boyfriend. He opened it. *I found a picture of the man I mentioned.*

Atticus scrolled down and waited for the picture to download. He tapped it to bring it up to full size.

He stared at it for a moment, too stunned to think.

'Atticus?' Allegra said.

It was a group shot: Cassandra and a group of six others. It looked as if they were out on the town, all of them dressed up in party clothes and some of them holding drinks up for the camera. Cassandra was in the middle of the group, and a man – older than the rest of them – had his arm looped around her waist.

'Atticus? What is it?'

He took a moment to consider how best to reply. The others were all looking at him.

'I've been going over the evidence, like I said,' he explained, his tone vague as he ran the angles through his head. 'I wanted to approach it from a different direction, so I started looking into Cassandra. It felt like everyone had ignored her, and I had a feeling there might be something there. I reviewed her social media history for the last three years and contacted some of her older friends. A lot of them disappeared between the first and second years of university – they were there; then they weren't.'

'She dropped them,' Allegra said. 'Ralph told me.'

'Did he tell you why?'

'She went off the rails. Juliet got her into the church, and she decided that she needed a clean break from the people she had been seeing.'

'That's what I heard,' Atticus said.

'How did you find them?' Allegra asked.

'Facebook.' He shrugged. 'It wasn't difficult. One of the old group got back to me – this lad, George. He's an ex-boyfriend from her first year.'

'You've spoken to him?'

'I went to Bath last week to see him. It turns out Cassandra wasn't always clean-living. Drink and drugs.'

'Usual student stuff,' Cadogan said. 'Kids being kids.'

Atticus turned to him. 'Why didn't you make reference to it in the defence?'

'Like I said – student stuff. It's hardly unusual.'

'No,' Atticus said, 'it isn't. But by saying nothing, we've let the prosecution paint her as if she was an angel, and she wasn't. There were four people in that house who might have had something to do with what happened. Hugo, Juliet, Cameron and Cassandra. You've only focused on Cameron. What about the others?'

'Because he's the most likely to have done it,' Cadogan said.

Atticus could have retorted, argued that the strategy had ignored three potential sources of reasonable doubt, but there was no point now; that ship had sailed. Recrimination could come later. He had to work with the hand that he had been dealt.

'One of Cassandra's friends died,' Atticus said.

'I remember,' Allegra said. 'Ralph mentioned it. Drugs?'

'Her name was Stacey Dickinson. It was on the news – she took ecstasy and then basically hydrated herself to death. George told me about it and I looked it up. Cassandra came straight home after it happened. She started going to church around that time. It seems like the experience changed her. She decided everything in her life had to be different. Church every Sunday, no more drinking, no more drugs, no more going out. When she went back to university for the second year, she didn't want anything to do with her old friends.'

Allegra frowned. 'I don't get it.'

'Neither do I,' Cadogan said. 'How does this have anything to do with the murders?'

'George and Cassandra were seeing each other for the first six months they were at university,' Atticus said, 'but then she finished with him and started seeing someone from home.'

Allegra shook her head. 'Ralph never told me that. Who?'

Atticus turned the phone around and held it up so that the others could look at the screen.

Allegra's mouth fell open. '*What?*'

'Show me,' Crow said.

Atticus angled the phone in his direction.

'That's Jimmy Robson.'

Atticus nodded. 'The last person to see Hugo alive on Christmas Eve.'

Allegra took the phone, stared at it and then handed it to Crow. 'Robson was seeing Cassie?'

'That's what George told me,' Atticus said. 'You didn't know?'

She shook her head. 'I had no idea. Ralph never said – I doubt he knew. But it's relevant. Right?'

'It is,' Crow said. 'Very.'

Atticus collected the phone and put it back into his pocket. 'George told me that it was Robson who got Cassandra into drugs. He was selling to all of them. Including Stacey. George says that he never saw Robson again when Cassandra came back for the second year. It seemed like he was out of her life, just like the rest of them were. So that got me to thinking: why would the relationship stop like that? And why would she start going to church? Then he told me about Stacey Dickinson and it made sense. Let's say Robson supplied the pill that killed Stacey. What if Cassandra confided everything to Hugo and Juliet? That seems likely. He was working for the family then. It's not that hard to imagine how Hugo would have reacted.'

'He would've lost his shit,' Allegra said. 'Perhaps he confronted Robson?'

Cadogan had opened the trial bundle and had flipped back to the chronology of agreed facts. 'That was around the time that he stopped working at the farm.'

'So let's put it together. Maybe Robson has a grudge against Hugo and Juliet. They stopped him from seeing Cassandra and fired him from his job. Maybe he had a grudge against Cassandra, too, for not standing up to them. Who knows? But what we *do* know, because he has given evidence on it, is that he was near the house on Christmas Eve. He was there twice – once in the evening when he says he saw Hugo, and then the police have him on the log that night, too, when he said he came to check out what was going on. We know he doesn't have an alibi – he said that he was at home on his own. So he had the means and the opportunity to do it. He might have had the motive, too.'

'He probably knows the house,' Allegra said, talking over him with excited animation. 'He worked for the family for years.'

'So maybe he knows about the way out through the coal cellar.'

'Would he fit through it?' Crow asked. 'He's big.'

'We'd have to check,' Atticus said.

Allegra's cheeks were steadily reddening. 'Why didn't the police find out about any of this?'

'Their resources are stretched,' Atticus said. 'They have to prioritise where the assets they do have are deployed. They would have started with the people who knew Cassandra immediately before she was killed.'

'And then they just *stopped*?'

'I'm not surprised, especially if they'd decided Ralph was guilty. Why else would they keep digging deeper and deeper into her past when there was no obvious reason to do it?'

'Because they might have realised that Ralph didn't do it?'

'No,' Atticus said. 'It doesn't work like that. Look – I'm not ready to jump to conclusions. I'd like to know a little more about Robson first.'

'What are you going to do?' she said.

'I'll go and have a nose around. If I think there might be something there, we'll have to tell DCI Jones. They'll want to bring him in for an interview.'

Allegra grimaced. 'Really? We have to trust her?'

'She'll investigate it thoroughly,' he said, instinctively feeling the need to uphold Mack's reputation even though this wasn't a friendly venue in which to defend her so volubly. 'I'll find out if there's any scope for more, and, if there is, I'll call. You can decide what you want to do, but that would be my very strong recommendation.'

'You'll need to move quickly,' Crow said. 'Our evidence is not going to last more than another couple of days, and that's only if I spin it out. If there's anything to use, we need it before I sit down. Otherwise there's a chance he will be found guilty. If that happens, we'd have to wait for an appeal, and that could take months.'

Atticus pushed himself away from the wall. 'I'll get on to it now.'

'This is good work,' Crow said approvingly. 'Very good.'

Allegra smiled hopefully. 'Well done.'

'I'll let you know if I find anything,' he said.

*　*　*

Atticus saw Mack talking with Gordon Abernathy as he exited the building. The prosecution silk looked happy and he laughed uproariously at something Mack said. Atticus did up his jacket and strode on, Mack noticing him as he headed towards the car park.

Their eyes locked for a moment.

Atticus gave her a nod of acknowledgement and continued on his way.

73

Atticus drove around the ring road until he reached the turn-off for Wilton. It was coming up to three in the afternoon when he passed beneath the railway bridge and headed out towards Great Wishford. He reached the village, drove through it and turned onto the one-lane track that led to the parking space at the fringe of Grovely Wood.

The car park was empty; Atticus reverse-parked and got out. He took out his phone, navigating to the mapping application. He selected the satellite view and zoomed in until he could see the farmhouse. There was a track that ran to the south alongside the eastern boundary of the property, travelling for around half a mile through a heavily wooded area until it ended at another house. The second house was where Jimmy Robson lived. Atticus spread his fingers to zoom in. The house was modest, with a series of outbuildings nestled around it. There was a collection of vehicles near to the entrance from the track and a wide stretch of garden that ended at the boundary of a large field.

Atticus put the phone in his pocket. Bandit had been with him the last time that he had visited the woods, and he found that he wished he was here now, too. The sky was leaden and the air pressure had dropped; it felt as if rain was on the way. Atticus looked down the track that led to the Mallender house. It was gloomy and uninviting, and, as he zipped up his jacket, he realised that the birds were quiet, too.

He gave a shiver and set off.

The trail was muddy, and the slop stuck to Atticus's boots as he trudged into the forest. The light dimmed as he went deeper inside, the canopy of leaves thickening overhead. He walked on, crossing the Roman road and continuing along the narrower track that led to the farmhouse.

The place looked still and sombre, the sole witness to the murderous events of almost a year ago. The curtains were closed and the chimneys were cold and lifeless. Atticus knew that the house and its land were worth millions of pounds, but he couldn't imagine it ever being lived in again. He wasn't prone to superstitious thought, but out here, miles from anyone and surrounded by the enveloping wood, it was difficult not to imagine that the blood of the Mallenders had soaked into the fabric of the building, and that their screams would echo inside for ever.

Atticus continued, following the track around the large agricultural barn. There was an open field sown with crops on his left and another field full of sheep to his right; he pressed on until he was surrounded by thick trees on both sides once again.

He walked the track until he reached the boundary of Robson's property. The track ended in a metal gate that had been fastened with a padlock. Atticus walked up to it and looked into the space beyond. A muddy track led through an overgrown front garden that was littered with the rusting hulks of old vehicles and pieces of farm machinery. The place was in a state of some disrepair. It was a large two-storey construction and had, most likely, been a farmhouse at some point in its past. Those days were gone. The downstairs windows had been boarded up, and the windows upstairs were obscured by vertical blinds, the fabric slats of which were stained yellow. The roof was missing a number of slates and the others were covered with a carpet of moss. Wispy tendrils of smoke drifted up from the chimney. An old and battered Land Rover was parked on a patch of muddy ground just off the track. He could hear the sound of an engine from behind the property; it sounded like a generator.

A path led across the unkempt garden to the house. Atticus dallied at the gate for a little, waiting to see whether Robson was at home or not, but, as he paused, the front door opened and a man came outside. He was followed by a large, shaggy-haired Alsatian. Atticus hurried back and pushed into the gorse at the side of the track. He looked through the vegetation as the man made his way to the Land Rover. Atticus recognised him: it was Robson. He was big, over six feet tall and heavily built. He was wearing an olive-coloured anorak, a beanie on his head and a pair of muddy boots. He held a shotgun beneath his right arm, the breech cracked open.

Atticus watched as the big man opened the door to the Land Rover. The dog bounded inside and Robson hauled himself in after it. The engine started and the vehicle rolled out, splashing through the mud until it was on the track. The brakes wheezed as it came to a stop in front of the gate, the engine turned over with a temperamental grumble, the door opened and there was a splash as Robson stepped out into a puddle. Atticus heard the jangle of the padlock chain as it caught on the metal bars of the gate, the squeak of hinges and then the sound of footsteps and the vehicle's door slamming shut. The Land Rover's engine grumbled louder and the vehicle splashed ahead, passing through the gate. Atticus crouched down lower, grateful for the gloom and the thick vegetation.

He heard the vehicle's door open once more, the squelch of footsteps, the creak of the hinges as the gate was shut, the rattle of the chain and then the click of the padlock as it was secured. He heard Robson get back into the Land Rover, shut the door and rev the engine, and then the vehicle bumped and bounced over the uneven surface of the track and headed north. It passed close enough to Atticus's hiding spot that he could have reached out and touched it; the Alsatian was in the passenger seat and its yellow eyes flashed at him as the vehicle went by.

Atticus stayed where he was until the sound of the engine and the squeak of a rusty spring were no longer audible.

He took a deep breath and, after checking that he was alone, he turned and made his way back to the gate. It had been locked, just as he had thought. Atticus clambered over it, his feet splashing in the mud as he dropped down on the other side. The path to the house had not been cleared for months. Weeds had been allowed to grow unchecked, and the grass was tall enough to brush against Atticus's knees.

He approached the front door and tried it: it was locked. He went around the back of the property. All of the windows were boarded, with no way of seeing inside. A thick electrical cable was suspended from a second-floor window to a post in the ground from which it snaked along to a diesel generator that chugged away beneath a wooden lean-to.

Atticus reached the midpoint of the back wall and a second door into the property. It was flimsy, a simple frame that held three panes of glass. He tried the handle; the door was locked. He didn't have his lock picks with him and, preferring not to damage anything in an attempt to get inside, he started looking for a hidden key. It was surprisingly easy. Atticus noticed that a collection of loose bricks had been left against the side of the house. One of the bricks was angled away from the others and, as he knelt down to examine it, he saw that it had recently been moved. He lifted it up and, to his satisfaction, saw that a key had been left beneath it. He used the key in the lock, pulled down on the handle, opened the door and went inside.

74

The inside of the house was gloomy, with the only light reaching in from the side of the open door. Atticus closed the door and wiped his boots on the doormat. He took out his phone and started to record a video of his investigation. He was in the kitchen. There was a stove that was stacked with pots and pans, a counter that held a pile of plates and the detritus of used packaging, and cupboards that, when Atticus opened them, held only pre-packaged microwave meals. The linoleum floor was sticky with some long-spilled liquid, and his boots squeaked as he crossed the room to the door on the opposite side.

There was a corridor beyond, with doors to the left and right and stairs that ascended to the first floor. He heard a low humming sound from above and, as he sniffed, he thought he detected something acrid in the air. The corridor was dark, but light glowed down from the first floor. Atticus would investigate that last of all.

He started with the door on the left. It was a bedroom. There was a bed, together with a chair and a television resting on an old dresser. The interior was a dreadful mess: bric-a-brac littered the floor, together with clothes that had been discarded and left where they lay. Shelves had been fitted to the walls, and a collection of books and magazines had been stacked there. They looked precarious and, as Atticus reached up to take down one of the magazines, the pile slid off the shelf and spilled out across the floor. They were pornographic magazines from the '80s and '90s, the covers faded and the pages stiff.

He wasn't sure where to look, or even what he might expect to find, and he had no idea how long Robson would be away from the house. He knew that he had to move quickly.

He started on the left-hand side of the room, with the bed and the surrounding furniture and debris. There were more magazines, books that had been taken from the library and not returned, dirty plates that had never made it back to the sink to be washed, and fragments of paper that must have spilled out of pockets. The bed was unmade and the sheets were stained. Atticus ignored that and cleared a space on the floor so that he could crouch down and look beneath the frame. There was nothing of interest. He picked up a photograph from the bedside table; it featured three people on a beach, a man and a woman and a young child. The man was big and resembled Robson; Atticus wondered if it was Robson's father, the photograph a memory of a family occasion. He looked on the shelves above the bed, in the drawers of the bedside table, and inside the dresser.

He didn't see anything of interest.

He left the bedroom and checked the door to the right. It was a bathroom. It was filthy, but there was nothing of note here, either.

Atticus went to the stairs and climbed. He stopped on the half-landing, his mouth falling open.

Where the ground floor was dark, the first floor was unnaturally bright. Industrial lamps had been fitted to the ceiling, and light blazed out of them, a harsh white glare that had Atticus blinking his eyes until they had adjusted. He climbed all the way up and saw that the internal walls of the property had been removed to make for a wide-open space, the roof supported by struts and props and the space enclosed by plastic sheeting that made for a large tentlike structure.

The space was filled by hundreds of cannabis plants.

The heat from the lamps was stifling. The humming that he had heard from below was the sound of the extractor fans that ventilated the plants.

Atticus reached down for one of the plants, trailing his fingertips across the leaves. His mind spun, drawing lines between facts, teasing out conclusions. Robson already had one potential motive for wishing harm to the Mallenders: the possibility that Cassandra's parents had forbidden him from seeing their daughter.

Here, though, was another: what if Hugo Mallender had discovered the cannabis farm?

What if he had threatened to call the police?

What might Robson have done *then?*

Atticus's mind raced, seeking more connections, follow-up questions and enquiries that would have to be made, and, as he stood there, distracted, with the noise of the fans smothering any noise from outside, he forgot where he was and whose house he was in, and it was too late – *much* too late – that he heard the sound of footsteps below.

He heard a bark and then the slap of paws as Jimmy Robson's Alsatian raced down the corridor and leapt up the stairs.

The dog reached the half-landing, its paws slipping from underneath it as it quickly changed direction, scrabbling for traction again and then launching up the rest of the stairs. Its lips were pulled back and its teeth shone as it reached the top and started to bark.

Atticus backed up, but there was nowhere to hide.

He heard the sound of heavier footsteps coming down the corridor and then up the stairs, and then the mechanical click of something being snapped together.

Jimmy Robson reached the top of the stairs, the shotgun held level and aimed at Atticus.

'Who the bloody hell are you?'

Atticus backed up. The dog growled and padded after him.

Robson frowned. 'No – I know you. I remember you. I've seen you before.'

Atticus didn't answer and took another step back.

Jimmy followed. 'You're police.'

'I'm not.'

'You are – I remember. You nicked me.'

'I'm not police. I got fired.'

The dog barked, saliva dripping out of its half-open muzzle.

'Stop lying. I remember you. You did me for assault.'

'You headbutted a police officer, Jimmy.'

'What are you doing in my house?'

'I'm not police,' he said again. 'I was fired.'

'Bollocks. You just happen to be up here, nosing in my business?'

Robson was still advancing, the shotgun still aimed into Atticus's body. They would be picking bits of his corpse up for days afterwards if Robson fired at him from as close as this.

'You're Drugs Squad.'

'I'm not Drugs Squad. I'm not police. And I'm going to leave now.'

Atticus felt something against his back and, stumbling, he knocked it over. It was a trestle table upon which had been arranged a number of large bags of processed cannabis. The table collapsed with a loud crash, the bags of cannabis spilling open and scattering buds all across the floor.

'You ain't going nowhere,' Robson said. 'Not until you've told me what you're doing inside my house.'

Atticus stepped over the table and backed all the way up to the wall. He had nowhere left to go.

Robson followed. He looked even bigger close up.

'Come on,' Atticus said. 'There's no need for this to get nasty.'

'You shouldn't have come in here,' Robson said.

Atticus feinted right and tried to pass the big man to the left. It didn't work; Robson was faster than he looked, shoving out a meaty fist that struck Atticus in the chest. He staggered back, winded, and crashed into the wall. Robson closed in, his fist clenched and ready to strike. Atticus gasped for breath and tried to slide out of the way as Robson threw out a big right-hander. His knuckles caught Atticus on the side of the forehead; sparks of light detonated across his vision. Robson came up close and grabbed Atticus, both hands knotted in his jacket, and hauled him upright.

Atticus drew back his head and butted Robson in the face.

The big man swore. He grunted with effort, switching his weight from left to right and tossing Atticus across the room. Atticus slammed onto the floor. He tried to find his feet but couldn't, the soles of his boots sliding across the spilled buds.

The clamour stirred the dog into action, and, with an angry growl, it sprang forward and closed its jaws around Atticus's wrist. He tried to free himself, but the dog was tenacious and its grip was strong. Atticus booted it in the ribs; it yelped in pain and let go.

Atticus lost his balance and, as he put out his arms to try to prevent himself from toppling over, he turned back to Robson as the big man unloaded a right-hander flush into his jaw.

Atticus's knees went out from beneath him.

The lights started to fade, and then they blinked out.

75

Atticus drifted in and out of consciousness. The first thing that he was aware of when he finally came around was the pounding in his head. It was centred just above his right ear, an electrical pulse that popped through his skull and all the way down into his gut. He felt sick. He thought that he had opened his eyes, but he could see nothing. It took a moment for him to realise: his eyes *were* open, but, wherever he was, it was dark. The pain continued to throb, and he tried to put his hand up to his head so that he might be able to work out why, but, as he tried, he found that his arms were stiff and unmoving. He tried again, jerking from his shoulders, and felt something coarse abrading the skin on his wrists.

He had been tied up.

He remembered: Jimmy Robson.

He had tied him up and dumped him somewhere.

He blinked and waited for his eyes to adjust. The dark wasn't complete; he could see a line of grey down low, as though it were coming from under a door. He waited a little longer until he thought that he could make out the dim shape of a paint pot, and, next to it, what looked like a bucket. He remembered the storeroom that he had poked his head into as he had searched the house. Robson had put him inside there.

'Hey!' he called out. '*Hey!*'

He heard the sound of footsteps overhead – the heavy tread of a person and the scampering patter of a dog – but no one came to attend to his cry.

76

Mack grabbed her coat and made her way out of the court building. It was cold and damp, with a chill in the air that promised the snow that had been forecast. She wrapped her scarf around her neck and looked left and right, getting ready to cross the road. She would go back to the station and take care of the administrative tasks that needed to be got out of the way.

The afternoon's evidence had been enthralling, although without the explosiveness of the morning's session. Abernathy had finished his cross-examination of Ralph Mallender and had handed the witness back to Crow for re-examination. Ralph's anger during Abernathy's questioning had caused serious damage to the defence case, and Crow had done his best to repair as much of it as he could. Abernathy had been gleeful when they debriefed afterwards. It was, he suggested, a lost cause. The loss of Lamza's credibility didn't matter any more. Lamza had been important because he could say that Ralph had told him that he hated his parents.

Ralph had just confirmed that from his own mouth and, what was more, he had explained why: his father had abused him and his mother had enabled it.

Mack had been around briefs enough times to know that equivocation was their standard response when asked to prognosticate as to the odds of a successful prosecution. Abernathy had been no different during this case. Now, though? When she asked him what he thought were the chances for a guilty verdict, he had unhesitatingly and confidently replied that he thought it was eighty-twenty in their favour.

Eighty-twenty? Mack could live with that.

The road was busy and she had to wait to cross.

'Detective Chief Inspector!'

Mack turned in the direction of the voice.

'DCI Jones!'

It was Allegra Mallender.

Mack stiffened. Ralph Mallender had been put through the mill all day, and it wasn't difficult to imagine what his wife must have thought of that. Mack suspected she was about to receive another dose of Allegra's bitter abuse.

'Hello, Mrs Mallender. How can I help you?'

Allegra reached her. She was out of breath. 'I need to talk to you about something.'

'Of course,' Mack responded, as politely as she could. 'What is it?'

'Atticus Priest.'

Mack managed to stifle her sigh. 'What's he done now?'

'I'm worried about him.' Allegra paused. 'You know he's been working for Ralph?'

'I had gathered that,' Mack said as blandly as she could.

'Look – I don't think you know this. Cassandra Mallender was seeing Jimmy Robson.'

Mack frowned. 'What?'

'You know, he works in the woods. He used to work for the family?'

'I know who he is,' she said. 'What do you mean – Robson and Cassandra were in a relationship?'

She nodded. 'Atticus found an old friend of Cassandra's from when she started at university and he said that she was seeing Robson. Cassandra used to be wild – the friend thinks that Robson was the reason she started doing drugs. He says he was supplying them. One of the friends died after taking ecstasy, and Cassandra changed – she started going to church, ignored all her old friends, stopped seeing Robson.'

'Did your husband know about this?'

'No,' Allegra said. 'I mean, yes, he knew that she was a little wild, but that's just student stuff. I don't think he knew that she was seeing Robson. He's never mentioned it to me, anyway. But it's important. He was there that night – he said so himself.'

Mack felt the case shifting again.

'Robson might have had a reason to want to hurt them,' Allegra said.

'Maybe,' she said. 'If it's true. Why are you worried about Atticus?'

'He said he was going to go and speak to Robson.'

'When?'

'In the lunchtime adjournment. He would've been there by two at the latest.'

Mack looked at her watch. 'It's four thirty now. You haven't heard from him?'

She shook her head. 'I tried to call, but he isn't answering. I'm worried.'

'All right,' Mack said. 'I'll send someone over there. Thanks for letting me know.'

She unlatched her handbag, took out her phone and then walked around the corner of the building for a little privacy. She stared at the screen for a moment. Lennox had interviewed Jimmy Robson in the aftermath of the murders, and then he had been interviewed at greater length as they prepared for the trial. Mack recalled the detail of his file. He was a nasty piece of work, with three convictions for assault. The last one had seen him butt the officer who had tried to restrain him after a scuffle outside the Chapel at the end of a drunken Friday night out; Robson had been rewarded with six weeks inside for that. His evidence at the trial had been solely for the purpose of establishing a timeline; save the murderer, Robson was likely to have been the last person to see Hugo Mallender alive. He had no alibi for the evening of Christmas Eve, but, even with his record, they had seen nothing that gave them reason to consider that he might be a suspect.

They had not discovered that he and Cassandra Mallender had been in a relationship. Robson would have been accorded much more interest if they had known that.

Mack knew Atticus all too well. If he had discovered that there was a reason to investigate him, what would he have done?

He would have gone over there to speak to him.

Jesus.

She tapped through to Atticus's number and called it.

'It's Atticus. Whatever unfortunate chain of events has led you to call my number, please leave your story here and I'll call back if I find you sufficiently interesting. If you don't hear from me . . . what can I say?'

Mack hit cancel. She called Lennox.

'Afternoon, boss. What's up?'

'Where are you?'

'At the nick. What's up?'

'Atticus thinks Jimmy Robson might be involved in the murders.'

'The gamekeeper?'

'Yes. He's gone to check him out, but he's not answering his phone.'

'Seriously?'

'Look, Tristan, I'm worried and my car's broken down – we need to get over there. Can you come and get me?'

'Give me ten minutes.'

77

Atticus found it difficult to keep track of time. How long had he been in here? There was no way of saying. The light that leaked beneath the line of the door had the yellow tinge of a bulb, but, even then, the corridor outside the storeroom had been gloomy even when Atticus had broken into the house. He doubted that he would have been able to detect any natural light, assuming that it was still daytime.

'Hey!' he called out again. 'You're making a mistake, Jimmy. People know where I am. They'll come to look for me if I don't get in touch with them.'

He heard the footsteps overhead again.

'You'll go to prison,' Atticus yelled. 'Let me out of here and we can pretend this never happened.'

The footsteps pounded across the floor above. They faded out as Robson moved across the room, and then grew louder as he descended the stairs and approached the door. Atticus tested the rope that secured his wrists again, but the knots were too tight and there was no play in the bonds.

There was a click as a key was turned in the lock and then the door opened. Robson had changed out of his overcoat and was now wearing a T-shirt that revealed muscular arms that were covered with full sleeves of lurid tattoos.

'Jimmy,' Atticus began, 'come on. Let me go.'

Robson stayed in the doorway. 'I don't remember your name.'

'Atticus Priest.'

'That's right. DC Priest.'

'I'm not police.'

'Bullshit.'

'I got fired,' Atticus said. 'Months ago.'

'So what are you doing inside my house?'

'I'm working for Ralph Mallender.'

Robson's lip curled up. 'Yeah?'

'Yes.'

'How?'

'I'm a private investigator.'

Robson took a step forward. 'What does that have to do with me?'

Atticus had known that question would come, and had wondered how he should answer it. There was a balance to be struck between tact and honesty. Not enough of the first might anger Robson; too much of the second would be dangerous.

'Ralph Mallender is on trial for murder.'

'I know that. Killed his family.'

'He says he didn't.'

'He would, wouldn't he.'

'He employed me to investigate the police's evidence.'

'That still don't explain why you'd be snooping around in my house. That's got nothing to do with me.'

Robson was slow on the uptake. Atticus could see that he would have to nudge him in the right direction, but knew that he would need to do it very carefully.

He nodded to Robson's right arm. 'That tattoo,' he said. 'Just above your elbow.'

Robson looked down at his arm. It was a mess of ink, with what looked like a likeness of an Alsatian drawn on top of something else.

'That's Dave,' he said, laying his finger on his arm.

'Dave?'

'My dog. Dave.'

'I don't mean the dog. You used that to ink over a name.'

Robson stared down at the tattoo. There was no name visible beneath it.

'Cassandra,' Atticus said. 'Her name was there. I saw a picture of it. You were in a club in Bath with her and her friends.'

'Nah.' Robson looked as if he was going to say something else, but he shook his head instead.

'You were seeing her, Jimmy. I know. You were going backwards and forwards to Bath. One of her friends told me.'

His eyes narrowed. 'That was ages ago.'

'What happened? Why'd you stop?'

'The girl died.'

'Stacey. That's right.'

'But that weren't my stuff. What happened to her had nothing to do with me.'

'I believe you.'

'I didn't even have pills with me that weekend. I don't know where she got it from.'

He was defensive and off guard. Atticus saw a chance to get him to talk.

'Did Hugo find out about you and his daughter?'

Robson nodded. 'When she came back after the girl died. She told him about us.'

'And he wasn't happy about it?'

'Fired me,' Robson said. 'Worked for the family for ten years, ever since school, and he got rid of me, just like that.'

'Did that make you angry, Jimmy?'

'Course. Wasn't fair.'

'How angry?'

Robson frowned, and, after a moment, realisation dawned across his face.

'You think *I* did it?' he said, gesturing in the rough direction of the farmhouse. 'You think I killed them?'

His anger flared, and Atticus worried that he had gone too far. 'I didn't say that.'

'No! *No.* That ain't got nothing to do with me. Nothing.'

'But you didn't tell the police that you had a history with her.'

'They never asked.'

'Don't you think you should've said something?'

'Would you have told them?'

Atticus nodded. 'Probably.'

'I got a record,' Robson said. 'Like you say – I been done for assault, more than once. I tell them about me and Cassandra and how Hugo and me didn't see straight about it, and then I give them a reason to think that I might've done it. And someone like me, I can't afford lawyers or private investigators to look into *my* evidence.'

He invested the term 'private investigators' with sarcasm.

'Hiding it from them ends up the same way. It makes you look guilty.'

'It wasn't me,' he said with sudden heat. 'You say that one more time and . . .'

The sentence drifted off, but his anger did not. His cheeks throbbed with blood, and he clenched and unclenched his fists as if he wanted to hit something with them.

'I'm sorry, Jimmy.' Atticus swallowed. 'Tell me what happened. Maybe I can help. Did Hugo say something to you? Did he know what you're doing here? Did he threaten to go to the police?'

Robson leaned in close enough so that Atticus could smell the odour on his body and feel the spittle that sprayed from his lips.

'I didn't kill them,' he repeated.

78

Robson paced the room. Atticus could guess what was going through his head: he was wondering what to do.

'I'm not police,' Atticus said again. 'And I don't care about what you're doing upstairs. I'm sorry for breaking into the house, but you gave me a pretty hefty whack by way of punishment. Can I make a suggestion?'

Robson kept pacing.

'Untie me and let me get out of here. This doesn't have to get any worse – for either of us.'

He shook his head. 'Can't do that.'

'So what are you going to do?'

'I need to talk to someone.'

'Who, Jimmy?'

'Bartley.'

'Bartley Cooper?'

Robson grunted.

Atticus knew that name. Bartley Cooper lived up on the Gypsy site at Oak Tree Field at Odstock, near to the hospital.

He was bad news, with interests in drugs and prostitution and anything else from which he could squeeze an illicit profit. Salisbury, like every other city, had an underworld. Cooper sat atop it: ruthless, cruel, and protected by the fear with which everyone – police included – regarded him. Atticus had arrested him three times in his brief career in the CID, and he had walked every time when witnesses decided it wasn't in their best interests to give evidence against him. Cooper was mouthy and full of himself, and Atticus had taken pleasure in making the arrests as humiliating as possible. That seemed like a mistake now. Cooper would recognise him.

'I need to go to the bathroom,' Atticus said.

Robson bit his lip, thinking.

'Please,' Atticus said. 'I'm just going to piss all over the floor otherwise. I'm not going to do anything stupid.'

'Wait,' Robson said.

'I'm hardly going to go anywhere, Jimmy.'

Robson reversed out of the room, leaving the door open, and returned a moment later with his shotgun.

'I'll untie you,' he said. 'But if you mess me around, I swear to God I'll put both barrels in you. Understand?'

'I do.'

Robson went around behind the chair, and Atticus felt strong fingers working against the knots. The rope loosened and Atticus was able to pull his hands free.

'Toilet's down there,' Robson said. 'I'll be right behind you.'

Atticus got up and stepped out of the storeroom. The light in the corridor was harsh, and it stung Atticus's eyes after being in the gloom for so long. He turned right and walked along the corridor to the bathroom.

'Leave the door open,' Robson said.

Atticus didn't protest. He held up his hands and looked at his wrists. The skin was abraded from where the rope had rubbed up against it, and the dog's teeth had punctured it in three places. There was a dusty mirror on the wall, and Atticus turned his head to look at his reflection; the side of his face, from the corner of his right eye and up into his scalp, was discoloured with a livid purple bruise.

'Get on with it,' Robson said.

'You really hit me, Jimmy,' Atticus observed.

'Shouldn't have broken into my house.'

'There's something we can agree on.'

Atticus patted his pockets for his phone. It wasn't there.

'I got it,' Robson said. 'You can forget about calling for help. Now have your piss or don't have it. Whatever, but make it quick.'

Atticus unzipped his trousers and relieved himself.

'I was here that night,' Robson said from the corridor.

'What night?'

'Christmas Eve. I saw Hugo when I was doing my late rounds, and then I came back here. I had . . . things to do.'

'With what I saw upstairs?' Atticus suggested.

'Kind of thing I can't mention to the pigs,' Robson said. 'All that matters is that I was here, not at the house. What happened to them has nothing to do with me.'

'You must have been upset,' Atticus said. 'About what happened to Cassandra.'

'I wouldn't have wanted anything to happen to her. But it wasn't like we were serious or anything.'

Atticus zipped up and washed his hands in the grimy sink.

'And look at what she did to me. Her daddy tells her she can't see me no more. It's like I didn't even exist.' There was bitterness in his words. 'She didn't care about me. I'm sorry about what happened to them, but it didn't have anything to do with me.'

'So Hugo didn't know about the dope farm?'

Robson shook his head. 'Why would he? I keep it on the quiet.'

Atticus was wiping his hands on the back of his trousers when he heard the sound of knocking on the front door.

Robson heard it, too, and turned away. A voice called out, 'Mr Robson?' Robson froze.

'Help!' Atticus yelled.

Robson swung around. 'Shut up!'

'*Help!*'

Robson surged into the narrow space, filling it, and clamped a big hand over Atticus's mouth. The shotgun clattered as he dropped it onto the floor. Robson pressed down, muffling Atticus as he tried to call again.

'Mr Robson? It's the police. Open the door, please.'

The dog barked, the sound muffled; it must have been shut in another room.

Atticus jerked his head up so that Robson's index finger was between his lips and bit down on it, hard. Robson bellowed in sudden pain and yanked his hand away.

Atticus yelled as loudly as he could. 'Help!'

Robson drew back his fist, but Atticus was quicker. He raised his knee, driving it deep into Robson's groin. The big man crumpled forward, but his bulk still blocked the way ahead.

Atticus heard the sound of something crashing against the front door.

Robson stumbled ahead, wrapped his arms around Atticus's waist and hoisted him aloft. He rag-dolled him, yanking him left and right and then cracking his head against the mirror. The glass shattered and Atticus felt a sharp scrape against his scalp. Robson turned them around, and Atticus managed to get his feet up against the wall, shoving as hard as he could and sending them both staggering out into the corridor.

The crashing against the door came again.

The effort of bearing all of Atticus's weight had unbalanced Robson and, despite his strength, he staggered back into the kitchen. Atticus felt warmth on his face and tried to blink the blood out of his eye. Robson still had his arms wrapped around his waist, and he drove him into the wall again. The edge of the stove bumped against Atticus's hip and, recalling his investigation from earlier, he reached down with his right hand. His fingers traced across the dirty surface of the stove, tracking through the crumbs and the grease until they brushed up against the cold cast-iron of the skillet that he had seen there. He found the handle, gripped it, and, before Robson could stop him, he used all of the strength that he had left to swing it up and behind him.

The skillet cracked against Robson's skull.

Robson's grip loosened.

He hit him again.

Robson released Atticus and collapsed to the floor with a heavy thump.

Atticus fell to his knees and scrambled out of the kitchen into the corridor. He turned back, the skillet heavy in his hand; Robson was face down and unmoving.

The front door burst open and Tristan Lennox stumbled inside.

'Christ,' he said.

Mack was behind Lennox.

'It's all right,' Atticus gasped as he tried to catch his breath. 'I've got it covered.'

79

Atticus had knocked Robson out cold and, because of that, Mack decided to put him in the first ambulance that arrived. Bob Carver and Vernon Edwards had appeared just before the ambulance, and Mack sent Carver to the hospital with Robson, the latter cuffed to the trolley.

Atticus was sitting in the back of Lennox's car. Mack went over to him.

'Let's have a look,' she said, indicating the cut on his head that he was trying to staunch with a scarf that she had found in her handbag.

He took the scarf away. There were three distinct cuts, each starting up beneath his hairline and reaching down onto his cheek.

'How is it?'

She winced.

'Is it going to ruin my looks?'

'Women like a man to be scarred up a little.'

'That so?'

She rolled her eyes as he winked at her.

Lennox came out of the house and walked over to them. 'You're not going to believe it,' he said.

'You find it?' Atticus said.

Mack looked away from her inspection of his cuts. 'What?'

Lennox gestured up to the first floor. 'Turns out that Robson has turned his house into a cannabis farm. The whole first floor – he's knocked the internal walls down, rigged up lights and irrigation.'

'What?'

'I know,' he said. 'It's a big one.'

'We didn't go inside when we spoke to him after the murders, did we?'

Lennox shook his head. 'We didn't have any reason the first time; then he came to the station for the formal interview.'

'You think he could have anything to do with the murders?'

Lennox shrugged. 'Don't know.'

'It's worth looking at,' Atticus said. 'Maybe Hugo found out?'

'I'd rather we'd known about it a lot sooner than this,' Lennox said.

Mack said, 'It gets worse. Atticus thinks Robson and Cassandra had a thing.'

'What? Seriously?'

'It's true,' Atticus said.

Mack sighed as Atticus ran through what he had found for Lennox's benefit. She had been confident of the case against Ralph Mallender – she was *still* confident – but there were shades of grey now that had the potential to complicate things. Robson had no alibi for Christmas Eve, and now he had two possible reasons for wanting harm to come to the Mallenders. Revenge and greed. Both seemed credible.

She felt the insidious touch of doubt and dismissed it with a shake of her head. She knew exactly what they had to do: investigate Robson, remove any suggestion that he might have had something to do with the deaths, move on.

Or conclude that he had a case to answer and adjust accordingly.

Atticus pulled the scarf away again. The blood was still weeping out of the cuts.

'You're going to need stitches,' she said to him.

'Later,' he said. 'I want to have a look in there.'

'No. Hospital – now. I'll take you. Wait there.'

She walked away from the car and, at her gesture, Lennox came too. 'I'll take him,' she said.

'You don't have to. I've got another ambulance coming.'

'It's okay. I want to talk to him – you can handle it here.'

'What about the house?'

'A cannabis farm is grounds for it to be searched,' she said. 'Call the drugs boys in Melksham. Get them down here as soon as you can.'

'Yes, boss.'

'Who else is on shift tonight?'

'Patterson and Scarlett.'

'Tell them to get over here, too. Wait until Drugs arrive and then have a poke around. See what you can find.'

'Will do.' Lennox angled a glance back at Atticus. 'You know I think he's a dick, don't you?'

'You've always made that very clear,' Mack said with a weary smile. 'Cancel the ambulance. This'll give me a chance to find out what he's been doing. Call me if you find anything.'

80

Mack drove Carver's squad car out of the woods, turned right on Great Wishford Road and headed towards Wilton.

Atticus was in the passenger seat. 'I'm sorry.'

'About what?'

'This,' he said, indicating the scarf. 'I'm going to ruin it. I hope it wasn't expensive.'

'You tell me.'

'What?'

'Don't you remember?'

'Should I?'

'You bought it for me.'

Atticus removed the scarf so that he could look at it more carefully and remembered; it was from Hermès and had been a Christmas present the year before last.

'You're right,' he said. 'I'll buy you another one.'

'Don't do that,' she said. 'Not sure how I'd explain it to Andy.'

Atticus chuckled. 'Fair point.'

They passed through Wilton, following the main road towards Salisbury.

'Why were you there?' he asked her. 'I mean, I'm not ungrateful. I'm just curious.'

'How did I know you were doing something stupid? Allegra Mallender told me. She said you'd gone there and that you weren't answering your phone.'

'She told you about Robson and Cassandra?'

'She mentioned it. I'm annoyed with myself. We didn't go back far enough.'

'It's not your fault,' he said. 'You have to draw the line somewhere. There was nothing to suggest what happened had anything to do with her. And definitely nothing to suggest it had anything to do with him.'

'It still might not,' she said. 'All we have is the suggestion that they were seeing each other.'

'It's more than a suggestion. He admitted it to me. He has her name on his arm.'

'Do we know that Hugo told them they had to stop?'

'Hugo fired Robson right after she came home – what other reason would there be?'

'I doubt Robson took that particularly well.'

Atticus shrugged. 'He's got a temper,' he said, tapping the side of his head.

'And a criminal record,' Mack added. 'He did time last year.'

'I know,' he said. 'I nicked him.'

'You did,' she said. 'Forgot.'

They drove on.

She glanced across the cabin at him. 'Did you break into the house?'

'No comment, Detective Chief Inspector.'

'Jesus, Atticus.'

'Are you asking me officially?'

'Does it matter?'

'Officially, I had an argument with Robson outside his property. He attacked me and, when I woke up, I was inside.'

'Unofficially?'

'I may have gone inside for a look around.'

She sighed. 'Just like Lamza.'

He made a gesture to suggest that he was zipping his lips.

'Nothing is ever easy with you, is it?'

'Does it matter?' he said. 'I got you a way to look around, didn't I? You heard someone calling for help from inside. You decided that you had grounds to effect an entry under section 17 and, whereupon forcing entry to said property, you found me being assaulted by Jimmy Robson. Now, if you happened to find anything *else* of interest while you were there – the cannabis farm, for example – I'm sure that would be evidence that could be used against him.'

Mack shook her head and chuckled wryly. 'And people wonder why you were fired,' she said, glancing over at him with a smile.

'I get results,' he said. 'I can't help it if that intimidates others.'

She shook her head and smiled. The bump on the head hadn't done him any lasting damage.

'Did you find anything that might be helpful on the murders?'

'No,' he said. 'I had a quick look; then I went upstairs. Of course, that's the other possible motive. Let's say Hugo found out about the drugs – maybe he threatened to report Jimmy, and Jimmy decided that he couldn't let that happen.' Atticus let the

393

thought run away a little. 'Or, if it wasn't Jimmy, maybe it was Bartley Cooper.'

'What's this got to do with him?'

'Jimmy's been working for him. He's not smart enough to know how to sell the amount of product that he's been growing, but it's right up Cooper's alley. And we know he's got form for violence.'

'But murder?'

'I'd be looking into him,' Atticus suggested.

'Leave the policing to us,' she said, then, regretting her tone, she added, 'Sorry. Didn't mean it like that.'

'It's all right,' he said. 'My work here is done.'

'Allegra Mallender is going to be *so* pleased,' Mack said with a bitter laugh. 'We're not going to be able to proceed against Ralph now. There was already reasonable doubt. And now this. You have single-handedly destroyed my case, haven't you?'

He spread his hands. 'Sorry.'

'Forget it.'

They turned onto the Odstock Road and the run down to the hospital.

'What do you think will happen?'

'On this evidence?' Mack sighed wearily. 'Abernathy will have to throw his hand in. The judge will direct the jury to enter a not guilty verdict. And that's *all* I need.'

81

Accident and emergency was busy. Atticus looked around at the others who were waiting to be seen: a teenager looked as if he was the worse for drink, a young man looked like he might have broken his arm, and a worried mother and father cradled a young child with a temperature. The TV hung from the wall was tuned to *EastEnders*, the volume turned down low and subtitles scrolling along the bottom of the screen. The lights were harsh and a woman was moaning in pain in one of the treatment rooms out of sight around the corner. There was a lingering atmosphere of surly depression.

Atticus took a seat while Mack showed her warrant card and spoke to the nurse.

'There's going to be a wait,' she said.

'I've got no plans,' he said.

'Guess what? Jimmy Robson's in the back. Likely concussion. How hard did you hit him?'

'Hard enough. You do know how big he is, don't you?'

'I do.'

'Built like the proverbial.'

'So call the police next time,' she said.

'Yes, boss,' Atticus said.

'I'm serious, Atticus. You could've been killed.'

Atticus was ready with a pithy response, but he bit his tongue. 'You don't have to wait with me.'

'It's okay,' she said. 'I don't mind.'

Mack picked up a tatty copy of *Woman's Own*, flicked through the pages without really looking at them, then dropped it back on the table.

'You haven't told me how the kids are,' he said.

'They're good,' she said.

'School?'

'Both doing well,' she said. She stretched out her legs. 'Daisy is really into writing. She loves it. We bought her a diary for Christmas, and she's filled it already. It's funny . . . Some of the things that she says.' She stretched out her arms. 'Sebastian is still into football, just like he always was. We're lucky, I know – he's good at school, too, always does his homework before we let him out in the park to play.'

'He's a good kid,' Atticus said. 'They both are.'

'How's your family?' she asked him.

'Dreadful. My old man's talking about selling the business. You can imagine how excited that's made my brothers and sisters. It's like tossing bloodied meat into a tank with four piranhas. It is *extremely* unedifying.'

'You still haven't worked it out with them?'

'I don't think that's going to happen,' Atticus said. 'I'm the black sheep. I never fitted in, and I don't think there'll ever be a time when I can be bothered to do what they want me to do so that I could. And I'm happy with that.'

'Are you sure?'

'What do you mean?'

'You don't *look* happy,' she said. 'I'm not sure you've ever been happy since I've known you.'

'There have been times,' he said, holding her gaze, and, as she realised what he was talking about, she looked away.

'I was happy, too,' she said unexpectedly. 'But it can't happen again. You know why. We talked about it.'

'The kids – I know.'

'I'm not going to change my mind. I'm sorry – I don't want to hurt you, and I know that I have. But . . . well, it's just how it has to be.'

She reached and rested her left hand on his elbow.

'I know,' he said.

Atticus laid his hand atop hers and, to his surprise, she didn't pull it away.

Her phone buzzed. She gently removed her hand, got up and put the phone to her ear.

'Who is it?' he said.

'Lennox,' she mouthed.

She turned away and walked down the corridor towards the vending machines. Atticus watched as Mack gesticulated animatedly, her left hand stabbing the air as she punctuated whatever it was she was saying to Lennox.

She finished the call and came back again. Her eyes were alive with excitement.

'What is it?' Atticus said.

'They've found something.'

'What?'

'A box of nine-millimetre rounds. Lennox thinks it matches the brass we found at the farmhouse.'

'Seriously?'

'Yes,' she said.

'Where did he find them?'

'Didn't say. Why?'

'Because I didn't see them.'

'How long were you looking?'

'Not that long.'

'Exactly.' She shrugged. 'I've got to go – I need to get over there.'

'Let me come,' he said.

'Atticus – you know I can't do that.'

A doctor came into the waiting area. 'Mr Priest?'

'You wouldn't have found any of that without me,' he said.

'Come into the station tomorrow,' she said. 'I'll give you everything I can then.'

The doctor looked around impatiently. 'Is there a Mr Priest here?'

Mack pointed. 'He's here.'

'Tomorrow morning,' Atticus insisted. 'Promise me.'

'Bright and early. I'll see you then. I promise.'

82

Mack retraced the route back to the farmhouse and then to Jimmy Robson's property. There were more vehicles there than before: two squad cars, a forensics van and two unmarked vehicles that she assumed belonged to the drug squad. There was no space to park inside the gate, so she reversed back out again and found a spot at the side of the track.

Crime-scene tape had been suspended between the trees in front of the house, and a scene log had been set up. Mack showed her warrant card to the constable who was in charge of the log, and signed in. The man held up the tape, and she ducked beneath it and went over to where Lennox was waiting for her.

'Boss,' he said.

'What have you got?'

'You'll want to see,' he said.

There was a box of plastic forensic suits at the entrance to the house, and Mack pulled one of them on over her clothes. She added plastic overshoes and followed Lennox into the house.

'So we've finished the first search,' Lennox said. 'There's a large cannabis farm upstairs, like I said. The drug squad are up there now. If we didn't find anything else, there'd still be enough up there to put Robson away for a stretch.'

'But you did find something else,' she said.

'We did. This way.'

Mack followed Lennox along the corridor to a room that was evidently being used as a bedroom. It had been kept in a slovenly condition, with clothes strewn over the floor, magazines scattered around, empty pieces of packaging and scads of newsprint. Lennox stepped through the debris to the bed and knelt down at the foot of it. He indicated a Tesco carrier bag.

'That was underneath the bed,' he said.

'You find it?'

'No – one of the lads did.'

He pulled on a pair of forensic gloves and carefully opened the bag. Mack looked in and saw five items: four small cardboard boxes, coloured blue and white, with MAGTECH emblazoned across each one, and a red velvet bag.

Lennox took one of the cardboard boxes. It was already opened; he flipped back the lid and turned it so that Mack could look inside. It contained nine-millimetre rounds, slotted vertically, half of them missing. Mack stared at it. Her mind was spinning. She remembered the detail from the ballistics report: the Browning was a nine-millimetre, and here was a tray of the same calibre rounds. She was already thinking: she would send the shells to NABIS, the ballistics intelligence service at the Met, so that they could be compared with the brass that was recovered from the farmhouse.

She pointed to the velvet bag. 'What about that?'

Lennox pulled a drawstring to open the bag, reached inside and took out a silver crucifix on a chain that was fixed with a diamond clasp. He picked it up between gloved fingers and held it in the slant of artificial light that lanced in from the corridor.

'Is that what I think it is?'

'It is,' he said.

Cassandra Mallender had taken to wearing a necklace with a crucifix in the year before her death. Her surviving relations had testified that she never took it off, and had noted its absence when her body and then the farmhouse had been searched.

'Jesus,' she said. 'It wasn't Ralph, was it?'

Lennox shook his head. 'I don't know, boss – it's looking much less likely.'

Mack took the necklace and let it dangle. 'It was Robson. He did it.'

83

Bandit was on the mattress, curled up in the space between Atticus's legs. He sat up, his sore head throbbing, and scratched the dog behind the ears.

'Morning, boy,' he said.

The dog slithered up the mattress on his belly and offered his muzzle so that Atticus could scratch it. He probed the side of his own head with his fingers. It was tender, and he was glad of the codeine that he had been given at the hospital last night. He used his thumb to press two of the tablets from the blister pack and swallowed them, washing them down with a glug of water from the glass next to the bed.

He heard the buzz of his phone. The ringtone was muffled and it took him a moment to locate it beneath the duvet.

He put it to his ear. 'Hello?'

'Atticus?'

'Mack, where are you?'

'Outside,' she said. 'Let me in?'

* * *

Atticus boiled the kettle and made two cups of coffee as Mack took off her coat and cleared the sofa of papers so that she could sit down.

'Here,' Atticus said, handing her one of the cups.

'Thanks.'

'You look done in.'

'I've been up all night,' she said.

'What happened?'

'Like I said – we found ammunition. I'll get the ballistics report back at lunchtime. They're running mass-spectrometry tests to compare it with the cases we found in the farmhouse and, maybe, match it. I'd be shocked if it's not the same.'

'Why?'

'Because that wasn't all that we found.' She sipped her coffee and exhaled. 'I needed this.'

'Come on,' Atticus said impatiently. 'What else was there?'

'There was a velvet bag in the same bag as the ammunition. It had a necklace that matched one that we couldn't find in the house. A crucifix. The family told us Cassandra wouldn't take it off.'

'Is it the same?'

'It's at the lab. But it'll match. I'm sure of it. We got the whole thing wrong – we arrested the wrong man.'

Atticus paced the room. 'Where was it?'

Mack looked up wearily. 'Where was what?'

'The bullets. The crucifix.'

'Inside a Tesco carrier bag.'

'And where was that?'

'Under the bed.'

Atticus closed his eyes and tried to remember. 'Under the bed?'

'That's what I said.'

'Do you have a picture?'

'Yes,' she said.

She took out her phone and swiped through her photographs. She found the one that she wanted and handed the phone to Atticus. He examined the picture and recognised where it had been taken: Robson's bedroom. He swiped left to bring up the next shot. Mack had taken a series of pictures, changing the angle slightly each time so that she could capture all of the room. Atticus found the photographs of the unmade bed and, as he swiped, the vantage point dropped down so that he could see beneath it. There was a plastic bag at the end of the bed furthest from the wall. The mouth of the bag was open and, inside, he could see the edge of a cardboard box.

He stared at the screen. 'Atticus?'

He laid his thumb and forefinger on the screen and moved them apart, zooming in on the bag.

'What is it?' Mack pressed.

'Nothing,' he said.

'Come on,' she said. 'What is it? Something's bothered you.'

'It's nothing,' he repeated.

'I don't believe you.'

'Where is he now?'

'Robson? In custody.'

'What's he saying?'

'He's denying it.'

'How does he say he got the necklace?'

'Says he has no idea how it got there.'

He slumped down next to her. 'What are you going to do next?'

'I spoke to Abernathy last night. We're going to apply for the case against Ralph to be dismissed. We can't proceed after this.'

'Have you told the defence?'

'Not yet. Abernathy is going to speak to Crow at seven. Have you told Allegra?'

'About what happened last night?'

She nodded.

'No. Not yet. I was waiting for you.'

'You might as well get the credit for it. You found out about Robson and Cassandra. This is all your work.'

She reclined against the back of the sofa and he did the same. She turned to look at him and he turned to her.

He spoke first. 'Are you okay?'

'Just tired,' she said. 'I interviewed Robson for three hours last night.'

He could see that she was blaming herself for the way things had played out. 'Don't beat yourself up. There was no way that you could have known about Robson and Cassandra.'

'You found out,' she said.

'I got lucky.'

She smiled. 'I could say a lot of things about the way you work – not all of them complimentary – but I wouldn't call it luck.'

'Have you told Beckton?'

'No,' she said, getting up and smoothing down her trousers. 'I'm saving that particular pleasure for when I get back to the station. He's not going to be happy. I wouldn't say that I know

Allegra and Ralph particularly well, but they strike me as the vindictive type.'

'Hmm. I think so, too.'

'They'll go straight to the press; then they'll get Cadogan to come after us. I can see an inquiry into how this investigation was run in my not-too-distant future. And that is all I need right now. Things between me and Andy aren't the best . . .' She stopped, looking away.

'Mack?'

'Forget it. I shouldn't have said.' She straightened up. 'Right. Back to it.'

Atticus got up, too. 'Thanks for coming over,' he said. 'I appreciate being kept in the loop. I'll do the same for you.'

'Something *is* bothering you, isn't it?' she said.

'I just want to think about it a little,' he said. 'Is that okay?'

'Don't keep me in the dark again. Please?'

'I won't,' he said.

84

Mack drove to court after leaving Atticus. A conference had been scheduled for eight. Abernathy was irritated and made no attempt to hide it. He reported that he had just endured a humiliating meeting with his opposite number, during which the two of them had concluded the procedure for bringing the trial to a close.

'What a waste,' he said. 'Three months' work and all for nothing.'

He said it while he looked at Mack. She was shedding allies left and right. She saw it for what it was: Abernathy was abandoning her, leaving her to carry the can for the wasted resources that had been invested in a trial that should never have begun. Like rats, they were fleeing the sinking ship.

* * *

Allegra Mallender was already in her seat when Mack came into the courtroom that morning and took hers. Allegra stared gleefully across the room; Atticus must have told her about what had happened, and now she was ready to enjoy her moment of vindication.

Allegra got up, crossing the floor until she was next to her.

'I'm glad you're here,' she said. 'This last year has been the worst year of my life, and that's just me – think of what your incompetence has cost my husband. He's been in prison for months because of you. I told you there was no way that he could have done what you accused him of doing. I told you, again and again and *again*: my husband is not a violent man. He never has been. But you wouldn't listen, would you? And now, here we are. Ten months later, ten months of our lives wasted, goodness knows how much money wasted, and we're right back where we started.'

'I'm very sorry about how things turned out,' Mack said. 'If we'd had this evidence earlier, things would have been very different. As it is, as soon as we found out what we did last night, we made sure that the case was dismissed as quickly as we possibly could.'

'That's it? That's your apology?'

'I *am* sorry,' she said. 'We've conducted this case with the same amount of care as any other. That's all I can say.'

'That's not good enough,' Allegra said.

'I understand.'

'We're going to want compensation for what you've done.'

'Of course.'

'Compensation and a formal apology.'

'I'm sure Mr Cadogan will be able to help you with that.'

The associate came inside. 'All rise.'

Allegra looked as if she wanted to say more, but, instead, she shook her head in disdain and went back to her seat.

Somerville sat down and invited the court to do the same. Mack looked around: it was full to the rafters, with the journalists who had been declaiming against Ralph Mallender for the last nine months now ready to write the story of his acquittal and the disgrace of an investigation that had gone so badly wrong.

85

Mack followed the crowd of people out of the court, aware that they were looking at her. Some were curious, others derisive; she was the public face of a botched investigation that had cost a man his liberty for ten months and might have cost him even more. She wanted to get away from them.

Atticus was waiting outside the court when Mack emerged. He looked across the crowd, held her eye and then nodded towards the corner of the building. He disappeared around it and Mack followed.

He made his way to the back of the building and waited for her outside the custody entrance.

'Atticus?' she said. 'What is it?'

'You're right. Something *is* wrong.'

'With what?'

He gestured to the building with a flick of the wrist. 'Everything. Robson. Mallender. Everything.'

'What do you mean?'

He looked straight into her eyes. 'Do you trust me?'

He was earnest, his characteristic playfulness – that ready sarcasm that was attractive and irritating in equal measure – was all gone.

'You know I trust you,' she said. 'What is it?'

'I haven't been able to stop thinking about it.'

'About what?'

'Everything, Mack – everything you told me. It's all so *convenient*. Don't you think so?'

'I don't know,' she said. 'It seems obvious now.'

'Exactly. It's too neat. I don't buy it.'

'What does that mean?'

'I think we've been set up.'

She put a hand to her head. '*Now* you tell me. We just had the case against Mallender dismissed.'

'Ralph didn't do it,' he said. 'That's the only thing I'm completely sure about.'

'Well, at least *that's* something.'

'I need you to help me. There are going to be some questions I can't ask – but you'll be able to.'

'Like what?'

'Give me a couple of days to get my thoughts straight,' he said. 'I think I know what happened, but it's not going to be easy to prove. I'll call you when I've got everything clear in my head – you'll be able to help me then.'

He had a faraway look on his face. She had seen him like that before. He retreated into himself when he was obsessed with a problem, as if the act of unravelling it required him to withdraw, to close down and remove himself from all external distractions.

'Atticus,' she said, waiting for him to click back into the now.

'Sorry,' he said. 'Million miles away.'

She put a hand on his elbow. 'I trust you. Be careful. Call me when you're ready to talk.'

PART III

86

Atticus was up early. He had found it difficult to sleep and, as he turned to and fro with no prospect of drifting off, he had eventually given up. Bandit had trotted over to him as he brandished his lead, and had wagged his tail enthusiastically as Atticus clipped it to his collar. Atticus swallowed his pills, grabbed his overcoat, added a thick scarf to ward against the freezing cold, and led the way outside.

The gates to the Close were still locked, so Atticus continued on to Crane Bridge, crossing over it and then taking the hard left turn onto the path that followed the Avon into Queen Elizabeth Gardens. There had been a hard frost overnight, and the trees and plants were heavy with ivory rime. The forecast was for snow by the end of the week, and as he looked up, he saw that the clouds were dark, suggesting that the snow might arrive a little sooner than had been advertised.

He unclipped Bandit's lead from his collar and watched as the dog hared away. They had spent a lot of time together in the week since the conclusion of the trial. Atticus had needed time and space to think, and he had always found that one of the best ways to do that was to go on a long walk. Bandit was always happy to come along, and the two of them had enjoyed ten-mile hikes through the countryside around the city. They had been back in Grovely Woods on three separate occasions, visiting the farmhouse that still stubbornly held onto its secrets.

Atticus had broken into the house again on the first visit, going down to the cellar to check the coal hole and, in particular, the nail that he had noticed the first time he had been there.

He noticed activity inside the house as they strolled past it the second time and, as he watched from behind the cover of an old wide-boughed oak, he had seen Ralph and Allegra as they made their way around the rooms, opening the curtains and letting the light back in.

He had returned a final time yesterday afternoon and had seen a white van embossed with the logo of a local painter and decorator parked up alongside Allegra's car. The front door was open, and Atticus watched the tradesman as he ferried his equipment – a trestle table, pots of paint, brushes and brooms – inside. Atticus made a call to a contact at a local estate agency and was told that the house, and the associated farmlands, would soon be put on the market with an indicative price of six million pounds.

A lot of money.

He had spent a lot of time with Mack, too. They had assembled the information that he analysed on those long walks. He had been to London, visiting the American Embassy in Wandsworth. They had both worked with the CPS before making an application to court for two separate search warrants. Mack had pulled information from the Resource Management Unit that administered the comings and goings at the station. She had liaised with the forensics laboratory in Exeter so that the fragment of Tyvek that Atticus had found beneath the coal hole at the farmhouse could be analysed, and then had reviewed the scene log for anything that might have explained how that material had come to be there.

Mack had also collated every single photograph that had been taken at the farmhouse by the crime-scene examiners. There had been over a thousand of them. Atticus had spent an entire day isolating those that he wanted – whittling the total down to eleven, when he was finished – and then analysed each of those in close-up detail.

The problem was a difficult one to solve. He had an idea of what the solution might look like, but it was no more than a sketch. It was a jigsaw with missing pieces, and it made it difficult to imagine the whole picture. He worked at it, adding in pieces as he found them and taking away pieces when he realised that they didn't fit. He kept at it until he had a better idea of what he was looking at and, once the outline was in place, he started to extrapolate. Disparate pieces of data – dates and times, relationships, possible motivations, records pulled from various administrative databases, not all of them in the UK, post-mortem and autopsy reports – were gathered, assessed, tested, tested again and, once he was confident that they were relevant, slotted into place.

It had taken him ten days to find certainty, but he was there now.

The picture was complete.

He knew what had happened that night, and he was ready to bring the whole sorry charade to a close.

There had been extensive preparation for what would happen later today. Mack had made an urgent request to the chief constable under the Regulation of Investigatory Powers Act and, following his assent, a tech support unit had been deployed to gather the evidence that Atticus expected to find when his trap was laid.

All that was required now was to bait the trap.

He was lost in contemplation again and snapped back as Bandit launched himself into the river in pursuit of a duck that had had the temerity to cross his path. Atticus put his fingers to his mouth and whistled, then waited as the dog changed course and paddled back to the bank. He clambered out, shook himself dry, and trotted over. Atticus knelt down to rub his damp fur.

'Let's get back, boy,' he said. 'Busy day today. I've got things to do.'

87

Mack went downstairs and bummed a cigarette from Cathy, the civilian who worked the front desk. She didn't really smoke any more, except for moments – like this – when she was particularly nervous. Trials didn't do it to her any more, nor interviews that she knew would be important. She had a modicum of control over those, through careful planning and preparation, and she could find solace in that. This, though, was different. She wasn't in control here, and never really had been. She had allowed herself to be swept along with events, tricked and fooled every step of the way, and now the only possible way to find resolution was to invest all of her trust in a man she had promised her husband she would have nothing to do with ever again. She felt guilty and vulnerable; her career and her personal life were at stake and she had no ability to influence how things might play out.

So, yes, she was nervous. Very. And she needed a moment to think.

She went outside into the cold, wrapped her coat more tightly around her in a futile attempt to stay warm, put the cigarette to her lips and lit it. She set off, headed into the Greencroft, and walked in the direction of the children's playground.

The days following the collapse of the trial had been difficult. Abernathy had abrogated himself of all liability for what had happened, with his rejection quickly mirrored by the CPS. Both blamed the quality of the evidence that had been assembled by the police and, as the senior investigating officer, responsibility for that attached to Mack. Chief Superintendent Beckton had been bollocked by his boss, and now there was talk that Mr Justice Somerville was going to order an inquiry into the conduct of Wiltshire Police.

Mack knew it: shit rolled downhill, and she was going to get all of it.

She sucked on the cigarette, held the smoke in her lungs and then exhaled it, coughing a little as she did. Work was bleak and she found no solace at home, either. The work with Atticus had necessitated late nights, and Andy hadn't even protested when she had told him that the long hours would have to continue for another week or two. He was still resentful and the atmosphere between them remained chilly. They put on a brave face for the sake of the children, but she knew that they were going to have to work at it if they were going to put things back the way they had been. She had looked online for couples' therapy, but had decided against suggesting it; she would have given it a try, but Andy had never had much interest in things like that. Instead, she had tried to leave her worries about work at the nick, to minimise the late nights as much as she could, and to concentrate on being present when she was at home.

She reached the playground, watched a single kid swinging back and forth under the jaded supervision of her mother, and then turned back.

Mack had tried to distract herself from her troubles by wrapping up the file for the CPS on an assault that she had been overseeing, but the exercise had been only partially successful. The Mallender case loomed large, always just a moment away from occupying her thoughts, and, as today had approached, it had been difficult to ignore. She had spoken with Atticus the night before, taking the call on her mobile away from the office, and knew that what was likely to happen this afternoon had the potential to be difficult. Their planning had been thorough. She had second-guessed herself over and over about the good sense of taking his advice, vacillating between confidence that the course of action that they had chosen was the right one, and the fear – despite everything that they had put together – that they were wrong.

She reached the station, dropped the cigarette and ground it underfoot.

It all came down to trust. She had to trust in her own assessment of Atticus's talent, in her ability to separate the professional and the personal, and in her judgement that what they were proposing to do would bring the case to a close rather than just make it worse.

She looked at her watch.

Ten minutes to eleven.

She had already waited too long.

She had to do it now.

* * *

Mack took the stairs to the CID room and made her way across to Lennox's desk.

'Boss,' he said, 'what's up?'

'What are you doing this afternoon?'

'Nothing that can't wait – do you need me?'

'I think so.'

'What's the problem?'

'It's about the Mallenders. Well, Allegra specifically.'

'Right. What about her?'

'There's something that's never really sat right with me.'

He frowned. 'Like what?'

'Like . . .' She paused. 'Look, this has to stay between me and you, okay?'

'Of course, boss. Goes without saying.'

'So, I might have done a little digging around into her background over the course of the last couple of days.'

'Why? The case is over.'

'I don't know. Intuition. That's the only way I can describe it. But every time she came in here, I ended up feeling the same way – that there's no way she was telling us everything. Didn't you feel it, too?'

He pursed his lips as he thought. 'I know I never trusted her.'

'Exactly.'

'Did you find anything?'

'I did,' she said. 'I don't think she's who she says she is. The wedding register has her maiden name down as Allegra Cook. Early thirties, originally from the United States. I started looking for her in the databases.'

Lennox nodded for her to go on.

'So, the only Allegra Cook I could find who would've been her age today died aged six in 1990. I can't say for sure, but I'm about ninety-five per cent confident she stole the dead girl's birth certificate and then built her new identity from there. If I'm right, we'll be able to charge her for possessing documents – birth certificate, passport, driving licence – for use in connection with fraud. And that's at the very least.'

He leaned back and shook his head in disbelief. 'Bloody hell, boss.'

'Tell me about it. And it got me thinking: *why* would she do something like that? What does she have to hide? That's what I want to talk to her about.'

'If she's been lying about who she is,' Lennox said, 'what else could she be lying about?'

'Exactly. We have to bring it up with her. But not here, at least not to start with. You know she and Ralph have already moved into the farmhouse, right?'

'I did,' he said. 'Doing it up before they put it on the market.'

She nodded. 'I'd rather speak to them there. You know what it's like – I'll be able to be a bit more *liberal* with what I say and how I say it if I do it away from the nick.'

Lennox winked his understanding. 'And you'd like me to come?'

'I really would. I was thinking of going over there this afternoon.'

'No problem, boss. I'll drive us over.'

88

Lennox drove them out to Wilton, and then beneath the railway bridge and out into the countryside beyond. Mack was nervous, and her mood had seemingly spread to infect her sergeant, too. Lennox had asked her how she was intending to play the conversation, but, once Mack had explained, the two of them had settled into a pensive silence that wasn't really alleviated by the bonhomie of the Spire FM DJ as he linked songs by Katy Perry and Miley Cyrus.

Lennox drove through Great Wishford and then turned onto the track that led into the woods. It was four o'clock now and the gloom of dusk was deepening into darkness, with the tops of the trees fringing the join between land and sky. It had grown colder as the afternoon had progressed, and now snow started to fall. They were thick, fat flakes and, with the ground already icy hard, they started to settle. The snow gathered on the windscreen to be swept off by the wipers.

'Going to be a white Christmas,' Mack observed.

'As long as it's better than last year, I don't care. Working on Christmas Day? They don't pay us enough.'

'Tell me about it,' she said.

Lennox passed the car park and continued into the wood, following the track to the farmhouse. He pulled up behind the gate to the property and they both got out. The temperature had plummeted during their drive, and Mack clapped her arms about her in a vain attempt to generate some warmth. The branches overhead – even denuded of their leaves – were enough to shelter them from the snow, but little flurries of it fell through gaps where the sky was open. Mack looked beyond the gate to the house and saw that the rooms on the ground floor were lit. The curtains had not yet been drawn, and warm light shone out, casting golden oblongs on the white. She saw a silhouette pass through the kitchen, reappearing in the sitting room a moment later.

'Ready?' she asked Lennox.

He nodded. 'How'd you want to play it?'

'I'll ask the questions. Just look ominous.'

'I can do that.'

* * *

Mack took a deep breath and knocked on the door.

Her stomach twisted as she waited. They had gamed this out, but there was no way of predicting how it would go for real.

She heard the sound of footsteps and then Allegra Mallender opened the door.

'Hello,' Mack said.

Allegra should have been surprised, but, if she was, she mastered it quickly. 'Detective Chief Inspector,' she said, 'what do you want?'

'I've got a few additional questions,' she said. 'Do you mind if we come in?'

'What questions?'

'It'd be much better if we could speak inside.'

Allegra stayed in the doorway, blocking the way. 'What if I don't want to?'

'Please, Mrs Mallender. I'm trying to make this as easy for you as I can. It would be much more convenient for us both if we could speak here. I don't want to have to take you to the station tonight, but we can do that if you'd prefer.'

'What? Why would you do that? I don't understand – the case is finished. Don't you remember? It was dropped.'

'I'm hoping this is just a misunderstanding that you'll be able to clear up. But we really do have to speak about it.'

Ralph was standing behind his wife. Neither of them looked happy to see her, but that was hardly a surprise. The police had turned their lives upside down for the better part of a year.

'Fine,' Allegra said. 'Fine. You'd better come in.'

Ralph led them through the house. Mack looked around as they passed through the rooms. The Mallenders had already made good progress. The kitchen units had been freshened with new doors, and the carpet that had been laid through the hall had been torn up to reveal the floorboards beneath. These were in the process of being polished; half of the boards had been sanded, and a buffing machine had been pushed up against the front door in anticipation of finishing the job.

'Excuse the mess,' Ralph said. 'We're in the process of getting the place ready to be sold.'

Allegra glared at her husband, as if annoyed that he had been civil with their tormentors. She was evidently not interested in small talk; she opened the door to the sitting room and indicated that they should go inside.

The room was very different from how Mack remembered it. It had been gloomy before, even when the curtains had been pulled back, with tired furniture, walls that were in need of redecoration, and dirty glass in the windows. More vivid in her memory, of course, had been the three bodies that they had found there: Juliet, Cassandra and Cameron. She remembered the blood that had soaked into the fabric of the armchairs, and the insides of Cameron's head sprayed out across the walls. She had been back after the bodies had been removed and recalled the swathes of carpet that had been removed and the tincture of red that had stained the boards beneath.

Today, all of that was gone. The room was clean and modern, with a polished oak floor and brand-new furniture. A flat-screen TV had been hung from the wall; there was a sleek dining table and chairs and a Scandinavian sofa and armchair collection. A Christmas tree stood in the bay window, half-dressed; there was a tray of mince pies on the table, and Bing Crosby was singing 'White Christmas' on the stereo. It appeared that their visit had interrupted the festivities.

'Sit down,' Allegra said, waving her hand in the direction of the table and chairs.

Mack thanked her. Allegra went over to switch off the music when there came a knocking at the door.

'Who's that?' Allegra sighed. She glared at Mack. 'You don't have anyone else coming, do you?'

Mack shrugged.

'I'll get it,' Ralph said.

89

Atticus was waiting on the track that led to Jimmy Robson's house. He was standing behind the same ancient oak as before, close enough to watch the farmhouse yet shielded from observation by anyone on the track. He saw Mack and Lennox going inside and collected the leather satchel that he had hooked on the branch of the adjacent tree, dusting the snow off it. He made his way back up the track, passed through the gate and walked up to the front door. He knocked and waited.

The door opened.

Ralph Mallender was there.

'Hello, Ralph,' Atticus said.

'What are you doing here?'

'I need to come in.'

Ralph frowned. 'What?'

'May I?'

Ralph was about to protest, but Atticus forestalled him by stepping inside and closing the door.

'This isn't a good time,' Ralph said.

'It's the perfect time.' He took off his jacket and handed it over before Ralph could demur. 'Where are they? The sitting room?'

He didn't wait for a response, making his way along the hallway to the room that he remembered from his last visit. Ralph followed in his wake.

'This really isn't a good time,' he said. 'The police are here.'

'I know,' Atticus said. 'I told them to come.'

He stepped into the room. Mack and Lennox were sitting down at a new dining table, and Allegra was standing by the fireplace. Mack looked over at Atticus and gave a shallow nod. Lennox's face crumpled in confusion and Allegra stiffened.

Her eyes widened. 'Atticus,' she said, surprised.

'Hello, Allegra.'

'What are you doing here?'

'I thought I should come.'

'I'm sorry – I don't understand. Why? What for?'

'The conversation we're about to have.'

'No – you've lost me.'

'I've been digging into what happened here a little more.'

'There's no need for that. It's over. They dropped the case. You've already done more than enough.'

'I don't know about that. There were a few things about what happened that I couldn't stop thinking about. I tried, I really did, but I couldn't get them out of my head. Ask the detective chief inspector – it's one of my weaknesses. Once I see a problem, I can't stop thinking about it until it's been solved.'

Atticus pulled out the chair at the head of the table and sat down. Lennox's face was blank, almost studiously so. Mack was rubbing her left wrist with the fingers of her right, a gesture that Atticus remembered from before; she did it when she was anxious. The atmosphere in the room was tense.

Allegra looked confused. 'I still don't understand. What *things?*'

'That's what we're here to talk about,' Mack said.

'What?' she fumed. 'This is *ridiculous*. You said that you had questions for me to answer.'

'I do,' she said. 'Lots of questions.'

Allegra's face flushed with anger. 'You already put us through an ordeal for something that Ralph didn't do. He's been in prison all year, and then the trial . . . Isn't that enough? Why can't you just leave him alone?'

'It's not about Ralph,' Atticus said calmly.

'Of *course* it's about him.'

'It's about you.'

Allegra stayed where she was and, for a moment, Atticus thought she was going to grab her husband and drag him out of the room. She didn't. Perhaps it was the tone that Mack had adopted with her – stern and inflexible, a show of her authority – that persuaded Allegra that she had no choice but to hear Atticus out. Perhaps it was the surprise of being ambushed like this, in their own home. Or perhaps it was the shock of an ally – Atticus – now a seeming turncoat, ready to betray her.

She sat down, crossed her arms over her chest and smiled a thin, condescending smile. 'You're working with *her* now?' she said to Atticus. 'With the police?'

'No,' he said. 'Not any more.'

'So?'

'I don't like being used. And, like I said, I've never met a problem I didn't want to solve. This was a good one.'

'Fine,' she said. 'Whatever. We've dealt with police incompetence once. Police *misconduct*. We can deal with it again. Get on with it – say whatever it is you think you have to say and then leave us alone.'

'Thank you,' Atticus said. 'I will.'

90

Atticus got up. He took another breath, put the leather satchel on the table – taking a moment, letting Allegra wonder what it might portend – and then unzipped it. He took out the bundle of photocopies that he had been collecting over the course of the last week. He put them on the table.

'We'd better start with the basics,' he said. 'Your name isn't Allegra, is it?'

'Yes, it is.'

'Sorry,' Atticus said. 'Let me qualify that. It is *now*, but only for the last two years. You were Rachel before that.'

Ralph frowned.

'And you were Catherine before you were Rachel. That's your birth name – Catherine McCoy. Born on 15 January 1985 to Nicholas and Laura McCoy in Framingham, Massachusetts.'

'What?' Ralph said.

Atticus shuffled through the papers until he found the copy of Catherine McCoy's birth certificate. He and Mack had petitioned the Registry of Vital Records office in Dorchester, Massachusetts, for the papers. They had required a court order to do so, eventually receiving the certificate last week. Next, he picked out the bundle of legal documentation that confirmed that Catherine had changed her name by petition; Catherine had become Rachel. He shuffled through the papers again until he found the third document he wanted: the copy of the wedding register that had Allegra Cook marrying Ralph Mallender.

Atticus put all of the papers on the table and flicked them across so that Allegra and Ralph could look at them.

Allegra didn't take her eyes from Atticus. 'My personal history has nothing to do with what happened to Ralph.'

'I think it does. You stole the identity of a dead girl when you became Allegra Cook.'

'That's a crime,' Mack said. 'It's fraud.'

Allegra should have been surprised by the revelation, or at least put onto the back foot. Atticus watched her reaction carefully and, although she *appeared* to be shocked, he could see that it was an act. The hand to the mouth and the wide eyes were an approximation of what she suspected her audience would have expected – a psychopath's reaction – but her eyes showed calculation, not fear. Her body language, too, gave away more than she would have liked. Her eyebrows should have curved upwards, her brow should have wrinkled, and the whites of the eyes should have been more visible as they opened wider. Atticus looked for those small cues, but he didn't see any of them.

'You've been married twice before.'

Atticus glanced over at Ralph; his shock *wasn't* manufactured.

'And?' Allegra said.

'And both of those marriages ended in unfortunate circumstances. Your first husband was a man called Richard Wilson. You were nineteen when you met him, I believe. A ceremony in Las Vegas. His wife had died the year before and, since he was lonely and wanted to share his life with someone, he placed a profile on a website that specialises in matching older men who have the good fortune of wealth with younger women. You saw his profile and contacted him. You met, seemed to get along, and, after what could only be described as a whirlwind romance, you got married after knowing each other for just six months. All very romantic.'

'Allegra?' Ralph said.

Allegra glared hard at Atticus, ignoring her husband. 'The unfortunate Mr Wilson died two months later. A tragedy, of course. I would offer my sympathy if I didn't think that it would be wasted on you. Mr Wilson was a wealthy man, and, since he died intestate, his estate passed to you. Several hundred thousand dollars.'

'That must have helped take the sting away,' Mack suggested.

Allegra glared from Atticus to Mack and back again, but she held her tongue.

Atticus went on. 'You changed your name to Rachel McCoy and then you moved to London. You grieved for a month or two before you met the man who would become your second husband. Rupert Yates. Again, you met him online. A different community, this time, but one with the same aims: sugar daddies looking to meet younger, attractive women. DCI Jones went to court for an order that the website's messages be shared, so she has a record of what you said when you approached him.'

'Rupert Yates,' Mack said, taking over. 'Another whirlwind romance. You made contact in January of the year before last. You'd moved into his home by June, and the two of you were married that

September. Another well-to-do older man who had lost his wife, looking for someone "bubbly" and "fun", according to the profile. You said that described you to a tee and he seemed to agree. We've been able to access your emails from back then, too.'

'You can't do that.'

'The court felt that there were grounds,' Mack said. 'You'll be able to complain at trial if you disagree.'

She frowned, the anger draining away a little to be replaced by what looked like panic. 'Trial?'

Atticus continued. 'Mr Yates died three months after your marriage. He was hospitalised with serious nausea and died soon after. Awful tragedy, but he was older and not in the best of health, just like Mr Wilson. These things happen.'

'I know what you're doing,' Allegra said. 'And you should be ashamed of yourselves.'

'Allegra,' Ralph said, 'is it true? You were married?'

'Yes, Ralph, it's true,' she snapped.

'*Twice?*'

'Yes. *Twice.*'

'Why didn't you—'

'Because it has nothing to do with you,' she snapped. 'Jesus. It has nothing to do with *any* of you.'

'I'm your husband. How can you say that?'

Allegra seemed to find a moment of self-awareness amid her anger. She reached out a hand and laid it atop Ralph's. 'I should've told you,' she said. 'But that was in my past. What happened was painful. I didn't want to have to talk about it – to bring it up again.'

'But you're my *wife*,' he said pleadingly.

The arrogance and conceit that he had shown when Atticus had met him before was gone; he sounded lost and confused, the foundations upon which he had built his life now shaky and unstable. Atticus had wondered if there might have been a better way to confront Allegra so that Ralph might be spared, but had concluded that there wasn't. He needed Ralph there when he started to crank the wheel, slowly tightening the vice around Allegra and her lies. He wanted pressure on her from all angles.

'That's right,' Allegra responded. 'I *am* your wife. And, whatever they might say, I love you.'

Mack intervened. 'Do you?' she said. 'Really?'

'Do I love my husband?' Allegra snapped. 'What kind of question is that? Of *course* I do.'

Allegra stood up and her eyes flashed. Atticus saw anger there, but now there was fear, too. She had stumbled, her leg was in the snare, and the only way to extricate it would be to proceed with caution and care. But that, he could see, was going to be beyond her. He had goaded her, just as he had intended, and now the predatory cunning upon which she had relied for all of her adult life was out of reach. She was caught; all they had to do was prod her a little more, and let her tighten the trap until there was no possibility of escape.

'Sit *down*, Mrs Mallender.'

Mack's voice was firm, weighted with the authority of her rank and the conviction – instilled in her by Atticus and the evidence that he had supplied – that they had penetrated the veil of deceit that Allegra had deployed to such great effect for so long. Allegra sat.

Atticus made to look through his papers even though the facts all came easily to hand. 'Ralph,' he said, glancing up at him. He was red-faced. 'You met Allegra on a similar website, I believe.'

'Yes,' he said.

'And you, like Mr Yates and Mr Wilson, were lonely and seeking someone to share your life with.'

'There's nothing wrong with that.'

'Not at all. Your wife contacted *you*, I believe?'

'Why are you asking him?' Allegra snapped. 'You have those emails, too, I presume?'

'We do,' Mack said.

'That's right,' Ralph said. 'I was flattered. I couldn't understand why she would be interested in someone like me.'

'An eligible bachelor who stood to inherit a small fortune when his parents died?' Mack said, smiling at Allegra. 'No, I can't think why.'

'Don't listen to them,' Allegra said. 'They're trying to make us doubt one another. I stood by you through all of this. I did that because I love you, Ralph. I always have loved you. I always will.'

'You would've been next,' Atticus said.

'What are you talking about?'

Mack took out a sealed evidence bag. She rested it on the table. The bag was clear and, inside, there was a second clear bag that held a greyish-white powder.

'What's that?' Ralph said.

Mack pushed it towards Allegra. 'Tell him.'

'I don't know what it is.'

'Really? We found it in your car.'

'No, you didn't. I've never seen it before.'

'What is it?' Ralph said.

'Thallium,' Mack said. 'Used mostly in manufacturing electronic devices. It's a poison, too, made especially effective because it's odourless and tasteless. It's also very difficult to trace in the system. Graham Young used it – the Teacup Poisoner. He killed at least two colleagues by lacing their tea with it. An unpleasant way to go.'

'Good God,' Allegra said. '"Thallium." "Teacup Poisoner." That's enough. I'm not standing for another moment of this.' She got to her feet. 'I want you to leave.'

Mack and Atticus stayed where they were.

'Ralph!' she said. 'Tell them to go.'

Ralph stayed where he was, too. He didn't speak.

Allegra turned to Lennox, as if in hope that he might say something, but, seeing that he was studiously looking the other way, she slumped down again.

'You were careful before,' Atticus said. 'Wilson and Yates were old and in poor health. It's not beyond the bounds of credibility that they might have died of natural causes. Of course, it would have aroused suspicion if *both* of them had died so soon after marrying the same woman, but those new identities helped, as did moving to a different country. Making the connection between the two deaths would have been almost impossible. But then you got greedy. I think you thought Ralph had more money than he said. You used up all of his savings very quickly, and then you looked at what you might be able to get your hands on in the event that his family died. You took on something a little more challenging. A project.'

Ralph looked as if he was in physical pain.

'Fantasy,' she said. 'Honestly – absolute fantasy.'

'Is it?' Atticus said. 'I don't think so.'

'It's the most ridiculous thing I've ever heard.'

'The bodies of your two previous husbands have been exhumed,' Mack said.

'*What?*'

'Trace amounts of thallium have been found in their systems,' Atticus said. 'That's right, isn't it, Detective Chief Inspector?'

'That's what the labs are saying,' Mack said. 'It's not easy to spot, especially if it's been administered by someone who knows what they're doing and there's no reason to look for it . . . But if there *is* a reason to look?' She shrugged. 'You'd be surprised what you can find.'

'You can't prove a word of any of this.'

'I got it wrong last time,' Mack said. 'I won't make the same mistake twice.' She stood up. 'Allegra Mallender, I'm arresting you for the murder of Rupert Yates. You do not have to say anything, but anything you do say may be used against you in court. Do you understand?'

'Lawyer,' Allegra said, staring coldly at Mack. 'I want my lawyer.'

91

Ralph looked as if his world had fallen in upon itself.

'I don't understand,' he said. 'What's happening? Allegra? What are they saying?'

She didn't look at her husband. Instead, she shared her scorn between Mack and Atticus.

'Ralph's parents saw through you, didn't they?' Atticus said. 'What did they say? That you were a gold digger?'

'We've never made a secret of what his parents thought of me,' Allegra said.

'No, you didn't,' Atticus said. 'But you couldn't really deny it, either. Other people knew about it – Hugo's family and the cleaner. They didn't know how deep it went, but they knew you were bad. I imagine that must have been frustrating for you. You're used to taking whatever you want, and they were in the way. How dare they. Did it make you angry?'

'Lawyer.'

'It would be more difficult to murder Ralph's parents the same way,' Atticus said. 'There were two of them, for a start. You had to think of another way to get rid of them. And you decided that you'd need help.'

'Didn't you hear me? *Lawyer.*' Atticus looked over at Mack. She nodded.

He reached down into his bag, took out an envelope and laid it on the table. He slid his finger inside and withdrew the contents: a selection of photographs that he had taken to be printed at Snappy Snaps on Catherine Street two days before. He flicked through them, making a show of it, before he dealt them out, spinning them the way a croupier would dispense cards.

They came to a stop on the opposite side of the dining table, close enough for Ralph to look down at them. He frowned, his expression becoming even more confused as his gaze slid from one to the other, left to right and then right to left.

'What is this?'

'That's your wife,' Atticus said.

'I can see that,' he snapped, but then the anger drained away as quickly as it had arrived. 'But what am I looking at?'

He knew.

'You don't recognise that house?' He shook his head. 'No.'

'There's no reason why you would.' Atticus turned to Lennox. 'Detective Sergeant? Do *you* recognise it?'

Lennox was frozen, his face pale and bloodless and his hands clutching at one another on the tabletop before him. He was clenching his jaw, and a muscle in his cheek twitched and pulsed, in and out, in and out.

'Lennox?' Mack said.

'Come *on*,' Lennox said, his voice thin and reedy.

'What's going on?' Ralph pleaded, his tone suggesting that he knew very well where this was headed, hoping against hope that he had jumped to the wrong conclusion, but knowing that he had not.

Atticus dealt the photographs that he had been holding back. He had relied upon his telephoto lens, zooming in close enough to show Lennox and Allegra embracing at the door, the golden light from inside framing their clinch.

Ralph looked distraught. He held onto Allegra's hand and nodded across the table at Lennox. 'You and . . . him?'

Allegra turned back to her husband, and, as if at the flick of a switch, the cold stare was replaced by damp-eyed penitence. 'I'm sorry, darling. It was a terrible mistake. I was lonely. You were locked up. It meant nothing to me – I promise. I love you. I love you and I always will.'

It was an impressive show. She was an emotional chameleon, able to morph from sour anger to tearful regret, seemingly at will. Another symptom of her personality disorder. Atticus had been fooled, but that had been before; he knew better now. Ralph, though, was still trapped within the ambit of her malign influence.

'What does this have to do with my parents?' he said.

'I'm going to tell you what happened here on Christmas Eve,' Atticus said. 'The whole story, not the lies that you heard before. I've already established that your wife had a motive for wishing your family dead. Money. Your mother and father had joint wills – if one died, the other inherited the share of the deceased. When that surviving parent died, the property would be shared between the children. Of course, if you were the sole surviving child, you'd inherit all of the estate. A very significant amount of money.'

'No,' he protested. 'That says nothing at all.'

Atticus ignored him. 'You and your family argued about your relationship with Allegra. They were unhappy – they didn't trust her and warned you that she was manipulating you. You disagreed. The argument became heated and you left.'

'This was all established at court.'

'As is what follows, but I like to be thorough. I find it helps to have everything laid out before you.'

92

Atticus glanced over at Mack and then continued. 'So, Ralph – you came back here, where you saw your father's body in the kitchen. You called 999 and Detective Sergeant Lennox was the first officer at the scene. I always found that odd. It's not impossible that he would have been driving nearby and heard the call, but it did seem unlikely.'

'I was in the area,' Lennox said. 'I heard it on the radio from dispatch.'

'What were you doing out this way?' Mack asked him.

'I wanted to speak to a suspect in another case.'

'Who?'

'Dylan Eastman,' he said, easily enough for it to have been true or very well-rehearsed.

'And did you speak to him?'

'I did.'

'What time?'

'I can't remember,' he said.

'I spoke to him. He remembered. It was early evening. He said it was a strange conversation and that nothing came of it. And then I looked at the rosters. You volunteered to work that night, Lennox. You volunteered on *Christmas Eve*. No one does that.'

Lennox looked ready to protest, but closed his mouth.

'It was a ruse,' Atticus took over, 'an excuse for you to be out this way. I thought it was convenient, and it became more of an issue the more I looked into it. You were finished with Freddie by seven or eight – you stayed out this way and waited for the green light.'

He glanced over at Lennox; the DS just stared back at him, hate radiating from his eyes, yet unable to move, a fly caught in a web as the threads of silk were wound about its body.

Atticus continued. 'So, the truth. You were first at the scene because you had never really left. You'd been here all evening. I don't know exactly when you arrived, but my guess would be after Ralph called Allegra to tell her about the argument. I suspect that she told you that Ralph had left the house and that you should make your way there to put your plan into effect. And you did. I'm not sure how you got inside – Ralph, you said that your father was paranoid about security, but there would be no reason to be wary of a police officer with a warrant card. Allegra had already taken the missing pistols from Hugo's collection, and she'd given them to the detective sergeant to use. And so you did, Lennox. You shot him.'

'*This*,' Lennox said derisively, 'is why you got fired. Have you been on the weed again?'

'Unfortunately not. Maybe later.' Atticus reached down for a piece of paper. 'The killer was very accurate that night. Sixteen shots fired, sixteen hits. That's impressive. Cameron, so far as we were able to ascertain, had never fired a weapon before.

He wouldn't have been so precise. But you, Lennox – you're a trained firearms officer. You were on the firearms unit for a year before you switched to CID. The DCI pulled the logs from the range to see if you'd been there recently, and it turns out that you had. Three sessions in the three weeks before the murders. The first for eighteen months. Here.'

Atticus pushed the paper across the table. It was the log from the firing range. Yellow highlighter picked out the three times that Lennox had signed it.

'I want to keep my qualification,' Lennox said. 'I need to practise to do that.'

Atticus ignored that – it was an obvious and poor excuse – and turned back to Ralph. 'Your father was badly injured. The detective sergeant made his first serious error in not confirming that he was dead, and left him to go and attend to the rest of the family in this room.' He swivelled in his chair and pointed to where the sofa and armchair had been. 'He shot your mother and your sister first. I imagine Cameron would have been last.' He pointed to the wall. 'He told him to sit there, then shot him at close range. The intention, of course, was to make it appear as if your brother was responsible for the murder of the family before turning the gun on himself. Allegra knew that Cameron had issues with his anger. Out of the four of them, he made the most likely stooge.'

Allegra was sweating now, a light sheen on her forehead that she could not hide. She was an accomplished liar – good enough to have fooled Atticus once – but now she was unable to prevent her body from betraying her. The little cues were spilling out, getting bigger, more and more of them, all out of control.

'I imagine you must have heard movement from the kitchen and realised that Hugo was still alive. You went through, perhaps saw that he was trying to call 999, and tried to shoot him, but the pistol jammed. You bludgeoned him to death instead. You were in the process of ensuring that everything appeared just as you wanted it when you were disturbed by Ralph's knock at the door. That, Ralph, was the problem that your wife and the detective sergeant did not anticipate. You weren't supposed to be here. You should have been on your way home, miles away by then, but, instead, you showed up just after the murders.'

Lennox cleared his throat, but didn't speak.

'You panicked, Lennox. Perhaps the person at the door has a key? You have to leave before you can be discovered. Of course, Allegra told you about the way out through the coal hole. Ralph – you told your wife about that and she told me that she knew, one of the very few slips that she made during this whole complicated scheme. Very impressive, but those mistakes are instructive to someone who has the eye to see them. The detective sergeant was always going to go out that way so that it looked like the killer was still inside. He hurries to the cellar and lets himself out, taking care not to alert whoever it is he has heard outside. In his haste, however, he catches his shoulder against a nail that has worked free of the boards that secured the entrance. Mack?'

'I saw it,' she said to Lennox. 'You said that you caught it when you were fixing the fence at home.'

'Probably the best excuse that he could come up with on short notice, but he was unlucky. Lennox – you're in several of the crime-scene photos. I examined them very carefully and saw the tear. I'd seen the nail when I looked around the cellar before, so I went back and checked. It's at *just* the right level for a man of your height to snag the right shoulder of a jacket. A small thing, but instructive when added to everything else.'

'Come on, Priest,' Lennox said, finding his voice at last. 'A rip on my jacket? You're accusing me of murder because I ripped my *jacket*?'

'It's a little more than that. I found a small piece of material on the floor of the cellar, beneath the nail. We sent it to the lab in Exeter. They confirmed it was polyethylene – the sort used to make forensic suits.'

'There were a dozen men and women in those suits that night and the day after,' Lennox protested. 'More than a dozen. One of them must've caught the nail.'

'None of them reported it in the log as you would've expected.'

'Because they didn't want to admit they messed up.'

'Again – possible. But, then again, maybe not. Mack?'

'The police use Tyvek suits from DuPont,' she said, 'and the lab said that the sample definitely did not match that chemical composition. We had a look at your bank account. You paid £6.59 to Screwfix on 15 December. We looked at your account history and found out what you'd bought.'

Atticus took out a printout of a Screwfix sales page and read out the headline. '"Disposable coverall with elasticated hood, full-length front zip and elasticated ankles and waist." The lab compared the sample with a suit that I bought. Both contained a very distinctive spunbond non-woven fabric. They're confident that the sample I found in the cellar matches the material used to make the suit that you bought.'

'Coincidence.'

'*Lots* of coincidences,' Atticus said. 'Shall we pick up the story again? Let's go back to what happened here, in this room. You left in a panic and, in your haste, you put the pistol just a little too far away from Cameron Mallender's body.'

'That was all explained,' Lennox said. 'It could easily have ended up there after he shot himself.'

'Ah, yes,' Atticus said. 'The involuntary twitch. The defence made much of that suggestion and, yes, I concede it is possible. But the prosecution's evidence was that it was a stretch. I agree with them. It's not likely. My explanation is more likely.'

'You're full of it.'

'I imagine you took off the oversuit when you were outside. You went back through the woods to the car park where you'd left your car, muddying your shoes in the process. You stowed the suit and left enough time so as not to appear too quickly, but, nevertheless, you ensured that you were first on the scene. You met Ralph outside the house and then went to the door, where you observed Hugo Mallender's body. You pulled back and waited for support. The two constables arrived and spoke to Ralph. This is where you diverged from the plan. You realised that it was entirely possible that the finger of blame might point at him. Perhaps you remembered that the gun had been left a little too far away from Cameron's body. Perhaps you worried about the rip on your jacket or the mud on your shoes. I can't say – I've never murdered four people before; I don't know what might run through my mind. But what I do know is that I would want to do something to divert possible blame from anyone *outside* the property by making it seem as if someone is still alive *inside* the property. Because if someone is alive inside, then, *quod erat demonstrandum*, it must surely be much more likely that that person is the murderer, and not someone who is outside. The problem you had is that no one else – not Ralph, not either one of the constables who attended – saw anything. It was just you. And, in the absence of any other evidence, that small detail would be insignificant and easily overlooked. You might have considered it a necessary risk. But now we have the gun being too far from the body. The speed with which you reached the scene. The torn jacket. The material in the cellar that matches the coverall that you bought. A narrative is beginning to form.'

93

The tension in the room was palpable.

Lennox turned to Mack. 'Really, boss? You're allowing this?'

'Shut up, Tristan.'

Atticus continued, on the home straight now. 'The case looks like it is going to go your way,' he said. 'Cameron seems like a credible suspect – there isn't anyone else, in any event. But then the family get involved. They demand that Ralph be investigated. They say that he didn't get on with his parents. The argument that afternoon comes to light. Mrs Grant says how vicious it was. The evidence against Cameron starts to look tenuous: the gun falling where it did is problematic; there's no gunshot residue on Cameron's hands; no blood other than Cameron's own on his body, odd given that Hugo clearly tried to put up a fight; Cameron was not familiar with firearms, yet he was a perfect shot that night. The investigation widens. Ralph is investigated. Freddie Lamza sees the case on television and realises that he has a chance to get revenge for what he sees as poor treatment, while also making a large amount of money into the bargain. The case against Ralph ooks more and more serious. He's arrested, interviewed and charged.'

Atticus got up, reached across the table and collected the photographs.

'But this just won't do,' he said. 'This is the worst possible outcome. If Ralph is convicted of murdering his parents, he can't inherit. He forfeits what he would otherwise have received.' He looked down at Allegra. 'I can only imagine what you must have been thinking. You must have been desperate. The police had built a credible case against him. Good enough. You couldn't risk it, so you hired me. A last throw of the dice. And it very nearly worked. I attacked the prosecution's case. I showed Lamza for what he was, and then, after Ralph's outburst undid all of that good work, I found out about Cassandra Mallender and Jimmy Robson. A second stooge for you to exploit.' Atticus crossed his arms over his chest. 'And you were desperate enough then to take a foolish risk.'

'Do I need someone from the Federation to sit in on this?' Lennox said.

Atticus turned to him. 'Are you guilty, Detective Sergeant?'

'Of course I'm not bloody guilty.'

'We can get a rep if you want,' Mack said. 'Or you can hear Atticus out.'

He shook his head. 'Whatever. I don't care. Get it over with.'

Atticus turned and paced to the window. The snow was still falling, a shifting curtain that was suffused with the golden glow from an exterior light.

'I told Allegra about Jimmy and Cassandra. He was perfect – the idiot who could take the fall for Ralph. He had already testified to the fact that he had no alibi for Christmas Eve; he had a record for violent crime as long as your arm; and now we had evidence of a relationship with Cassandra, and the possibility that he might have been the bad influence that caused her mother and father so much grief. We know he was dismissed from the farm around the time that Cassandra had her religious conversion. Isn't it possible that Hugo might have warned him off and told Cassandra she was forbidden from seeing him? And, if he had done that, isn't it possible that a man like Jimmy might bear a grudge?

'You hoped that the suggestion that there was a better suspect might have been enough to cast enough doubt on the prosecution's case, but then I got into trouble while I was investigating Robson and you decided to go for broke. You took Cassandra's necklace from her body for specifically this purpose: a last-ditch strategy when everything else had failed – fit up someone else. Robson was perfect, and I had given you the ideal opportunity to roll the dice. Allegra – you told DCI Jones that you thought I was in trouble; then DCI Jones saw DS Lennox, who was conveniently at court that afternoon and able to get there with her. Robson holding me inside was justification to break in and, in the confusion that followed, you' – he pointed at Lennox – 'planted the necklace and the nine-millimetre rounds that were from the same box as the ones you had used to murder the family.'

'Really?' Lennox said. 'You can't prove any of it.'

'I'd already searched the property,' Atticus said. 'I know that the necklace and the rounds weren't there before. I have video on my phone that shows that they weren't under the bed where they were found. It's possible that Robson could have deposited them after he had locked me up, but why would he do that then? It's more likely that someone who entered the property between then and the start of the full search did it. You could have done it, Lennox. The ripped jacket. The target practice. Being at the farmhouse first. Being at Robson's house first. So many little coincidences. When you add them up and look at them, they don't look like coincidences any more. They look like a pattern. Add in the relationship with Allegra, a woman who has already killed two men, and they look like motive, means and opportunity.'

'Bullshit,' he exclaimed. 'None of that proves anything.'

'There's one other thing,' Mack said.

She reached into her pocket and took out a digital recorder. She put it on the table, stared at Lennox, and pressed play.

Lennox's voice played back. 'Allegra.'

'What is it?' Allegra replied.

'We're in trouble. I just spoke to my boss. They've been investigating you.'

'Why?'

'She says that she can prove you stole someone's identity. Is that true?'

There was a pause.

'Allegra – is that true?'

'Yes. When I got here. So what?'

'That's fraud. And it's made her suspicious. She's going to come over this afternoon and question you.'

'Shit. Shit.'

'You should've told me.'

'Shit.'

'It'll be fine. It's just this, as far as I know – she doesn't know anything else.'

'That's easy for you to say. You were supposed to stop this from happening.'

'Relax. I'll find out if she knows anything else. I don't think she does.'

'There's more,' Mack said, 'but you get the idea.'

She pressed stop.

'You bugged me?' Lennox said. 'You can't do that.'

'We asked the chief constable and the surveillance commissioner. They said we could.'

'No,' he said, vigorously shaking his head. 'No bloody way.'

'Your car, your house, the office,' Mack went on. 'Your work emails. Everything you'd expect. It was Atticus's idea. Give you something to worry about and wait to see what you do. You went down to your car this morning and called from there. Fifteen minutes after we'd spoken. And on speakerphone – that was helpful.'

She reached over and collected the recorder just as there came a heavy knocking on the front door.

'What now?' Ralph said.

'Let me guess,' Lennox said. 'Some of the lads from the nick?'

'Bob Carver and a couple of others,' Mack said. 'Ralph – could you go and let them in, please?'

'Lawyer,' Allegra said, a little pointlessly.

'You're under arrest, Lennox.'

What happened next took Atticus completely by surprise. Lennox sprang out of his seat, reached around his body and pulled out a pistol. Atticus recognised it: a Smith & Wesson, presumably the one that had been stolen from Hugo Mallender's gun safe at the same time as the Browning.

The one that they had never found.

Allegra screamed.

Lennox backed away from the table, pointing the gun at Mack and then at Atticus.

'Put it away,' Mack said. 'You're making things much worse.'

The hammering at the door came again.

'Lennox,' Mack said. 'Tristan, come on – put it down. There are three big blokes outside. How far are you going to get?'

Lennox aimed at Atticus again. His finger was around the trigger. Atticus could see the tension in his body: the clenching of his jaw, the knotted cords in his neck, the tremor in his outstretched arm.

'I told you,' he said. 'I told you, but you didn't listen.'

It took Atticus a moment to realise that Lennox wasn't talking to him. The gun was trained into his gut, but Lennox flicked little glances across at Allegra.

'I told you,' he said. 'I told you that Robson was a step too far. You didn't listen. You never bloody listened to me and now look what's happened.'

'I'm sorry,' Allegra said. 'I should've. You're right. I'm sorry.'

'Yes, you should've listened. You should've left it as it was, taken your chances with the trial. Ralph was going to get off. We didn't need to make sure. It was already done.'

Mack stood up slowly. 'Put the gun down, Tristan.'

Lennox was crying. He swung the gun back to cover Mack.

'I'm sorry, boss. I got caught up in it all and now I'm lost.'

He backed away from them, covering the room with the pistol.

'Don't,' Mack said. 'It's over. Put it down.'

He backed out of the room and they heard running footsteps.

'Shit,' Mack said.

Atticus got up. 'He's going to run,' he said. 'Carver doesn't know he's got a gun. He'll get shot.'

He ran to the door.

94

Atticus remembered the layout of the house, and guessed that Lennox did, too. There were two main entrances – the front door and the door to the kitchen – and a third, used less often, that opened from the study into the garden. Carver had knocked on the front door, and Lennox would have expected him to have put a man on the kitchen door, too. Perhaps not the study door, though.

Lennox had a head start, and he was armed; Atticus followed carefully. He heard the sound of a key turning in a lock and then the squeak of unoiled hinges and knew that he was right.

'Atticus!' Mack called out from somewhere behind him.

Atticus ignored her.

He reached the door to the study and pushed himself against the wall, edging to the opening and then risking a glance around the frame and into the room beyond. The study door was open, the wind rustling the curtain that shielded it from the rest of the room. Atticus gulped a breath, and, without thinking too much about the fact that Lennox might still be inside, he stepped into the room.

It was empty.

He crossed it at a trot and, ignoring a second warning from Mack, he parted the curtain and stepped outside.

His feet crunched into the thin layer of snow that had fallen while he had been inside the house. It was dark, with the only light coming from the exterior lamp that he had seen from the sitting-room window. The light did not extend far, quickly swallowed up by the gloom and the snow that was falling heavier and heavier. There was enough, though, for Atticus to see the footprints that extended from the doorway and into the vegetable patch at the side of the house.

Atticus heard another vigorous rapping on the front door.

'Carver!' Atticus called out. 'He's made a run for it.'

He didn't wait for the uniform to respond. Lennox was running, and, unless someone went after him quickly, they would lose him in the woods.

He followed the tracks, clambering over the uneven ground of the vegetable patch and sprinting hard into the inky black that was thick between the trees. His feet slipped on the ice beneath the powdery snow.

The footprints reached the track and then, with no light, they disappeared. The snow had fallen heavily here, and Atticus almost tripped as his feet ploughed through it. He kept on, just able to make out the boundaries of the track, hemmed in on both sides by the darker shapes of the trees.

His thighs started to burn from the effort and the cold air stung his lungs as he gasped it in.

He staggered to a stop and turned. He couldn't see the house any more. There was no light. The trees crowded in, shades of black and the darkest grey, absorbing him.

He closed his eyes, listening.

He heard steps, crunching through the icy surface somewhere ahead of him.

'Lennox!'

The footsteps stopped.

'Lennox! There's no point in running.'

He heard the crunch of footsteps.

He thought he saw movement.

A grey shape sliding through the black.

The shape stopped.

Atticus stumbled and fell, tripping over a frozen rut in the track and crashing down onto the snow.

There was a flash.

Something sliced through the air just above his head.

The crack of the gunshot was accompanied by an impact behind him – the bullet blasting into a tree, perhaps – and the panicked shriek of an animal nearby.

'You should've kept your nose out of my business,' Lennox said.

Atticus tried to move to his left, to get into the bushes that he knew were at the side of the track, but his feet and hands scrunched through the hard snow, much too loud, and he froze.

'You never knew when to stop, did you?'

Atticus bit his lip.

The footsteps started again.

Coming down the track towards him.

One.

'Always putting your nose where it didn't belong.'

Two.

'You didn't know when to stop then and you still don't know now.'

Three.

Atticus was frozen to the spot. 'You're going to regret you ever—'

He was interrupted by a solid *thwack*, the sound of something striking against something solid, and then a crunch as a heavy weight collapsed onto the snow.

'Atticus?'

It was Mack.

'*Atticus?* Shit, Atticus, where are you?'

He spat snow. 'Over here.'

Light shone out as Mack activated the flashlight on her phone. The light shone downwards onto Lennox's motionless body and then reached down the track to where Atticus was sitting. He blinked his eyes against the light until he could make out more. Mack had a thick branch in her right hand. It ended in a knuckle of gnarled wood.

'Are you all right?'

'He missed,' Atticus said. 'I'm fine. What about him?'

Mack knelt down and pressed her fingers against Lennox's neck. 'Still with us,' she said. 'It was just a love tap.'

'"Just a love tap?"' He got up and brushed away the compacted snow that had adhered to his clothes. 'Remind me never to get on your bad side.'

'Bit late for that,' she said, although he could hear the smile in her voice.

She searched Lennox for additional weapons, running her hands up and down his torso and over his pockets.

'Anything?'

'Nothing,' she said.

'Where's the gun?'

'He's dropped it.' She shone the flashlight over the snowy ground until she located the weapon. 'Here.'

Atticus exhaled. 'What a mess.'

'I can't believe Lennox would be so *stupid* as to have done something like this.'

'Money,' Atticus said.

'You think?'

'I had a little look in his account.'

'Should I ask how?'

'Probably best not to.'

'But?'

'He had gambling debts. Quite big ones. I imagine Allegra promised that she'd pay them all off.'

'She's quite a piece of work,' she said.

'She is.'

'Boss?'

Atticus recognised Carver's shout. He looked back down the track and saw three more torches bouncing towards them.

'We're over here,' Mack called back. She reached out and took Atticus by the arm. 'You're sure you're okay?'

'Just annoyed.'

'Apart from your pride?'

'I'm fine, thanks to you. He would've shot me.'

She squeezed his biceps. 'Don't get mushy. I was just doing my job.'

Carver reached them. He was breathing hard, out of breath. 'You okay, boss?'

'All good, Bob.'

'Priest?'

'Didn't know you cared,' he said. 'I'm fine.'

'What about DS Lennox?'

Mack gestured into the darkness. 'He's over there,' she said. 'Better call an ambulance. He's out cold – took a bit of a bang to the head.'

'Right you are.'

'He had a weapon,' she said, shining her light to where the gun had fallen. 'Take a picture of it in situ and make sure it gets packaged properly.'

Mack dropped the branch to the ground. Carver and one of the other uniforms stayed with Lennox while Mack and Atticus followed their tracks back to the house. Mack delivered instructions as they walked. She spoke in a clipped and terse fashion, no wasted words, no emotion, efficient and businesslike. She called the station and had them dispatch SOCOs and a search team to both the farmhouse and to Lennox's house. She called Beckton and quickly updated him as to what had just happened. She was organised and incisive, qualities that Atticus knew that he did not possess. He found that his legs were weak as the shock of what had nearly happened finally registered.

'What about Allegra?' he said.

'Patterson is with her.'

'And Ralph?'

'Betts.'

'My God,' he said weakly.

'Let's get a coffee,' she said. 'You need to warm up.'

PART IV

95

The farmhouse had been turned into a crime scene for the second time in a year, and, as officers arrived to start the investigation, Mack took the decision to send Atticus to the Royal Oak in Great Wishford. Francine Patterson went with him to the car park and drove them both down the road to the village. The pub was an old building at the end of the track that had recently been done up, with a few cars in the car park and a modern floodlight on the wall that washed the snow in white. Two elderly men stood beneath the porch and watched as a pair of police vans, their blue lights strobing, drove quickly into the woods.

'You know what's happening?' one of them asked as Atticus approached.

'No idea,' he said.

Atticus went inside. The pub was quaint despite the updated décor, the room warmed by a huge fire that blazed in the hearth. Patterson went to get them both coffees and then sat with him at a table in front of the fire, both of them slowly warming up.

Mack arrived after thirty minutes. She shared a word with Patterson and waited as the junior officer made her way out and back to the house. She sat down at the table.

'You had a drink yet?'

'She got me a coffee.'

'Well, that won't do.'

Mack went to the bar and returned with two whiskies. She sat down, held up her tumbler and waited for Atticus to touch it with his. They downed the shots quickly. The alcohol burned its way down his throat, but it had the desired effect.

'You okay?'

'I'm fine.' He nodded in the direction of the farmhouse. 'You under control there?'

'We're good,' she said. She pointed at his glass. 'Another?'

'Go on, then.'

Mack went to the bar and Atticus got up to put another log on the fire. The wood was damp, and it hissed and spat as the flames wrapped around it. Mack returned with a coffee for herself and another shot for him.

'Not joining me?' he said.

'One's enough. I've got a busy night ahead.'

'I'm sure you do,' he said. 'I used to love this kind of stuff.'

'How do you mean?'

'The moment when you get a break in a case. You have someone who you know did it, and the only thing left to do is to get them to confess. It was fun. Getting them to lie, tying them up in knots, persuading them the only way out of the mess that they were in was to tell the truth.'

'A battle of wits?'

He nodded. 'Exactly.'

'You were good at it,' she said. 'I don't remember many who gave you much trouble.'

'Alfred Burns,' he said.

'He was something else,' she said.

Atticus knew the way his mind worked, and did not want to trigger his obsession with Burns.

Mack saw it, too, and moved the subject back to the evening's events. 'Lennox is on his way to A & E.'

'Under guard?'

She nodded. 'I'll question him when they give him the all-clear.'

'It won't be hard. He couldn't be more guilty.'

She sipped her coffee. 'The gun – that was the other one from Hugo's safe?'

'Most likely,' he said. 'She gave him both and he kept that one just in case. What about Allegra?'

'They've just taken her back to Bourne Hill. I'll question her tonight.'

'You get enough to make up for the stuff that was inadmissible?'

'I think so. I haven't checked yet, but the device in the sitting room was working fine when they tested it this afternoon. I can't imagine there'll be a problem. I've got the CPS complex case unit coming in tomorrow morning – they can review it then.'

'Abernathy is going to be happy.'

'He's a shit,' she said. 'Happy to throw me under the bus when it went wrong, but I bet he'll be there to take the credit now you've solved it.'

'We,' he corrected her.

'Sorry?'

'Now we've solved it. I couldn't have done it without you.'

She smiled, but didn't answer. They sat in companionable silence for a moment, sipping their drinks.

'What about Ralph?' Atticus asked her.

'Victim support. He's had a difficult year.'

'He won't see it yet,' Atticus said, 'but he had a lucky escape. I'd test his blood.'

'For thallium?'

He nodded. 'I bet she started already. Probably the day he got off. She'll have added it to his champagne.'

'A black widow.'

He frowned. 'What do you mean?'

'Eats her own husband. Actually, she's eaten two.'

'Nearly three.'

*　*　*

They stayed there for another half an hour. Atticus ran through what he believed had happened for a third time, setting out those parts of the story of which he was certain and underlining those that Mack would need to investigate further. He had no doubt that a full investigation into Allegra and her past would furnish more than enough additional evidence to make the case against her certain beyond any prospect of doubt, not that that was going to be relevant after what had happened. The evidence from Allegra's own mouth, recorded by the bugs in the house and practically a confession, would be enough to damn her.

They got up and went to the door. The snow was falling heavily now, a thick curtain that reduced visibility to just a few feet.

'You'll let me know when you've questioned Lennox?' Atticus said.

'I will.' She drew closer and kissed him on the cheek. 'Thank you. I'll call you tomorrow.'

96

Atticus parked the car in Central and walked back. The snow was falling steadily now, covering everything in a white mantle that smoothed away the edges and hid imperfections. His feet crunched through it, his toes quickly frozen in boots that weren't intended for weather like this. The late hour and the weather conspired so that the roads were almost empty, with a solitary gritter spraying salt behind it as it made its way through the city.

He reached the office and pushed icy fingers into his pocket for his keys. He fumbled them into the lock and went inside. The temperature as he climbed the stairs was not much warmer than the street, and he was glad of the warmth from the storage heaters inside the office. He switched on the two cheap oil-filled radiators that he had purchased from Tesco to keep the worst of the chill away, and knelt down so that Bandit could come forward for an embrace.

'It's cold out there,' he said.

The dog pressed his wet muzzle into the cleft between Atticus's chin and shoulder, and Atticus rewarded him with a vigorous rub.

'What a day,' he said as he stood and made his way into the bedroom. 'You're sleeping on the bed with me tonight. We can help each other keep warm.'

Bandit didn't need to be asked twice. Atticus took him out into the garden to relieve himself, and then led the way back up the stairs to the bedroom. The dog trotted behind him obediently and curled up on the bed.

* * *

Mack tried to ring Andy's mobile, but the call went to voicemail. She stared at the display as his familiar message played out, but pressed end before the beep. She knew that she should have called earlier, but she had been distracted by what had happened. That was reasonable, she thought, given the circumstances. She wondered whether Andy would feel the same way. She had been working too hard and coming home too late for weeks now – months – and she knew that his patience was wearing thin. That made her angry – what was she supposed to do? This was her *job*. So she always put off the conversation that she knew that they desperately needed to have. She put it off, too, because she knew what he would say. He would tell her that she needed to prioritise their family over her career, and that was a decision that she didn't want to face.

She chuckled bitterly. Who was she kidding? After the catastrophe of the Mallender case, what kind of career did she have left?

She got up.

'Francine?'

DC Patterson spun her chair around. 'Yes, boss?'

'I'm going home.'

'What about Allegra?'

'Let her stew. I'll do the interview in the morning. You heard anything about Lennox?'

'They just called,' she said. 'He's concussed and they want to keep him in overnight. He's got two blokes guarding him until he's ready to be transferred to custody.'

'His PACE clock hasn't started,' Mack said. 'We've got plenty of time, not that we'll need it. We'll have holding charges for both of them by the end of tomorrow.'

'Right you are, boss.'

'You look tired, Francine. Go to bed. I'll need you to be fresh in the morning.'

'I'll log off, then.'

'Good. See you tomorrow.'

Mack took her jacket and bag and hurried to the exit.

* * *

Mack stopped at the store attached to the twenty-four-hour garage on the way home to pick up a bunch of flowers and a bottle of wine. She suspected that Andy would already have gone to bed, but at least it would show that she was sorry for her recent inattention. Perhaps they would be able to drink the wine while they discussed the things that they needed to sort out; she would make sure that they did that tomorrow. It would be a priority, as soon as she had interviewed and charged Allegra. No excuses.

The house was dark as she approached the front door. That wasn't surprising, given the hour, but she had harboured the hope that perhaps Andy might have stayed up so that he was downstairs when she returned. Never mind. She unlocked the door and, as quietly as she could, stepped inside. The children were sometimes difficult to get to sleep in the evenings, and the last thing that she wanted was to disturb them now.

She took off her jacket, hung it from the hook and dropped her keys in the bowl next to the telephone. She waited at the foot of the stairs, her eyes closed, just listening. The house was very quiet. She used her toes to press off her shoes and padded through into the kitchen. She was thirsty and wanted a drink of water, but, before she had even taken the glass to the tap, she saw the envelope that had been propped up against the micro-wave. It was addressed to her.

Her stomach fell. She felt sick as she reached for the enve-lope, sliding a finger inside and tearing it open.

Andy had written her a short letter. He said that he had taken the kids to his parents' for the weekend. He thought that he and Mack should have a short time apart so that they could each consider what they wanted from their relationship. He told her that he loved her, but that he was increasingly unhappy; he concluded by saying that he needed to work out whether he would be more unhappy if they were apart than he was when they were together.

Mack slumped down into the chair next to the kitchen table. She stared at the letter, her eyes skimming over the words without really reading them. Her mouth was dry. She laid the piece of paper on the table, went to the drawer and took out the corkscrew. She opened the bottle of wine, poured a large measure into a glass, and drank it quickly.

Then she poured again.

Her phone rang.

She picked it up and put it to her ear without looking at the screen. 'Andy?'

'Sorry, no. It's me.'

'Atticus?'

'Yep. Sorry it's so late.'

'What is it?'

'Can't sleep.'

'That'll be the adrenaline.'

'I keep running what happened through my head.'

'It's not every day you get shot at.'

'What about Lennox?'

'Concussed. They're keeping him in.'

Neither of them spoke for a moment. Mack gazed out of the window, absently listening to the pops of static on the line.

'Are you still at the nick?' Atticus said.

'No. Just got home.'

'Oh – shit. I'm sorry. You shouldn't have picked up. I don't want to disturb you.'

She was about to tell him that it was fine, that she welcomed the sound of his voice, but she bit her lip. She knew where that conversation would lead and, as she looked down at Andy's letter to her, she knew that was something that she couldn't allow to happen. She was vulnerable now. Sad and lonely. It would be simple to fix that, but the damage that it would cause would be long-lasting and would more than out-weigh any short-term relief.

'Mack? You still there?'

'I'm tired. I'd better get to bed. You too. Get some sleep.'

'All right. Good night.'

'Good night, Atticus.'

She ended the call and laid the phone down on the table, staring at the screen until the display faded and then died. She put the wine glass in the dishwasher and the wine in the fridge and made her way up the stairs to bed.

*　*　*

Atticus put the phone down and lay still. He still couldn't sleep. He doubted that was going to change.

He found his thoughts returning to Grovely Farmhouse, and the events of almost precisely a year ago. Would Ralph ever be able to return to live in it? Atticus doubted it. He wasn't superstitious, but it would be an impossible task to ignore the echoes that would for ever sound around those rooms. It would have to be sold, or razed to the ground, or left to stand empty as a monument to the family that had been murdered within it.

He turned over and then turned over again. It did no good. His mind was buzzing.

There was no point in just lying there. He needed to distract himself and, remembering that he hadn't checked the game that he had started with Jack_of_Hearts, he got up and padded through into the office. He switched on the desk lamp, woke the keyboard and clicked across to the game.

Jack had pushed his knight to f3. Atticus mirrored the development on his board on the coffee table and mulled over his possible responses, referring back to what he had read of Bobby Fischer's travails against Spassky. He slid a pawn out to g6 and confirmed the move.

He stared at the board and tried to picture the way that the position might play out from here when a message appeared in the chat box.

> *An interesting move, Atticus.*

Atticus stared at it for a moment. He frowned. On this site he had only ever been known by his username, just like everyone else. His real name was hidden. He had never shared it with anyone that he had played against.

He typed.

> *How do you know my name?*

The cursor blinked to indicate that Jack_of_Hearts was composing a reply.

> *I'm afraid I haven't been very honest with you.*
> *What does that mean?*
> *I should apologise.*
> *Why?*
> *I know who you are. Where you live. I know about your career – the old one and the one you are pursuing now. I've been following your work for some time. I'm a fan.*

Atticus was on edge. This was starting to feel unpleasant, even a little threatening.

He typed.

> *I'd like to say that I was flattered, but this feels creepy.*
> *I'm sorry about that. That's the last thing I want.*

Atticus reached for the keyboard to reply, started to type, then stopped. He didn't know what to say.

Another message appeared.

> *I wanted to congratulate you. I was concerned that you might believe that Robson was guilty. It was always obvious that he was a stooge. The wife and the detective sergeant were shrewd, but they panicked. Wouldn't you agree?*

The cursor flashed. Atticus's mouth was dry. He reached for a plastic bottle of fizzy water that he had left next to the keyboard and drank down the tepid half-inch that was left in the bottom.

He typed.

> *Who are you?*
> *It's best that you don't know that.*
> *Best for who?*
> *For both of us.*

Atticus stood and went to the window. He looked out into the street below. It was deserted. The snow had been falling all night and now even the road was smooth. There were no tyre tracks or footprints to disturb the white. He had the uncomfortable feeling that he was being watched, yet could see no evidence to suggest that it was more than just a premonition.

He went back to the desk and saw another message was waiting for him.

> *I just wanted to say hello. Properly. I'd like to be able to be honest with you.*
> *How can you be honest if I don't know who you are?*

Another message flashed up at the bottom of the chatbox.

> *JACK_OF_HEARTS HAS LEFT THE CONVERSATION.*

EPILOGUE

Atticus waited in the same café where he had taken Allegra Mallender on the first day of her husband's trial. He had stopped at court first of all, but, as he had expected, there was a scrum of activity both inside and outside the building. Television outside broadcast vans had parked along the side of Wilton Road, and reporters were filming pieces to camera as bemused members of the public made their way around them. There was a queue of interested parties waiting to pass through security, and the usher – a man Atticus knew from his days in the police – had told him over a cigarette that the public gallery and the space reserved for the press were both full, and that no one else would be admitted.

The Crown's case against Allegra Mallender and Tristan Lennox started today. Both stood accused of murder, and the magistrates were sitting in order to send the case straight to the Crown Court. Even though the hearing was purely procedural, this was still the biggest show in town. Ralph's trial had been a cause célèbre, but this – adding his murderous wife and her illicit lover to the existing tragedy of the Mallenders – had given proceedings a salacious edge that went beyond what had gone before.

Atticus had two polystyrene cups of coffee on the table. He blew on his to cool it down before gingerly taking a sip. He heard the sound of the door opening and, as he turned his head, he saw Mack as she came inside. She raised a hand in acknowledgement, took off her coat and sat down opposite him.

'Morning,' she said.

He pushed the other coffee across the table. 'For you.'

'Thanks.' She put the cup to her lips and sipped the coffee. 'I need it.'

'Long morning?'

She smiled wanly. 'Long few days.'

Atticus didn't doubt it for a moment. The law allowed Mack twenty-four hours to interview Allegra and Lennox, but she had secured an extension for thirty-six hours before making the decision to charge them both. He remembered what it would have been like during that initial period: a concentrated burst of questioning, investigation and more questioning. The case might have appeared straightforward, but there were questions of the admissibility of the evidence that had been gathered at the farmhouse that needed to be discussed with the CPS. That, together with the inevitable media attention that the case would attract, would have been enough to give Mack a full plate.

'Did they give you an idea what they might plead?' he asked her.

'Not guilty,' she said.

'A trial in the summer, then?'

'At the earliest. I've got months of this to look forward to. I've already done it once before. Now I've got to do it all again.' She shook her head and laughed bitterly. 'Listen to me. Maybe I ought to come and work with you.'

'*For* me,' he corrected her. 'I have an established business now.'

'Sorry,' she said, smiling. 'Of course.'

'Actually, I'm not completely joking. I could do with the help.'

'You have work?'

'Don't sound so surprised. The phone's been ringing off the hook.'

Atticus had been approached by the BBC's *Look South* news show yesterday and had accepted their offer to be interviewed about his role in the case. He had been careful not to prejudice the fresh investigation, but had discussed how he had unravelled the case against Ralph. It was only a local programme, but he had immediately noticed a spike in traffic to his website, and the phone calls had started soon after. A good number of the enquiries were easily dismissed – crank calls, those looking for help in finding lost pets, someone who asked whether he could help investigate a possible haunting – but there had been half a dozen that were promising.

'Look at you,' she said. 'On the TV and now you're a big shot.'

'Hardly,' he said, although he enjoyed the acknowledgement that was hidden within her gentle sarcasm. 'What about Ralph?'

'Haven't seen him. Probably best – the rumour is that he's getting lawyers on board to make a civil claim.'

'It'll settle,' he said, trying to sound reassuring.

'Probably.'

Atticus thought that she looked tired. It wasn't surprising. Mack had had a difficult two weeks with the disintegration of the first trial, and he didn't doubt that she had been given a rough time of it by Beckton and the other senior officers. The BBC reporter to whom he had spoken had suggested that there was going to be an external investigation into what had gone wrong, and he had heard rumblings that Ralph was gearing up for a civil claim against the police. Mack was the face of the investigation, and that would all have taken a toll.

'Everything else all right?' he asked.

'Fine,' she said.

'Home?'

Her eyes flicked up and to the right. 'All good. The kids are a handful, but that's par for the course. We're doing good.'

Atticus knew Mack well enough to know the baseline for when she was being honest, and her body language was a million miles from that. She shifted a little, there was a slight crack in her voice – almost imperceptible, but not to him – and there was the shirked eye contact. The self-deprecating shrug of helplessness when she mentioned the children came after her words, rather than accompanying them; it had been added after the fact to reinforce the lie, rather than being contemporaneous, as would have been the case if she was answering truthfully. Atticus knew that she was hiding something.

'I can't imagine how difficult it must be,' he said. 'You've been through the mill the last few months. Don't forget to look after yourself.'

'What is this? Detective Sergeant Priest thinking of others?'

He wondered whether now was the time to tell her about the conversation that he had had with Jack_of_Hearts, but decided not. Mack was up against it, and there was no sense in burdening her with something else now, especially since it was probably just a crank. Atticus had given the online exchange a lot of thought and had come to the conclusion that it was someone who was messing around with him. It was elaborate, certainly, and could only really have been someone with knowledge of the investigation and the events of that evening in the woods. A police officer, then. He had made a lot of enemies during his time in the force, and it wouldn't have been difficult to fill a list with those people who would have both the motive and inside knowledge to spoof him.

That was what he was telling himself, anyway. It hadn't stopped him from obsessively checking his account for further messages, but, so far, Jack had made no further moves in their game nor sent another message. Atticus would watch and wait. There was nothing else that he could do.

'I'd better get back to the nick,' Mack said. She stood. 'Thanks for the coffee.'

He got up, too, and watched her go. It had started to rain again and she stood outside the door and stiffened the collar of her overcoat before disappearing around the corner. Atticus scattered the coins in his pocket on the table as a tip, swiped his own jacket from the back of the chair, and put it on. Bandit needed a walk and he had made an appointment with a potential new client that afternoon. Something about a missing person, with enough in the initial email to suggest that it might be interesting. He thanked the woman behind the counter and went outside just as one of the news vans with a satellite dish on its roof rolled around the roundabout and headed away in the direction of London.

Atticus was reminded of something that his father used to say: 'Today's news is tomorrow's fish-and-chip papers.'

There was truth in that. The Christmas Eve Massacre would soon fade from the news, to be replaced by the next lurid scandal. The benefit to Atticus's brief fame, such as it was, would soon fade, too. He needed to take advantage of it while it lasted.

Life went on.

And Atticus had things to do.

Acknowledgements

Thank you, as ever, to Team Milton for their diligent inspection of the manuscript and suggestions for improving it. Special thanks to former detective (and current thriller writer) Neil Lancaster for making sure I didn't embarrass myself with my policing and to a criminal barrister who wishes to remain anonymous for dispensing advice when it came to the courtroom action.

And, of course, to my wife for her sage advice. The ending is a little different because of it.

Atticus will be back.

Mark Dawson
Salisbury 2023

MARK DAWSON is the bestselling author of the
Beatrix Rose, Isabella Rose and John Milton series
and has sold over four million books. He lives in
Wiltshire with his family and can be reached
at www.markjdawson.com

www.facebook.com/markdawsonauthor
www.twitter.com/pbackwriter
www.instagram.com.markjdawson

A message from Mark

Building a relationship with my readers is the very best thing
about writing. Join my VIP Reader Club for information
on new books and deals, plus correspondence dealing
with Atticus's departure from the police. Find out
what really happened with this exclusive reader content.

Just visit www.markjdawson.com/AtticusPriest

WELBECK

PUBLISHING GROUP

Love books? Join the club.

Sign-up and choose your preferred genres to receive tailored news, deals, extracts, author interviews and more about your next favourite read.

From heart-racing thrillers to award-winning historical fiction, through to must-read music tomes, beautiful picture books and delightful gift ideas, Welbeck is proud to publish titles that suit every taste.

bit.ly/welbeckpublishing

WELBECK

ANDRE DEUTSCH

MORTIMER

MORTIMER

WELBECK